To the God

Apologies if this offends

anyone — I'm afraid that

it's a talent.

John Alston

A graduate of the University of London, John Ashton studied geography and geomorphology as he wanted to know how hills were created and planned to avoid any form of career involving desks.

John qualified as a chartered accountant in 1984 and promised himself that he would escape from the exciting world of auditing by 1990.

In 1985 he travelled to the Middle East on an eighteen month contract; he returned to the UK in 1990, thereby allowing Saddam Hussein easy access to the Upper Gulf region. "He waited until my wife was back in Europe before invading," explains John, "as he didn't want her nagging in his human shield."

In 2002 he finally underwent the frontal lobotomy reversal required to recover some of the personality and character he had been forced to have removed when becoming a chartered accountant. Now best described as a "recovering human being", John spends his time between the insides of various hostelries, on a number of (failing) business interests, and at his keyboard (where he vainly searches for that Pulitzer winning idea).

His previous works include a delightful publication on the operation of insurance companies in the Middle East, a humourless piece entitled "*The Tax Regime of the Kingdom of Saudi Arabia*", and a range of newspaper articles on subjects as challenging as "Succession planning in the family business", "The effect of the euro on North East business" and "How to have fun with a calculator" (a rework of his 1998 masterpiece "Having a laugh with an accountant").

Struggling to support the wives and children of the employees' of his favourite brewery, he is searching for a second wife and hopes to be able to describe himself as a "contented, mature and successful" individual before his fiftieth birthday; being short, fat and bald, he has given up on being "tall, dark and handsome".

DINNER
WITH MANDELSON

John Ashton

DINNER
WITH MANDELSON

Vanguard Press

A CIP catalogue record for this title is
available from the British Library.

ISBN: 978 1 84386 387 8

Photographs © 2007 Dirk van der Werff / AQphotos.com

http://www.aqphotos.com/

Vanguard Press is an imprint of
Pegasus Elliot MacKenzie Publishers Ltd.
www.pegasuspublishers.com

First Published in 2007

Vanguard Press
Sheraton House Castle Park
Cambridge England

Printed & Bound in Great Britain

Dedication

For CJ. Simply the best. A Gentleman. A Scholar.
All round nice guy. Under appreciated. Much loved.
My own Superman.

Acknowledgements

To Paddy..........this is your fault; you told me to
shut up and get on with it!
Thanks to Dr Steve for the title – it's all I can remember from
another good night in 'The Urra'!
And my kids - thanks for trying to keep me sane; you failed. But
Emma, Kate and Tom, you are 'the best'. And you
still make me laugh and smile.
To Pete – part-time proof-reader, super-hero and drinking buddy.
You really are a ****.

And Lynn – thanks for the affection and all that soft stuff when it
was needed. If it wasn't for your love and encouragement, I'd still
be counting things.
And Dick – Buster will have his thrills! In Book 4.
Dirk – thanks for the photography.

And many thanks, for many things, to Welder, Ian Grant, Bruce
Watson, Tony Butler, Mark Brzezicki, Stuart Adamson, JW
Cameron, Alan Hull, Daz, Vic, Lee Patterson, Dr Fauzi F Saba,
Miles Middleton, Dick Slater, Ritchie Humphreys, Brian Honour,
Derek Freeman, Glynn Wealleans, Joe Joe Joe Allon, Franko,
Hawk, Cookie, Smurf, the Theakston family, and David Newstead.

And all the usual thanks to the likes of my hair stylist, dietician,
wardrobe specialist, personal trainer and feng shui consultant. Oh
yes, and Mazz rocks!

And a very special thank you to the brewers of fine ales and all
importers of quality red wines (from anywhere other than France).

Cheers.

You will never be happy if you continue to search for what happiness consists of. You will never live if you are looking for the meaning of life.

Albert Camus.

One

"Look at 'em," moaned Grant, "kids, stinking food, aggressive mastication and an unwelcome amount of bare skin, this is supposed to be a quiet country pub, not the inside of some dingy seaside caff."

Grant, when he wasn't sitting in judgement in the public bar of The Urra Arms, was some form of accountant (a cue for his oft repeated comment that 'I've never been good with numbers though'), was virtually bald (and not as the result of some styling decision), possessed an extended stomach upon which a suitably talented individual could balance a full pint glass, was never seen in public with his long suffering wife (to whom he rarely referred) and could bore for England on the subjects of lower division English football and late twentieth century rock music (mercifully, even he was too bored by everything to do with accountants and accountancy); he, like the majority of those with whom he was acquainted, drank too much and was occasionally something of a wag (or, to be more precise, thought that he was).

"Quite" was the only response which Buster, a local farmer with a questionable workload, could muster. In fact the description 'local farmer' was totally misleading: Buster hailed from the south, had been educated at public school and still possessed (and worked on) the accent, phraseology and mannerisms of the text book, gentrified oaf, and appeared to 'farm' for only two or three days per year. Liked and respected by all, Buster was a true character (still delighting in tales of his school days and his class nickname 'Gargoyle'), short but exceedingly stocky and with hands like those of your average heavyweight mountain gorilla, he was very much a 'fixture' in The Urra (subject to 'sporting' commitments and the 'feeding times' specified by 'the little lady'[1]).

Getting to his feet, with some considerable effort, Grant grunted "same again for everyone" and, sighing, pushed his way through the pack of 'learner drinkers', family flotsam and 'early-doors' locals to the bar.

"Do you know," started Buster with an exotic waving of his lower arms, "the people who annoy me are those who hold extended conversations with cash dispensers, usually in the rain and always in front of me."

No one replied; it was too much of an effort.

The Urra Arms was a substantial public house, which was rarely full for nine months of the year, serving locals from the surrounding villages and the occasional visitor from one of the towns to the north. The Urra was the only watering hole in the five villages comprising the local parish; at one time each village had supported its own pub but the economic consequences of an ageing (retiring and dying) population, the closure of the various major industries which had once filled the villages with all types of managers and their families, Gordon Brown's prudent tenure as Chancellor of the Exchequer and the drink drive laws[2] had resulted in the eventual closure of all but The Urra. And so, subject to the weather, every Bank Holiday and throughout the summer school holidays, The Urra was filled with visitors from the towns to the north, all determined to use the interior of the pub (rather than the

---

[1] The 'little lady' was small in stature but this did not prevent her from ruling through fear – and not just on her long suffering spouse. All of the locals treated Mildred – for that was her given name – with total and unquestioning respect – ideally from at least two miles.

[2] Which had taken some twenty years to have any impact on this part of North Yorkshire; and it had even then taken a rather spectacular incident one warm Sunday afternoon involving a powerful Jaguar car owned by a local doctor, an over-powering but possibly unnecessary urge to change the contents of the in-car CD player, forty feet of white picket fencing along the front perimeter of the village infants school, and a bored pensioner of the flicking lace curtain variety.

adjacent beer garden and children's play area) to exercise their children (without any form of parental control or discipline) and committed to the rapid consumption of pints of fizzy lager, chips and something (or, if adventurous, something and chips), alcopops, and the various types of crisps offered by the financially pleased landlord, Alf; or Alf the Arsehole as he was known by his many despairing customers. And so, on this evening, the second Friday in August, the sun and barmy temperatures had attracted several dozen townies[3], and their children, to The Urra; much to the frustration of the Regulars[4], a group of locals, drawn from a variety of backgrounds with little in common, who all enjoyed a few pints too many on most evenings of the week, and most certainly on Wednesdays, Fridays and Saturdays. And Sunday afternoons. And Bank Holidays. And Tuesdays. And Thursdays.

The Urra occupies a commanding position overlooking the beck, which runs through the middle of the picturesque village of Watson Humphrey. An ancient village with a long and interesting history (involving all kinds of rampaging foreigners from Romans and Vikings, through to the US Air Force during the Second World War and, more recently, tourists looking for anything to do with Captain James Cook; the latter generally being disappointed), Watson Humphrey boasts a cosmopolitan population of almost five hundred souls, few of whom actually hail from the village or its surrounding area. Clinging to the northern edge of the Hambleton Hills, the majority of properties are old and constructed from local

---

[3] 'Townies' is not a term of endearment. Often used by those who believe that they have a monopoly on all things 'rural', the term covers everyone from the much loved car radio removal mechanic through to the much abused members of the medical profession (who, by dint of ill fortune and the budgetary mistakes of successive governments, are forced to live in urban areas).
[4] Welcome, dear reader, to the alcohol fuelled world of Elliott, Grant, Frank, Buster, Bill, Ben, Pete, Neil and Biggles, and the rest of the sad pack of locals who frequent The Urra most Wednesdays, Fridays, Saturdays, Sundays and Tuesdays. The term 'regular' has no connection to bowel movements, although their output is pretty similar.

17

stone and, if the paraphernalia of the modern era (such as television aerials, road signs, caravans littering driveways, executive motor cars and street lights) were to be removed, the village could have been stuck in the Nineteen Thirties. To the unceasing delight of all, the village had not (yet) been invaded by any developments of what Grant refers to as 'executive warehousing for kids'.

"You'll soon be buying rounds on credit given the prices in this place, and it wouldn't be so bad if the ale was consistently good, but that's nowt more than a pipedream," grumbled Grant on returning with the usual round of two pints of 'Sheep', three pints of 'Worthy' and two pints of the guest beer (which this evening was called something like Old Codger's Whitby Armpit). This was pretty much the standard round which only changed when Old Bill was approaching capacity ("I'll have a wee Grouse if I may"…which was always met by a variation on the theme of "well, we can't stop you complaining"), whoever was at the bar was reasonably well oiled leading to a never refused invitation to Ben (who had not bought a round in anyone's memory and accordingly was usually excluded from rounds, despite his sudden coughing and Saint Bernard dog impersonations) or Uncle Frank requested a lager (prefacing the order with attempted excuses, which never failed to result in even greater 'yah lager supping poof' type comments) rather than a 'Sheep'.

Bill was a retired pharmacist, who had retired to the nearby village of Cringle when he had sold his shops to a national chain of chemists; and hence was often accused of living off the ill-gotten gains of a career in drug-pushing. Phenomenally healthy for someone in their late seventies, and still with a full head of thick white hair, Bill was a cultured moaner and a man of firmly held views; in fact some would call him bigoted, he, on the other hand, would dismiss such accusations as ill-considered tripe. Grant was frequently heard explaining that, when he gets old, he wants to be as miserable as Bill – and sufficiently alert to enjoy his (and therefore everyone else's) misery.

Grant was rambling, "There is something decidedly thick in asking for three pints of lager."

"Explain," instructed Elliott; it was not a question or a request.

"We ask for our beer by brand," Grant paused, "These townies ask for however many pints of lager and the poor barmaid always has to ask what type." Grant took a pull from his pint "The townie will always reply, irrespective of how many times he has previously visited the bar with 'what have you got, pet' or something equally banal."

"And your point is?" asked Elliott.

"You're an intellectual snob, that's what you are," observed Bill.

Ben also lived in Cringle; although some would argue that he 'existed' rather than lived. Also retired and in his late-seventies, Ben literally hobbled about, due to two false hips and the effects of what he referred to as 'a hard milk round'. He had owned a variety of businesses, ranging from a petrol station to a chain of clubs (of ill-repute according to those who were old enough to remember them; no one ever admitted to visiting them), but now appeared to be approaching some form of senility; he possessed an eccentric dress sense (in that he never changed his clothes), always appeared unwashed and had avoided the inside of any hairdressing establishment since before the Falklands War (few assumed that the growth beneath his nose and around his chin was an intentional beard; and some had suggested that it was, in fact, home to a pair of Great Tits). The perception of senility was derived from the fact that he allegedly kept his immense wealth in a box in his greenhouse (he certainly never spent any of it), and because of his limited conversation; in fact Ben appeared to have a limited number of phrases, which he could manipulate to a degree, and thus, whatever direction the conversation was taking, and whenever it suited him, Ben would interject with a gem such as: '*there's some that say they're all wogs south of Harrogate,*' a phrase used when mention is made of anything to do with London or the South.

Other 'Ben favourites' include the following – many of which Grant found himself reciting in the long cold hours before dawn, when he would find himself lying in bed, alone, lonely, annoyed, scared, and generally miserable:

'*I think that this is off*' or '*a tadge too cloudy, pet*' phrases used when returning a half-consumed pint to the barmaid.

'*What was that*' or '*What did you say*' or '*What did he say*' used when mention is made of any form of distress or problem affecting a resident of Cringle.

'*Ta-rah, as they say in Hartlepool*' or '*Ta-rah, like well*' or '*Sees you later, as they say in Middlesbrough,*' used when leaving to go home, any of which would elicit nothing more than grunts of acknowledgement or, rarely, a response along the lines of 'Giz yer wallet, as they say in Liverpool' (or wherever the fancy took the speaker; Darlington being a particular favourite of Grant).

'*There's some that say that the Romans should have built the wall on the Tees,*' a phrase used when any mention is made of Scotland, Tyneside, Wearside, Durham or any place or person situated north of Yarm[5].

'*Five million with a speech defect,*' a favourite, used at any mention of, or reference to, Birmingham.

---

[5] A quaint market town on the banks of the River Tees once marking the boundary of the counties of Durham and the North Riding of Yorkshire, Yarm is now home to various massively overpaid footballers; this attracts totty from all over the area; this in turn attracts the young warm blooded male to the area; Yarm is now full of drinking establishments of varying pedigrees, boasts gutters full of vomit most weekends, has a large police presence due to the level of alcohol-fuelled and totty-caused violence, and is thus an over-priced shit hole. To quote Grant, not the author.

'They hung a monkey in Hartlepool you know,'[6] a comment which Ben expected to produce laughter or enlightenment, dependent on his audience, but which usually resulted in a deathly silence, which Ben would then attempt to fill with tales of the German navy bombarding Hartlepool and of Zeppelins dropping bombs on the Hartlepool football ground; again he would expect amusement or further enquiries but would merely stimulate a comment such as 'shame the krauts didn't do the job properly' or 'was the Kaiser a Darlington supporter?'

Frank was really Martin, but had assumed the name of Frank after one liquid evening when, during increasingly fuelled (and failing) attempts at sincerity, he had repeatedly used the phrase 'can I be frank'; he got his wish. Tall, with a ruddy complexion caused by countless hours on golf courses, Frank sincerely believed that he was something of an intellectual giant and was one of the 'more cultured' of the regulars in The Urra; as Elliott had pointed out previously, Frank had read the complete works of Dick Francis. A retired engineer, Frank frequently amused the likes of Grant and Elliott by his apparent slowness, but was always quick to remind them that he had managed to retire, early…and with a big wallet.

"Yer not wrong," agreed a sullen-looking Ben.

"Magic pint that," concluded Frank at the completion of a half pint pull from his fresh drink, "better than sex"

"Wassat?" said Grant, hoping for a reaction to what he felt was a mildly amusing riposte, but receiving the silent gazes he deserved.

"Whilst I fear that I may regret asking," started Buster using, as usual, a strangely old fashioned, but not affected, language,

---

[6] And they did too! A long and sad story involving the wreck of a French vessel in Napoleonic times and the one survivor being a simian character dressed as a cabin boy. Some would argue that it was lucky that they only hung it.

spoken in a perfect south coast accent, "but what is aggressive mastication?"

"Oh no," interjected Frank, but it was too late; Grant leapt at the opportunity to jump on one of his countless soap boxes.

"Have you ever seen anyone eat with their mouth open in a friendly way?" Grant paused for effect, "or demonstrating any level of intellectual credibility?"

"Sorry, but I don't follow," admitted Buster.

"Look at the relationship between number one haircuts[7], high heels with short skirts on middle aged mules[8], loud kids...you know, Borstal puppies[9]... stupid stickers on rear windscreens...you know... 'divvent dunshus wor Geordies'...or 'Boro for Wembley'... 'My other car is a Porsche'...shell suits...Barcelona football shirts after the post holiday wash...people going into Indian or Thai restaurants and demanding steak and chips, well-done with a pint of fizzy lager...come on, you know what I mean...this is open mouth eating country...all the hard knocks, showing that, yes, they could eat your innards if you happened to look at them at the wrong time."

Before the now hyper-ventilating Grant could continue Bill lifted his hands in mock surrender, "Well the things you learn, were you taught this at school?"

Elliott, a teacher who was originally from some backwater in Kent but was now proud to live in the cottage adjacent to The Urra, saw his opportunity, "No, no, no Bill, remember that you can't use the words 'Middlesbrough' and 'Education' in the same sentence."

---

[7] Short cropped hair - possibly, but not necessarily linked to an outbreak of nits – often associated with a short temper, experience of the use of fists in cases of disagreement, and a thorough understanding of the benefits system.

[8] A term often used for a beast of burden but in this case referring to a member of the 'gentler' sex who is used to carrying babies/ excess fat/ unreasonable attitudes/ inadequate male partners (delete as appropriate).

[9] Children being groomed for careers in detention centres and other government run institutions rather than educational establishments.

"Mmmmm, well," concluded Buster rising from his chair, clearly intent on returning home and not to the bar "must dash, 'fraid I'm playing golf near Leeds tomorrow, cheerio."

"I've never liked those stupid sticky labels you get on apples, that won't come off or, if they do, they stick to your thumb," commented Ben, to no one in particular, although Elliott nodded, in agreement or acknowledgement, but probably not both.

"And why, tell me," continued Grant, "do they have 'our dinner or our dinners' instead of 'my lunch or trough-time', eh?"

"I like the terms 'bait' and 'snap'," offered Bill.

Grant started with a flourish, "Me Mam, Our Mam, Nana, You know, Our this, You know, Our that, Our Place, bet they never passed Latln!"

"You didn't study it, did you," a statement, not a question, from Elliott.

With some effort Ben exclaimed, "There's some that say they should have built the Roman wall along the Tees."

"Who built it in the wrong place then?" asked Elliott.

"Would keep the buggers out if it had been built there," continued Ben, ignoring or not understanding Elliott's attempt at humour.

"Why was it built on the Tyne anyway?" asked Grant.

Shaking his head in despair, having missed the point that Grant and Elliott were acting stupid, Bill stepped into the debate, "Children, children, children…it was to keep out the Scots."

"But, in Roman times the Scots weren't the Scots," argued Grant.

"So who were they then?" asked Frank, smugly, confident that, for once, he had outwitted the gruesome twosome.

"Members of various warring tribes who would have eaten a gangly shit like you for breakfast," replied Elliott, keen to return to some Ben-baiting.

"No, but they were Scots," pleaded Frank.

"So, was Boudica, the Queen of the Iceni, the Queen of England or Margaret Thatcher's Great Great Grandma?" asked Grant.

"The latter you daft twat," answered Elliott, before continuing to develop his theme, "Look, the Italians, who've always been cowards, built the Wall…and remember that they had two attempts at it…to keep out the northern based ignoramuses and hooligans…to assist in their attempts to bring civilisation to what was then an outpost of their empire…it just so happens that we now know those warring masses of wode covered perverts to be Scots."

"What do you mean, gangly shit?" asked Frank.

"Why is Italy the shape of a Wellington boot?" asked Grant.

Elliott shook his head, "Dunno, give up."

"'Cos you wouldn't get that much shit in a training shoe…boom boom." Grant slapped Bill's back in an act of mock hilarity. Bill shook his head, his despair deepening.

"So, anyway," Elliott tried to regain control, "why didn't the Romans build the wall at, say, York…thereby keeping out those tribes we now know as Geordies[10], Machems[11], Poolies[12], Darloids[13], Smoggies[14] and so on?"

"Maybe they wanted to be in with the Poolies and were going to exterminate the Darloids," suggested Grant.

---

[10] Someone from Newcastle upon Tyne, not Gateshead. The name having some historical connection to a King George.

[11] Poor sods from the Sunderland area. The name apparently refers to the "making" of things (takes all sorts, doesn't it?).

[12] Those fortunate enough to be from the Borough of Hartlepool, the merger of the now long forgotten British West Hartlepool and the home of the cod-heads, Old Hartlepool.

[13] The tribe based in the southern-most market town of County Durham, Darlington; which should be destroyed and rebuilt, possibly in the Urals.

[14] Anyone travelling towards the Teesside area, by any mode of transport, cannot fail to be horrified by the smoke cloud hanging over the industrial towns of Billingham, Stockton, Middlesbrough and Redcar; true smoggies are drawn from the northern and eastern areas of Middlesbrough and, like their brethren in the East Cleveland area, are instantly recognisable by the single eye in the middle of the forehead. Be afraid, be very afraid.

"But places like Darlington didn't exist in Roman times," pleaded Bill.

"Well, that will have made their life easier then," concluded Grant.

Elliott grinned, "Yes indeed-ee…so that will be why they didn't build the Wall on the Tees…see Ben, it's obvious."

"Little Tommy needs an airing," announced Frank, unnecessarily as he stubbed out his cigarette and rose from his chair.

"As does young Rupert," agreed Bill.

"Rupert?" queried Frank.

"Aye," nodded Grant, "Rupert the Redundant."

Grant Bannister was in his mid-forties and had never forgiven his parents for his name. During the later stages of her pregnancy his mother had been reading a romantic novel, set in a 1950s hospital and had decided that, if a boy, 'it' would carry the name of the doctor winning the heart of Staff Nurse Cameron. The story focused on the rivalry between Doctors Grant Singleton and David Thomas; Grant wanted to meet the author, but in the meantime blamed his mother. His father, who should have ensured that his mother was reading a more appropriate novel, was at fault for all those 'didn't we meet on the stairs' and 'going up?' type comments. Grant was now definitely on the way down.

His life, which to the outsider may have appeared successful and comfortable, was, at best, a shambles: his wife despised him, his eldest daughter took after her mother, work and family pressures had resulted in him losing contact with many of his friends, his professional life was becoming intolerable, and his only 'escapes' were following one 'of the worst fucking teams in the league' all over northern England, and beer. Beer; not lager ('fizzy alcohol for young bucks and puffs'), no spirits, never white wine ('just like water but you get the shits after two bottles') and never any fashion-led bottles or cocktails. A bottle of decent red each evening (on returning to the silence of the marital home) was purely medicinal; *and it goes off if you leave it in an uncorked bottle doesn't it,* so it had to be a full bottle (or two if 'she' had been more difficult than usual or work had been worse than intolerable). His health was less than good, partly due to the pressures of work and a dysfunctional domestic life. The excesses of work-related socialising and a non-work social life focusing on beer were clearly beginning to take their toll.

Where had 'it' all gone wrong? Grant wasn't even sure when 'it' had all gone wrong and accordingly was at a loss to work out why…but, when he was willing to explore the darker parts of his life he could work out why 'it' had got progressively worse.

He had loved her and had tried. "Everything I do I do for you" had been a frequent, light-hearted comment, to which she had reacted negatively long before he had appreciated it.

Had she ever really loved him? "Buggered if I know" would be his response. A poignant memory was her telling him that one of her family, on being told of his proposal of marriage, had advised her that 'given her age, she was on a high shelf and might not get many more chances', and to 'remember his American Express Gold Card'.

Had it ever been right?

Had it been fundamentally flawed from the start?

This morning had been typical.

He had fed the cats.

He had walked and fed the dogs.

He had shouted his farewells from the foot of the stairs.

His departure was brought to a crashing halt.

"Grant, I want a word with you!"

"Can it wait until this evening?"

"No! I hear that you got some tickets for the Rolling Stones"

"Yes, what about it? You don't like them!"

"How do you know!"

"Sweetheart I'm in a rush. I know you don't like them because you told me so when I took you to see them before we got married."

"So you gave them away! To your bloody secretary!"

"Not quite. I got them for Heather's brother. He is a life-long fan, a decent guy and-"

"So what, I would have gone with Samantha. She loves them."

"And he has an incurable brain tumour and I very much doubt if Samantha likes anything more sophisticated than the latest boy band."

"That's out of order. Get the tickets back or else!"

Grant had closed the front door. With an unnecessarily loud bang.

Always needing the last word, she had shouted out of the bedroom window **"And you'll never get to shag her!"**

Had she always been so unreasonable?

"Mullets,[15]" continued Grant, "another sure sign."

"Don't budgies have them?" asked an increasingly perplexed Bill.

"No, no, no, my little drug-pushing friend," replied Elliott. "I believe that he is referring to the strange haircut worn by the likes of the footballer Chris Waddle[16] and many, many females from places such as Hartlepool."

---

[15] A type of hair cut, favoured by members of both sexes during different periods of twentieth century history.
[16] A "famous" footballer from the North of England who wrecked his reputation by agreeing to sing in a duet with a Mr G Hoddle, of whom Grant could pass many a rude comment, but the author won't (today).

"They hung–" but before Ben could finish Grant continued at speed.

"Babies out-numbering parents by the ratio of four to one, uncontrolled mongrels, an inability to queue, a failure to understand the simplicities of the capitalist system, as in you should starve if you're a lazy parasitic bastard and, and," Grant was beginning to lose himself, "tight denims over fat arses."

"You've little room to talk," interrupted Elliott.

"Everything alright at home Grant?" enquired Frank.

"Excuse me," replied a completely confused Grant.

Bill stood up and commented, "Perfect circles."

"You what?" asked Grant, somewhat more aggressively than necessary.

"Arab queues," replied Bill.

Normality was returned by Bill announcing that it was his turn to buy a round.

"Shit, Haley must be returning," commented Elliott.

"Who's she?" asked Frank.

"The comet," replied Elliott.

"Halley," corrected Bill.

Frank was, and looked, totally confused. Grant tried to assist.

"As in squadrons of pigs."

Grant failed.

Frank, shaking his head, reached for his cigarettes and, to avoid the possibility of looking stupid, changed the subject.

"Anyone fancy a game of golf tomorrow?"

A variety of true and poor excuses for not watching Frank throw his clubs off several tees followed.

Bill returned from the bar and carefully placed the assorted drinks in front of the enthusiastic drinkers.

"I do like these darker ales," commented Grant as he held up his pint to the light. "Clear as a bell."

"What a daft phrase," commented Frank.

Elliott sat forward. "I believe that good health is nothing more than the slowest way to die."

Grant giggled; he had an infectious laugh and his face glowed when he was laughing at, or telling a joke. Humour could show Grant's best side: and his worst. "Aye, can you just imagine all those health nuts lying in hospital, proper parasites on the system, dying of nothing!"

They visited the pub for different reasons.

For Ben it was habitual; seven days a week, an hour or so at lunchtime and one and a half hours every night.

It was the same for Buster; out for a few pints every night, unless one of his sporting interests prevented it, although he occasionally visited the pub in the nearby village of Wyke on the Hill. The hostelry in Wyke on the Hill, The Lion Rampant, was a far more welcoming establishment than The Urra; the landlord was an amiable and witty individual, the beers were well-kept and cheaper, and no bar meals were served. It was, however, a little too far away for the locals to regularly chance the drive, given that it involved three miles on a major road; for Buster, however, this was a reasonable gamble.

To Bill it was a social occasion; a thrice weekly opportunity to meet and enjoy a few slurps of the amber nectar; and to moan, if anybody would listen.

Elliott, in the opinion of many, was an alcoholic; this unreasonable view being based on the simple premise that when anyone visited The Urra, Elliott would be in residence. Those who knew him realised that he was very much a people person, craving the sullen wit round the bar room table, and that he would regularly visit The Urra and drink only alcohol-free beverages. The definition of the word 'regular' is, of course, determined by the user of the word; regular could be once a week, once a year, or once this side of the Millennium.

Frank, if he had been anything other than successful, would have been the 'village pisshead', or idiot. An attractive wife and superb house, with bar and snooker room, Frank would visit The Urra most nights of the week, often after several post-round ales in one of the many golf clubs he frequented. The village whisper was that all was not well with Frank's marriage; his wife apparently being bored and increasingly uncomfortable with Frank's presence in the family home.

Grant just didn't want to go home and found the relaxed haze of a few pints too many to be the only peace he achieved.

"You know," continued Grant, "I can't stand women who toss back their hair and then run their fingers through it, like that bint over there."

"The 'I'm a free spirit' look?" suggested Frank.

"Nah, it's the 'I fancy a shag' look and what pisses Grant off is that it's 'I fancy a shag with anyone other than that fat, bald slob over there', isn't that right Sunbeam?"

"Piss off Elliott!"

Elliott sat back and folded his arms; he was in full control of the table, was marginally inebriated and was totally happy. Grant sat shoulders slumped, staring into his beer, deep in thought.

"Why?" asked Elliott.

"Piss off," repeated Grant.

Two

An extremely mild late-August saw trade booming at The Urra –
even on this third Wednesday of the month; the bar was becoming
virtually a no-go area for the locals and on at least one occasion an
overly emotional Grant had threatened to call the licensing
authorities; his complaint being the number of children "playing" in
the bar. Loud though he may have been, Grant had never summoned
the courage to discuss this issue with 'management', and this
subject had merely become another source of his regular
grumblings; grumblings which were often initiated and encouraged
by Elliott.

   In his late forties and significantly overweight, Elliott always
appeared to be in complete control of his life, totally satisfied with
his 'lot' and never depressed. Occasionally referred to as Sheila, as
in Ferguson, on the basis of his three degrees[17], Elliott was clearly
an intellectual heavyweight who, from a career perspective, had
obviously chosen the routes of least resistance; that is not to say that
he was fundamentally lazy, but he would always choose an
opportunity for a few slurps and a chat, avoiding anything remotely
connected with the concepts of responsibility or graft. Now a highly
experienced teacher, he had managed to avoid any form of
departmental, year or functional responsibility, and retained the
somewhat challengeable view that the pupils were there to entertain
him and, if they learnt anything from him they should regard it as a
special bonus. In reality his laid-back style (and lack of dress sense;

---

[17] The Three Degrees were a female singing trio, popular in some quarters during
the later part of the twentieth century – HRH The Prince of Wales liked them
(apparently/ unfortunately).

31

dark, almost grubby chinos, baggy dark coloured shirts and suede boots – which he would argue were made from the scrotal sacks of camels – seven days a week, whatever the venue or occasion) made him a highly effective teacher and although his lunchtime visits to neighbouring hostelries caused some grief for school management, he was highly respected (and liked) by pupils, past and present. The combination of his intellect driven wit, and the ability to stop a herd of rhino with one of his withering looks, made Elliott a formidable drinking companion and a popular client of The Urra; but for all of his seeming contentment, his closest companions (he had few true friends as he was a very private person) always felt that he had failed to meet his potential; mind, he could drink just about anyone under the table and was never caught out in any verbal jousting. He would revel in the story of the day that he was called priapic[18] by one of his female colleagues, an intended insult but, in fact, the highest of compliments to a man such as Elliott; and when telling the story he would never, being an awkward cuss, explain the meaning of the word.

Just past seven in the bar of The Urra and Elliott is in full flow...

"The fact that I wear anoraks has nothing to do with your misguided view, based on a singularly poor education, that anoraks can only be associated with individuals of the train-spotting variety; and anyway, what is wrong with collecting numbers for Gawd's sake, Christ look at you, you're a bloody number cruncher."

Grant smirked, keeping his memories of watching Deltics[19] power out of Darlington station to himself and took a long pull from his pint of Hedgehog Remembrance Ale; it had been yet another shit day at the office.

---

[18] Persistent erection of the penis. Insult or compliment? Interesting question!
[19] A class of extremely powerful diesel locomotive once used on the East Coast mainline, famous for breaking down with alarming regularity.

"Look…you have to be bloody brave to wear an anorak with the hood pulled up…particularly if the toggles are pulled tight…it is a scientific fact that wearing anoraks can be injurious to one's health."

Grant shifted uneasily, his new suit already looking slept-in and, perhaps to stop himself from falling into a state of half consciousness (a regular problem usually caused by the long hours he worked rather than the amount of alcohol he had consumed) he joined the discussion in his own intellectual style.

"Bollocks."

"Look you cretin, the average anorak hood significantly impairs vision and, therefore, the wearer is at risk from being knocked down by a juggernaut every time he crosses the road."

"Why…do they make you deaf…as well as look stupid?"

"Wearing an anorak with the hood up results in severely impaired vision and you therefore need to be brave to wear one…it is bloody obvious innit…the binocular visual field is what it's all about…you ask any optician."

Elliott relaxed and his face took on an all-conquering look; Grant was having none of it.

"I was in the opticians this morning…you'll never guess who I bumped into?"

Buster, who had been remarkably quiet thus far, reacted.

"No, who?"

"Everyone," replied Grant, delighted with himself and failing to control his child-like giggles.

Buster, slack jawed, stared into space before waving his spade-sized hands and introducing a new topic of conversation, immediately getting Ben's attention. "Righto, my turn, what's everyone having?"

Ben dived in before Buster could clarify who his question was being addressed to.

"I'll have half a Worthy if you're asking."

33

Buster looked heavenwards and, with some effort, pulled himself up to his full height of just over five foot.

"Come on Man, stand up and get the beers."

"Elliott…why don't you bugger off…two Sheep, three Worthy, two Hedgehogs, I guess?"

This was met with a variety of grunts and Buster span round, making full use of his low centre of gravity, and shimmied to the bar.

"And a half of Worthy," called Ben.

"Fancy a round tomorrow?" asked Frank in the general direction of Elliott.

"Golf, here we go…bloody golf," mumbled Ben

"Got to be an early start," replied Elliott, "got some work to do tomorrow afternoon, but an early morning game would be very nice."

"I don't know, bloody golf!"

"How about you Grant?"

"No thanks Frank, too busy."

"Less of the Frank. My name is Martin!"

"Sorry Frank."

"Fuck off."

"Now, now."

Buster started putting pints on the table; as always, and in the view of some, on purpose, he mixed them all up resulting in a round of "This is Worthy; This must be yours; The Hog's nice innit; Sorry this is yours; Have you got any infectious diseases?; That must be Sheep; Where's my half?"

"Talking about disease," interrupted Grant, "As life is sexually transmitted, does that make it a disease?"

Buster looked pained.

Frank looked lost.

Grant raised his eyebrows; genuinely amazed at the absence of any response.

"Have you noticed," started Elliott, "that every time Buster sits down, stands up or merely lifts a pint, he makes a peculiar throaty noise."

"Do I really? Well, well, and what, per chance, do you believe to be the cause of these alleged noises, it can't be ill health or any form of unfitness given my agricultural occupation," responded Buster.

"Agricultural occupation my arse," was the deeply considered contribution from Grant.

"It's the same thing that is causing your hair to migrate from the top of your bonce to your nostrils and why you, like Ben, frequently start conversations with 'Nowadays' or 'When I was a lad' or something equally oldmanish," continued Elliott.

"You know," interrupted Grant, who was beginning to annoy Elliott, "Frank told me that as he got older, well, I mean old…"

"Fuck off," commented Frank as he reached for his cigarette lighter.

"Thanks Frank," continued Grant, "as the man himself told me, as you get older you learn never to waste a hard on, never decline an opportunity for a pee, and never, ever trust a fart."

Elliott, "Another valuable contribution from Grant."

Frank, "My erections are hard enough to knack you, Grant."

Grant was struck dumb by the wit of Frank's comment.

Buster, "Well actually, I realised that I was getting old when I noticed that the little old dear that I was helping across the street was the wife."

Elliott, "Exactly…and I expect that your bathroom cabinet now resembles the inside of Superdrug."

Buster, "Well now you come to mention it."

Ben, "When I was younger drugs weren't for headaches."

Bill, "What's this got to do with anoraks?"

Elliott, "And then there is the issue of concentration and memory...do you know that you become progressively more stupid by the year after the age of thirty two?"

Frank, "Isn't giving up lager and drinking stuff that is flat, brown and cloudy a sign of old age?"

Grant, "Nah, that's about your sexuality."

Frank, "Fuck off bean-counter."

Elliott, "And then there's the ability to formulate reasoned arguments, to construct complicated sentences, making full use of the vast English vocabulary and..."

Frank, "Like piss off you patronising southern shit head."

Elliott, "Definite signs of improvement there Old Boy."

Grant, "Being serious, I'm getting old...I go to bed before my kids, I keep thinking that I sound like my old man, my memory ain't..."

"Yup," interrupted Frank, seizing the opportunity, "it's your round."

"Are you ever wrong?" replied Grant

Frank drained his pint and looked Grant in the eyes, "Well, I think I overslept once."

"Mine's a half of Worthy, if you're asking?" sighed Ben, more in hope than expectation. Whilst he hadn't worked out the plot, he had noticed that, with an increasing frequency, people were forgetting his drink when they bought a round.

The front door of The Urra opened, accompanied by a blast of cold air tinged with the smells of rural activity, announcing the arrival of Dave 'Biggles' De Vere. Nodding towards Grant in a manner translating to "Yes, I'll have a pint of the Durham Light Infantryman Special", Biggles joined the table, immediately taking a pack of duty free cigarettes from his flying jacket pocket, and lighting up in his best James Dean manner.

Biggles had two jobs: his main occupation being a pilot for a company providing services to the RAF. 'Bloody madness' was Grant's considered opinion – as an accountant, Grant simply could not accept the logic behind outsourcing public sector services to private, profit-making organisations. In his ample spare time Biggles flew private jets for a local businessman. Having learnt to fly at a relatively late age, Biggles was clearly saddened by the fact that he had never been an RAF ace, had never flown sorties against bad men, and had not been young enough to develop a career flying long haul aircraft for a major flag carrier (with the obvious perks of sun, hostesses, exotic locations, hostesses and hostesses). Still, flying executive jets was an improvement from piloting the Short 330 'Flying Vans'[20] of his previous employment with a regional airline. (As he would tell anyone who would listen, the company only had two chances of success: 'none and fuck all'). He had always felt that piloting Flying Vans was beneath him (an interesting conceptual position for a pilot), and had never been amused by questions such as 'did you build that yourself' and 'can I use that as a chock; he was now easily annoyed by Grant.

In his early forties, Biggles had changed careers in his early twenties and had then met the daughter of a local millionaire; he now didn't need to work, saw putting up with his nineteen year old stepdaughter as a reasonable pay-back for his opulent life-style, and was, in his own eyes, something of a playboy. Sadly, his expanding waistline and relative shortness, together with the general absence of any form of suave, sophisticated personality, failed to give others the impression that he was the local equivalent of James Bond; still, he could always find solace in the facts that he wasn't a fat, bald, ugly accountant, he was a superb golfer, and he was totally in control.

---

[20] A small commercial aircraft built out of balsa wood or something similar, and looking remarkably like a garden shed with wings.

"Can I have four hundred Benson & Hedges, a bottle of Gordon's and a model 737 please," said Grant as he placed the first pints of his round on the table, "and a large G and T from your trolley please?"

Biggles tried to ignore him but failed, badly: "Piss off Grant."

Grant returned to the bar, pleased with Biggles arrival and comfortable in the knowledge that there would be some easy sport this evening.

"Where've you been today," enquired Frank, who was genuinely interested.

"Yes, yes, anywhere exciting?" added Buster.

Grant placed a further three pints on the table, including the DLI Special for Biggles, "Like over dams in the Ruhr valley or the marshlands of southern Iraq?"

"Piss off and thanks for the pint," replied Biggles, his hackles obviously rising.

"Did you forget my half?" enquired Ben.

Helping Grant out of a difficult, but frequently encountered situation, Elliott changed the subject.

"Went for a haircut this morning, down in the town…the place run by the two blonde girls."

Everyone nodded knowingly, each having their own private fantasy. They weren't particularly attractive. Neither had much personality. And any personality they had wasn't particularly warm. But, take any group of sexually frustrated, fundamentally immature males, be they in Sixth Form or a pub, and the juices or the imagination will flow[21].

"She says 'How do I want it?' and I reply 'In complete fucking silence'."

---

[21] It must have been a woman who realised that males have only two emotions: Hungry and Horny. And it must have been a woman who then concluded that if one sees a male without an erection, make him lunch.

Buster shook his head, "No, no, no, that's an urban myth or whatever."

Grant, who had clearly brightened up with the introduction to the discussion of the two blonde hairdressers, re-entered the fray "It's funny…every time I go I get asked what I want and I always say 'A number two, please' and one of them always replies 'Not that, I was asking about your hair' and everyone bursts into laughter."

"You don't need a haircut, a polish more like," replied Elliott.

Warming to his subject, Grant ignored him, "It's a great shame that a number two is so quick…I wish I had a fringe which needed trimming…what a view that would be…and I wouldn't mind if she had to brush past me at head height…oh yes…and this isn't a bald patch anyway…this is a solar panel for a sex machine."

"I saw that on a cushion," interrupted Buster.

"Two firm cushions, ripe for plumping," continued Grant.

"Down Tiger," laughed Elliott.

"Eindhoven," said Biggles, stopping the merriment in a flash.

"What?" asked Frank.

"You asked where I'd been today," replied Biggles.

Frank looked temporarily lost, "Wasn't that yesterday?"

"What cushion?" asked Bill.

"What's it like?" enquired Buster.

Elliott made the obvious reply, "The cushion or Eindhoven?"

"Eindhoven of course," stuttered Buster.

"Well, I guess a dark coloured runway, a terminal building with shops, a tower so people can see, and a big garage for the planes to rest in…is that right?" Elliott looked at Biggles.

Biggles knew that whatever answer he gave, however serious or stupid, it was he was going to be the butt of more jokes and insults, so he simply nodded.

"No, no, no…the city…it's where they make radios isn't it?" pressed Buster.

Biggles took a drag on his cigarette and nodded.

"Oh come on," begged Buster.

Biggles took a deep breath, "It's nice, took a battering during the war so much of it is rebuilt, it's flat… relatively warm at this time of year.…but your clogs will freeze off in winter …very much a housing estate for Philips like Billingham used to be for ICI…and the airport is pretty small and modern…typically Dutch."

"The airport?" asked Elliott.

Biggles looked lost.

Elliott persevered, "In what way is the airport typically Dutch?"

Biggles shook his head.

Grant joined in, "You said the airport was typically Dutch."

As everyone knew, there were times when the best policy to adopt with Elliott and Grant was silence; particularly when the double act were in drink, bored and looking for sport. Biggles failed to read the signs.

"I did not," pleaded Biggles.

Grant took his glasses out of his pocket, placed them on the lower part of his nose and folded his arms in a judicial manner, "Sorry, but you did."

"Did you have to land on a dyke?" asked Elliott.

Grant looked over the top of his glasses, "A Dutch airport with strange sexual preferences?"

"And what does Eindhoven mean? What is a Hoven? As it sounds as if the airport has only one," Elliott took up the questioning.

"No, no, no," interrupted Grant, "Must have two as it's Dutch."

Biggles and Elliott both looked confused.

"Double Dutch," continued a self-satisfied Grant.

Elliott looked pained; he expected a greater level of sophistication in humour and sensed that Grant had peaked for this evening.

Getting up with some effort, "Ta ra well like as they say in Hartlepool," said Ben, to no one in particular, which was perhaps for the best, given that no one was listening to him.

Grant looked at his watch. The kids would be going to bed soon. He missed them. Wanted to know them better. He had tried; he had reduced his workload to spend more time with the family; that was, after all, what she had said she wanted. But the more time he had spent at 'home' the worse matters had become. If he went home, she went out. And she was out more and more; and she regularly arranged for the kids to be elsewhere; result: he got home, no wife or kids, just notes telling him where and when he had to collect them.

He had two daughters. He had been besotted with each of them from birth. He had tried – succeeded in his mind – to be a 'modern father'. She had always been in control but he had been able to spend many happy hours with them; walks in the country, kite flying, story telling; playing; acting the fool; nappies; everything; for the first few years. Things; everything, had changed about the time of her father's death.

He knew that his going to the pub frustrated her, in part due to the continuing memories of her alcoholic father, but it annoyed her if he went home; and he didn't expect any tea to be made; no, he enjoyed cooking and would happily make a meal for them; but she didn't like him in the kitchen. He was full of fluid and had endured a long and frustrating day at work; all he wanted was to sit in front of a nice warm fire, socks off, music playing in the background, and to share a bottle of Medoc or similar with his wife and talk. Well, she wouldn't have any of that. Alternatively, he'd keep the fire and

Medoc and change the background music for some loud rhythm and blues. Well, she wouldn't have that either.

Grant drained his pint and placed the empty glass on the table with an exaggerated flourish.

Biggles took the hint "Thirsty?"

Grant nodded in the style of an over-excited Labrador.

Elliott persisted "So, do all the ground staff wear clogs in this typically Dutch airport?"

"Same again," said Biggles, a statement, not a question, as he stood, collected a few empties and then made for the bar.

Three

The first Wednesday in September brought with it the delightful emptiness caused by the return to school of the screaming hordes and, what Elliott referred to as, the post-holiday bankruptcy of your average family man. The Urra was virtually free of visitors and a full squad of locals was expected this evening.

"Life is what happens when you're busy making plans." A serious looking Elliott took a long draw.

"Deep," was the only comment Grant could muster; yet another bad day at the office and he was clearly up for a couple of quickies before returning home to numerous loud children and a silent wife.

"John Lennon, I think."

"Fucking Deep Man," replied Grant, in a truly awful scouse accent. Many people had told him that he could not do impersonations, or any accent other than his own (which he liked to describe as 'educated Teesside'), but he couldn't help himself. In fact, on occasion, he would find himself mimicking whoever he was talking to…no malice or forethought would be involved…it just sort of happened…but this was of no solace to his wife and her Irish family… 'to be sure' was no way to say 'yes please' in such company. And then there'd been that awkward situation with the cab driver in Glasgow…Grant hadn't meant to speak like a poor man's Billy Connolly[22]...it just sort of happened...and the cab driver had made his feelings felt...and it bloody well hurt the following morning.

"So I make no plans," continued Elliott in an effort to provoke Grant, who had committed the cardinal sin of talking about work and had bored Elliott on the subjects of business plans, strategic plans, action plans, financial plans and people plans, until he had been saved by the timely arrival of Buster.

"What are you on about?" enquired Buster.

"Plans my boy...plans...we don't need them."

"Well I don't know about that...I need to know what I'm going to plant."

"Do you plant set-a-side?" enquired Grant.

"And when I need to harvest or take beast to market."

"And when you need to put your red coat on for a gallop round the fields with your chums," added Grant.

"Quite."

"Well, I need no plans," continued Elliott, "As Johnny Lennon said."

"What, to you personally?" interrupted Ben. This was his first comment since joining the table, pint in hand, sometime previously.

---

[22] Billy Connolly, The Big Yin, was born and brought up in Glasgow, Scotland. He left school to work in the shipyards where he became a welder, joining the Territorial Army (in the Parachute Regiment) at around the same time. He developed an interest in folk music, eventually becoming an accomplished banjo player and a member of the band "Humblebums" with Gerry Rafferty (later of "Baker Street" fame). The jokes he told between songs eventually took over his act and he became a full-time comedian. Already a big star in Scotland he became a household name across the UK after appearing on "Parkinson" in the early nineteen seventies. This was, and is, an unfulfilled ambition of your poor novelist. Billy has released many recordings of his concert performances over the years as well as several videos. He has expanded his repertoire to include acting, appearing in a number of television dramas and films, more recently in the USA. In the 90s he made two documentary series for the BBC about Scotland and Australia respectively and in 1997 he starred in the award winning film Mrs. Brown (1997). He, according to his friends, is by some considerable margin UK's top comedian. Known for his long, messy hair, 'Goatee' beard and lots of bad language in his stand-up show.

Elliott continued, "I'm free me... I float like a bird high in the sky... do what I want, when I want... no ties no plans...people who can't do, plan."

Grant reacted, as Elliott knew he would, "Bollocks, not planning, in whatever circumstances, is akin to planning to fail."

"What's family got to do with it," asked Ben.

"Eh?"

"Kin...you mentioned kin."

No one ever told Ben what they really thought, or suggested that he leave to enjoy some sexual activity with himself, but Grant was coming close...he took a deep intake of breath and continued, "No, what I meant...I remember now...failing to plan is planning to fail."

"Thanks G."

"What Elliott?"

"You are working too hard Sunbeam," replied Elliott in an almost sympathetic tone, "and you need to remember that, as some bugger said, there is more chance of a camel passing through the eye of a needle, than a rich man passing through the pearly gates."

A bemused Grant stared at Elliott. "Eh?"

"It's your round...do you need it writing down?"

"Ho Ho."

Grant roused himself and walked purposefully to the bar. Alf eyed him with some disdain. Grant had often wondered what it was that made Alf such an awful publican; greed was an obvious answer, but Grant was becoming more certain that Alf's dislike of the rest of the human race was a major contributing factor. This accounted for Alf's inability to retain any quality staff, his habit of sacking staff who ask for holidays, and his well-known habit of attempting sexual relations with any reasonably attractive female member of staff, irrespective of their age or relationship to any of his clientele; to Grant's disgust, such attempts were more often successful than not. Disgust and intense envy. He couldn't remember the last time…his mind started wandering…but couldn't find much to concentrate on.

The order complete, Grant returned to his seat and listened, with some interest, to Elliott's views on a number of television presenters and Buster's predictions for the following days' horse races at Southall. The arrival of Frank was, of course, marked by another round of drinks, as was the entrance of Bill. Bill looked even grumpier than was usually the case and the size of his round made him appear even more annoyed "Do you buggers sit there with empty glasses, waiting for some retired and poverty stricken man to arrive?"

"No, but it's worth trying out," replied Elliott.

"Who's retired and poverty stricken?" asked Grant, setting up the almost immediate retort from Elliott, "Buster's all but retired."

"No, no, no…I'll have you know that I work exceedingly hard…but, working on the land does leave me virtually poverty stricken."

Elliott laughed, "Define 'virtually'."

"Well, er" Buster stuttered "as in 'almost'."

Grant replied on behalf of all those present, "Bollocks."

The conversation around the table had taken its usual illogical and almost mind-challenging path through such unconnected subjects as the shower of unwanted leaflets that fall out of newspapers, the deadweight price of cattle, racing bike handles and the prospects of Alf providing free drinks on Christmas day until, with the clock approaching nine, Biggles arrived.

"You're late…did you get lost?" enquired Elliott; any degree of sincerity or interest missing from his voice.

"Hun over the channel?" asked Grant.

Biggles sighed, shook his head in mock pity and pulled his wallet out of his jacket pocket "You won't be wanting a pint then."

"From your trolley or the bar?"

"Piss off Grant."

"Not for me, more's the pity," Buster stood up, "She who must be obeyed will have supper on the table and I'm off to Cumbria tomorrow, to see some prize cattle, so you know, must show willing, cheerio."

Rousing himself with some effort Ben addressed the table "Sees youse later as they say in Hartlepool"; as usual these parting comments were met with a silence broken only by a grunt of acknowledgement from Grant.

The welcome departure of Ben was followed by the arrival of the shuffling giant known to all as Big Pete; a retired banker (as in the bank retired him at the earliest possible juncture). Pete had invested wisely in bedsit type properties and now spent his days as a class room assistant – not out of any love of children – he hated them – but in the misguided hope that he'd be able to teach some young female teachers a lesson or two. His shuffling gait – which he denied and Grant was fond of impersonating – was the result of a number of hip operations and two dodgy knees – the latter being, according to Pete, the result of countless tremblers – old age was more probably the cause. A difficult bloke to dislike – although all of his bosses appeared to have mastered this skill – Pete was one of the most popular people in the area; always cheerful, frequently rude and always equipped with a bad joke, he had a 'special' love – hate relationship with Grant. They had both enjoyed 'under achieving' rugby careers and had 'fought' each other on numerous occasions in their younger years. In his late fifties and standing at well over six feet, Pete saw himself as a handsome beast and refused to acknowledge the fact that he had more facial hair than cranial hair. He refused to accept, or even acknowledge, any suggestions of baldness. Prone to stroking his grey, short cropped beard (he argued that it was a sophisticated silver) when thinking,

Pete was completely unable to manage the little hair that remained up top – so however much effort he put into his appearance, he always looked scruffy.

"Evening Pop Pickers." Pete stood behind Grant, looking round the table, making a mental note of the round he was about to buy. "Has Grant told you about the ring he bought his wife because of her mood swings…so he'd be able to tell what mood she's in?"

Grant shook his head, "Fuck off Pete."

"When she's in a good mood it glows blue…and when she's in a bad mood it leaves a big red mark on his vast forehead." Pete chuckled and signalled to Biggles that he would get this round.

Biggles nodded and sat down, "So, what have you chaps been up to?"

"Fuck all," replied Grant.

"You really must work harder at your command of the English language," suggested Elliott.

"Too right," agreed Bill, "for an educated professional your language is pretty much sewerage standard."

Pete chuckled, "They're right Fat Lad."

Grant shrugged his shoulders. He knew they were right. He smiled and looked up at Pete, "But, as they say, he who laughs last, thinks slowest."

Pete guffawed and wandered off to the bar, nodding in acknowledgement and back slapping as he went.

Grant was more tired than usual this evening and this manifested itself by his quicker than usual decline into a state of alcohol induced bigotry. He'd spent all day at his desk, with an early start, having left home before 6 am. A day of little intellectual challenge, but numerous frustrations. He had once enjoyed his job and had positively thrived on client created pressures and technical problems; but now the increasing number of management issues which he was forced to address, together with the number of staff

48

and client complaints, was making his life a working misery. Many of the client complaints, from which he was supposed to defend his firm, were, in his opinion, justified, and all appeared to stem from two service areas, both of which were not his areas of speciality, interest or responsibility; but he was in charge of the office so he had to deal with them.

But he was unable to solve the underlying causes, which caused him even greater angst; both service areas were populated by staff who, in his opinion, failed to deliver appropriate levels of client service, had the communication and interpersonal skills of Attila the Hun, and were managed by politically adept but fundamentally useless managers. And so the same problems continued to arise and, not unsurprisingly, clients were now leaving. Was he being unreasonable? Self doubt was beginning to affect him. But the level of client complaints could not be challenged and surely he was correct to believe that it was not his fault; he had explained the issues to more senior partners and they had failed to take any action. But he was still 'banging his head against the proverbial brick wall' …and it was beginning to hurt. Another shitty day and nothing to rush home for; he needed a break but was beginning to feel that he couldn't punch his way out of a paper bag.

"Righto, it's my round," shouted Grant, heaving himself from his seat before walking purposefully to the bar.

" 'bout time," commented Bill, "can you make mine a small Grouse please?"

"Okay you whingeing git," replied Grant, at an unnecessarily high volume.

Bill shook his head. "Can't remember when that was last funny."

Pete nodded, sagely, "Grant is an auditor you know."

"What's that got to do with the number of monkeys in Hartlepool?" asked Bill.

Pete answered with a smile "Well, they don't let auditors have coffee breaks...as...if you did...they would need retraining!" Clearly pleased with himself, and in his best Santa Claus style, Pete giggled for some minutes.

Elliott giggled, "GOG...grumbling old git."

Bill shook his head and drained his pint glass.

"I thought that he was a seniorish partner with a large firm of accountants and spent his time closing or buying businesses, I can never remember which" offered Biggles, breaking his silence.

"True, true," replied Pete, "but no one ever admits to being an auditor you see?"

Bill attempted to return the discussion to an even keel "He never really talks about his job, does he?" And failed.

"Too right mate-io, GOG me old china," interrupted Elliott. "Well, would you go round announcing that you've had a personality by-pass and add things up for a living?....no sireee."

"Or that you're fat, bald and a total bastard?" added Pete.

Grant returned with the first beers of his round, placing them by the appropriate drinker.

Elliott was on a roll, "Can you imagine a normal, healthy seventeen year old deciding that they want to spend the rest of their living days adding up other people's money?"

Pete interrupted, "Or ticking things."

"Aye," agreed Elliott, "Wrongly."

"And then denying that it was your responsibility to spot fraud...even though that is what the customer thinks he paid for." Pete finished his point by folding his arms and sitting back in his seat, a large grin breaking across his face.

Grant placed the next three pints on the table, after ensuring that the drips from the glasses landed on Elliott's shoulder, this generating the usual response "Twat."

"So, what's it like being a useless, incompetent, over-paid parasite?" asked Pete as Grant sat down. Grant knew immediately that the jibe was being addressed at him but, after another day which suggested that Pete was probably right, he was in no mood for this sport. "Fuck off Granddad" was the best he could manage.

Grant sat back and let the conversation flow, oblivious to the details and nuances, merely alert for further personal attacks.

But it was true.

What he did for a living served little purpose for much of the time.

Yes, he was an auditor (when he couldn't find anything more interesting to do) and, as a result of cut-price fee quotes, it served little purpose, particularly for the businesses in his market place. He enjoyed the transactional work arising from deals; either when he was leading a deal or when he was undertaking due diligence work[23] for one of the parties to the transaction. He got great satisfaction from dealing with clients, providing business and personal advice to entrepreneurs, but.

And it was a big 'but'.

He was increasingly fed up of the hassle involved in managing an office, in terms of internal reporting, compliance with the increasing number of external regulations, and being answerable for the failings of staff who he could not control (as they reported to others). Today had seen another of these; a member of the HR department ('modern day Trades Unionists' he had once called them), based in his office, had failed to respond to a query from a former member of staff about his pension arrangements; not only that, but she had denied seeing any of the correspondence in question despite the fact that the copies now provided by the

---

[23] Although he regularly described due diligence work as nothing more than high pressure audits, where the results were wanted before the work was started and where the accountant was always at fault (for whatever went wrong). Usually required by a banker before he lends to an acquirer, a cynic would argue that the purpose of due diligence is to ensure that there is someone available to sue (with deep enough pockets) if the fantastically optimistic profit forecasts prove to be flawed.

disgruntled former employee referred to letters from her and conversations with her. In Grant's mind she was lying, he believed his former colleague, and was adamant that the paperwork proved both of these views to be correct. But, he had taken two 'bollockings' because of this; the first for being in control of an office where HR staff were not being properly supervised; and the second, from the head honcho of HR (the 'chief shop steward' in Grant's eyes – who was an untouchable, perhaps because of the 'favours' she had shown to certain individuals) for challenging the word of the HR girl in his office and explaining that it was a far from satisfactory situation. And between these two episodes he had been faced with the usual panoply of cock-ups and complaints; had he really been put on this planet to take this shit?

"Fuck." Grant thought out loud.

"Fuck what?" asked Elliott, with some justification, as Grant's comment bore little obvious connection to the matter now under discussion, that being the continuation of previous debates over the logic behind the Romans deciding to build a wall between the towns now known as Carlisle and Wallsend.

"Sorry, mate…I was miles away," admitted Grant.

"Wish you fucking were," agreed Pete, more harshly than he intended.

"Housesteads is bloody impressive, mind," continued Bill.

"Too right," commented Grant, sitting up and looking interested, for a change "And it's so bleak up there…and the wall along the edge of the escarpment is stunning."

"What you on?" asked Pete.

Grant shrugged this question away, "No, really…I go up there at least once a year…and Housesteads rather than Corstopitum, or one of the other places down in the valley."

"No shit?" enquired Pete.

Nodding Grant continued, "Aye…seriously, it's worth a trip…better in my opinion than many places of supposed interest."

"Durham Cathedral," offered Bill.

Biggles stirred himself from his apparent slumber, "I think Stonehenge is pretty impressive…considering the size of those stones and when it was built."

Elliott contributed, "York Minster."

"What about Beamish?" asked Pete without much conviction.

"Different sort of thing mate-io," the short, sharp reply from Elliott.

Grant sighed, "But the kids today are just not interested…are they…heads up their computerised arses."

"Were you interested in such things when you were a kid?" asked Bill.

"Too long ago for him to remember."

"Fuck off Pete" Grant continued "Had no choice, was taken to castles and things every holiday…the old boy used to take us all over, visiting castles, museums, that sort of stuff…quite enjoyed it at the time…perhaps because I didn't know any better…but I look back with happy memories of days out visiting such places…there were days I hated…only natural I guess…but you remember the highlights…the engine sheds at Carnforth, great steam locos, the shushing noise, smoke and the smell of oil…my recollections of that amazing place are in black and white…I always preferred castles to cathedrals mind…so the building work may have been more impressive on your typical cathedral…but there is something awesome about a castle…even a little one…like Helmsley…some of them along the Welsh border are impressive…up high above rivers…and that one where Charles was invested or infirmed or whatever it was… Arundel was a good one…but Dunstanburgh castle takes some beating…cracking walk along the beach to get there…massive, powerful looking stronghold….haunted…ghost of the Lady of the Grey Mare or something like that…cracking days out...yes, I was lucky." Grant stopped, everyone looked surprised, they had never heard him talk like this, he regained some control "But the kids of today...shit...they look at you as if you've got two heads if you say 'shall we have a day out at Richmond castle' or something similar...all they want is a trip to the computer shop, a new game of zapping aliens with lasers or picking up boys in night clubs... and a burger and fries on the way home...burgers and fries...no interest in trying anything different...unless it's on a pizza...with chips of course...or between two bread buns...anyway...I'd like to take my kids out to places like that...on days out...exploring...shit we've got a lovely country.....Barnard Castle...Holy Island...now that's a good trip...they're not interested...or their mother puts the mockers on it...I used to love those toasted sandwiches in plastic bags that you got in pubs...first place I tried curry...mind it wasn't proper curry...ham and cheese...the cheese melted and it was none of today's sliced muck...lived on them when I was a student...a real treat they were...and proper fish and chips...in the days before cod became virtually extinct...I remember days out to Whitby and Hartlepool and the harbours being full of trawlers and cobles...screaming gulls circling the boats as they returned from Dogger Bank or wherever...the sound of auctioneers selling the fish...crabs still moving...and the smells...and the treat...proper fish and chips...with mushy peas and buttered bread...magic...one of my all-time favourites...or crumpets with Dandelion and Burdock...remember that stuff...brown and fizzy and made you burp...we used to have crumpets toasted by the fire on a Saturday, after the wrestling...my granddad, a giant of a man, even when in his seventies, sitting by the fire...'till it was replaced by the bloody Baxi or whatever it was...yelling at the TV...like it was for real...the bloke with the black mask...always a baddie...Tally Ho Kaye...before Doctor Who...when it was good...the later Doctors were all pretty poor, particularly that little dark haired fella...I had

54

some of my first sexual thoughts about his young female assistants…the monsters were always pretty crappy…amazing how frightening a bloke dressed up in cling film and silver foil could be…yes, it was always Hartlepool United nil…the results on the teleprinter…you know the staff take the piss out of me now with lines like 'Tell us about your first telex machine' and 'Tell us about the days of the fading fax paper'…a walk in the countryside followed by a bit of Mick McManus and crumpets…sad, very sad."

Grant sat back, almost breathless, a spent force; the silence was deafening.

Pete looked at Elliott; the look was returned: they would leave him alone tonight.

It was raining heavily; sufficient excuse, unspoken, for one 'for the road'; Pete (never one to miss an opportunity to ogle the delightful Sally behind the bar) collected some of the empties which were now littering the table and sauntered over to the bar.

"How's your wife?" enquired Sally, completely ruining the moment for Pete, who was old enough to be her father, but overlooked such trivial facts when he let his imagination run to matters sexual.

"Still breathing…same again please and one for yourself."

Grant looked at his empty glass.

He knew that she hated his drinking.

Her father had died after a long fight against alcoholism. A painful end. Losing his dignity. But lying to all – and himself – until the end.

She expected him to become an alcoholic.

This opinion upset Grant.

He never drank spirits in her presence – he rarely drank them anytime – and tried to understand and respect her position.

During her father's final years they had spent many long weekends at his home; this had frustrated Grant, but he had never complained. Other than that once. He had been looking forward to a weekend at home; he had arrived home early; she had met him on the doorstep.

"Come on, get a move on!"

"Why! Are we going out?"

"No! Daddy is not well and I've booked us all on the seven o'clock flight."

"Oh, you're joking. I'm knackered and it is so long since we had anytime together."

"Stop being selfish!"

And he had cracked. He punched the doorbell. His strength shocked him. The plastic exploded.

"He's been ill for fucking years, he is the selfish bastard! We've spent the majority of our married life looking after him. So, if wanting some family time is selfish, sorry, I'm an inconsiderate bastard!"

"You are! You have fifteen minutes to get ready."

He had thought about that night many times.

Had it been wrong?

He had supported her – or so he believed. But had he ever really understood; or empathised?

It had placed intolerable pressures on his career; he had lost contact with many of his friends.

And when he had died Grant had found it hard to grieve.

He had allowed her to mourn.

He had looked forward to restarting his marriage. But it never seemed to go back to how it was before; or back to how he had thought it had been.

Four

Wednesday night was always a popular night in The Urra, the night that the part-timers joined the table.

Late September saw a return to relative normality after the stresses of the summer: few brats[24] charged through the bar, damp returned to the air for at least twenty three hours a day, Happy Hour returned between the hours of six thirty and eight (As Elliott would frequently comment "Thank God that Alfie Arsehole[25] can't tell the time"; and this would then often generate a discussion on the background and validity of his name for, as Frank would emphasise, 'my arsehole is quite useful').

Pete, who now saw his primary objective in life to be baiting Grant, was getting the extended round in, assisted by Neil[26], a builder. Neil was in his early forties and could not look or behave less like a builder; always immaculately dressed, he looked more like a lawyer than someone involved in the construction industry. Clearly under the thumb, Wednesday night was the highlight of Neil's week.

Frank sauntered in with Bill and Eric; Eric was one of the local 'gentry' having being born (many, many decades previously) into a family owning a substantial number of shops; from their ruddy and

---

[24] As Grant would describe them; to others, possibly their parents, they were delightful young things.

[25] It had been said, probably by Elliott, that Alf was the sort of host who, if he had been a waiter, would announce the day's specials at the moment that one reached the punchline of the best joke of the day. Grant would have used the phrase "shithead" to make the same point.

[26] Neil's surname was Watts - this lead to the unfortunate nickname of 'Forty', given that he wasn't bright enough to be 'sixty' or a 'hundred'.

windswept appearance it was easy to ascertain that a round of golf had been enjoyed that afternoon.

"My, my Frank, you're looking particularly hubristic this evening," commented Elliott.

"Thank you," replied Frank.

Bill sniggered, "Yes, he won again."

"You taking the piss?" Frank asked, unsure as to what was going on and being afraid of digging himself into a hole.

Bill turned to Eric, "It means full of pride or arrogant."

Eric, looking somewhat annoyed that Bill was questioning the size and quality of his vocabulary, shook his head and nodded greetings to those already around the table.

"I knew that," claimed Frank. No one was convinced.

"How did the daughter's wedding go Eric?" asked Elliott.

"Yeah…OK…everything went real well and Her-indoors seems happy enough."

"What about your speech?"

"Just under four minutes."

"Longer than it took to conceive her."

"That's why I rarely come in here."

"Want to rephrase that?"

"Grow up Elliott."

"OK Dad."

Eric sighed, "One day," he muttered, shaking his head.

Grant was driving along the A66, enjoying, as much as one could, the rugged beauty of Stainmore and the angry cloud patterns he could see in the east, over Teesside. He had endured a long but almost rewarding day; it had started twelve hours earlier in Newcastle, and he had then driven (raced would be a more appropriate word) along the A67 to Carlisle; there he had worked with the directors of one of his favourite clients, ultimately making the necessary decisions and setting out individual action plans. A good day – people he respected and liked; feelings which appeared to be reciprocated; interesting work; decisions were made and the way forward was clear – why wasn't every day like that? He felt that he had earned his pay today and could feel a large bill coming on. He was tired but invigorated: he felt that he had delivered good advice, felt valued and had enjoyed himself.

Yes, a good day.

And what was he rushing home to?

A nice family meal?

A warming conversation about their respective days. Showing a healthy and sincere interest in each other.

A laugh with his wife and children?

Bollocks!

It was beginning to rain and dusk was coming in quickly.

He switched on his lights and wipers.

Why did so many tossers drive with their fog lights on?

Why did so many people tootle along in the wrong lane?

He could feel his mood darkening, almost in parallel with the arrival of the night. Shit. He switched on his CD and let his foot push down on the accelerator.

The slapping drum sound of the opening section of 'In a Big Country[27]' started…and Grant immediately joined in with the haunting lyrics penned by his long lost hero Stuart Adamson

---

[27] With their ringing, anthemic-like guitars and the thought-provoking lyrics of frontman Stuart Adamson, Big Country emerged as one of the most distinctive and promising new rock bands of the early 1980s, scoring a major hit with their debut album, *The Crossing*; though the group's critical and commercial fortunes dimmed in the years to follow, they nevertheless outlasted many of their contemporaries, releasing new material into the next century. Englishman Adamson formed Big Country in mid-1981 following his exit from the Scottish punk outfit 'The Skids', enlisting childhood friend Bruce Watson on second guitar; Clive Parker and brothers Pete and Alan Wishart completed the original lineup, but were soon replaced by bassist Tony Butler and drummer Mark Brzezicki. Signing to Polygram's Mercury imprint, the band issued its debut single, "Harvest Home," in late 1982; a series of opening dates on the Jam's farewell tour increased Big Country's visibility exponentially, and the follow-up, "Fields of Fire," burst into the U.K. Top Ten.

Come up screaming

Come up screaming

One of his favourite bands, Big Country; The Crossing[28], an old album that he'd loaded into the CD at the weekend…

Ha!

I've never seen you look like this without a reason

Another promise fallen through

Another season passes by youooooooooo

Shah!

I never took the smile away from anybody's face

And that's a desperate way to look

For someone who is still a child

Hands beating on the steering wheel Grant's mind started wandering. What was the song about? It seemed so relevant, but he was buggered if he could work out why.

The Crossing appeared in 1983, its passionate, idealistic approach and Celtic-inspired arrangements far removed from the prevailing new wave mentality of the moment; the album not only went platinum in the UK but went gold in America as well, its success spurred by the Top 20 pop hit "In a Big Country." Critics raved, and in early 1984 Big Country returned to the British Top Ten with the single "Wonderland." Their second album, *Steeltown*, entered the charts at number one, but despite good reviews there were already (misguided) suggestions that all of the band's material sounded much the same; similar accusations were made against *The Seer* in 1986. A tour of the Soviet Union accompanied the 1988 release of *Peace in Our Time*, but the following year Brzezicki resigned and drummer Pat Ahern was enlisted for the single "Save Me." Chris Bell replaced Ahern upon completing 1991's *No Place Like Home*, the first of the band's albums not to receive an American release.

After parting ways with Polygram, Big Country signed with the Compulsion label for 1993's *The Buffalo Skinners*, recorded with yet another new drummer, Simon Phillips; the record launched a pair of British Top 30 hits, "Alone" and "Ships." Brzezicki rejoined the lineup in time for *Without the Aid of a Safety Net*, a live LP recorded in Glasgow. *Why the Long Face* followed in 1995, and after recording the acoustic effort *Eclectic*, Adamson relocated to Nashville in 1997. It was a further two years before their first studio effort in four years, *Driving to Damascus*, appeared in 1999.

Like many geniuses, Stuart Adamson had struggled with demons and was greatly under-rated during his short life.

On December 16, 2001 Adamson was found dead in a hotel room in Hawaii. He had been missing for several weeks from his Nashville, Tennessee home. A great tragedy.

[28] The Crossing, issued in 1983 by Mercury – 812 870-2; In a Big Country lyrics copyright Virgin Music Publishing Limited

In a big country dreams stay with you
Like a lover's voice fires the mountainside
Stay alive

Was it about being optimistic when your life turns to shit? He wasn't sure and increased the volume. Great guitar work by Bruce and Stuart…

I thought that pain and truth were things that really mattered
But you can't stay here with every single hope you had shattered

Grant hummed along to the E-bow and guitars. Great sound
I'm not expecting to grow flowers in the desert
But I can live and breathe
And see the sun in the wintertime

Had the song been written with him in mind? All of his hopes had been shattered. And he *didn't expect to grow flowers in the desert* – shit, what a great line.

The A66 began its fall into North Yorkshire and Grant could feel the relief and pain of approaching home.

So take that look out of here it doesn't fit you
Because it's happened doesn't mean you've been discarded
Pull up your head off the floor – come up screaming
Cry out for everything you ever might have wanted
I thought that pain and truth were things that really mattered
But you can't stay here with every single hope you had shattered

Grant fingered his nose; a good pick was relaxing. He thought about all the Big Country concerts he'd enjoyed – alone. When had they ever done things together?

I'm not expecting to grow flowers in the desert
But I can live and breathe
And see the sun in the wintertime

True. He had grounds to be optimistic. Didn't he? Shit! He realised that his speed had crept up to a ton. He took his foot off the accelerator and checked his mirror. He had eight points. And what would she say if he got anymore? You daft twat. He shook his head. The lights of oncoming traffic were beginning to hurt his eyes. Why did so many prats have their fog lights on? Bloody people carriers and boy racer machines. The rain was intermittent and the wiper was squeaking against the windscreen. Not long now. The strangulated guitar of 'Inwards' started.

I wouldn't want to go home on a night like this
When I find out that some of the past
Had been missed
And the light in the window has burnt out its fuse
I pull everything inward
But everything's loose

He nodded his head – in tune and in agreement[29]. He felt comfortable cocooned in the heated German built cabin. No nagging. No silences. No atmosphere. His thoughts and his music. Barnard Castle passed in the darkness on his right. Home, for that was its name, crept ever closer.

"I'm telling you," continued Elliott, "most married couples argue about two things...sex and money."

"So?" asked Frank.

Elliott took a long pull on his pint and wiped his lips with the back of his hand, "So, so...agree the price before you start! It's obvious, bloody obvious."

Frank shook his head. Neil nodded.

"See!" shouted Elliott, pointing one of his chubby fingers dangerously close to Neil's ruddy face.

Neil shifted uncomfortably in his seat, "You really are a daft bugger."

---

[29] Although, as usual, he was completely misinterpreting the lyrics: but then, he had always struggled with comprehension at school. He had to admit it, his head had been in the dark place from an early age.

"But always right, always and absolutely right," replied Elliott.

Ben arrived and, much to the annoyance of all present, started to move the table in order that he could sit on the bench with his back to the wall – the last place someone so ungainly on their feet should sit, but that was Ben; awkward, inconsiderate and a proficient pain in the proverbial. Neil wiped up the spillage.

"This is a bit cloudy," announced Ben, holding up his glass towards the ceiling lights, "And it doesn't taste too good."

Grant had once suggested that Ben's beer always tasted awful because he used fish and chip papers to dry his long unkempt hair and this resulted in old fatty substances falling into his glass – causing cloudiness and loss of the intended taste. Probably wrong but an interesting theory all the same.

Elliott finished his pint, "Mine was fine."

"End of the barrel then," replied Ben.

"Who has the honour of replenishing my glass," enquired Elliott. "Anyone celebrating anything?"

Eric stood up.

Outside The Urra it was beginning to rain steadily and there was an autumnal feeling in the air. Grant drove into the village, intending to give the pub a miss and to attempt some degree of social intercourse with his family. As he approached his house Grant could see that Samantha, one of his wife's best friends was visiting. He'd never worked out why, but she really seemed to despise him. Sexy in many ways, but with unusually hairy arms. A bonny face with a sexy mouth – until she opened it – she never had anything remotely pleasant to say about her husband – a bloke who Grant viewed as being too nice, harmless, a gent. Well, there won't be a welcome on the hillside tonight!

Grant virtually sprinted into The Urra, wearing a suit but still looking unkempt and hassled. "My round, what is it?"

"Half a Worthy," answered Ben.

"Now then Fat Bald Bastard," responded Pete. "I'll have a pint of the grossly over-priced Otway Really Bitter…and have one yourself."

Buster bounded down the steps into the bar, grinning like a Cheshire cat. "Perfect timing I see," patted Grant on the shoulder, "just the one for me thank you."

"That looks like a newish jacket" commented Pete to no one in particular.

Elliott nodded, took a long pull and, in an unnecessary loud voice, asked Buster, "Been a death in the family?"

"Sorry, what was that?"

"The new wardrobe…been to a funeral?"

"Oh yes, I see, well actually I did get this jacket from my cousin James, well from his widow to be more precise."

Howls of laughter.

"Shame you've gone bald," commented Pete, staring at Grant, who, unusually and to his credit, failed to react.

"Anyone see the dwarf tossing this morning?" enquired Elliott.

"'Cos Fat Bastard sounds much better than Fat Bald Bastard," concluded Pete.

Pointedly ignoring Pete, Grant turned to Elliott, "Surely that's discrimination against the vertically challenged?"

"It's attitudes like that, that can put your average dwarf out of work," was the immediate reply from Elliott.

"Where was this dwarf tossing then?" asked Eric, immediately opening himself open to ridicule.

"I mean, in the old days dwarfs could visit pubs and discotheques and make beer money by allowing themselves to be tossed around in competitions," explained Elliott.

"Tossed off?"

"Shut up Frank!"

"Thank you Grant my man." continued Elliott. "It is these bleeding heart Human Rights activists and politically correct new socialist MPs who are removing the livelihoods of these cuddly little people."

"Do both sexes compete?"

"Good question Billy boy, good question." Elliott paused, took a pull from his pint and continued "You've obviously got to be careful with the landing bounce in the case of the lady dwarf, that is in the case of the frontal toss and landing...damage to the face is accepted by the male dwarf... isn't that right Buster... but the female has to be careful of her face and chest."

"Sorry, you lost me there," mumbled Eric.

Howls of laughter.

"Oh, you josher."

Elliott stood up "From you Eric....I'll take that as a compliment...time to water the horses."

Some beers later and Neil, the desk driving builder, as Grant had recently named him, was moaning about his domestic life. For no reason other than that it had all been heard before, Neil received absolutely zero sympathy.

"It's the banging doors which are the worst of it," Neil explained, in a panting style of narrative which failed to garner any sensitivity from his audience.

"Take the bloody doors off mate," suggested Elliott.

"Even an office bound construction operative should be able to manage that," agreed Grant.

"Steady on Grant," interrupted a shocked looking Bill.

"Really?" replied a fear struck Neil.

"Absolutely Bob, next time the wife or daughter gives you grief and retires behind a slammed door...take it off the bloody hinges, put it in the garage and leave it there until a suitable apology is received from the daughter ...or the wife gives in to your manly charms…next round?" And Elliott rose from the table and staggered in the general direction of the little boys' room.

"Bob?" enquired Bill.

"Aye, Bob the Builder and now specialist room entrance carpenter," replied Grant.

Ben pushed the table forwards to create room for his escape; it was a constant source of frustration that he always did this, spilling beer as he went, and that it wouldn't be necessary if he sat on a chair or stool; but no, Ben had to sit on the bench seat by the wall. Grant had dared, on a few oiled occasions, to sit in 'Ben's seat' but had long since realised that this was a pointless and futile gesture and, more importantly, would always result in a series of sighs and comments about the seating arrangements emanating from the aforementioned Ben; a man who would act as if the bailiffs had evicted him or committed some other heinous crime.

"Ta ra like well as they say in Middlesbrough…or Middlesboro as the locals call it."

Bill shook his head. No one ever moved to sit in the seat vacated by Ben.

"Well," commented Elliott, staring pointedly at his now empty glass.

"Not for me, thanks," replied Grant as he summoned up the effort for the short trip to ice cold loneliness.

Eric stood up. For a man in his early seventies he was still an impressive height and now towered over the sullen looking Grant. "Go on…one for the road."

"Well, it would be churlish not to," agreed Grant, settling back into his chair.

Grant knew that he was becoming increasingly intolerant but was at a loss to understand why. No longer was it those understandable things like tossers who say 'yeah' after every other word as if you're stupid. Or arseholes that are fully able but park their cars in disabled spaces. Everyone was frustrated with the rolls of rubbish bags with invisible joints and the supermarket bags at checkout which are always stuck together and require a degree in nuclear physics to open them. But now everything seemed to annoy him. A woman sitting at the far end of the bar burst out laughing at her partner's story; now even women who cultivate earthy, thigh-slapping laughs were earning his wrath.

He hadn't always been miserable; or had he? Hadn't he once been a jolly, cheeky chappie? But now even a five mile car journey could turn him into a gibbering wreck, wanting to deliver suitable punishments[30] on the majority of those crossing his path; capital punishment, and why? Fog lights. Acceptable but a tadge extreme. Parking in disabled bays or on yellow lined corners. Again, acceptable but extreme. Centre lane hogging. Surely a short custodial sentence would suffice? Tail-gating. Well, no argument there.

But why? Was it some form of irritable bowel syndrome, but affecting the brain? Was it the pressure of work? He couldn't accept any suggestion of stress or any form of weakness. He would accept that he was working ridiculously long hours, however, but could not determine whether this was due to workload, personal inefficiency or the need to avoid 'home.' Was it Her Indoors and the daughters from Hell? Could it be the mid-life crisis?

Did people see him as some form of intolerant, increasingly impatient and ignorant bastard? He had enjoyed a couple of pints too many to form any structured thoughts, and he was becoming uncomfortable with the direction his cerebral wanderings were taking. The return of Eric, with beers, was a welcome relief.

---

[30] Death by slow and painful means, particularly if the car bears a Darlington number plate or a "stupid" sticker in the rear windscreen. Like many immature forty year olds Grant wanted to have machine guns fitted to the front of his car; for use in less serious cases of "motoring abuse."

Eric sat down "Cheers me dears."

"Ugh," grunted Grant.

"I said cheers me dears," replied Eric.

Grant looked at Elliott, a quizzical expression requiring some form of response.

Elliott raised his glass, "Cheers Eric."

"You know" started Grant as Neil wandered off towards the Gents, "if his brains were made of money, he'd have to get a loan to buy a round."

"Cruel…cruel" said Bill, nodding.

"I'm flying down to London tomorrow afternoon" explained Grant, to no one in particular.

"Why are TV cops always mavericks?" asked Elliott.

"Are they really?" replied a confused-looking Frank.

"And I always fall in love with at least one of the hostesses," continued Grant.

"Or they suffer from tangled webs of domestic lives," Elliott paused, waiting for a reaction.

Grant ignored Elliott, "I should have married a hostess."

"She wouldn't have worn her hat and uniform in bed you know," replied Frank.

"You never know Frankie Boy."

"Fat Bastards like you have no chance," countered Pete.

Grant continued on without pausing for thought or any form of reality check, "I don't know if it's the leather gloves, the shiny stockings and tight bottoms, the tied-up hair or what, but I just can't help myself."

"Why do you always get so much cutlery with airline meals?" asked Bill.

Neil returned from 'powdering his nose'.

"And more is spent on cleansing napkins and the wrappings than on the god-awful food itself," agreed Grant.

Elliott interrupted, "Is that American?"

Bill and Grant both stared at him.

"Is godawful some form of Yank grub?"

Grant shook his head, "Funny man."

"Is it?...I'd like to try it," commented Neil.

Elliott leant forwards, as if he was about to issue forth with some ground breaking disclosure "You know," he started, "I hate many things about holiday flights but the biggy, after the planks who applaud after the plane lands...the biggy is the people who stop at the cabin door, who don't just walk straight down the steps...and sort of stand there as if they are some form of star being photographed."

Bill, Frank and Grant nodded.

"You know" said Pete, staring at Neil "Grant says that if your brains were made of money, you'd have to get a loan to buy a round."

Neil looked perplexed.

"And," Elliott blustered, "then there's the pilots who talk drivel rather than steer the bugger...and announce that the local time is approximately whatever...rather than getting a decent watch and being able to tell the exact time."

"Shame Biggles is away," commented Eric.

"Is it my turn?" asked Neil, rising without waiting for an answer.

"Good boy," commented Elliott.

"Why are you going to London?" enquired Pete.

"I'm not," replied Elliott, "hate the fucking place."

"Beggars," agreed Buster

"Filth," commented Eric.

Grant nodded sagely.

"Asylum seekers everywhere," contributed Frank.

Bill shook his head, "I always feel the need for a shower if I've travelled on the underground."

Elliott giggled, "You bloody would."

"Bloody motor bike messengers," added Buster.

"Aye, and cyclists who think that they have the right to use the pavements and that all pedestrians are legitimate targets," agreed Frank.

Placing the round of fresh beers on the table Neil provided the cue for further hilarity, "I quite like London…and Helen and the girls love the shops."

"Shops!" exploded Elliott. "Fucking extortion establishments, owned and filled by bloody foreigners…like the rest of London."

Frank nodded and grunted, "Illegals."

"No…there are some impressive sights," suggested Eric.

"Nah," Elliott wasn't having anything positive, "It's a total shit-hole."

"Full of tossing accountants and lawyers," laughed Pete.

"Work," was the only response which Grant felt obliged to make.

Five

Early October and the number of locals available for a few beers is down.

Frank is away at his villa in Spain.

Grant is working on 'a secret transaction' and hasn't been seen, other than at weekends, for some time.

Pete is away on holiday somewhere; a fan of last minute deals, he had disappeared, wife in tow, the day before he was due to play Biggles at golf, leaving Biggles feeling frustrated and lonely (as Pete had failed to tell anyone other than his wife).

Buster is 'busy farming' resulting in his late or non-arrival. "How can you be busy when your entire farm is set-a-side?" Elliott would frequently ask, but never receive a reply.

"Absolutely lovely walk round Wireltune, lovely summer evening, not too many flies, the sheep calling in the fields, an all pervading sense of peace about the place." Bill stopped, no one sure if simply to take a breath or if his tale was concluded.

"The old church is something special...12th Century but on the site of a Saxon church...locked up due to bloody vandals but you can just make out the sleeping knight effigy through gaps in the old wooden door...fresh flowers on the altar."

Elliott "ready for a human sacrifice?"

"Be sensible for once will you."

"Well it is spooky, is it not, that Grant is missing tonight... and it's a full moon, and the clouds are high... and the Worthy has gone off."

"There are times, Elliott dear boy, when you really do need some medical help."

"That's why I married a doctor."

"But Tina is a doctor of philosophy or something…not medicine."

"Really…eleven years I have been shackled to her and I've never known that…never queried all the pills she makes me take…I feel somewhat unwell now."

Bill rarely swore, and thus when he did it carried far more effect. "Stop pissing about and get them in…I'll have a wee Grouse if you would be so kind."

Ben pushed the table away from himself and stood, somewhat hunched before staggering to the bar; as usual his definition of a round was not circular and Elliott followed him; ensuring that there could be no eye contact and the implication, however slight, that he would buy Ben a beer. Bill mopped up the beer spilt by Ben with a sigh and a shake of his increasingly weary head. Bill was beginning to show his age and was far less agile than had recently been the case.

Elliott returned with his round; as usual the bar staff made a point of serving Ben last (well, if he was going to return it, why rush to give him it?).

"Is it true" asked Neil "that Frank has different golf waterproofs for the various types of rain?"

In many ways Neil was simply too nice. He took most people at face value and believed what everyone said; despite the number of times that such an approach had landed him in trouble. Many of his friends wondered, nicely (nicely as it was difficult to think badly about Neil) what, if his father hadn't created and then bequeathed him such a robust, profitable company as Busby Moor Developments Limited, would Neil be doing for a living, outside of the priesthood?

"How many sorts of rain are there? It's all wet" offered Ben as he clumsily manoeuvred himself back into his seat (where he promptly started holding his pint up to the light, mumbling words and phrases such as 'cloudy', 'see that again in the morning' and 'end of the barrel'; he was resolutely ignored by all...as usual).

Elliott folded his arms with a flourish. "Well, Ben that's not strictly correct and, yes, Neil, partly as a measure of his ill-gotten fortune, partly indicative of his ego, and partly due to his churlishness, Frank does indeed have a large collection of golfing waterproofs." Elliott took a large drink before continuing "and, as you can't rely on the weather forecasts...the more kit these people get, the more technologically advanced it is, the less reliable are the forecasts...Frank carries most of his collection with him, on his motorised trolley which, as you may know, also features a drinks cabinet and satellite navigation equipment."

"Do you mean 'the less reliable the forecasts, the more kit you need'?" asked a bemused Bill.

"Isn't it obvious?" replied Elliott.

Neil sat open mouthed; he had arrived earlier than usual this evening – well, the female part of his family was away 'shopping', so he felt he could misbehave – a bit. And despite the fact that senior management was 'away', Neil still couldn't 'relax'; his clothes were immaculate and his tightly cropped hair, with left side parting, was held in place by gel – or was it fear?

Ben shook his head and returned to the close examination of his now half drunk pint.

"I thought everyone knew about Frank," commented Bill, bracing himself for the impending return of Ben to the bar.

Elliott nodded and winked in a knowing manner, "You don't get to park in the Captain's spot at two golf clubs for nothing!"

Neil stared at Elliott "But he'd have to be Captain to park in the Captain's space, Elliott."

"Correctomundo," replied Elliott, lifting his and Neil's glasses as Ben started to rise, to return his 'cloudy, undrinkable', but now half consumed, pint. The girls behind the counter, seeing him coming, both moved to opposite ends of the bar, busying themselves with unnecessary tasks.

Grant looked out of the twelfth storey window; the City, and Saint Paul's in particular, looked quite spectacular at this time of night. He held his umpteenth cup of coffee in his left hand, holding his mobile phone to his ear with his right hand. "Look, I'm not being difficult," he repeated. He was clearly becoming frustrated and tired. "But I cannot sign the prospectus off as it stands and certainly not until you and the underwriters have stopped making changes to it." He took a drink as he listened to the reply. His back ached and his eyes were sore. He shook his head and stretched before continuing, "You might think that the changes are cosmetic, and so they may be, but we must see them before accepting responsibility and giving the comfort that everyone wants." He looked at his watch; this was going to be an all-nighter and his stomach was beginning to rumble: not enough food or too much coffee? Bollocks he thought; ulcers were guaranteed.

Once upon time he had enjoyed this work; the buzz, the pressure, the technical demands, the exciting environment and the on call supply of refreshments; it had been the icing on the cake of an otherwise pretty monotonous professional desert of audit and other dry, tedious work; now his patience couldn't tolerate the City arseholes who seemed to issue nothing but ridiculous instructions, contribute little (other than by increasing his workload), but receive all the plaudits (and the 'big bucks'). And his brain and his body couldn't take the long, late hours, lack of thinking space and absence of decent sleep[31]. Once upon a time, not so many years ago, Grant had been able to laugh off just about any problem; he'd sit back, put his hands behind his head[32], swear, and, usually…well, nearly always, inspiration would arrive…as if by magic. And if he didn't know the answer…well, talk quickly, bully if you have to…buy time. Or tell a joke.

He finished the call. "Yes, we will restate the intangible values but we will also need to review the accompanying notes and stated policies…yeah, yeah…no…have to…bye."

One of his junior colleagues groaned with the realisation of the additional work that this involved.

Grant threw his phone into his briefcase and stretched his arms and back. He fantasised briefly about standing under a red hot shower; the water pulsing on his back and shoulders; his mind then wandered to the ice cold gin and tonic which would be waiting for him on the sink. His mind raced to the moment when the air hostess wandered into the shower room and started undressing. He shook his head. "Right chaps and chap-esses, let's get on with it. And remember; the P/E ratio is the number of investors who will wet themselves if they buy these effing shares." He started preparing a list of tasks requiring attention before sunrise; he still got a buzz from being in control and, whilst not as good as he once was, he

---

[31] Of course a doctor would add a comment about good food, fresh fruit or a balanced diet at this point. In Grant's case this would be an invalid point; given that he had not enjoyed a balanced, healthy diet for many years – primarily down to the fact that his wife cooked a meal involving his participation only once a week (Sunday evening meal) – and his only other cooked meals were at 'black tie' dinners – always a sauce with a chicken bone sticking out of it – hotel breakfasts, breakfasts on the early train or plane to London, or out of boxes, consumed in lay-bys or car parks.
[32] Now most psychologists would have you believe that the hands clasped behind the head routine illustrated a 'fuck you' attitude or one of complete openness; to Grant, who reckoned he was a bit of a frustrated psychologist at heart, it meant "look, my pits aren't sweaty".

continued to be a pretty effective operator. "Hey Gerry, is a market correction what happens the day after or the day before you buy?"

"Feck orf" drawled Gerry, Grant's co-lead on this transatlantic assignment. Gerry Braden was from the firm's Denver office; he and Grant had known each other socially for some years, but this was the first time they'd 'gone into battle' together. Grant grinned; he knew he could bug Gerry, but, more importantly, he knew they complimented each other – professionally. "You are some mother, you colonial fuck wit."

"Yeah, twice we've helped you officially, and you'd have lost the Falklands and your park pond fleet if it hadn't been for us, you fat Geordie shit."

"Cup of tea?"

Big Ben sounded midnight over by the Thames.

They were working in the brightly lit and exceedingly plush (as in exorbitantly expensive[33] and tasteless) office of the Lead Advisers to the flotation on which they were working; Lead as in they did little detailed work and were nowhere to be seen at this time of night. Having set out the work plan for what remained of the night Grant left the conference room in search of sustenance for his staff and some fresh air for himself; the latter he found on the roof, thanks to the assistance of a suitably bored security man, and the former was delivered by one of the 24 hour catering staff. He lost track of time on the roof, half sleeping, half running issues over in his mind, the bright orange shaft of light breaking over the eastern horizon (where he imagined Canvey Island to be) forcing his mind back to the reality of the task in hand. "Shit" he shouted "here we go again."

---

[33] So much had been spent on the carpets that the pile was so thick that, as Grant had commented to his client, "you need to be wearing fucking crampons to get across the reception area."

His attempt to enter the conference room 'purposefully' was completely lost. "Hey Grant, you been shooting your rocket or what?" yelled Gerry. Surprisingly, given his general dislike of professionals from the northern hemisphere colonies, Grant not only liked Gerry, but respected his technical knowledge. "Fuck off Tonto."

Gerry grinned "You know? Nothing is foolproof to a sufficiently talented fool, and you are one talented mother."

At the time that most people were starting work, and Elliott was beginning to consider rising, Grant and his team packed their bags, the float having been delayed; 'The mothers' had been Gerry's considered comment when the decision had been announced by the senior attorney from the Chicago based legal team; Grant had explained the technical problems giving rise to the delay several days previously, but had been ignored as it was far from palatable news. "Shit, shower, shave…then full greasy followed by some rapid ales?" had been Grant's mature and professional suggestion. "Can I pass on the greasy and swap the ales for a gallon of Medoc?" had been the response of Kate, one of Grant's juniors[34], and the only dissenting voice.

The team returned to their hotel… a grand sounding but ultimately disappointing establishment near Euston railway station…abluted[35] and so forth.

They congregated in the reception area while Grant settled the bill; his half hearted attempt at negotiating a discount for the

---

[34] A junior but important colleague; he relied on her so much that she resembled a Zimmer frame. Most importantly, she appeared to understand his sense of humour; in a Milliganesque moment she once vandalised the "Do not disturb" sign on his door by writing "'Cos he's disturbed enough already": Grant appreciated the act of vandalism whilst most others were horrified. Like Grant, she also possessed the ability to drink beyond the point of no return with consummate ease.

[35] 'Ablution' is a fine but under used word, don't you think?

unsoiled sheets failing. Gerry and Kate were engrossed in a conversation focusing on the lyrics of Bruce Springsteen while Paul, one of Grant's tax advisors and unofficial jester to the court of King Grant, and Simon, the team 'go-for' and 'Mr Dependable', were discussing the relative merits of Young's Best Bitter and Newcastle Exhibition Ale.

"So what did he mean 'they blew up the chicken man in Philly last night'[36]...eh?"

Gerry nodded "Dunno but I like the line 'well now everything dies baby that's a fact' and 'so put on your stockin's 'cause the night's getting cold', ahah it's one hellava album."

"Yank shite."

"Piss off Paul."

Paul threw his head back, grinning "You say so Kate."

"I fucking do."

"Ladies should never swear," suggested Gerry.

"There's many a thing a Lady shouldn't do," agreed Paul.

Simon looked lost. Never comfortable talking to people he knew well, he appeared stand-offish around people he barely knew, and positively rude to the rest of humanity. "I prefer Exhibition even though it causes morning after pebble dashing."

"Too right Simes." Paul clicked his tongue... a habit most people found annoying but, for some completely unknown reason, it made Grant grin.

"And there's chemicals in this southern stuff."

"Too right Simey baby." Paul clicked his tongue again.

Kate tried to recover the conversation "My favourite track on Nebraska is 'State Trooper'."

Gerry nodded. "The line 'In the wee wee hours your mind gets hazy' was written about Granty Baby you know."

---

[36] Part of the opening line of the tremendous "Atlantic City", a track on the 1982 Bruce Springsteen album "Nebraska".

78

Kate grinned. Grant had seemed a bit 'hazier' than usual the previous night. She was worried about him; in a purely professional way. She tried to convince herself. She could remember the day that Grant had first arrived in the office: a young, high flying partner, fresh from a five year spell on the international circuit. She'd been drawn to him almost immediately; compared to other partners he seemed more down to earth, keen to help, charming but not confident; clearly able and highly professional, but he still managed to inject a sense of fun into work. And those gorgeous blue eyes. He'd clearly been struggling in recent years – indifferent health and his home life seemed less than happy – although his face still lit up whenever he talked about his children, but there seemed to be some underlying unhappiness. But however busy or hassled he seemed, he could always make time to help people...but Heaven help anyone who tried to bullshit him! She looked over to reception; he'd made the receptionist laugh.

Gerry was talking to her "I got a brother named Franky and Franky ain't no good."[37]

"Why's that?" asked Paul.

"Jeez Paul." Gerry shook his head in mock despair "You're some mother."

"Nothin' feels better than blood on blood."[38]

"Feckin 'ell, you do know something Paul," replied Gerry in his awful mock cockney.

"Young's ESB is alright, if you like that sort of thing," offered Simon.

By lunchtime fatigue was beginning to set in and the team, laden down with bags and including a completely lost (physically and mentally) Gerry, arrived in the Royal Scot bar close to King's

---

[37] A line from "Highway Patrolman" from Springsteen's 1982 album "Nebraska".
[38] Another line from "Highway Patrolman" from Springsteen's absolutely superb album "Nebraska".

Cross railway station. The rate of alcohol consumption slowed and the jokes worsened; everyone being at pains not to mention anything remotely associated with the job in hand; Gerry broke ranks first.

"Jeez, the arse on that underwriter from the Big Apple was something else."

"Come to Pappa," was Paul's limp contribution; he was now wasted; mentally, physically and psychologically.

"I didn't think so," replied Kate, who had fleetingly considered flirting with Gerry but had decided to focus her declining attention on the lighter fuel masquerading as a red wine. Tall and blonde, Kate was bonny rather than beautiful, hard working rather than sharp, and totally devoted to Grant, professionally.

Grant had encouraged Kate to stretch herself and she had been amazed at how well she had done. He had always shown an interest in her – professionally and personally – he always asked about her weekends and her husband. He had given her a variety of opportunities and challenges. He had helped her to broaden her horizons. She had travelled more than she had ever expected. He had given her confidence. And he made her laugh.

Grant stood up "Time for a quick one before the one o'clock, or do we miss the train?"

"What time is the two o'clock?"

"Fuck off Tonto."

"Yoh, Granty Baby…so the three o'clock is the target."

"You can't beat that Pearl Harbour spirit, can you?"

"Too right Grant," agreed Gerry with a shake of his head.

"You know," continued an increasingly tired Grant "I cannot abide all these tourists and students with massive backpacks…they bump into you without knowing or caring…haven't paid for all the space they consume…and are often Yanks."

Kate interrupted enthusiastically, "And you can't get any worse than that can you?"

"You're all mothers."

"If you say so Tonto."

Whilst he was mentally and physically drained Grant did not want to go home. Although the bar was seedy in the extreme he was comfortable. Here he was in some form of control; was part of something. People talked to him. What he thought and said 'mattered'. All different to the case at 'home'. No one would show any interest. It would be quiet or unbearably noisy. It would be empty, or occupied in such a way as to make it terribly lonely. But he really did want to go home; if only home meant a warm welcome – and that didn't need to mean a nice meal, convivial conversation and then his conjugal rights. Just a sense of inclusion or involvement. A feeling that someone was interested. Even if was only to check that he still had a pulse.

Someone had started the jukebox; this would always cause an extreme reaction in Grant, simply dependent on whether he liked the music or not.

"Fuck that's loud."

The train journey north passed without too much incident. They all dozed. Few words were exchanged.

As the train pulled into Darlington's historic but mistreated station Grant could feel his stomach churning. Home was getting ever closer. The warmth of the bosom of his family. Bollocks.

No one was home. Even the cats ignored him. The dogs simply slept through his arrival. He thought about drinking something. He'd drunk enough. He could feel the adrenalin of the last few days going cold. There must be more to life than this! Grant bent over to undo his laces. "Fuck, why were slip-ons so uncool?"

Six

Mid October. The Urra is relatively busy, most visitors being young couples (fifty percent of which would get inspected by a leering Grant… 'Look at the baps on that', 'She deserves better than that', 'Christ, I'm falling in love', 'Those legs go on forever', 'Why couldn't I get something like that' and so on). Such comments were usually ignored; unless Pete was present (cue 'You Sad Fat Bald Bastard' and similar responses).

"No, I fancy being something like a shepherd, the freedom, the satisfaction…but I'm not into dogs, sheep hold little attraction…I have no Welsh blood in me…and it gets damn wet on the fells." Grant took a pull from his pint of Old Rounton.

Pete announced his arrival. "Alright all and Fat Bastard."

Bill corrected him, "You mean Fat Bald Bastard don't you?"

Grant persevered, albeit with little enthusiasm, "And I wouldn't have to deal with prats like you if I was a shepherd."

"Doesn't have to be sheep," replied Elliott, "you could have a herd of something else."

"Like wilderbeast you mean?" asked Pete.

"No, you've lost the plot," continued Elliott "say something small and slow, removing the need for dogs…like snails, with slugs to round them up."

"You could use a few trays…so you wouldn't have to walk the fells," added Pete.

Grant joined in, "What about the wool?"

"Daft sod," replied Pete.

"All those shells could be put to some use," Elliott was now warming to his subject "And you could use garlic for the annual dipping."

Pete "After de-shelling you could use crumbled breadcrumbs for the bedding."

Elliott "Correctomundo my man and the breadcrumbs could be specially flavoured…say with a Gallic mix of spices and herbs."

"How long have you jokers been here?" asked Frank, sitting down and not expecting any form of sensible response.

Grant obliged "Bog off!"

"Say, just how many chins have you got?" asked Pete, scoring a direct and immediate hit.

"Better than have none at all, like you" replied Grant, in haste.

"That's as maybe, but just how many do you have?" continued Pete.

"And how long does it take to grow one?" asked Elliott.

"A chin or a snail?" asked Pete.

Ben waddled into the bar. The two barmaids instantly became busy and everyone around the table entered into one of a number of deep conversations. Having determined that no one was about to buy him a drink, Ben approached the bar. "Pint of the usual," he grunted, without any form of grace, affection or amusement.

"I can't stand people who say 'simply' or 'the thing is' " explained Elliott.

"But the simple fact," started Grant before he was interrupted by Bill "What's wrong with 'the thing is'."

"Obvious," replied Elliott. Grant nodded, folding his arms as he sat back, spreading himself as wide as possible on the bench seat he and Elliott currently shared; it was to no avail. Ben returned from the bar; moved the table, spilling beer in the process, and pushed his ample body onto the bench "Well aye as they say in Gateshead, what are all youse buggers doing here, as they say in Stockton." No one replied.

"The thing is," continued Elliott "it's like people with trouser pockets on their knees and hips…seriously dubious…and people who say 'simply buy me a beer' or similar are, frankly, simple…it stands to reason."

"Where could I buy sufficient snails…as a starter stock…for breeding and so on?" asked Grant.

"You simply…" started Elliott.

"What's he on about?" interrupted Ben "Snails…did he say snails?"

"Eaten any children today?" enquired Elliott, too quietly for Ben's ageing ears.

"Eh!"

"He's going to farm them," replied Elliott, putting on a serious expression.

"Eh!"

"Grant's going to breed snails," replied Pete.

"Why?"

"Cos he doesn't want to be a shepherd," explained Elliott before he paused, then corrected himself "well, in a way he does, if you know what I mean."

Ben looked thoroughly confused "But he's an accountant."

Pete leant over "That's what some may think."

Ben looked at Pete, then at Bill, hoping for some form of logical explanation; none was forthcoming "You'll need planning permission."

Elliott poked Grant in the ribs. "You'll need permission."

Ben was warming to his theme "And you won't get it around here you know."

Grant turned towards Ben "Why not? The buildings will be pretty small."

"Eh?"

"I said 'why not'."

"You can't just go and build a snail farm around here…I mean what would be next?"

"Giraffes," offered Elliott.

"Eh?"

"Only joking…I meant rhino."

"Eh!"

Grant had returned home earlier than usual; and had quickly regretted it. He had been greeted by the usual silence and chilly atmosphere. He had attempted to start a number of conversations but now found himself sitting alone in the dark.

What was the point?

He fancied a glass of wine and something tasty to eat.

Should he go and cook himself something?

He used to really enjoy cooking. Until she started complaining about everything and then, when she decided to be a veggie, well, what could a growing boy do? He still enjoyed cooking, when she was away, although he was never sure if the stuff tasted good because he had done well, or because of the bottle he would have emptied during the cooking process. Should he do himself a stir fry? No, whatever he used would have been earmarked; for the kids or the dogs. Even the dogs ignored him, other than on mornings when they needed some exercise and an opportunity to relieve themselves.

The only time anyone seemed to communicate with him was when they wanted something.

There must be more to life than this.

He stopped and stared through the lounge window; the garden looked in need of some attention.

Memories arrived of sunny July afternoons; playing with his daughters, laughter, happiness. They had all seemed happy. His wife sharing a bottle of wine. A burnt barbecue. Bedtime stories. And, occasionally a touch of affection at bedtime!

So long ago.

Why?

He shook his head.

He had asked. Unconvincing replies. Perhaps he had not asked the right questions; or asked them in the right ways.

Perhaps he didn't really want the answers.

He closed the curtains and wandered into the entrance hall. A pile of letters and the day's newspapers lay on the table.

He pushed the letters, mostly bills by the look of the envelopes, to one side.

He flicked through the evening paper. Nothing attracted his interest. There was nothing on the television. He fancied listening to some music; but could not be pestered with the grief that such behaviour would bring. He could go to his study and do some work. Bollocks.

He decided to opt for an early night and an early morning jog.

An early morning jog! He was deluding himself! When had he last gone for a jog?

Or done anything remotely healthy?

He grinned to himself. If the shoe fits, get another one like it.

He wandered through the house to say his 'goodnights'; everyone had already gone upstairs.

Cows.

He found himself in the kitchen, inspecting the wine racks. One quick glass. Just the one…

"So there I was, sitting in the bath, and I looked down at my balls and then up into my mother's eyes." Elliott had the total attention of everyone sitting around the table "so, says I, are those my brains? Not yet son, says my mother, not yet."

Frank laughed, almost spitting his cigarette out of his mouth; Pete chuckled and Bill sighed.

Elliott clapped his hands together "Just trying to entertain, you boring bastards, if you don't like it, have a go yourselves!"

"Grant used to tell a good joke," started Bill "but I can't remember the last time he pained us with one of his awful shaggy dog stories."

Pete nodded "Aye, he does tell a good story when he's in the mood."

Elliott agreed "That one about the woman urinating in Hartlepool Marina and the canoe like reflection nearly finished me off!"

Pete laughed.

"Can't remember that."

"You're lucky Bill, very lucky," concluded Elliott.

He sat on a bar stool in the kitchen. The wind was whistling at the back door. He looked around. The kitchen was immaculate. Well designed. Well stocked. Almost like an exhibit in a furniture store. It wasn't homely. It didn't feel 'his' – he might have paid for it all, but he'd had no input in any other way.

He took a large mouthful and rinsed the Medoc around his mouth. Shit, this was cheap fire water.

Seven

The Urra, as a building, was some five hundred years old although a myriad of landlords, ably assisted by numerous builders, architects and pre-National Park bureaucrats had knocked away most of the character and charm it had as a hostelry, leaving a functional eating and drinking establishment, focused on one central bar area. The old snug with its massive fireplace, leading to it always being too hot, had been knocked into the general lounge area, much to the despair of the locals. The darts and pool room had also been removed and replaced by tables and chairs comprising a general smoking area; the removal of these facilities by the current landlord had not been forgiven. His building of a children's play area (including various climbing frames and swings) had also caused much hand wringing and whingeing; and it is questionable whether he would ever be popular[39] with the locals, even if he addressed his much criticised price list. In fact his lack of popularity was reaching the depths attained by the one infamous landlady in The Urra's history; she was that unpopular that it became known as the Udder in recognition of her nickname.

A cold wet October night had brought few customers other than the usual flotsam from the business day.

Frank was at the end of the 'regulars' table, by the fire (moaning that it was too hot) in order that he could use it as an

---

[39] Did he care? His son attended private school, he had a challenging collection of "lady friends", and he had just acquired a new villa in southern Spain. So, that would be a "no" then!

ashtray. Straight from work[40], Frank was smartly turned out in jacket and (golf club) tie.

Elliott had been home prior to attending The Urra; many, such as Frank and Grant, never visited home prior to visiting The Urra for fear of being kidnapped[41] or captured by a menopausal spouse. Elliott was looking relaxed; partly due to his attire of over-sized jeans and baggy smock-type jumper, and partly due to the lingering effects of a liquid lunch.

Grant was simultaneously present and absent; his increasingly over-weight body was filling a shabby blue pin-stripe suit, the smart hand-made shirt and tie ensemble probably looked good in the Sunday paper advertisement but now reflected what had been a long hard day; mentally he was miles away. Significant effort was being expended to sit upright, take the occasional drink and focus on the photograph of the Urra in the early part of the nineteenth century, which hung above Bill's seat.

Bill had enjoyed a day of relaxation with his female companion and was being collected in an hour (fifty eight minutes and counting); he was approaching the wee grouse time of day.

Pete was explaining (to no one in particular) that his hips needed replacing (again) and was half-heartedly attempting to provoke Grant "What rhymes with You Fat Bastard?"

Ben as usual looked unwashed, unkempt and half cut; the results of working from home.

Biggles was absent; flying his employer to some exotic destination, or Liverpool.

Buster was late, but expected.

The usual badinage prevailed.

---

[40] Well, he called it "work", some, if not many would disagree. If attending the occasional directors meeting, or corporate golf day is work, where is the queue for these jobs?

[41] As in being forced into quality time with one's progeny

Neil arrived, via the bar, and sat next to Elliott, obviously keen to join the conversation.

"I did it, you bastard, and it just caused more trouble."

"Evening Forty," replied Elliott, with a child-like snigger.

Neil "No, really, it didn't work."

Elliott "What didn't work?"

Grant "His workforce."

Bill "Are many called Bob?"

Elliott "Managers are called Robert."

Neil "No you bastards, taking the door off."

Howls of laughter.

Elliott, with concerned face "So what happened?"

"You know" interrupted Ben "I hate those drivers who double park, then switch on their hazard lights to make it alright."

Neil "Well I took our bedroom door off, just like you told me to, remember, to stop her slamming it whenever she went off on one!"

Ben "Happened on the High Street this afternoon…caused chaos."

Elliott "Steady on now, what do you mean by "like I told you to"…it was a mere suggestion, an attempt to help and nothing more."

Neil "Well anyway, I took it off and she gave me nine bells and then, a week later…"

Bill interrupted "Nine bells?"

Grant "Later Bill, this is great."

Neil continued "So we'd been out, to her sister's, and she seemed game when we got home so, well…"

Bill "You were right Grant."

Neil "Well the bedroom door was in the garage so she refused on the grounds that the kids would hear…and made the point that it was my fault for being so bloody stupid."

Grant "She has a point Neil."

Elliott "Couldn't you have used a sock?"

Bill "Doesn't she just lie there in silence anyway?"

Grant "An interesting observation Bill…is it based on personal experience perhaps?"

Elliott "With Neil's wife?"

Grant "Possibly a lifetime's experience of the fairer but more dangerous sex?"

Neil "So she's not talking to me and I can't find the screws to put the bugger back up."

Elliott "Have you thought about calling a builder?"

Frank "This reminds me of the story of when Pete was fed up of his kids leaving their clothes all over the floor…and some bright spark suggested that the way to solve the problem was to go into their bedrooms and put all the clothes on the floor into bin bags and throw them out…after a suitable warning to the Little Petes I guess…anyway Pete goes home after a few wets and does the deed."

Pete was sitting bolt upright, arms crossed unnaturally high, grinning insanely.

Neil "So what's the problem?"

Frank "Well Bob, firstly he hadn't warned the kids or consulted Missus Pete…and secondly, it was a Tuesday night when he put the bags out."

Neil "Shit…the bin men come round early Wednesday morning."

Frank "Correct, and being efficient servants of the community they removed the majority of the kids' clothes."

Pete nodded "Cost me a fucking fortune."

Grant "And his nuptials for months."

Pete looked at Grant "So, why did you get named after a form of Government assistance?"

Elliott "She Who Must Be Obeyed still doesn't see the funny side of it…daft bint."

Neil "Really?"

Grant "Sure, as it's your round."

Neil did as he was told. His wife had trained him well.

"Anyone for trick and treating then?" asked Elliott.

"Get real," was Grant's considered reply.

"Ignoramous"

"Thanks Elliott," replied Grant.

"Well," started Bill "I quite like Halloween."

"Does it run in the family?" enquired Grant.

Bill ignored him. "Started by the Druids I believe, building bonfires."

"Like in the olden foot and mouth times," suggested Grant.

Bill continued, "Was it not something to do with the dead returning on the 31st?"

Elliott interjected, "Where is Buster?"

Bill persevered "There was a Celtic celebration of Samhain and a Roman two day event of Feralia and Pomona."

"Straight up?" asked a clearly impressed Pete.

"I thought Feralia was a sexual position," offered Grant, weakly.

Elliott moved closer to the table "You're right, and the symbol of Pomona was the apple...which is why in cruder times we got apple bobbing."

"No shit!" exclaimed Pete.

"And didn't one of the Popes introduce All Saints' Day in an attempt to get rid of Halloween?"

Elliott nodded "I think that's right Bill, and what do we do today? Pah, we send kids out in pathetic outfits, begging for sweets."

"I thought Halloween was actually derived from All Hallows Day, which is All Saints' Day" Grant paused for effect "Samhain was a Celtic celebration and the Romans merged it with Pomona and Feralia. All Souls' Day was all about honouring the dead and the whole thing goes back to the change from Summer – light, harvest, all that shit and Winter – dark, death and so on. Anyway, it's time for me to return to another type of pagan ritual," and with that he left a temporarily silent table.

Having wandered around the house, attempting to show interest in his wife's stories of what her friends had been buying and saying, and in the school days endured by his offspring, Grant sat slumped in his usual chair, staring at the dying embers in the stone fireplace. At least they had all spoken to him. But, they had to, as he couldn't mind read and they all wanted cash. Not one of them had enquired after his day.

It had been a mixed one as usual; it had started well, and had then gradually deteriorated through to just before 9 a.m., when the day had started becoming seriously crappy. 9 a.m. marked the time when the phones started ringing, the post arrived on his desk, and staff started pestering.

The two hours before 9 a.m. were when he got most work done and this morning he had even managed to raise a few bills; still, after twenty years in the profession, preparing bills gave him most satisfaction. He had put the finishing touches to a report on an ailing business; he had raised a number of new issues and, he believed, had identified a number of 'escape routes' for the bank; avoiding the dreaded liquidator! He had checked over a draft report on the idiot proposals of a failed motor dealer who was now planning to make it 'big' in the world of novelty pizzas; the stupidity and arrogance of some people in business never ceased to amaze him; and there were only a limited number of professional ways to say 'this is shite'.

Much of the morning had been taken up by a local civil servant who had been working on a project to provide financial support to an Asian businessman who was proposing to move his factory to the

North of England. Grant was less than convinced and had struggled to control himself when the civil servant had explained that several other accountants had looked at the project and had failed to deliver. Could that be because the project was fundamentally flawed? Eventually, more out of frustration than enthusiasm, Grant had agreed to 'make something happen' (although he had no idea 'what') and to do what, in his opinion, the civil servant should have done months ago and go and visit the Asian and develop the necessary business plan. Subject to someone agreeing to pay! He didn't expect a call back.

The afternoon had been taken up by a myriad of 'niggly' problems that others, more junior, should have dealt with, and the icing on the proverbial cake had been the receipt of a writ shortly before the close of business. The writ, issued on behalf of a local businessman of some repute, whom Grant felt should never have been allowed to become a client, related to some tax planning work undertaken some years previously; by an individual who had been 'moved on'. Whilst it looked to be unjustified, the writ would result in significant 'defence' work and, to his disgust and frustration, this would fall on his shoulders. And, being the 'boss' he had no one to grumble to. And he couldn't talk about his work with any of his friends. Oh, to have a relationship like a marriage. Bollocks.

Where were the cats when he needed to deliver a good kicking?

Is this what loneliness is all about?

Whatever, it wasn't too good.

He felt dead inside. Like he was rotting away. His insides being eaten away. Maggots feeding on dead flesh. He shook himself. And he was getting bored with himself.

Bored of the same frustrations.

Bored of the same self pitying voice in his head.

Bored of the same problems.

Did he feel sorry for himself?

No!

But he wasn't sorting anything out.

He wasn't moving forwards.

Shit, shit, shittedy shit shit.

He craved some healthy, home-cooked food; fat chance, his darling wife had effectively excluded him from family events, such as meals, some time ago, and he was too tired to bother looking for something to cook.

He was too tired to read and was not in the right frame of mind to attempt any work. One of the dogs had destroyed the evening papers; probably on purpose.

There was nothing of interest on the television and he was not allowed to listen to 'his awful music' (other than in his car!).

Shit, shit, shit.

There was more to life than this; there must be.

A glass of wine. Just one. Then he'd retire. Perhaps she might be in his – their bed.

Where were the cats?

Eight

Early November and the general depression caused by the few daylight hours was having an effect on the locals. Just past seven and the table used by the regulars was already well populated.

Grant was clearly 'up for a few' and drained his second of the evening well in advance of his drinking partners. "Righto, that's got the dust down, now for a pint or three, same again?"

He wandered off to the bar without waiting for a reply.

Ben wandered in; Grant made a point of not noticing him.

"Another death in the family?" asked Elliott as Buster sat down, having assisted Grant with the beers.

"Well actually," replied Buster in an almost breathless manner "my Uncle's son recently left us and, yes, he had bought this jacket."

"So that's your dead cousin's coat?" cut in Elliott.

"Well one could make that assertion."

Grant interrupted "Say, have you heard about the latest archaeological find, the Third Testament?"

"Here we go!"

"Sod off Frank, this is no joke," pleaded Grant.

"Yeah yeah, heard that before."

"No, seriously, they have just found the Third Testament, the follow on to the New Testament."

"Who or what is they," enquired Pete, but Grant, now in full flow, refused to be diverted "and the first bit translated is the Second Book of Noah."

Pete again "Didn't know there was a first book."

"Anyway, the story goes that one day God calls down to Noah and says Noah me Old China or words to that effect, I want you to make me a new Ark. Noah replies No Probs Boss and God replies that he wants some modifications to the design. OK Gaffer, says Noah, what do you want?"

Grant takes a quick draw providing sufficient space for Pete "Say Fatman, have God and Noah moved to Sunderland since the New Testament?"

"Who said 'dreams are illustrations from the book your soul is writing about you' or words to that effect?" asked Bill.

"You make that up?" asked Pete.

"Sunderland?" Ben stirred himself "There are some that say…" Before Ben could finish Grant continued.

"Bog off Pete, so God explains that this time he wants the boat to have twenty decks, one on top of the other and asks if Noah can oblige. Tall order agrees Noah but he agrees to have a go. So sometime later God calls down and asks how it's going. Finished announces Noah, what shall I do… fill it with animals like last time? Sort of, replies God…but this time I want it filling with fish. Fish asks Noah. Yep, fish answers God…but not just any old fish…no sirreee…I want Carp, every type of Carp going…Are you sure asks Noah…yes says God…I've always wanted a multi-storey carp ark," Grant breaks out in his best Basil Brush[42] laugh.

"Oh shit," announced Pete.

"Six finger jobbies you know," commented Elliott, folding his arms and winking, knowingly at Grant.

"What?" asked Pete.

---

[42] "Boom, Boom"….throws head back and guffaws! You could only get a character like Basil Brush in Britain! Making his television debut in 1963, his cheeky volpine antics soon attracted audiences of more than 13 million and his "Boom, Boom" catchphrase became a national habit. An early indication of the dumbing down of the British population? Perhaps. One great parallel between Grant and Basil is his rubbish jokes, punctuated by his annoyingly boisterous laugh.

"Those strange folk from Sunderland," replied Elliott, leaning forwards to attract maximum attention "it's all the interbreeding you know…and long distance travel amounts to a day out in South Shields…poor bastards…guess they've got no chance…one must be sympathetic but, well, you know, it's all a bit weird."

"I never actually met my cousin when he was alive," continued Buster, huffily.

"Are you planning on meeting him now he's dead?" asked Elliott.

"Well, that would be quite a feat wouldn't it," agreed Buster.

Pete "I didn't believe in the after life…that was until I met Grant."

Buster smirked "Yes I can understand that."

"You know," started Ben "that new barmaid has an awful habit of handing over the change with all the coins balanced on top of the fiver."

"There's a moral there somewhere" replied Pete.

Elliott grinned but decided to sidestep the obvious riposte "I hate it when they say 'there you go' when they give me my change…I mean, where am I going?"

"Moral?" asked Buster.

Pete smirked "Nah, given that I'm dyslexic, I meant 'marble'."

Grant poked Pete on the shoulder "Heard that one before."

"Eff off."

"Eddie Izzard I believe."

Pete flicked his fingers in Grant's general direction. Grant guffawed.

Grant had enjoyed a good day; the sort of day that one would like to share with one's wife. She was 'out' with one of her girlfriends and the kids were both away on school trips; the opportunity for a romantic escapade later on? Dream on. A couple of beers with the boys then a 'chicken ding'[43] and off to bed on one's own. Yes, he'd have a few more beers and pass on the chicken ding...perhaps.

Neil arrived, suited up, obviously on his way home from work and, as usual, looking in fear of his shadow "Evening chaps, what's what, guess it's my round."

The usual series of responses followed, including a successful request from Ben "Well, if you're asking, I'll have a Worthy."

Neil repaired to the bar; Alf was waiting for him. "Yoh, inn-keeper, my fine fellow, I'll have a pot of your finest and the same again for my erstwhile colleagues."

In the spirit of bonhomie the regulars had come to expect Alf replied "You taking the piss or what?"

"Well, you sell it," replied Neil, leaving Alf silenced and the regulars dumb-struck by the speed and wit of Neil's retort. Stupidly, Alf made a point of failing to properly fill the beers in Neil's round; stupidly as they were all sent back for topping up and he had to suffer a series of barbed comments from Ben 'If I wanted a half I'd have asked for one', 'Short measure and it looks cloudy', 'Straight out of the Tees this...and there's some that say the Romans should have built a wall along the Tees.'

Grant wondered whether he should retire; chicken ding and a bottle of red suddenly appeared very appetising. Elliott gave a passing thought to the concept of euthanasia and Pete was considering giving up breathing.

Neil completed the round and returned to the table.

Grant was the first to congratulate him "Good one, my son."

"Why yah bugger" continued Ben "as they say..."

---

[43] Chicken "ding" as in anything involving chicken and capable of being cooked in a microwave. Pierce the film, press the buttons, then "ding", it's done. Possibly hot, certainly tasteless.

Pete interrupted him "Bet you daren't talk to her indoors like that."

Neil blushed; brightly.

Ben, Grant and Pete applauded him.

"How's Neil" enquired Elliott as Neil struggled to remove his jacket and move a bar stool simultaneously. "Shit" replied Neil, not to the question but following the wetting of his suit by half of his pint "she'll know I've been in here now."

"So, anyone going to the village firework display?" asked Buster.

Elliott sat up, in mock horror "What? You selling tickets Neil?"

Neil looked perplexed.

"Cos there'll be fireworks when she sees that stain," finished Elliott.

Buster waved his shovel sized hands in an exaggerated attempt to calm Elliott. "Gentlemen, I have always wondered if the purpose of Bonfire Night is to celebrate the capture and execution of Guy Fawkes or, and this may be somewhat apt, to honour his attempt to do away with the government."

"Well," started Elliott in a surprisingly firm voice "it was that Robert Catesby who started it and he wanted to kill the King and the Prince of Wales, as well as the rabble of MPs."

"Thanks for that Sheila," concluded Buster.

Grant stood up. He was visibly weary. "See you later."

"And you know," continued Elliott "that Guy Fawkes was known as Guido by his friends."

"Thank you Sheila" repeated Buster.

Grant was sitting in his sun lounge. The rain was making a drumming noise on the glass roof; it reminded him of nights spent under canvas; happy days; days with no responsibilities; a complete freedom but one that wasn't properly recognised at the time.

He had tried to read a newspaper; it was too much of an effort. He had thought about cooking; that was too much of an effort. He had taken the dogs for a walk – he had never wanted a dog, but had been assured that he would not be required to look after it – they had ended up with two black Labradors and, typically, the three female members of the house had soon lost interest in them. The girls had named them 'Dusty' and 'Rags' – to Grant they were 'Eric' and 'Ernie' – and he was pretty sure that the 'boys' preferred these names.

He wanted to talk; his children were on trips – he had no idea as to where or why – all he was told was how much cash they needed - and his wife had retired to her room as soon as she had arrived 'home'. He could hear her now, despite the rain, her shrill tones creeping through the stone wall as she spent even more time on the telephone, to her friends.

He sighed and took his shoes off, kicking them under the sofa. This can't be right. He smiled, remembering the first time he had met her. She had been talking to one of his colleagues; he could remember it clearly. Her long, mane-like curly hair and bright brown eyes against a typically Irish complexion; her almost perfect teeth in a mouth keen to break into a warming smile. She had been wearing a tight black skirt – not a pencil skirt, but one tight enough to show off her womanly thighs – she had never been slim but she had less than a fuller figure. She'd been wearing black tights – he had fantasised that they were stockings, but that was probably just another symptom of his intrinsic immaturity.

And a red jumper, showing off her ample, but not large, bosom. And he had 'tingled'.

And he struck lucky.

She was his first girlfriend for over three years. She had recently ended a very long relationship; one going back to her school days. Grant had never got near a girl during his school days. In fact his sex life, as it was, had been focussed on three outrageous

102

years at university. Was he scared of women? Was he dysfunctional in some way? Or was he just unlucky? Pete would suggest that being fat, bald and ugly didn't help.

And time had moved on. He stood up and stretched his back; he was tired and he had an ache in the kidney area. Should he go to bed? He wandered into the kitchen and opened the fridge door – never eat standing up or with the fridge door open – bollocks, he rummaged around but his search was unsuccessful. He returned to the sun lounge and slumped onto the sofa.

She hadn't worn one of those tight skirts for many years. In fact he couldn't remember the last time he'd seen her legs. Stockings. On their wedding day; but she'd got amazingly drunk and that had been the end of that. Two, maybe three times, in the early years, she had got dressed up for him; but it had been frustrating as she was clearly uncomfortable with 'it all'.

What was that phrase? Memories are the key not to the past, but to the future. He didn't understand it. Did it mean that having happy memories would mean that it would all come good? Bollocks!

That smile and laugh. No, he hadn't seen or heard them for many a year. Well, he would hear her laugh when talking to her friends on the telephone; but it wasn't a warm or friendly laugh. And now it got the hairs on his neck rising for the wrong reasons.

The shiny eyes. Well, they seemed permanently angry.

Conversation; they used to talk for hours, about nothing. Now, nothing would be said for hours.

Sex? Had they ever had a good sex life? He wasn't sure. There had been times when he felt that they had been really close; but, more often, it had seemed to be a chore to her; and increasingly, over time, an unwelcome chore. When was the last time? He couldn't recall. Sad. Very sad.

Was it his fault? He hadn't done anything wrong that he knew about. He'd never been unfaithful or violent.

Was he insensitive? He felt that he'd been more than understanding and patient.

He had never complained about the absence of affection in recent years.

Perhaps he should have?

They had rarely kissed. She had complained about this. He had tried; but he couldn't see the point in kissing if it didn't develop.

They had never shown much tangible warmth towards each other.

Was this his fault?

He knew that he was fundamentally afraid of women.

They had rarely cuddled.

He should have tried harder.

They both should have tried harder.

Had she changed? Had he changed? Had they both changed?

Would it get better? He couldn't put up with this lifestyle much longer. He grimaced. She was probably thinking similar thoughts.

"So, if you had a band, what would you call it?" demanded Elliott.

Pete was speechless.

Frank had lost the plot.

"Bad breath dogs?" suggested Elliott.

Buster was confused "Well, er, I'm not sure what point you are trying to make."

"The Strangulated Hernias?"

Frank shook his head.

Elliott persisted "The Amazing Skinned Aardvaarks?"

Nine

The rain was torrential and had been for several hours, resulting in a number of the back road fords being impassable and forcing a number of regulars to stay home or risk a short 'drink drive' along one of the main roads: a risk few would take after the early scrapping of the doctor's Jaguar.

Neil, Elliott and Grant sat round their usual table in silence. For the second Wednesday in November, a night which would usually be relatively lively, the number of locals present was disappointingly low. The occasional sigh or slurp was all that broke the virtual silence that gripped the Urra.

Grant rose and, without question or comment, walked to the bar.

"Now then Tiger," enquired the landlord, who served the necessary beers without the need for any form of instruction.

"All right Alf?" enquired Grant, with minimal effort or interest.

Grant had enjoyed an interesting but exhausting day. Meetings with clients, and clients he liked as people and whose businesses interested him, in Carlisle and Durham had filled his day; only the mobile phone spoiling what would have been one of his better days; he hated the ring, as it rarely heralded anything other than a new problem, and he disliked the feeling that he was permanently on call for the idle overheads that populated his firm. Staff would call him up about minor issues, avoiding thinking about the matter at hand or making a decision, creating a form of mental interference which clouded his mind when he was supposed to be using his grey matter on fee generating matters; whoever invented the mobile phone should be shot. He had a similar view of email; a useful and powerful medium, completely wrecked by plonkers using it to avoid direct conversation or to publicise themselves. Shit, shit, shit. It never ceased to amaze him that the next logical development from email was actually the bloody phone; people to talk to each other rather than send written messages; a great technological leap backwards! The hours spent alone in his car provided scope for his mind to wander and to exaggerate whatever his mood was. He sometimes wondered if the music he listened to affected his moods; 'perhaps' had been his learned conclusion. He knew that he speeded up if he was listening to punk rock or driving music like ZZ Top; he reckoned that his driving became more considerate if he was listening to soulful, melodic music; the music with the stronger, personally provoking lyrics possibly made him a danger to other road users – he did have a habit of 'losing himself' in music written by the like of Stuart Adamson and Alan Hull. He looked at the selection in the multi changer; why did he only ever change it when he bored himself of his favourite tracks? Bored almost to the point of sickening himself. 'Bone idle'. Well, that's how is father used to describe him.

Today had been good until the bloody phone had started ringing…

At the table Neil leaned over towards Elliott and, in conspiratorial tones enquired. "Look, I've wanted to ask for ages but…why is Selwyn called Buster?"

"Well, it's a long story going back to his time in the Bournemouth and Wittlesea Fusiliers."

"I didn't know that he'd been in the Army."

"Ah…not just the Army…the Bournemouth and Wittlesea Fusiliers were special…a specialist regiment drawn from the public schools along the south coast."

"Specialist in what?"

"Secret," replied Elliott in hushed tones.

Grant returned from the bar and, in silence, placed three pints down before wandering off to, one could reasonably assume, the Gents.

"It was when he won his medal," continued Elliott "A little known episode during the last Omani uprising when, as you will know, special British forces assisted the Sultan's army in fighting off an invasion of Yemeni based tribes."

"Oh yes," agreed Neil.

"Well Buster, or Selwyn as he was then called, managed to gain entrance to a desert fort, held by the enemy, using a Sherman tank…"

"But they're American tanks," interrupted Neil.

"Aye, they were involved too…it was all hush hush you know," continued Elliott without pause for thought or drink "and Selwyn disguised the Sherman as a combined harvester, using all of his agricultural knowledge and south coast upbringing, so outwitting the Sultan's sworn enemy, the Maharajah of Sebastapol."

"That's in Turkey," countered Neil.

"Correct," agreed Elliott "All to do with the history of the Persian Peninsula, the Turks and Lawrence on his camel."

"Of course," whispered Neil.

"So Selwyn, and his fellow subaltern who, I believe, was some form of minor duke from the Hampshire area, were awarded medals for this inspired approach towards military equipment."

Neil took a long drink.

"But why Buster?"

"Obvious, you can't call a hero Selwyn."

"Yes, but why Buster?"

"Cos he bust through the fort walls."

"You're having me on."

"Ask Grant then."

His timing immaculate as ever, Grant returned and announced "Landlord owes me for three pints of lager."

Neil, struggling to control himself, launched himself towards Grant "Is it true about Buster?"

"What?" asked Grant.

"About him disguising a tank as a combined harvester and breaking into a desert fort!"

"You mean the battle with the Arabs?" responded an unsure Grant. Elliott's frantic attempts to catch Grant's eye, without alerting Neil, having been successful.

"That's it…is it true?"

"Too right…Selwyn was a bloody hero."

"Still is, you mean," interrupted Elliott.

"Have you mentioned the medals?" Grant asked Elliott.

Elliott, waving his hands, palms down, "Ssssh, you know that Buster doesn't like people to know about his bravery."

Neil, shaking his head in a mixture of disbelief and awe, "But he's never mentioned it."

Elliott, now in complete control of the conversation and comfortable in the knowledge that Grant had picked up the theme, "Heroes never talk about their deeds."

Grant, in hushed tones, re-emphasised the point, "Most people don't talk about their wartime experiences…unless they were in the Catering Corps at Catterick, and want to sound like they saw action."

Elliott, "Just look at Grant here…he never talks about the flak of a particularly tricky audit does he?"

"Piss off Elliott."

"I'll try."

"Are you sure about all of this?" continued a still uncertain Neil, "I mean, I didn't even know that he'd been in the Army, let alone seen any action."

Elliott, "But you wouldn't know would you…as he doesn't broadcast it."

Grant, "Just like Bill flying jets in the Korean War."

Neil, "But he was a chemist in Middlesbrough!"

Elliott, "Yes…after he did his active service."

Neil, "You're having me on."

Elliott, "No way…ask them, they won't like it…given that both of them don't like talking about it…but if you don't believe me…or Mister Bannister here… who corroborated the combine harvester story without prompting…just ask them."

Grant drained his glass and placed it, loudly, in front of Neil

"Oh yes, must be my shout."

Neil went to the bar.

Elliott, "Still raining?"

Grant, "Cats and dogs."

Elliott, "Great, isn't he?"

Grant, "Not the brightest light in the village."

Elliott, "Like a six pack without the plastic bit at the top."

Grant, "Just a couple of sarnies short of a picnic."

Neil, returning from the bar, "Someone hungry, do you want some nuts?"

Elliott, "The lift doesn't stop at the top floor either."

Grant nodded, "But he's a decent enough sort."

Eric and Ernie had been pleased…no, delighted to see him. In need of relieving themselves, of some exercise, of some attention and some food; the parallels to his own situation were striking; the big difference being that Grant hadn't fancied a drenching in the name of walking the boys.

As for the rest of the family; one of his daughters had managed a 'Hi Dad', the other was clearly unable to communicate due to some upset involving a boy in her class. As for his 'dearly beloved'…she was 'out'; 'out' being defined as 'not at home', 'not contactable', 'no idea of where she was' and no indication of 'when she would return'.

Grant sat in the sun lounge (he refused to call it 'the conservatory') and had been a rogue in allowing Eric and Ernie to join him – once they had dried out. He glanced at the mail – bills, bills and more bills.

He would never be able to retire at this rate.

Did she need so many clothes?

He never saw her wearing any of these expensive outfits.

And shoes.

Shit.

She must have bought more than Imelda Bloody Marcos.

He poured himself a glass of Chianti and put his feet on the table; so, she was 'out'; he could remember when they used to go 'out' together.

Usually with or to her friends. Never with 'his' friends. And he'd lost touch with too many of them than he cared to remember.

He, more than often, would be judged to have misbehaved in some way; occasionally by making an ill conceived comment or attempting a risqué joke, but usually by making an impressive dent in the hosts' wine supply.

When had they last gone 'out' together?

He struggled to remember.

He could recollect various unsatisfactory trips out when the girls were younger; the lack of satisfaction usually emanating from his inability to mind read.

Shit, it was unfair that the abilities to transmit and receive brain waves and to read other peoples' minds had been vested in a restricted number of people, and all of them were female.

He grinned; there had been a time when a 'night out' had usually ended with a fumble in bed; often short lived and clearly less than satisfying for her, but a degree of affection was involved if nothing else. Shit. He poured himself another glass. There had been that time when, out of the blue, she had asked him to tie her hands behind her back. He had done as he was asked but it had probably excited him more than her...and certainly him too much! And she had refused to ever speak about that incident again. Fucking shame really; he'd really fancy that again.

Ten

The last Friday in November; the bar was relatively quiet but it was still early.

The village was no longer covered by a glorious mix of browns and golds, the fallen leaves having now been compressed into undignified piles of mush. This was one of the dirty times of year; the plentiful rain, itself often less than clear, was no match for the autumnal debris, particularly when mixed with the early season road salt and the oil and rubber which collected on the ground during the cold dry spells. No, not a nice time of year; which is why the roaring fire in The Urra was even more welcoming than usual…

Grant sat with a look of fevered concentration; Elliott awaited his response with a broad grin stretching across his ruddy face.

"Got it…this is a journey not a destination."

Elliott nodded; obviously impressed with both Grant's response and his continued involvement in the evening's game. "Of course," replied Elliott, "but are you grazing from the fruit hanging from the lower branches?"

Grant shifted uneasily, took a quick draw from his pint of Southside's Fever Ale and continued, "Certainly not, but we must find the corn amongst the cornflakes."

Bill looked at Buster, shook his head and grumbled, "Tossers."

Buster nodded, "But it is your shout I believe."

Ignoring the pair of them Elliott retaliated, "Ah yes, but have you been thinking outside the box?"

Grant looked shocked, surprised and disappointed at the weakness of the reply, "You clearly need more face time, Sunbeam."

Elliott grinned, knowing that Grant knew that he had won, "You can cut that Sunbeam stuff out, straight out, I'll have you know that where I come from that is far from a term of endearment."

"Have they got it out of their system yet," enquired Bill.

"Sorry, just a half," interjected Ben.

Frank arrived, "Now then playmates."

"A half, if you're asking."

Frank made a point of blanking Ben.

"Head-rent, that's it," exclaimed Grant.

"What's he on about," asked Frank

"A new term for management consultants?" offered Elliott.

"That would be 'Wankers', wouldn't it?" suggested Frank.

Grant was clearly enjoying himself, although everyone else had lost track of his cerebral wanderings, "Spot on, Daddio!"

"There's some that say," but Ben was stopped by Elliott before he could get into the flow of the conversation.

"If you rent your head to someone, what do you do?"

"Good point," replied Grant, "Let's ask Old Two Brains," After a brief pause to take breath, he cleared his throat. "Frank, just how do you manage to walk and talk at the same time?"

Not realising that another wind up session was about to start, and with him as the target, Frank took the question seriously, "Well, it's automatic isn't it, you learn it as a baby, it then comes naturally doesn't it"

Elliott moved in "Sorry Frank, do you learn it or does it come naturally…it can't be both can it?"

"Well, you learn it…then it becomes automatic…so it seems natural."

Elliott shook his head, slowly, "Sorry Frank, me no comprendes."

"Look, when you're a baby you learn to make sounds, right?"

Elliott nodded, a serious expression on his face.

113

"You then learn to move around, you with me?"

Elliott nodded.

"Over time you learn to speak and to walk, then it's natural."

Elliott nodded slowly, rubbed his chin and asked, "But how do you do them simultaneously?"

"Oh fucking hell," Frank reached for his cigarettes, a give-away sign that he was getting frustrated.

"So you learn to move… then you learn to speak…or is it the other way round?" asked Grant.

Waving his right index finger towards Frank, Elliott continued, "Or, and this is the point, do you learn them together?"

"Or do they come naturally?" offered Grant.

"And, whatever, together or individually?" added Elliott.

Pushing the table away from himself, to create room for him to get up, and thereby knocking Frank and Elliott's knees, Ben bade his farewell for the evening. "Ta-rah, like well, as they say in Hartlepool."

"You know," said Bill, "the phrase I hate is when people describe an experience as being part of 'Life's learning curve'."

Elliott took a quick, excessively enthusiastic slurp "Good one…but what about 'Mwa' or 'Mwa Mwa?' " he finished with some theatrical kissing gestures.

"Chance would be a fine thing," replied Grant.

"Crackerjack that," agreed Elliott.

Frank smirked, a smirk of frustration, not humour, and wandered off to organise the next round of refreshments.

Frank returned from the bar. Conversation had come to an unusual end. The quiet was uncomfortable.

"Any plans for the weekend?" asked Frank, to break the silence.

"A little something," replied Elliott.

"It's the wife's birthday," offered Grant.

"How old?" asked Frank.

"The big four zero."

"Much younger than you then?" asked Elliott.

"Fuck off, I'm a toy boy."

"Doing anything special?" Frank seemed genuinely interested; or was he angling for an invitation to some free booze?

"Yes, I've organised a surprise party for her...couple of old school friends...they are meeting up at the Hutton Hotel tonight...and her family should be arriving in a couple of hours."

"And she doesn't know?" asked Elliott, with an expression of horror.

Grant nodded, proudly.

Elliott shook his head, "She'll kill you if she hasn't cleaned the toilets."

"Nah, it'll be cool," Grant took a long pull of his pint before continuing, "I've stocked up on everything, have organised a pamper day for the women tomorrow, have sorted a table at the Hutton tomorrow and...and this is the big brownie point winner... a kids party for Sunday!"

Elliott bowed his head and shook it gently, "You're dead my dear friend."

"Should be great," suggested Frank.

"Better be," replied Grant, "Mind, I've not risked inviting any of my friends or family. That would be a step too far."

"So, no chance of..."

Grant stopped Frank before he could finish. "No, but you might be able to help me finish the barrel that I've got in the garage."

"You're doomed," continued Elliott.

And so, Grant returned home. Somewhat earlier than usual.

Surely they were wrong? This would be a great weekend? It would prove he cared. It may re-ignite the flames of affection. Passion even.

She was in the lounge, 'sharing' a bottle of wine with her friend Susan. Grant had never 'warmed' to Susan – he would argue that this was because she had never made any attempt to hide her disdain for him; how she seemed to make him feel unwelcome in his own home; how she seemed to demand – and receive – 'first call' on his wife. It had almost seemed as if they were competing for his wife's attention – and affection. He knew that he had 'lost'; but wasn't quite sure when. He had consoled himself with the thought that, fundamentally, Susan was a relatively unattractive, completely unappealing, man detesting bitch. But this was only a temporary consolation.

It had always puzzled Grant why his wife would never entertain, shop with, or generally do anything with Samantha and Susan together.

Perhaps they both hated each other?

Proving Grant's feelings to be fair.

Perhaps his wife was some form of control freak?

He smirked; she was always 'in control'; too controlled.

But it was strange; how she never let her friends mix. He shrugged. Mind, at least she had not barred them – like his friends and family.

He had grown to hate Susan – ever since she had appeared his relationship with his wife had gone from pretty average to pretty awful; but, in his moments of clear thinking, he challenged the thought that it could be all her fault. But anyway, here he had a potentially exciting night for his wife…and she had to be here!

He attempted to initiate conversation.

He commented on the weather.

He asked how Susan 'was': a question out of common courtesy, not genuine interest, but still deserving of a reply: she ignored him and made some form of eye signal to his wife.

He enquired after her day.

He offered Susan a drink: she declined.

He asked about her plans for the weekend.

He mentioned the dripping tap in the garage.

He made a number of suggestions. *Joint activities. Shopping. Quality time with the children.*

He listened to her excuses and criticisms.

He'd fix the tap then!

He tried to talk about his day.

He asked after his children.

The door bell rang. He was saved. No, he wasn't. It was her family; en masse.

Her sisters; all identical in appearance and all with a downtrodden 'partner' in tow. Rachel, the youngest was through the door first – she gave Grant a friendly peck on the cheek before hugging her eldest sister. Grant viewed Rachel as a 'nice kid' who had endured a difficult childhood. He couldn't be as understanding of her husband; Denis was, in Grant's considered opinion, a foul mouthed waster who he wouldn't trust as far as he could throw him.

"Now then Denis," said Grant, gripping his hand firmly, and shaking it like he was a long lost brother, "the booze is through there, make yourself at home." And he would, thought Grant.

Next came Teresa with her 'friend' Tabitha. Grant gave Teresa a gentle hug. It was not reciprocated. Tabitha grinned at Grant and he smiled back – the two of them hated much about the others' principles but, through a mutual honesty they had developed a sort of respect and admiration for each other. "You alright, you capitalist bastard?" asked Tabitha.

"Still paying for too many social workers?" replied Grant.

117

The next to force their way in were her father's sister and her husband – Gladys and Seamus – Grant had liked Seamus from the moment he had first met him – a cultured gentleman, mild mannered, courteous to a fault, a warm sense of humour and a mischievous glint in his eyes. Gladys was something else. He took Seamus's outstretched hand and shook it warmly, before giving Gladys the requisite kiss on the cheek.

Jennifer, the last of the sisters, tumbled into the house, laden down with baby paraphernalia. Grant thought about helping her but then saw her boyfriend, Robert, lingering outside: Grant liked Robert and took the opportunity for a brief escape.

Grant and Robert had spent many hours, over the years, discussing the common problems of their female partners; always over an ale or six. Grant had always enjoyed the visits back to her 'home' – even though he had, at first, been treated as some form of novelty item; a target for witticisms and japes. Unfortunately for Grant, Robert seemed withdrawn this evening; not talkative, not particularly happy.

"Baby has cried all the way over and Jennifer is going through one of those phases."

Grant nodded, "Come have a drink then."

"Better not thanks," replied Robert, "you know that anything that looks remotely like enjoyment gets banished at certain times of the month and I'll only get accused of being drunk in charge of a baby."

Grant agreed and sympathised with Robert. Well, he thought, this is turning out well!

He walked into the lounge; he could feel a searing pain in the back of his neck; that would be Susan's eyes. He surveyed the mayhem and made an attempt to act the part of genial host. Where was his wife? Where were his children?

He 'worked' the room like a professional – well, that was part of his 'day job' – and soon everyone had a drink, the snacks were already being eaten or trodden into the carpet, and he had managed to avoid Gladys. Where was his wife?

The door bell rang and further guests appeared. It was as if half the population of the Republic of Ireland had decided to relocate to his front room. Where was the party girl?

Noise. Noise with an Irish accent. Where was the volume control? It rapidly spiralled out of control. What had he done? Why did they all have to talk at the same time?

"Eeeeh, what a surprise!"

"And I was saying to yon Seamus…"

"That'll be the Bushmills,"

"So Grant, how are the numbers?"

"Where's the birthday girl?"

"Stone dead he was, right where he'd been standing,"

"There's something wrong with that new priest,"

"Have you lost the nappy bag already?"

"And I said to him I said, you'll not be for the wanting with her, don't you know,"

"Too young, don't you know,"

"I prefer the crisps back home,"

Grant caught a glimpse of his wife returning, with Susan. Where had they been? Bloody typical. And where were the kids?

"Happy birthday!"

"Hello sweet heart,"

"Hi Sis,"

"This is going to be some weekend!"

"Where are the children?"

"Priests should be old,"

"Bit of a shock, you wait, there's more to come,"

"Uncle Silas, well, it's his hips,"

"You looked lovely when you were carnival queen,"

"Forty, who would have thought,"

"Well, says I, if I was to be going there, I wouldn't be starting here,"

"How long has it been?"

"Did you make that yourself?"

"Haven't the girls grown?"

"You look just like your mother did,"

"And I said to Harry down in Cork,"

"Now Grant, I'll be wanting a kiss off you soon enough,"

"You must miss the blarney,"

"Any Guinness?"

"And marrying a successful Englishman as well,"

"Your cousin Mary is having problems with her Tyrone,"

"And down in County Kildare,"

"Do you remember?"

"Red wine please."

"You look well,"

"Any Babycham?"

"Look at the state of me, I had no idea,"

"Wasn't it nice of Grant?"

His 'world' would shortly end. Amidst much girly screaming and hugging he caught a flash from her eyes; anger, pure, unadulterated anger.

Eventually, once they all had full glasses in their hands, Grant made good his escape. He had thought about offering a brief respite to Robert – but had thought better of it. There were times when he positively loved Eric and Ernie and tonight was one of those times; and tonight they would get an especially long walk.

He wandered along the main road through the village before deciding to sit on a bench overlooking the beck; he let the boys loose and leant back. The clouds were high and he could see the millions of stars; he followed the paths of a few high flying jets – he felt a pang of sadness, remembering when he used to travel widely – and happily. He looked round the village; what was going on behind those drawn curtains? Sex? Violence? Love? Laughter? Or were many of them as pissed off as he was?

It had been almost two years since he had given up smoking but tonight…no, he'd beaten the habit, he hoped.

He was in the garage collecting some drinks when the door opened.

"What the fuck do you think you are doing?"

"I thought you'd love it, your birthday with your friends and family. They all thought it was a great idea and isn't it nice that they've all come over?"

"And do I have any say in this?"

"Well, if you had it wouldn't have been a surprise now, would it?"

"So what about my plans?"

"Sorry, didn't know you had made any."

"You inconsiderate bastard."

"Oh, that's a bit unfair, look, do you want your presents now?"

"All I want is…oh, you would never ever understand."

She switched off the garage light as she left.

Eleven

The snow was beginning to lie; it had been falling since darkness fell, some three hours ago. It was unusual to get this amount of snow before late January; but the forecasts had been correct and the end of November would long be remembered for one of the biggest snow storms for many years.

"Global fucking warming," had been Elliott's observation on his arrival in The Urra.

The Urra was rarely cut off, but it was a distinct possibility this evening and, as a result, the bar was virtually empty. The fire by the 'Regulars' table was burning brightly, aided by the wind from the North East; the same wind which was rattling the windows in their ancient frames and was beginning to create a sizeable mound of snow by The Urra's back door.

"You know how we worried about nuclear war when we were kids?" started Elliott, "well, do you think today's kids worry about melting ice caps?"

"I can't remember worrying about nuclear war," replied Frank.

"That's an age thing," acknowledged Elliott.

Neil helped the conversation along, "I know what you mean, I certainly remember thinking about the Cold War and how we might all die in a nuclear blast."

Frank laughed, mockingly, "You never did, you toss-pot!"

"Haway Frank," started Elliott, "we all did, I remember talking to Grant about it and he made the point that it was like spending your teenage years with the Sword of Damocles hanging above one's head, and how his girls should carry similar fears of seeing polar bears in their garden."

The thought of polar bears marauding through the village brought a temporary silence to the table.

Elliott sat back and studied the ceiling.

Neil was lost in his thoughts – probably worrying about how he would explain to Helen that the roses have been eaten by a flock of penguins.

"I doubt that even Grant would be daft enough to venture out on a night like this," said Frank, breaking what had appeared to be a lengthy silence.

"Aye, expect he's hiding in his study with a bottle of red," agreed Elliott.

"Poor bugger," replied Frank, continuing, "have you heard that one of his kids, Charlotte I think, has got epilepsy?"

Neil appeared to wake from a trance, his dark eyes staring at Frank, "Doesn't that mean she should be on an island in the Indian Ocean?"

"You tosser," replied Elliott, "that's leprosy, she's got epilepsy."

"So where do they live then?" asked a now clearly uneasy Neil.

"Time for me to throw my hand in," announced Frank.

Warming to the subject Elliott took on the challenge, "Aye well, better than laughing your head off."

"Pull your finger out...or is it off," replied Frank.

"Doubt you'll get your cars out of the car park tonight," announced the snow covered Pete as he placed the requisite beers on the table. "The snow is coming down heavy now and the wind is causing drifting."

"Shit," Neil was looking somewhat uncomfortable. "I was supposed to collect a take-away on the way home. Shit shit shit. Helen wanted a Chinese and the girls wanted pizzas. Shit shit shit."

"You could try serving humble pie," suggested Elliott.

"Aye, there's plenty of icing about," agreed Pete.

"Shit shit shit." Neil stood up and bid his colleagues a good night, "Well, see you later if the wife or a polar bear doesn't get me first."

"Wanker!" shouted Frank, at Neil's disappearing back.

"What's up with Frank?" asked Alf, the Landlord.

"He's not too happy with your fine ales," replied Elliott.

"You what! The little fucker."

"Steady on Alf."

"Shit shit shitty" concluded Neil, before making for the front door without any form of farewell.

"He's fucked," commented Frank.

"Not tonight he won't be," replied Elliott.

"So, what's wrong with my beer?" pleaded Alf, sitting down without invitation and clearly ready for a row.

"Where shall we start Frank?" asked Elliott.

"You can keep me out of this?" replied Frank, looking at Pete as if for help and support. Pete obliged.

"No, come on Frank, we've all heard you say that Alf doesn't clean his pipes often enough, that his beer is over-priced and watered-down, and that you regularly get the runs after sampling the guest ales."

"Oh thanks Pete," was all Frank could manage before Alf started on him.

"Come on then, what's wrong with my beer?............the pipes are done virtually daily and anyone who says I water my beer will get barred, 'cos I don't, and, other than for Ben I always change a drink if someone's unhappy…and no one ever complains, other than Ben…so what's your problem Frank?"

"See you tomorrow," said Pete, rising from the table

"Aye, you'll be buggered now, as they say in Barrymoreland," added Elliott, in his best 'Ben voice' as he too rose to leave.

"I take great care in maintaining my cellar and all the plumbing," continued Alf, oblivious to the now departing Pete and Elliott, who were both reversing out of the front door, saluting Frank in camp military styles.

Grant leant back in his chair and surveyed his office; every inch of desk space appeared to be covered by files or loose papers, other than where his keyboard and screen stood. He would argue that he knew where everything was, and that there was order to the seeming mess; bollocks, this may once have been the case but not anymore; he was losing it.

He wandered through the other offices on the floor; the only lights were where the cleaners were working (or gossiping...or reading something that they shouldn't); his colleagues had all left for the evening, many of them early to avoid the snow. He should have left hours ago as his was one of the longer and potentially more treacherous journeys; bollocks, what was the point? He wandered into the boardroom and poured himself a gin and tonic, without ice or lemon but far too much gin. Slumped in the leather chair at the head of the table he let his eyes wander round the panelled walls, skipping from picture to picture; the smiling, almost benevolent faces of his predecessors stared down at him. Some of them he had known, he had worked with a number, but most were remembered only for their achievements, failures or eccentricities; how would he be remembered? Would his face ever stare down on this table? Bollocks.

He looked at the old fashioned-looking spring file which lay in front of him; the hand written words on its cover said it all: 'Office Restructuring'. With a sigh he opened it and began leafing through the numerous sheets of A4 paper. He totally disagreed with the proposals. The underlying logics of rationalisation and centralising specialist staff into key centres were unchallengeable; but they could not work in a geographically diverse region, where offices worked in separately defined economic and cultural regions. He was charged with implementing the plans; his objections had been noted, but not listened to. He was certain that the actions would ultimately lead to his own 'dumbing down' and to the eventual closure of his office; as it would not be able to compete with other national, and several local firms, all of which were investing in specialist staff and services. He fought the urge to raid the cigar supply in the drinks cabinet.

He looked at the lists of staff; those who were to stay in the down-sized operation, those who would be asked to move (and if they said no…), and those who were to be made redundant. How long would it be before he was on the third list?

He got up and walked to the window; the panoramic view of the Tyne and its bridges always impressed him. How did he get here? He shook his head. He had never wanted a career in accountancy. And when he'd fallen into one, almost by chance, he had always promised himself that he would make good his escape before his thirtieth birthday. But here he was, almost forty and stuck in a proverbial rut. He had enjoyed the work – until when? When had it changed? He had always got a 'buzz' from meeting new people and visiting new places, factories, offices, whatever…but few things were 'new' these days.

The job was changing – and it was changing in ways that he didn't welcome. He accepted some as necessary evils; others were pains in the arse; and some were total and unacceptable bollocks.

He looked at the papers on the table. He despaired. Should he go home? Should he start preparing a rebuttal? What was the point? He felt he should try. He gathered up the papers and returned to the 'safety' of his own office.

He rang home to find out how bad the snow was. No answer.

He surfed the net for a few minutes.

126

He could feel himself becoming frustrated and angry. Angry with himself. He wasn't sure why. He just felt that he must have done something wrong. It must be his fault. But what?

That was it. Decision made. He was going to prepare a set of counter proposals and would show the idiots why their ideas were flawed. But first, he needed to replenish his drink......and opted for a freshly ground coffee as, for once, he knew he needed to keep a clear head.

Grant's path to his current position – he would have used the word 'predicament' – was one of unplanned luck and misfortune. After leaving university he had drifted aimlessly for the best part of a year – simply, he had no idea what he wanted to do with his life.

He worked as a mobile ice cream salesman[44], before moving on to be a lamp fitters mate[45] and worked in numerous bars. Perhaps out of a feeling of duty to his parents he started making attempts to get a 'proper' job. He was offered a place on a teacher training course – but had a good word with himself and accepted the fact that this would be the first step on the road to jail – as he would surely assault a student within days of being let loose in a class room. He applied for a management trainee role with a railway company but was struck by uncontrollable giggles when the subject of trainspotting came up. Eventually, almost by accident, he applied for a place as a trainee accountant and, to the horror of many, he was offered the position. In Grant's view, that was the beginning of the end.

The pay was never good and the work was turgid – but he had expected nothing else so was not unduly concerned.

---

[44] Meaning he drove an old ice cream van around numerous housing estates, playing a worn out version of Greensleeves and selling watered down ice cream.
[45] Effectively the slave/ go-for for an under-qualified Council electrician – but, at least the pies were good.

127

The studying was a pain. As a graduate he felt that it was his divine right to go out every night. But the studies and low pay effectively curtailed that.

He was no star at the examinations and struggled greatly with statistics and a number of other subjects which seemed to be in foreign languages, fundamentally pointless and earth-shatteringly boring. Suffice to say, his exam record was far from perfect but, a year later than he should have, he qualified and became, to the shock of many, a chartered accountant.

And during that four year process, despite numerous drunken efforts, he had got nowhere near a woman!

So the world was his oyster! Well, hardly. He was stuck in the industrial back water known as Teesside and had no special skills (unless you counted his abilities in various drinking games). And then he had seen her. She was an accountant, had qualified before him, was clearly proficient and had recently joined the same firm as him. And that Irish accent and those 'come to bed' eyes. He was smitten. Badly. Big style. He didn't know it, but he was well and truly fucked.

He bought new clothes. He tidied up his car. He dieted. He started showing an interest in twentieth century Irish literature. He tried to be 'interesting'. He started playing rugby after a break of four years – pure madness.

And then he started trying – some would call it 'stalking'. After weeks and again, as if by accident, he found himself alone with her in a public house – everyone else had gone. "Well, what the hell" he had thought and had summoned up the courage to ask her…what she was doing at the weekend?........nothing had been her response.

And that was that.

He had embarrassed himself on the Saturday night by attempting to grope her bottom in a night club.

On the Sunday evening he had struggled with her blouse buttons in the style of a terrified fifteen year old.

On the Monday night they both drank too much and…

On the Tuesday night he had broken his four year 'duck' in less than impressive style – given that speed is not impressive in such circumstances.

And whatever she thought, he had fallen madly in love.

And from then a strangely one sided relationship had developed – where he had always made all of the running and she occasionally disappeared.

But he was in love, so who gave a flying fuck!

He did now.

Fifteen years too late!

Twelve

The first Wednesday in December; the Christmas crowds were not only in the shops but, to the frustration of the regulars, in The Urra. The inclement weather continued but pretty much a full turn out was expected this evening; henceforth a number of the regulars would stay at home or make late night visits to The Urra, to avoid the crowds of Christmas drinkers and the all pervading smell of bar food (and children).

Elliott was warning his cousin, Steve, who had joined him for a few beers, "Drinking too much will turn you into a woman."

Steve shook his head in disbelief, knowing his cousin well enough so as to sense some form of wind up may be in the offing.

"It's all to do with the phystrogens in the hops, isn't that right Buster."

Buster agreed.

"It's been tested…and we could reperform that scientific test this very evening."

"Really?" enquired Buster, looking worried.

"Yessiree…all we need is six pints in an hour and the case will be proven."

"Well, I'm game," offered Frank.

"So what will happen?" asked a somewhat nervous Steve.

"Well, my boy," continued Elliott "You'll gain weight."

Steve nodded.

"You'll begin to talk excessively."

Steve nodded.

"You won't make any sense and you may be loud…are you getting the picture?"

Steve nodded.

"You'll become emotional."

Buster joined in "You won't be able to drive."

Elliott agreed enthusiastically "Yes, yes and you won't be able to think rationally."

Neil contributed, "Like my Helen, you'll argue over nothing."

"Absolutely," agreed Elliott, but he was unable to wrest control of the discussion from Neil.

"And, just like her, you'll refuse to apologise even when it is bloody clear that you're wrong."

"And," an excited Buster interrupted, "you'll have to sit down to have a piss!"

Elliott made a face of mock horror, "Buster, I'm disappointed in you."

Pete arrived, nodded at his drinking companions and made straight for the bar, "Evening Sally my little pet lamb, how are you this delightful evening?"

"Same as usual?"

Pete was at a loss momentarily; was she answering his question or confirming the round?

"And one for yourself."

As she started pulling the various pints Pete found himself staring at her perfectly formed breasts… visions of loveliness in need of a delicate massage with natural oils, her smooth skin, long neck in need of a gentle nibbling by his mouth, those long delightful legs…

"Anything else?"

Pete jumped and hesitated, "Er… no… thanks, have one yourself."

Grant had gone straight home. In fact he had left the office promptly and had been determined to create social intercourse with his family. He was travelling to China in the morning and wanted to spend time with his family.

On arriving home, after the demands for cash by his progeny had been satisfied, she had announced that she was going out; to spend the evening with her friend Susan.

"It's Fat Bald Bastard's birthday today," announced Pete.

Elliott raised his glass, "His round then."

"Who's going to put in on Grant's tab?" asked Buster.

Pete rose to his feet, "Have no fear, Pete is here."

"Will he be in tonight or will he enjoying a romantic evening somewhere?"

"Daft question Neil."

"Sorry Pete."

"Well, don't do it again," and with that Pete marched purposefully to the bar.

His daughter Charlotte mentioned, almost as an afterthought, that she was being tested for epilepsy – she had taken a few 'funny turns'; Grant was shocked and appalled.

Why had he found out like this?

What was the cause?

Would she be alright?

What could be done?

Why hadn't his health insurance been used?

He had tried to find out more but his daughter was being less than forthcoming.

He took Eric and Ernie for a walk: they seemed happy enough.

He packed his case and tried to explain where he was going and why; neither daughter seemed particularly interested. He asked if they wanted a phone number in case he was kidnapped. In unison they explained that they wouldn't be that lucky.

He had an early start so, avoiding the urge to open a bottle of red, he decided to retire. He wandered into the lounge to say his farewells to his daughters.

"Night Pops."

"Have a good trip…bring us back some nice presents."

"Oh yes, your birthday presents and mail are on your desk in the study."

He'd forgotten with all the rushing around to get his visa and sort out his flights: it was his fortieth birthday. No chance of a cake and candles then?

He slumped into his study chair and surveyed the presents; without opening them he could see that his sister had remembered, as had a few old friends…and Pete.

A jumper from his beloved and a number of books from the girls. Happy Birthday Grant. He opened one of the desk drawers and took out a tumbler and a half empty bottle of malt: Happy Birthday you daft old bugger. And in the silence of his study he drank a toast to himself. And then he drank a toast to a safe and rewarding trip. And then he had a 'proper' drink.

"Where is he?" asked Frank.

"I saw his car on his drive," replied Neil.

"On the nest?" suggested Buster.

Pete guffawed, "Aye, and you'll be having rumpty tumpty later as well!"

"Rumpty tumpty?" asked Steve.

Elliott whispered, "Don't ask, it will only lead to embarrassment."

"I saw Mrs Bannister driving out of the village," explained Neil "at some speed."

Frank shook his head, "So, it's his birthday, she's out, where is the bean-counting prat?"

"And it is the big four oh!" announced Pete.

Frank slammed his glass down, "We should have bought him a prostitute then!"

Thirteen

Watson Humphrey was an unforgiving place in December; the wind whistled through the village from the tundra region of continental Europe or off the moors to the immediate south; whatever the direction, it was always windy (and when it wasn't windy, it was blowing a gale); and the wind was always freezing. If it wasn't raining, it was about to. The trees were bare and the drains were filled with decaying leaves. The Urra was at its most welcoming for locals at this time of year; few visitors ventured out to the village during the late autumn and winter months (other than for festive celebrations), the fire was always lit, and Alf, the landlord, was almost sociable.

"The complete and utter twats," concluded Frank, having described the events of the previous week to Buster, Eric and Ben. Pete and Elliott sat smirking, enjoying the obvious discomfort that Frank still felt.

"No sign of Neil tonight," commented Biggles.

"Gone Christmas shopping with Helen, poor bugger," replied Buster.

"There's been no sign of Grumpy Grant for some weeks," added Biggles.

Eric cleared his throat with the style and panache of a reformed smoker, "I think that he said that he was going to China."

"Aye, the daft fucker will be working so hard that his head is up his arse...or will be boozing that much that his head is in a gutter somewhere," commented Pete, who, despite all the insults and abuse he directed towards Grant, seemed to be genuinely concerned.

"Cert for a heart attack, stroke or worse, that fucker," offered Buster.

Ben looked at Eric, "China!....it's full of bloody foreigners."

"And when he's not working his tits off, he's entertaining or being entertained...which I don't think he enjoys anymore...or he goes home to what doesn't seem to be the most harmonious of domestic lives," continued Pete, who immediately changed the subject for fear that he may have said too much, "Anyway, my round and I see that Alf has got the Mistletoe Mild and Santa Special on."

"Half a worthy for me," replied Ben.

Buster, "The Mild for me, although I fear that I'll regret it in the morning."

Frank, "Same, ta."

Bill, "I'll have a wee Grouse if I may."

Elliott, "Well, it being the season to be jolly, well, almost, I'll try the Santa...and I wouldn't want to hear the wife say that."

"What about you Mandy?" enquired Pete.

Bill, "What's with the Mandy?"

Pete, "As in I'm Mandy, Fly me."

Frank, "Wasn't a Mandy a drug?"

Biggles, "I'll have a Mild please...and cut the Mandy shit, you're as bad as Grant, wherever the fucker is."

Ben, the master of the stupid question or comment, "What's he want to go to China for?"

Eric, naively, tried to answer a question based on ignorance and bigotry by common sense and fact, "He's gone to look at a business which might open an operation over here."

"What's it do...make noodles?"

"I'm not sure...you know how Grant has to be careful what he says about client affairs...but I think that it's something to do with electrics."

"Have they got electricity in China?"

136

"Yes, erm, I'm quite sure that China has become a very developed country."

"Full of bloody paddy fields and dead babies."

"And I believe that there could be significant job creation if a new factory is built."

"Who for…us or them?"

"Well, the people over here…I assume," Eric was beginning to lose the will to continue this line of conversation.

"So what's Grant doing?"

Eric looked around for help; Elliott came to his rescue, "Perhaps he will get himself kidnapped and, to celebrate this possibility, I will buy the next round."

"Isn't it his birthday soon?" asked Bill.

Grant was asleep on a couch in a Business Class lounge in Hong Kong's airport; exhausted from his trip into China and two days of sight-seeing in Hong Kong; two days which had largely consisted of visits to various hostelries, as shopping was not one of his favourite pastimes and the torrential rain had had a dampening effect on his sight-seeing efforts. He had arrived at the airport early and his plane was late; having consumed an appropriate quantity of complimentary drink he was now in a state of complete mental and physical exhaustion. He absolutely adored the pampering of international business class air travel; not least that the stewardesses, albeit that they are only doing their jobs, but they always seemed to care, to be interested in his well-being, and some actually talked to him. Unlike the women in his life.

Grant smirked. The hostesses on North American airlines weren't quite so hot. Generally more mature. Always seemed to disapprove of passengers trying to enjoy themselves. "You want another drink?" "Another drink" an observation rather than a question. He shrugged. It was time for another drink.

Elliott was in full flow, "So, the customer says: I want some nails. And the ironmonger replies: How long do you want them? And the customer replies: I thought I'd keep them."

Pete was the first to reply, "Crap."

Frank shared the view, "As bad as Grant."

He had bought presents for the children; at least they had wanted to talk to him when he had called home. She didn't. Probably sitting on her arse, drinking his red wine, shopping through some ruddy catalogue. He'd better get some perfume; perhaps something which removes skin, painfully.

Elliott persisted, "So, Mick returned from a doctors visit one day white-faced. Turning to his wife Sally he says: 'I've been told I have only 24 hours to live!' He took a long pull from his beer. 'Wiping away her tears, he asked her to make love with him.Of course she agreed, and they made passionate love," Elliott paused for effect. "Six hours later, Mick went to her again, and said: 'Darling, now I only have 18 hours left to live. Maybe we could make love again?' She agrees and again they make love," Elliott paused again. "Later, when Mick was getting into bed he realised he now had only 8 hours of life left. He touched his beloved's shoulder and says: 'Please? Just one more time before I die.' She agreed, then afterwards she rolled over and fell asleep. All Mick could hear is the clock ticking in his head, and he tossed and turned until he was down to only four more hours. He tapped his wife on the shoulder to wake her up. Babe, I only have four hours left! Could we...? His wife sat up bolt upright, turned on him and said," Elliott stopped, looked around the table, confirming that he had everyone's attention. "For fecks sake Mick, I have to get up in the morning, you don't!!"

Pete scratched his forehead and pronounced his verdict "Awful!"

Buster shook his head.

Frank took a long drag, coughed and agreed "Fucking awful."

Grant awoke from a suitably sordid dream; the usual storyline, involving him living alone and suddenly being attractive to women. But he remained besotted and faithful to the new woman in his life; a cabin attendant, amazingly, on the Heathrow to Teesside[46] shuttle, who was unable to control herself whenever they met (which was most nights of the week). Could he survive the nightly multi-bonking sessions? What a way to go. If only he could start his life again.

"Do you want another one?" asked Elllott.

"A beer yes, a joke no," replied Frank.

"Spoilsport."

Frank flicked cigarette ash into the tray and smiled at Elliott, "If you say so."

"Oh yes, indeedee, you are one serious spoilsport, but I'll forgive you. So, there's this green monkey, a yellow parrot and two spotted goldfish."

"Oh give it a break," pleaded Pete.

Elliott giggled, "Anyway, the parrot says."

Frank rose "Enough!"

He stretched and looked around, wondering what his fellow travellers did for a living. It was the over-weight Americans in badly fitting jeans, but with phenomenal laptops who always gave the greatest challenge. The loud-mouth Yank lawyers always pissed him off; mind, so did British lawyers. He couldn't stand the guys who felt the need to shout at colleagues, thousands of miles (and

---

[46] Or Durham Tees Valley as it is supposed to be called. A name which Grant had immediately dismissed and had henceforth decided to live in the past: as was his wont on many things.

many hours) away, by phone. They always seemed to talk such self important crap, or trivia, and always felt the need to repeat themselves. Shit. Then there were the young looking cyber merchants – complete geeks who had invented or developed something. But worse were the brainless pretty boys and girls with rich parents. He could feel that he had drunk enough; for the moment.

Time for a quick toodle round the duty free shops then another drinkie or two and then, if he had got his consumption correct, several hours of uninterrupted sleep before a delicious breakfast at 30,000 feet over Georgia or some other Central European statelet.

Fourteen

The second Friday in December was always a popular night with the locals. The festive celebrations were beginning to impact on those still in active employment (long lunches, Christmas drinks receptions and, for the more organised, shopping) but The Urra was not yet too busy; as Grant would say 'filled with part-time and learner drinkers, getting in the way of the purists such as ourselves'. As Biggles had recently observed, 'Grant is having increasing problems with his fellow human beings'. The weather was cold, wet and generally horrid; making the fire and barmaids inside The Urra all the more welcoming.

Frank, Bill, Elliott and Biggles were deep in conversation, the subject matter being as loose and varied as usual. Ben sat staring at his drink, willing someone to finish theirs and thereby generate a round-buying situation. Neil was sitting closest to the fireplace, stroking his pint glass whilst staring into the middle distance, his mind clearly elsewhere.

Pete was reading the local evening paper, more out of an attempt to avoid boredom than any interest in the written matter.

"Yes, here's Fat Bastard," announced Pete, as a somewhat dishevelled Grant wandered into the back of the bar.

"Sod off," was the limited response as Grant turned to the bar, "Evening mine host, same as usual for the rabble please...and I'll have a pint of the Otway."

"Otway's off."

"Your beers usually are!"

"Thanks Grant but that is not what I meant and you know it."

"Sorry, a cheap shot, I'll have a pint of the Santa please."

Grant looked over to the table where his drinking companions had congregated; it was good to feel a part of something. My, he was a sad bastard wasn't he? He sighed.

"All right Grant?" enquired Alf, more in the style of an automaton than a genuinely interested landlord.

"No problem," replied Grant before resting his head in his hands and staring at the beer being poured into seven pint glasses…at least Alf had not picked up a half pint glass, so something was going alright, thought Grant.

"Where've you been today then?" enquired Pete as Grant sat next to him.

"Started the day in Penrith, then went to Tyneside, then Wearside," replied Grant, more quietly than usual.

"They're not proper places," interjected Elliott, giving all the impression that he was about to "go off on one".

"Not only have you got to have a history, but you have to have something named after you to be a proper place…the bloody officials can't just go round thinking up new names for places and be allowed to get away with it…no sireee."

"Sorry," interrupted Bill, "you've lost me."

"Well," Elliott took a large gulp before continuing, "you have Red Leicester, Scotch Eggs, Welsh Rarebit, Cornish Pasties."

Pete joined in, "Cheddar Cheese."

"Danish Bacon?" asked Frank, attempting to join in, but not really sure what was going on.

"Tadge dubious that one," suggested Elliott before continuing. "Yorkshire Puddings, Kendal Mint Cake, Whitby Cod…you get my point?"

"No," replied Bill; Grant shook his head

Elliott spread his arms out, as in victory, "Well, you don't get Tyneside Tiramisu do you?"

"What's that?" enquired Ben.

"Something shitty you get in pretentious restaurants," replied Pete.

"Or Cleveland Cheesecakes, eh!" exclaimed Elliott.

"Cleveland clap," offered Grant.

"I quite like cheesecake," offered Ben as he stood up to go to the bar.

"But not clap?" asked Grant.

"The point is... these newly named places can't be taken seriously," concluded Elliott, before he drained his pint.

"Teesside tapeworm."

Grant was ignored.

"So a place has to be famous for something...or have something named after it for it to be a proper town?" enquired Bill.

"Yes indeed-ee," agreed Elliott.

As he rose to buy the next round, shaking his head in dramatic disbelief, Bill attempted to conclude the discussion, "Fascinating, the things you learn."

"Like the Hartlepool Monkey then?" proposed Ben, returning with his half of Worthy.

Rather than simply ignore Ben, as everyone else was inclined to do, Grant challenged him, "Do you mean that the Monkey was named after Hartlepool...or was Hartlepool named after the monkey?"

Not realising that Grant was being awkward, and as everyone else cringed inwardly, Ben started to recount the tale of Hartlepool and the monkey, "No, the idiots of Hartlepool caught a monkey and thought it was a French spy, so the daft buggers hung it."

"You're being unfair Ben," interrupted Grant, somewhat harshly.

Grant usually let Ben's ramblings pass him by but this evening he seemed to be spoiling for something and, without any indication of humour, he continued, "You need to get your facts straight...it was the Napoleonic era...O Level French wasn't on the National

Curriculum, Attenborough wasn't all over the TV screens with pictures of animals screwing each other in exotic locations…so how did they know what it was?…eh?…and they'd been told to watch out for spies…a ship was wrecked off the coast and the only survivor was dressed up like a sailor, walked on two legs and went 'Ooo Ooo Ooooo'…PG Tips weren't around then you know…and sentence was passed by some Lord or Bishop from Durham…so you leave Hartlepool alone…and, if it had caught on, and hanging Froggies had been encouraged, the twentieth century would have been more peaceful, we would be more comfortable about the Euro… and Arsenal would still be boring."

"But how did they know it was French," blustered Ben, somewhat unwisely.

"Bloody hell," seethed Grant, "What do you want…it was ugly…it was hairy…it smelt." Grant paused, wondering whether he could draw a comparison between the monkey and Ben and, mercifully, thought better of it. "It was loud in an indecipherable way, and it wasn't welcome…of course it was fucking French!"

Ben laughed nervously; he was far more comfortable being ignored.

Sensing an atmosphere, and the need to lighten it, Elliott asked if anyone had seen Buster recently, inviting a variety of comments along the lines of 'he can't be working', 'he did two days in August' and 'maybe Mrs B has grounded him at last'.

"So did you have a good day?" Pete asked Grant.

Grant's day had been pretty good; he had enjoyed the work, felt he had delivered quality advice and had been looking forward to a weekend with his family; until she had called him on his way home.

"Is that you Grant?"

"If it isn't I've nicked your husband's car."

144

"Ha Ha, look can you do some shopping on the way home? Only I've just arranged to go over to Knock for part of the holiday and so I need some more presents, I have a list here."

"So when are we flying over?"

"You're not, you're too busy and someone needs to look after the animals."

"It would have been nice to…"

"No, you don't need to bother yourself."

"It would be no bother, I'm sure that I'd enjoy it and the break would do me good."

"Perhaps, anyway, I need you get this shopping as I couldn't do any today, what with having to go to the gym and then Susan called round."

"Couldn't we do it together tomorrow?"

"Look, I'm in a rush. I'm going out with Susan tonight. Have you got a pen so I can give you the details?"

"I'm doing seventy in the outside lane of the A19."

"Aren't there any lay-bys?"

"I hate Christmas," started Grant, "Pubs full of learner drinkers, grannies and brats."

"Full of the festive spirit, then?" enquired Biggles.

Elliott interrupted before Grant could reply, "I'm with Grantee-Pops, do you know that the name Santa Claus comes from the Dutch word Sinterklaas?"

No one replied.

"And Sinterklass was, as we all know, a fourth century Turkish holy man."

The silence continued.

"So put that in your pipe and smoke it when you next wear a stupid flashing hat in the name of Santafuckingclaus!"

"Too right," agreed Grant, "and wasn't St Nicholas the patron saint of prostitutes?"

Bill waved his hands in the air, "Now come on Grant, there's no need for that."

Elliott leant forwards, quickly and aggressively, pointing his right index finger at Bill, "But he's right, Grantee-Pops is right, Santa is nothing more than a pagan lush who, when he's not getting his arse stuck down chimneys, is a red-coated pimp!"

"Oh my," was Bill's limited, but well-advised reply.

Fifteen

Christmas Eve in The Urra, as in the vast majority of other public houses in the land, was a lively occasion, filled with exaggerated laughter, the sounds of loosened jaws and the noise of well-meant bullshit. And wives. And the presence of wives brought with it a myriad of different behaviours – from the cringe worthy flirting to an almost child-like shyness. Grant in particular always seemed uncomfortable in the presence of women; almost to the point of rudeness; Buster was the opposite; he clearly loved the company of women and would flirt uncontrollably and embarrassingly. Like everything else, nothing seemed to affect Elliott.

Pete was talking to Elliott's wife, Tina. "Yes, I have a very musical background, I was born in a flat and, being in Gateshead you had to be sharp…"

Pete was interrupted by the arrival of Elliott with a tray of pint glasses and a bottle of the house white; seizing her opportunity to escape, Tina quickly turned to speak to Frank's wife, Carole.

Christmas Eve, like New Year's Eve, Good Friday, May Day and any other public holiday or celebration was an opportunity for Elliott to 'misbehave'[47] on a grand scale.

"You know," whispered Elliott, leaning unnecessarily close to Neil's wife's chest, "I was made an orphan at the age of eight."

"Oh no," muttered Neil.

"And tell me this," Elliott paused for effect, "what's an eight year old want with a fucking orphan!"

---

[47] As in, repeat stupid jokes, drink too much and upset at least two wives (excluding his own).

Helen looked shocked and looked around for some form of escape; Neil failed her, as expected, and would surely 'pay' for it later. Elliott laughed…loudly. Helen visibly cringed.

"See Ken Dodd[48] died yesterday," announced Frank.

"Did he?" asked Helen, in the vain hope that this was the start of an exit route from the unwelcome attentions of Elliott, and the associated aroma of several hours of entertainment in The Urra.

"No…Doddy," exploded Elliott, who was joined by Frank in a sudden outbreak of exaggerated laughter. Helen smiled. She hadn't heard that Ken Dodd had died and was at a loss to see what was funny.

Grant was sitting in his car. He had been the last to leave the office; he couldn't risk joining his staff for a few drinks, given that he had to drive home. He hated leaving on Christmas Eve; as leaving meant the start of a few days of festive purgatory. Mind, that would be short-lived, given that his family were going away on Boxing Day.

He couldn't go to The Urra; he wasn't in the mood and he always felt out of place, being a sad lonely bastard when everyone's wives were present. He wanted to go home and 'be Christmassy' with his kids; but her friend would still be there and he would be even less welcome than every other night.

He was parked in a lay-by on the hill above Watson Humphrey. It was a clear night and he could see the lights of the urban area stretching away to the north. The yellow lights and red glow of the industrial areas and the masses of white lights

---

[48] Ken Dodd started his career as a ventriloquist but his success came through his exaggerated on-stage persona – the manic hair, protruding teeth, tickling stick and ridiculous vocabulary…..ooh tattifilarious missus – a successful stage and television career, together with a number of nauseating ballads was topped with a court appearance in the 1980s on a tax dodging case – a subject close to Grant's heart – "proof that jury trials are fundamentally flawed," would be his final comment on the subject. Dodd was found innocent. Grant also worried about jury trials as the juries were comprised of individuals who had been unable to avoid jury duty.

comprising the many housing estates; there was a low cloud over to the east and this was coloured by a dull reflection of the lights below and occasionally flickered red as operations continued in the steelworks and chemical plants.

His chest felt tight and his brain felt numbed. He had promised himself last year (and on numerous other melancholy and alcohol fuelled occasions) that he would get himself out of this "rut"; another year of mental anguish, zero affection and working frustrations had passed and he had achieved nine tenths of bugger all.

The car was like a warm, safe cocoon. He manipulated his seat towards the horizontal and moved it backwards; he lay back, stretching himself out, and closed his eyes. He could just drive straight off the edge. No. He couldn't leave the children; and certainly not at Christmas. And it might hurt. And he was a yellow-backed weakling who didn't have the courage to top himself. And, it would be too much like a favour for his dearly beloved.

He folded his arms across his chest with a sigh.

How many other people, out there in the land of lights, were hurting like him?

Had been so fundamentally messed around, but could not move on?

Because of continuing love.

Or fear.

Or were having sex?

Right now.

Or were dying?

Or were watching a loved one pass away, in horrific pain?

Fuck. Give yourself a good talking to Fatboy. He adjusted his seat, switched on the interior lights and looked in the mirror. You ugly bastard. Let's roll.

"Anyone seen Fat Bastard?" enquired Pete.

149

"No chance of him making an appearance tonight," replied Frank, "he hates nights like tonight for some reason."

"Name something he doesn't dislike," suggested Bill. All nodded in silence.

"You know," started Elliott, "that I read somewhere that the name Grant means 'horny, but so sweet you can talk to him about anything' which is, of course a load of absolute codswallop, whatever that is."

Buster grinned; he stared at Neil's wife; unnecessary and futile thoughts passing through his mind.

"And this effing survey had the temerity to conclude that the name Elliott, a fine name don't you agree? Yes, Elliott means 'full of himself', which is clearly crap."

"And the source of this unusual set of definitions?" enquired Bill.

Neil folded his arms, "Not the normal Nordic or Viking type of meanings are they?"

"Fuck, he's awake!"

"Thanks for noticing Elliott," replied Neil.

"And Neil means 'likes men but is in denial', isn't that right Helen?"

Helen replied, tight-lipped, "Sorry, wasn't listening."

"No problem darling, what I said was that Neil likes men and is in denial."

Tina came to Helen's rescue, "Elliott sweetheart, are you wanting to play this Christmas?"

Elliott understood the implied threat, "Righto, my round I believe."

Elliott stood up.

Tina shook her head, "Once upon time he was a great lover, but he's never managed it since his mind was stolen by aliens."

Pete guffawed.

Frank looked shocked.

Bill broke the temporary silence, "You poor child Tina, how you must struggle with the pressure of trying to keep him in touch with reality."

"I heard that you old bastard."

Tina shook her head at Bill before looking up at Elliott, "Be a good boy now, go get the drinks."

Tina turned to Carole and quietly asked, "So, what's going on in the Bannister household?"

Carole leant towards Tina, "I've heard she's traded him for another model but he hasn't worked it out."

"That's what I had heard."

"Shame really, he used to be a really nice bloke, you know, safe and reliable, probably pretty average at everything but bad at nothing, and I think she has made him slightly mad," Carole took a sip of her wine, "And Frank thinks the world of him, you know he helped us save a fortune in tax and sorted out the sale of our business, and he's never asked for anything or talked about it."

"Elliott really misses him now that he's rarely in here and never manages time for a round of golf."

"Frank has reckoned that he's not been well for some time."

"What did you say?" interrupted Frank.

"Nothing darling."

Frank decided not to pursue the matter, "So, how's Tina?"

"Magic thanks."

Grant sat in his study. Still wearing his 'work' clothes, although his waistcoat was unbuttoned and his jacket lay, crumpled, on the sofa bed in the corner. His bright yellow tie still tight around his neck.

How often had he slept on the sofa bed? Many times before they had separate rooms. Many times when work or alcohol fatigue had made it too much of an effort to go to 'proper' bed.

The girls were 'out'.

His wife and her 'friend' were in the lounge; laughing; loudly. He thought it was Samantha but he didn't recognise the car on the drive – in his place – and the laughing wasn't familiar.

He loaded London Calling[49], his favourite album by The Clash, into his CD player and poured himself a glass of Medoc.

He briefly considered a supper of crisps but opted against solids.

He toasted himself, "Happy Christmas Fat Boy!"

He pushed his shoes off and leant back into his leather chair; the first mouthful, as is often the case with cheap reds, tasted foul. "Fuck."

What was he going to do over the festive period?

No work? He knew he would. It was an escape.

Fresh air, exercise, walks in the hills? He'd made similar plans previously and had never taken advantage of the neighbouring countryside. He knew that he would regret this appalling lack of effort in the years to come.

Spend time with his wife and kids? Yeah, good idea.

Catch up with old friends?

Do some reading?

Listen to music?

Do some jobs around the house?

Go watch some football and rugby?

He had the opportunity; the time was his. He sighed; he knew he would waste it.

Shit, he felt lonely.

And sorry for himself.

Sad bastard; there were times when he didn't really like himself. He took a large swig and winced.

"Fuck."

---

[49] The seminal 1979 album, released by Columbia.

Sixteen

The night before New Year's Eve and The Urra is full of locals, but with fewer visitors than would be expected; possibly due to the high winds and squally showers, but more probably as a result of people recovering from Christmas and preparing for the rigours of New Year.

Elliott was talking to Alf, while Alf watched one of his staff pour the beers for Elliott, Buster, Bill, Frank, Neil and Pete.

"Have you seen Grant this week?"

"Aye, he was in earlier on…came in about five thirty, sat at the end of the bar, read the paper and must've drunk four or five pints in the hour or so he was in here," Alf helped lift a few pints onto the bar before continuing, "Seemed a bit down, didn't want to talk really, just stared at the paper and drank without it touching the sides."

Elliott returned to the 'Regulars' table, his timing perfect as Ben walked through the back door as he sat down.

"Have you heard about the two nuns being attacked in Stockton?" asked Pete.

A concerned-looking Buster immediately replied, "No, what happened?"

The bait having been taken, Pete continued, "Seems they were walking down a dark alley near the High Street when they were jumped on by two rapists…one nun looks heavenwards and shouts 'forgive him Father for he knows not what he is doing' and the other nun then shouts 'Oh but this one does'." Pete grinned widely at Buster as the others simply groaned and Buster shook his head in horror and disgust.

"Was that in the paper?" enquired Ben as he gingerly edged himself onto the bench behind the table.

"Was Santa good to you?" asked Frank, to no one in particular, fishing for an opportunity to tell everyone about his expensive new driving iron and tailor-made putter. Realising this, Bill tried to redirect the conversation away from anything to do with golf or Christmas. "Did anyone see '*The Great Escape*' the other day?"

"One of the highlights of the Christmas season," noted Frank, "that and *True Grit*."

"Strange how Christmas is always marked by war films and westerns…people getting shot…in fact the first twenty minutes of *Saving Private Ryan* could be used to replace the Queen's speech," suggested Elliott.

"Sick twat," was all Frank could manage in response.

"It's *633 Squadron* for me," confided Neil.

Pete joined in, "*The Dambusters* more like…what was the dog called…him that led it, what was his name…in his early twenties he was…and my twenty year old bairns won't leave home…it's not on."

"Oh cheer up you old git," was the considered view of the previously silent Buster, "Can you imagine if our very own Squadron Leader had been involved? The Germans would be flying out of Heathrow today."

Elliott, "Where is young Biggles…anyone seen him?"

Neil, "I saw him at the driving range this morning."

Elliott, "Were you playing?"

Neil, "No, I was taking Helen down for her lesson."

Buster, "She can drive can't she?"

Neil, "No, the lesson was to help with her driver."

Buster, "No no no, I meant she can drive a car."

Neil, "Of course she can!"

Frank, "Is *633 Squadron* the one with the Mosquitos?"

Pete, "Yeah…made from plywood you know."

Elliott, "*The Longest Day*…with John Wayne."

Buster, "Is that the one where he is the centurion… 'He really is the son of God'."

Elliott, "No that was about D-Day."

Buster, "No, it was about the crucifixion."

Elliott, "No, *The Longest Day* was about D-Day!"

Ben, chuckling, "Does anyone care?"

Frank, "So is Biggles coming in tonight?"

Neil, "I didn't ask him."

Pete, "Well, you were concentrating on driving Helen weren't you?"

Bill, "I love the Steve McQueen character."

Ben, "Was he in the D-Day movie then?.

Bill, "No, *The Great Escape*."

Neil, "What do you mean?"

Pete, "Hiltz!"

Neil, "Pardon."

Pete, "That was his name…Steve McQueen in *The Great Escape*."

Frank, "No, it was Shultz."

Elliott, "Wasn't that a dog."

Pete, "Nuts."

Elliott, "Very good."

Frank, "And the big question is what was his first name?"

Pete, "It was Charlie…Charlie Brown."

Frank, "No, in the movie."

Bill, "Rooster Cogburn?"

Elliott, "No, not John Wayne…Steve McQueen!"

Ben, to everyone's astonishment, "It was Virgil…and the name was used only once in the film."

A brief but deafening silence was only broken when Bill rose, "My round, the usual for everyone? A half is it Ben?"

Ben, "Well, it being Christmas and all that, I'll have a pint of Worthy thanks."

Bill wandered over to the bar and the table then became divided between two conversations: Neil, Frank and Pete discussing the festive footballing fare; and Buster and Elliott arguing over which John Wayne film was best.

By the time Bill returned Elliott was lecturing Buster on the relative merits of *The Sands of Iwo Jima* and *The Alamo*, and Neil was totally confused as Frank and Pete debated which corporate entertaining facilities were the best.

Bill distributed the beers and returned to sit next to Ben; he pondered the risks of catching fleas or worse as, despite this being the festive season, Ben had clearly not been given any new...or clean...clothes.

"*Stagecoach!*" shouted Buster.

"Not one of his better ones...thanks for the beer Bill," responded Elliott.

"*Fort Apache,*" continued Buster in a vain attempt to recover some form of control or dignity.

"*The Quiet Man*...now that is a classic," volunteered Bill.

"Oh yes indeed-ee, a late run on the standside and we may have a winner."

"I love the fights in the pub and Maureen O'Hara is excellent," continued Bill, clearly warming to his subject, "of course it's all a bit twee, the rural idyll and all that .....but top notch entertainment."

"Do you ever go home and tell your family about the conversations we have?" asked Neil.

"They think I'm at work," joked Elliott.

"They're just happy that I'm out," commented Frank.

"It's nothing to do with Mrs B...and she wouldn't understand anyway," concluded Buster.

Neil persevered, "Come on now chaps...this is all bollocks isn't it?"

Adopting a stance somewhere between seriousness and upset Elliott retorted, "I'll have you know that no John Wayne film was bollocks."

"Lighten up," suggested Frank, "Here comes Mandy."

Biggles sauntered in, "Bit bloody cold out there."

"The Riverside, St James's or The Stadium of Light?" asked Pete.

"*The Quiet Man* or *McQ*"?" asked Elliott.

"Cheating," suggested Buster.

"Been here long," replied Biggles; a statement not a question.

Frank, "It's got to be St James's."

Biggles grinned broadly, "*The Stadium of Light* and *The Alamo*."

Buster, "Rubbish, complete nonsense…no, totally unacceptable."

Elliott, "Total tosh."

Pete, "You cannot be serious!"

Frank, "I'll have a pint of the most expensive guest ale."

Elliott, "Me too."

Grant was at home, sitting in their lounge, the only light being from the flickering TV screen; he had no idea what was on, his mind jumping about, trying to stay calm, to stop himself from sobbing out loud. He could hear his children laughing in the room next door, and the occasional instruction from his wife…how her voice now grated, a sound that he had once longed to hear. She had been awkward all day, ignoring him and belittling him. She had barely been polite to him when he had collected them from the airport.

Have you had a good time?
How's Seamus?
Good flight?
I missed you.

157

What did you do?
I expect that all the kids are growing up fast.
What was the weather like?
It's been pretty miserable here.
Did you get anything to eat on the flight?
I've got a brunch ready for you at home.
Susan called several times. Was she checking up on me?

Barely a grunt in reply. He had given up after a while and the journey had been concluded in a cold silence.

What had he done to deserve this? Christmas at home…home alone…his stomach ached with the pain of it all…and he was fighting the urge to find a bottle…red wine, anything…to help ease the pain…and to help him sleep. Why did she hate him…when did it all go wrong…why couldn't he accept that there was no way back? His head was spinning with the agony of it all…and the questions, the many questions, why, why, why?

She had started on him in the morning; not long after they had arrived home, explaining that he wasn't as good at DIY as her friend Donna's husband; he had no argument, she was right.

Then she moved onto more material matters: he wasn't as successful as her school friend Graham; they weren't as affluent as they should be, unlike so many of her friends. For all of his hours at work, he still didn't seem to earn enough.

Next were personal issues: he wasn't as sophisticated as Jennifer's Robert; Scott was much funnier; her ex, Josh, was so much better looking. "And look at you," she had screamed, before starting a monologue on his hair loss, expanding waist, lack of style and complete lack of sensitivity.

They had all gone out for the afternoon; the girls with friends. Her? He had no idea. He had read the newspapers, he had ironed some shirts, he had considered tidying the garage, he had walked the boys (twice), and had successfully avoided the pub until late afternoon.

She had eaten out so wanted no evening meal; she had made the girls some pasta. He had been ignored. Well, no change there then.

He found himself humming the tune of 'Just A Shadow'[50]

It's just a shadow of the man you should be
Like a garden in the forest that the world will never see
You have no thought of answers only questions to be filled
And it feels like hell

And it feels like hell alright! He sensed his anger was rising and knew that he needed to avoid any form of conflict, for she would surely win. Whatever 'win' meant.

A time for some serious resolutions.

He grinned. Yeah, just like last year.

---

[50] "Just A Shadow" a thoroughly haunting track by Big Country, found on the "Steeltown", "Through A Big Country", "Without the Aid of a Safety Net" and various compilation albums.

Seventeen

The first Wednesday in January was a cold and unwelcoming evening. The north-easterly wind had caused some drifting after the early afternoon falls of snow and the temperature was now dropping rapidly.

"Enough to freeze your nuts off," commented Frank, slapping his hands together for warmth. Or was it for effect?

"If you had any," replied Elliott.

Frank looked at Elliott. Elliott looked back. They both knew that both comments had been facile and worthy of no further comment.

Frank looked at the half empty glasses in front of Pete, Elliott and Bill, "Guess it's my shout then."

"Seems like a good idea to me," agreed Pete.

"Yes," mumbled a clearly tired Bill, "but just a wee Grouse for me."

"I'll have his pint then," proposed Elliott.

As Frank moved away towards the bar Pete turned to Elliott, "Seen the Fat Bastard recently?"

"Not for some time," was the succinct response; unusually for Elliott, there was no sign of irony, insult or intrigue.

"He staggered past my place yesterday morning…'bout six thirty…looked for all the world like he was jogging…well, trying to…wearing a rugby shirt which may have fitted him twenty years ago," Bill finished and all were silent until Pete, attempting to hold back a guffaw, and failing, broke the spell, "Daft bastard will kill himself."

"It's the kids and sheep I fear for," commented a serious looking Elliott, "he'll frighten them something rotten."

"Is his wife having an affair or something?" asked Bill, to the surprise of all those present. Given the silence he continued, "Well, there's always a blue mini there during the day, you never see her with Grant, and well, I just thought, perhaps, well, you know."

"The blue car belongs to one of her friends…bonny woman, great chest," replied Pete.

"I know the one," agreed Elliott, "Don't think Grant likes her too much, she's always there, makes him feel unwelcome in his own home, once told me that she was very shaggable, until she opened her mouth, and that she has very hairy arms."

Grant was sitting in one of the plethora of business class lounges at Heathrow; his flight was late – nothing unusual there – so he wouldn't get back to The Urra before everyone had gone home – frustrating. Free drink but he had his car at the airport. Well, he could have one gin and tonic; couldn't he, and then one on the aircraft to accompany the plastic mini-meal.

He sat on one of the sofas, placing his briefcase next to him – the 'don't sit there' approach to his fellow passengers – and looked around. The lounge was full of the usual 'sorts' and his gaze eventually focussed on the long, lycra covered legs of a blonde woman who was making herself a Bloody Mary. Vodka – quite a lot of it. Tomato juice. Worcester sauce. Salt. Very tasty. High heels. Pencil skirt and cropped jacket, the colour of dried blood. A very feminine woman, aware of her sexuality and not afraid to enjoy herself. He shook his head. Why wouldn't his wife ever try to…what was the point in even thinking about it? He stood up, well just one more gin and tonic…a small one.

The blonde moved away from the bar as he approached. He now saw her face; older than he expected from the rear view; tired, but still attractive. Confident? Competant? Why hadn't he ever? Just thinking about his sex life annoyed him, made him feel 'robbed', got him angry…

He sat down and tried to concentrate on the evening newspaper. All the usual stories.

Misbehaving officials; misbehaving celebrities and, on page twenty something, bottom right, seven hundred killed in another third world disaster. Grant closed the newspaper in an anguished flourish and returned to people watching.

The blonde in the red outfit was touching up her lipstick – class, pure class. She oozed sex, or at least in Grant's frustrated and sad little mind she did.

He scanned the room. Every other person, or so it seemed, was shouting into a mobile phone; jeez, what did they do before the bloody things existed. Why did they all look so self important? He reckoned he could spot those on expenses; those working in the public sector were always the easiest to spot – flying business class, reading a red top and always talking in the 'he said, so I said' style.

Was he a snob? He had no grounds to be. But he did sometimes wonder. Was he, fundamentally, at the end of the day, simply barking mad? Or was he, as his beloved family kept reminding him, an immature, self-centred, inconsiderate, patronising bastard? And then you always got the young media or IT types, scruffy, ignorant bastards, ignoring any signs about the use of mobile phones, kicking off their shoes at the first opportunity; he stopped himself as he caught sight of an earnest looking gentleman, tweed suit, highly polished brogues…a City something Grant decided…perfectly manicured hand holding a top of the range mobile phone…one which could track intercontinental ballistic missiles, plot your movements through the known solar system…but could never get a signal in rural Yorkshire…
"Hi Darling…yes…yes…no…no…sounds yummy,"

Wearing a well-worn, but perfectly tailored mackintosh, he was pacing around a tatty but expensive looking suit carrier and matching document case.

"One must grill it, briefly, to get the bread crusty, but make sure you don't make the pudding itself get dry,"

Bet he hasn't had to work hard. Shit, that's not fair. Grant worried himself at times.

"Well tell Tarquin to behave for mummykins,"

Sitting near the pacing City something was a well-fed, pompous looking type – well, he looked pompous to Grant's tired and increasingly cynical eyes – a thick personal organiser lay on the table next to his drink – a coke, probably of the low calorie variety decided Grant, who was approaching the end of his second large gin and tonic. For a moment he felt guilty at listening in to their private conversations; no, it was their fault for being so loud.

"Hi, Bill Monk speaking,"

Which conversation did he focus on? The big bloke in the woolly jumper and slacks, or the City boy?

"We can attend to that when we go down to the country this weekend,"

He finished off his drink, taking the remaining ice cube into his mouth. Mobile phones were the fog light of the business class lounge. Good line that, must remember it.

"Yes, Scott gave me your number and suggested that you may have a position for me,"

"I'll ring ahead and ask Dorothy to make sure that she has a spare,"

"Just finished a consultancy off and am looking to spread my wings,"

"It's so damn inconsiderate,"

"You can't beat my experience,"

"No, I told Toby to watch her,"

"But after that I was pretty successful at Arlington Meats,"

"Oh Clemmy give him a chance,"

Grant could feel his stomach tightening, *"Haven't touched a drop in months,"*

Well, Bill Monk seemed like a decent fellow decided Grant, but Mr Clemmy was clearly a plank. Jeez, what right had he to judge people? He gave his head a rhetorical shake and proceeded to get another drink.

There will be a further delay to flight MM340, we apologise for any…

Shit shit shit. Grant decided to absorb the alcohol by now consuming as many ginger stem biscuits as the airline could afford.

"Father will be driving down next Tuesday, once he has dealt with some dispute at the Manchester factory, terrible place,"

Grant looked around for another sight of the blonde. He really had a thing for classy women; women who dress as women; power dressers or hostesses. He fell in love…or was it lust…every time he flew. They all had lovely hair, long shiny legs, glistening eyes…he took a long pull from his drink. His fantasies… and that was all they were likely to be…such was the nothingness of his sex life…and his past…always seemed to start with a tight skirt, with a tasteful split, just exposing the stocking top and giving an occasional flash of slightly tanned skin. She was always superior, verging on dominant and he was nothing but her simple play thing. She let him touch, when and where she wanted. She made him kiss and lick to fulfil her needs first. She was always in control and…

"Flight MM870 to Edinburgh is now about to board through gate 8b, would all passengers with young children or requiring assistance please come forward now,"

"Ask him for a brace whenever he can,"

"And I said to her," a young, plumpish female of the travelling student variety sat down next to Grant...no particularly attractive features, thought Grant, and an intolerable personality, **"it is your problem, I spoke to Justin, what a tosser, and told him too, so there you have it."**

Loud, self-focussed and scruffy – in a well-shod way – decided Grant. But why did she have to invade his sad little world? He coughed, hoping that she would, at least, quieten down.

"No."

Grant sighed.

"No."

What large flabby breasts she had.

"Yes, late."

Grant grimaced. She would be on his flight and, yes, of course, she would sit next to him and regale him with tales of her gap year, paid for by Daddy, helping the wide mouthed toad of lower jungle land.

"No."

And they were so big. Both of them. He couldn't help but stare. She was wearing an ample sized cotton shirt with a flowery sort of pattern; which did nothing to hide the shape of her expansive chest and the item holding them in place; which, from where he was sitting, looked like it was made of industrial quality steelwork with anti-gravity special effects. A feat of engineering.

"No."

That must be why she's so loud. He'd always been a bottom man; well, that's how he would have described himself. Never been a fan of big chests. And when they sag!

"And he was less than a man, if you know what I mean."

Grant blushed internally. He knew exactly what she meant. Had that been his problem? He'd always been conscious that 'his' wasn't as big as others', but, but……memories of his days playing rugby flooded into his now alcohol relaxed brain; trying to hide 'it', being shy in the showers and plunge pools, always aware of it. And then there was that bloody girl in the first year at Uni…cow…why did she have to tell everyone about his little boy! Effing bitch.

`"Didn't know what to do, did he! Two`
`grunts and a squirt."`

He remembered, but didn't want to…

There will be a further delay to flight MM340, this has been caused by a lightning strike to the inbound aircraft, we apologise for any…

"I CAN ALWAYS CHOP 30% OFF A COST BASE, ALWAYS, THAT'S WHAT IT'S ALL ABOUT." A pinstriped unshaven twenty-something swept by, the latest micro sized phone appearing from his right ear…why did these people never feel uncomfortable, walking around talking loudly into nothing? Was jealousy his problem? Grant wasn't sure, but he was intelligent enough to appreciate that some of these people must be OK! It wasn't really a case that he was the only normal, well-balanced individual in the room.

"I always delivered for Arlingtons, you could say I brought home the bacon, oh yes."

But he didn't have a stupid ring tone, he didn't need a licence and a wide load sign to transport his computer bag through crowded areas…and what about those nerds with massive rucksacks, oblivious to the need for a wide turning circle and the dangers of such items in confined spaces. Bet they're talking to answerphones or imaginary friends.

"I CAN ALWAYS TELL THE GOOD GUYS FROM THE BAD GUYS IN SECONDS – I'M A PEOPLE PERSON, ONE OF MY MAJOR SKILLS IS PEOPLE MANAGEMENT, HAVE I NOT TOLD YOU ABOUT, HOLD ON, BATTERY IS GOING, I'LL CALL YOU IN TEN."

"Poor boy wanted to please me so much."

"Yar, it is just so grim but one must go there occasionally...one can't leave it all to father you know."

"IS ANYONE SITTING THERE?"

"So I said, what do you call it when you're damned if you do and you're damned if you don't, eh?"

"He'll just talk dirty."

"Aye, marriage I said, marriage."

"IS ANYONE SITTING THERE?"

"So are you going to collect me from the airport?"

"Hello Tiger, its Daddy."

"Why not?"

"We simply need to repackage the proposition and ask all parties to return to the table."

"Oh sod."

Grant felt like screaming. Were all of these conversations necessary? Were these just bored people, boring others? Including him! He grinned. What about the damage they might be doing to their brains. Like microwaved chicken. Brain ding! He shifted in his chair and let his eyes wander...was it time to play spot the celebrity look-a-like? Or spot the biggest, firmest titties? Or the widest arse? Or should he get another drink?

"Oh sod."

He gazed at her ample chest. Bet they've never been nuzzled or bitten. He pulled himself up, adjusted his belt and sagging trousers and walked, purposefully, towards the bar.

"IS ANYONE SITTING THERE?"

Grant looked back, suddenly aware that someone was talking to him. It was red suit. He met her eyes and immediately looked down. His tongue filled his mouth and his jaw refused to work. She was drop dead gorgeous. He shook his head and retreated to the comfort zone of the bar. Fuck fuckety fuck fuck.

Ben wandered in through The Urra's front door and bought himself a pint before joining the now quiet table.

Elliott grunted a form of acknowledgement.

"Bit bloody sharp that wind," was Ben's offering before silence returned.

Neil then positively breezed in, "Evening chaps, whose round is it?"

"Yours," was the collective response of Elliott, Frank and Bill, causing Neil to spin round on his heels and skip towards the bar and the sullen looking Alf.

"What's he so happy about," was Ben's limited contribution.

"He's just been shagged by sixteen beautiful women," replied Elliott.

"Really?"

Elliott nodded his head.

"Really?" repeated Ben.

Eighteen

The third Wednesday in January and the snow was several inches deep. Whilst the village was nowhere near cut-off, few townies were venturing out and The Urra was virtually empty – save for the usual congregation at the table by the fireplace.

"So I rang up the town swimming baths. I said 'Is that the local swimming baths?' And the cheeky bugger on the other end replies 'It depends where you're calling from.' Boom Boom." Elliott sat back, looking proud of himself.

Pete shook his head, "Shite!"

Buster agreed, "Terrible!"

Elliott grinned.

Pete stood up, "The only positive thing I can say is that it was better than any of Grant's stories...same again?"

"Where is he?" enquired Neil.

"Gone to a Burns Supper[51] I believe, some corporate entertaining do," replied Pete.

"I've been to a few of them in my time," offered Frank, "Freeze-dried haggis was never one of my favourite dishes...but the booze was usually top class."

"Aye, the noo," Pete could always be relied on for an unnecessary accent and his Highland warrior was one of his favourites. "I love the piping in of the wee haggi mesell."

---

[51] The Burns Supper is an institution of Scottish life, a night to celebrate the life and genius of the national bard, Robert Burns. These nationalistic suppers can be everything from an informal gathering of like-minded friends to a huge, formal dinner full of pomp and circumstance. The question is, of course, how come the English have no equivalent?

Ben took the opportunity, "The Emperor Hadrian was right…but he should have built the wall higher…and who wants to eat a sheep's bladder?"

Elliott placed his glass on the table with an unnecessarily loud thud, "Ben Ben Ben, but that is a myth…a myth started many centuries ago when Haggi numbers were low and the poor made do with the inflated sheep bladder, filled with offal, bread and any other surplus crap…but as they began to breed more freely and hunting was controlled, they became a part of the staple diet of your typical Highland Celt."

"Bollocks," replied Ben.

"No, it's true," replied Elliott, "Haggi are small furry, four legged animals"

"Wee beasties," interrupted Pete.

Elliott continued, "They live off moss and small insects…a varied diet as I'm sure you'll agree…an egg laying animal."

"And related to the Loch Ness monster I bet."

"You're not taking this seriously are you Ben?"

"Cos you're talking bollocks, that's why."

Elliot shook his head, "Oh Ben, how can a man of your age and undoubted experience be so unaware?"

"And I can't stand bagpipes."

"You know that the sound of the bagpipes is supposed to mimic the sound of a male haggis during mating season?"

"Piss off Elliott!"

"Straight up Ben."

Ben pushed the table to make space for his escape, "Tara like well."

No one bothered replying.

Grant was concentrating on the guest list provided with the menu and details of the evening's activities. He had looked at it before. Several times. He wasn't particularly interested in who else was enduring the dinner. Other than any of his clients who were being entertained by rivals. Disloyal bastards.

Focussing on the guest list stopped him, albeit only temporarily, from drinking anymore; he had had enough. He always drank too quickly when he was uncomfortable or bored with those around him; this evening it was a mixture of both.

To his right was a dreadful bore from one of the major clearing banks; clearly successful and pleased with himself, he appeared to delight in telling tales of his conquests with the fairer sex during the early part of his banking career. Grant grinned to himself. It rhymed.

To his left was the treasurer from one of the local hospitals; another accountant with whom he had nothing in common, much older than him in outlook and age. He was, thankfully, deep in conversation with the lawyer to his left; an attractive young woman who was surely wishing that she had been seated next to Grant; Grant grinned to himself again. She may well have a starring role in one of his fantasies later that evening.

Opposite Grant sat one of his rivals; who arranged these seating plans? There was nothing wrong with the bloke; he was a decent sort but not the type of person he wanted to talk to. Grant attended these functions to network with people who could be clients or providers of work; or to drink with friends; not to make small-talk with rivals. Twats.

Do you shoot?

Grant didn't realise that he was being spoken to.

I say, do you shoot?

Grant looked to his right and, not having heard the question, grunted in acknowledgement.

So, where is your gun?

"Sorry."

Your gun, your gun, where is it?

"In my holster?"

The banker laughed *Very good, very good, Grant isn't it?*

Grant nodded. Where do they get these pillocks from?

So, duck or grouse?

"I often find duck to be a tadge greasy."

The banker laughed *Very good, yes, very good.*

Grant took a sip of his wine and looked around, hoping for some form of rescue.

I have long wanted to travel to South America for the hunting, what about yourself?

Grant took a deep breath. "What would you hunt?"

Pete drained his glass, "It is a load of bollocks though…piping it in, reading it poems."

"Is there really a mating season?" asked Neil.

"Aye," replied Elliott, "immediately after the hunting season."

"Well," started Buster, rubbing his hands together, "I expect that Grant is having a thoroughly marvellous time."

"Or thoroughly miserable," offered Pete, who had spent many evenings with Grant at such functions.

"I guess that would be marvellously miserable."

Pete looked at Elliott, "You're a wicked bastard!"

Nineteen

The last Friday in January; an air of general depression.

Post Christmas bankruptcy.

Post New Year Hangovers.

Broken resolutions.

'Not again' depression.

"Anyone seen Grant?" asked Elliott.

The question was answered by silence.

"I miss him…I think," continued Elliott, "Seems like ages since he last entertained us."

"I think that he's been working away again," offered Pete.

"Playing away more like," grunted Ben, making a sound like he had a mouth full of fluids.

He was ignored by all.

Elliott stood to go to the bar, "Procrastination is the thief of time[52]"

"Eh?" was Pete's considered reply.

"Do you ever feel ashamed or concerned about how much money you've wasted on beer?" asked Bill

"Sometimes, sometimes," Pete shook his head and continued, "but then I think about the brewery workers and their families…and I think, shit, if it wasn't for considerate folk such as I, how would those families eat, how would their children go through university and how would they obtain vital medicines? And that's when I know that I should not worry about my wallet or my liver."

"Interesting," was Bill's response.

---

[52] Edward Young 1683-1765, English Poet and Playwright

Pete warmed to his subject, "Yes, as the Fat Bald Bastard would tell you, beer is the greatest invention in the history of the world. Sod the wheel and penicillin. And, of course, Grant was a founder member of the Brewery Workers Benevolent Fund, a very worthy cause indeed."

Bill grinned, "Grant likes the Benjamin Franklin argument that beer is proof that the Lord loves us and wants us to be happy."

"He never said that!" interrupted Bill.

"Who, Franklin or Fat Bastard?" asked a bemused looking Pete.

"Grant," was Ben's full and final response.

Grant was in Penrith – a town in Cumbria which fails to deliver the degree of attractiveness that one would expect, given the beauty of the surrounding area. He was attending the annual shareholders meeting[53] of one of his favourite clients: often a challenging evening, but one he looked forward to with a surprising level of excitement. This evening he had faced an interesting array of questions on subjects such as the company pension scheme, the remuneration of directors, and a spelling mistake on page 12 of the annual report and accounts. At the conclusion of the meeting he had mingled with a number of the more difficult shareholders, bought a few rounds of drinks for the directors and had then made his apologies and had left. He was now faced with the long journey home – dark and wet, the A66 was less than welcoming; and he was hungry.

Did he get something to eat in Penrith?

There would be nowhere open on the A66.

Did he wait until he got home?

Nothing would have been made for him.

---

[53] British public companies have meetings, at least annually, where the shareholders can question the directors and auditors – usually nothing more than a formality, in certain circumstances these meetings can "get out of control".

Should he pick something up on the way?

It didn't feel right, eating by yourself in your own home.

Did he rush back in the hope that someone would be in The Urra?

Drinking on an empty stomach.

He shook his head. He grunted out loud "What a fucking mess". He'd always liked anagrams and a favourite was 'desperation': 'a rope ends it'. He grinned at the thought and resolved to make it to The Urra, before closing time; if he could invest[54] in a sandwich at a petrol station on the journey.

"And why do they all have to have kitchen appliances in the front garden?" Elliott paused for a sharp intake of breath, "and I felt bloody uncomfortable driving through there cos I was in the only car which wasn't part of a chase!"

"You're exaggerating like bloody Grant does you are," replied Eric.

"You're exaggerating like bloody Grant does you are," mimicked Elliott, "What sort of English is that is it?"

"Bog off Elliott."

"Ah yes, the Lower Tees Valley lilt innit?" mocked a well-oiled Elliott.

"Perfection is the child of time[55]?" offered Pete.

Elliott looked like he'd been shot, "Fuck me Pete!"

"Thanks, but no."

"Seriously though, how come an ignorant banker like you knows a phrase like that?"

---

[54] He used the word "invest" out of respect for the prices charged at such roadside establishments. Alternative words, if correctly arranged, could be "bastards", "thieving", and "robbing". As Grant would argue, never has the term "highway robbery" been more appropriate.
[55] Joseph Hall 1574 - 1656, English Bishop

Pete grinned at Elliott; Elliott had obviously forgotten that Pete's daughters were students of literature and philosophy. "Elliott my dear man, it is the silent touches of time[56]."

"Have you got a fucking book under there?"

Pete smiled at Elliott; for once he felt that he was "in the chair".

"Just remember Elliott, what do the ravages of time not injure?[57]"

"Fuck me again," was Elliott's final response.

Buster broke his silence, "Dear me, I suppose that you'll be wanting me to buy a round."

Elliott looked at Pete.

Pete looked at Frank.

Frank looked at Bill.

Eric looked startled.

In unison they answered, "No!"

Buster went to the bar.

"Haway Pete," started Frank, "what's going on with Grant?"

Pete shook his head.

"Come on, you two have a special relationship."

Pete glared at Frank.

"No, nothing weird, just close…having worked together and all that."

Bill agreed, "Come on Pete, you know him better than any of us."

Pete looked uncomfortable, "OK, we do have a special relationship…in the style of a dog and a lamp post."

Bill laughed and clapped his hands together, "Nice reply, Pete."

Frank smiled and then leant forwards, "Come on Pete, we all like the bloke, you know that."

---

[56] Edmund Burke 1729 – 1797, Irish Politician
[57] Quintus Horatius Flaccus 65 – 08BC, Roman Poet

"I do," agreed Pete, "but I'm not going to discuss anyone's affairs, even the old Fat Bastard's, with anyone, no offence."

Frank nodded, "OK, but I'm telling you…something's up and I'm worried about him…and I haven't known him as long as you…but he's helped me out big style on a few occasions and I owe him."

Pete smiled, a tight smile of frustration, "I know Frank, he's such a good bloke that he sometimes gets clobbered…walked over… you know…I'm telling you…he deserves better…much better."

Frank sighed, then shook his head, "Too true, Pete."

"What are you two whispering about?" asked Bill.

"You, you daft old bugger," replied Frank, "it's your bloody round!"

Bill rose as Buster returned.

"One day, one day," Bill threatened.

Ten miles to the west of Barnard Castle, Grant was stationery. He had no idea why. The light drizzle had become heavy rain and the rear lights of the car in front were now making strange, almost painful patterns on his windscreen. He had switched off his wipers. He had consumed – he couldn't use the word 'eaten', as this implied some degree of enjoyment – a challenging 'Ploughman's' roll – well, that's how it was described and he had tasted something akin to a pickle on top of the plastic masquerading as cheese – and a cardboard-tasting ham sandwich. He now needed a drink, badly. Not an alcoholic drink, although one of those would be superb…no, he needed some fluids to counteract the general feeling of dehydration and tiredness. And, shit, he'd never get to The Urra at this rate.

Why did all these tossers drive around with their fog lights on? Twats.

Almost as bad as centre lane hoggers.

The lazy, ignorant bastards.

And prats driving 'people carriers' how they would drive a sports car…except they haven't worked out that they have no acceleration…or speed…

Fucking dickheads.

If the idiot in front doesn't take his foot off his brake light soon…

Fuck, fuck, fuckety fuck.

He thought about listening to some music.

No.

The radio.

No, unless…

He fancied some comedy. He needed a laugh.

At this time of night!

No chance.

Now, in the old days…

The Goons.

Jwonathwan Woss.

Dead Ringers.

The Hitch Hikers Guide to the Galaxy.

Now he needed to relieve himself. And he could see blue flashing lights approaching from behind.

Shit.

Some poor twat could be hurt up ahead somewhere.

On their way home. Wife and kids. Happy marriage.

Shame.

Sad.

He didn't know he was born.

He was the lucky bastard.

Should he ring home?

He missed them.

In more ways than he, or they could know.

He pressed the speed dial…

"Hello Charlotte,"
"What?"
"Is your Mum in?"
"Sorry, I don't think she told me,"
"Didn't know you had Luke round,"
"OK sweetheart, I'll speak to you tomorrow."
He put his phone back into its cradle.
Who the fuck was Luke?
What was his wife doing "clubbing?"
Who with?
He looked at the clock.
No chance of a couple of beers tonight.
Shit, shit, shittedty shit shit.

Pete was in full flow. "Wanda's dishwasher quit working so she called a repairman. Since she had to go to work the next day, she told the repairman, I'll leave the key under the mat. Fix the dishwasher, leave the bill on the counter, and I'll send you a cheque."

He paused for effect

"Oh, by the way don't worry about my bulldog. He won't bother you. But, whatever you do, do NOT, under ANY circumstances, talk to my parrot!" Pete shouted "I REPEAT, DO NOT TALK TO MY PARROT!!!" And then continued at a more comfortable volume, "When the repairman arrived at Wanda's apartment the following day, he discovered the biggest, meanest looking bulldog he has ever seen. But, just as she had said, the dog just lay there on the carpet watching the repairman go about his work. The parrot, however, drove him nuts the whole time with his incessant yelling, cursing and name calling. Finally the repairman couldn't contain himself any longer and yelled, Shut up, you stupid, ugly bird!"

Pete grinned before continuing, "to which the parrot replied, 'Get him, Spike!' "

Bill stood up to leave. "Did Grant tell you that?"
Elliott shook his head.
Frank laughed, after a worryingly long pause.

Twenty

Valentine's Day. The Urra is bedecked in garish decorations, every shade of pink imaginable; and a rose lies wilting on every table in the lounge area. A busy night is expected and the Regulars have arrived early in order that their escapes may be made before the pub becomes filled with love-struck couples and those going through the motions.

"Are you having a romantic meal this evening," Elliott asked Bill; Bill simply grinned back, the most effective 'sod off' known in these parts.

Elliott nodded, "Perhaps not then…what about you then Frank?"

"She's out tonight…golf club meeting…so the boy is collecting an Indian on his way home."

"But what are you having," pressed Elliott.

"An Indian…oh sod off," Frank lit a cigarette, to the obvious discomfort of Bill.

"Why can't you stop that terrible habit?"

Frank was used to being criticised for smoking; it had become worse since Grant had shocked everyone by quitting two years previously, although the fact that Biggles had recently started again deflected some of the wrath of the table of reformed smokers.

"Cos I like it," was his considered response.

"Oh I wish that you would stop it," continued Bill.

"Is Grant coming in tonight," asked Elliott, to no one in particular.

Frank flicked ash in the general direction of an ashtray, "Doubt it…saw him yesterday and he seemed a bit distracted, looked a bit under pressure."

"Just when he should come here then," Elliott smirked, "Our insult therapy is a proven cure for any form of mental anguish."

Bill shook his head, "What utter tosh."

"Now Bill, given your drug pushing background you should understand the medicinal and therapeutic effects of a good ale," Elliott paused for effect, "remember, alcohol can cause pregnancy," he paused, "and can cause you to tell your friends that you love them, many times." He paused, looked round the table and leant forwards, "and, and this is the biggy, beer makes you tougher, faster, smarter, sexier and funnier than anyone else in the whole wide world."

Grant was at home. He had arrived early. The previous night, in an attempt at thawing permafrost, he had suggested dinner out and, whilst he had received no form of clear reply, he had hoped and had made an effort.

The flowers were still in paper on the kitchen side.

She was upstairs getting ready; to go out with Susan.

The girls were out.

He hadn't eaten all day.

He'd been busy, but happy; a successful day in many ways.

He could make himself some dinner, do some reading, enjoy a bottle of Medoc whilst listening to music, or…he could eat the chocolates that he'd bought her.

He took Eric and Ernie for a walk.

"That's as maybe," stuttered Buster, "and whilst I have given this my fullest consideration…I fail to understand the connection between what you call 'upper class fanny' and stupidity."

Elliott grinned and leant forward, "I said intellect, not stupidity."

"Well, on even greater reflection I still fail to see the connection," replied Buster.

Elliott closed the palms of his hands as in prayer, "Do you accept that many upper class women, when young, have horses?"

Buster nodded.

"Do you agree that horses, bless 'em, need much attention?"

Buster nodded, unsure as to the route that Elliott was taking but now certain that he was in difficulty.

"And that this entails the aforementioned young ladies in early morning mucking out sessions?"

Buster agreed, was about to make a point but thought better of it.

"Now then, let us look at the likes of Neil's daughters."

"Careful," commented Neil.

"Teenagers lying in bed all morning, incapable of any form of effort before noon."

"Tell me about it," agreed Neil.

"Well, it is a medically proven fact that teenagers need this lying down time as their brains are still growing."

"Really?" asked Neil. Elliott nodded.

"Well, I'll be buggered," commented Neil.

Frank interrupted, "You're not lucky enough."

"Chaps, chaps," pleaded Buster, hoping for a resolution to the discussion.

"So," continued Elliott, sitting back and opening his palms in victory, "it stands to reason that these girls are not giving their brains time to grow, 'cos the horses need brushing or whatever you do to them, and so are necessarily less bright than the kids, usually middle and lower class, who spend all day lying around…letting their brains grow."

"Oh what tosh," replied Buster.

"Define 'lucky' Frank," asked Pete.

"You know why they called Elliott 'the Fox' when he was younger don't you?" asked Buster.

Speechless faces all round, a few shaking heads.

"Well, the only women that chased him were dogs," and Buster retired for the evening in an uncontrollable fit of the giggles.

"That was good that," commented Neil, before returning to the peace and solace of his pint of Brompton Six Iron.

"Jeeez," sighed Elliott, "Bring back Bannister, wherever the Fat Bastard is!"

Pete corrected him, "Fat Bald Bastard."

"Correctomundo," agreed Elliott.

"So, where is he?" asked Neil, "place is quiet without the Cantankerous Fat Bald Bastard"

"No, 'Fat Bald Cantankerous Bastard' sounds better," suggested Pete.

"Yes, well that's as maybe," countered Neil, "but whatever he is, where is he?"

"Kidnapped by aliens?" asked Elliott.

"Under arrest?" offered Frank.

"Now there's a thought," agreed Pete, "What would the Fat Cantankerous Bald Abusive Bastard be arrested for?"

"Bit of a mouthful," commented Bill.

"Aye, that's what the wife said," agreed Pete. Only Elliott guffawed.

"Child abuse," suggested Frank.

The considered view of Pete, "Expect he's thought about it, with just cause, on many occasions, but…no."

Elliott differed in approach, "Not necessarily with his own children per chance."

"Sheep?" asked Bill.

Pete disagreed, "Thought he left the road there clear for you…and Buster."

"No no no, as I've explained previously…I'm not Welsh, unlike Frank here."

"Fuck off Bill," countered Frank.

"Fraud," said Neil, seriously, producing a short silence; the quiet finally being broken by Elliott, "Possible, but not interesting."

"How about being too fat, too bald, too cantankerous, too illegitimate and an accountant…seem like reasonable grounds for punishment to me," suggested Pete.

"How can you be "too illegitimate"?" asked Elliott.

Ignoring Elliott's valid but unnecessary point Frank agreed, "Seems fair to me, should be down for a ten to fifteen stretch…now, time for a drink."

Grant was considering an early night. Watching television was a waste of one's limited life. He was too tired to read. And he had a nagging pain in the pits of his stomach. He was getting it more often. Usually in the middle of the night. Probably an ulcer, so no worries.

What had she meant when she'd called him 'the cork in the arsehole of success?' It was a great line, but what did it mean?

It had been a strange day for one liners.

Kate had puzzled him at work when she had asked him if 'he had been too long the fool'. Where did that come from?

What had she meant?

They had been talking about workloads and he had been talking about putting a full day in on the forthcoming Sunday. She had been talking about the rescheduled float and how much time they would need to spend in London. He'd been boring everyone, again, with his 'front load the work' mantra when, out of the blue, 'do you not think that you've been too long the fool'. She had quickly changed the focus of the discussion, but the line had stuck…

"So. Where is he then?" asked Frank.

"Dieting?" suggested Bill.

Elliott sniggered. "Jeez, that could put a few breweries and pie shops out of business."

"Maybe he's just been busy and is having a rest," offered Pete.

"Believe me mate," started Elliott, "If the boyo was resting, it would be in here with us and not at home with what's her name."

Frank nodded, "She is a bit of a one, isn't she."

"One what?" asked Neil, understandably.

Pete stood up, slowly, and stretched, "Right you pack of no-good wasters, time for a round in memory of the missing Mister Bannister, God help him and all those who add things up with him."

Grant lay awake. Why did he never feel this alert during the day? Sod it. Fuck but he was pissed off. Work was getting too hard. He had no 'home life'. In fact he had no 'life'. There were times when he felt like…well, like ending it. Yes, but not that way. Well, why not? No guts? The mess? The kids? Who would care? Who would miss him? What about his funeral? She wouldn't do anything. He'd better write it down.

Not a church service. No, a meeting of remembrance. A few mates telling stories. Some good music is played. Burn his remains. Then what about the ashes? On the pitch, near the corner flag, or into a rocket, a large firework, to be set off at midnight by his friends on the top of Whorl Hill, then everyone back to The Urra.

Or a lonely, cold, pauper's grave?

Did he still have mates?

It had been so long since he had seen many of his friends.

Would anyone come?

He had better arrange it himself.

He could plan the music; the booze; the food; perhaps he could 'leave' a few jokes?

Fuck. I'm not fifty yet!

186

Fuck. I haven't lived yet!
Too young to die.
Too old to live?
Bollocks.
But I better start soon!

Twenty One

It had been snowing continuously for two days. Any thawing was limited to heavily salted paths and major roads; the dirty slush stage was yet to start and Watson Humphrey was, to the innocent eye, pretty.

"You look like someone set fire to your face then put it out with a shovel!"

"Fuck off Elliott!"

"Only joking Grant, cool it."

"Sorry mate, fucking bad one, shouldn't take it out on you."

Elliott looked at Grant. He looked more dishevelled than usual – despite what was probably a nice suit and tie combination. And he looked like he had suffered a few very late nights.

"Snow is hanging around," Elliott offered in an attempt to move the conversation forwards.

"Fuck me, this fucking snow."

Elliott inwardly looked heavenwards – wrong subject.

Grant took a long pull of his umpteenth pint of Simian Heavy Ale and continued, "Got up early this morning, needed to be in Leeds for nine, shit, shower, shave, and out I go and the car is snowed in…wouldn't fucking budge…had to dig it out…then it got stuck on the bank opposite the church…fucking German crap."

"Rear wheel drive?"

"Fuck off Biggles, anyway, ended up having to leave the car once I got to the main road, had to go home and get changed as the wardrobe was wet and grubby…so I hit the outskirts of Leeds, fucking dump, at rush hour, fucking late wasn't I…anyway, on the way home the lazy bint rings me with a shopping list…she has a four wheel fucking Chelsea tractor but can't go out...so I get to the supermarket and get stuck in the snow...I mean shouldn't these places be gritted...get parked, do the shopping and, you guessed, I can't get out of the fucking car park...end up at an angle across this Volvo with a woman driver giving me the 'get out of my way you insignificant shit' look...and all I'm doing is burning rubber...stuck solid...some gadgie eventually gives me a push and off home I go...and, you'll never guess...yes! I get stuck on the hill coming into the village...and it's fucking rush hour innit! Oh yes, all the oldies returning from some bridge club or funeral planning session, all in convoy and yours truly is across the road at right angles...twats...no one helps and eventually the postman arrives and gives me a push. Left the car outside Pete's house, walked home, any thanks? Of course not! I forgot the toilet bleach! Shouldn't be allowed out should I? Can't wipe my nose, can I! So I took her car...car, it's a fucking tank...she calls it an inheritance...it's a gas guzzling pose machine...bitch...aye, the snow is hanging around."

Elliott agreed, "Quite."

"And where are the effing snowploughs? Eh? I'll tell you, I'll tell you...on the effing inner city estates...where the councillors get their effing votes...clearing the roads for the joy riders."

Biggles decided to take a chance, "And what are your views on global warming?"

"That's all a load of hot air," suggested Elliott.

Grant ignored Elliott's interruption and continued, "Fuck fuckety fuck fuck!"

Biggles decided to pursue his line of questioning, "Not quite sure I understand."

But it garnered no form of response. Grant stared at the remains of his pint; a sad, almost despairing expression on his face, like someone who knew he was about to lose a good friend. He drained his glass and placed it on the table with a bump. He looked confused for a moment and then looked at Elliott, "Want another?"

"Are you sure you do?" replied Elliott.

"I do, but…you're right…see you later," Grant rose unsteadily and left the bar without any form of farewell.

Elliott looked at Biggles, "Not well."

"Bad time."

"Poor bastard."

"My round?"

Of course, Grant had not recounted the full details of his day. His meeting in Leeds had gone less than well. It had been with one of his senior partners, a man who Grant loathed and feared; he generally referred to him as the 'Myopic Burton' – Burton had been in 'management' for too long in Grant's view; whilst he had made some great improvements to the way in which their firm operated he had, in Grant's opinion, failed to move on and had lost touch with the commercial and practical aspects of their business. So Grant viewed him with a degree of respect for his past achievements, but looked at his current agenda as being nothing short of myopic.

John Burton's view of Grant mirrored Grant's views of him. Burton, a fifty something scouser[58] admitted that he was 'tired' and it was time for the next generation to take the firm forwards. He had once agreed with others that Grant had such an important future; but not anymore. Grant had once…relatively recently…been one of the firm's best operators…with the best new client gains figures, with an ability to devise and manage new initiatives, and had taken his office from bottom of all the firm's league tables to the top of many. He didn't know why, but his firm belief was that Grant had somehow 'lost it', he wasn't delivering, he seemed unable to think strategically, and he appeared generally unwell.

---

[58] Someone from a certain area of Merseyside; often possessing a sharp sense of humour, a grating accent and a screwdriver.

190

Burton had called the meeting; he wanted Grant to specialise into what he saw as his best areas and wanted to combine the management of a number of operational units; this would free Grant to cover a wider geographic area. Grant had agreed to the overall logics but had argued against some of the specifics – particularly the idea of running all funding referrals through banks and finance houses in Leeds – Grant could see that the generation of a higher level of referral activity in this major centre would have clear benefits for colleagues working in other fields – particularly the receivers and liquidators – but he had argued that he would receive no referrals from his current contacts if he could not reciprocate. Also, he liked working his current network.

The meeting had ended in an impasse. Of sorts. They did not agree. So Burton had concluded that the only way forward was to force Grant's hand; Grant had told him to sexually pleasure himself.

Grant stood in his lounge; he loved this room. Spacious, well-lit, functional…home to some happy memories.

He could hear his wife talking on the telephone and the repetitive thud of music from his daughters' rooms.

He wanted to talk to some one.

Did he make himself something to eat?

Did he make a drink? He shook his head and wearily climbed the stairs. It was not yet 9pm and the day had beaten him.

And his stomach ached.

Was it too much ale? He had cut back. Very rarely drank the "hard" stuff.

Was it a bad diet?

Stress? Bollocks.

Was he just knackered?

He would be OK.

He shook his head. He was fed up, frustrated, possibly tired.

He got into bed but sleep would not come.

The volume of her voice on the telephone seemed to get louder.

The room vibrated to the sound of the girls' music.

Burton's voice seemed to fill his head.

And his stomach seemed to be eating away at his insides.

And whatever he tried to think about, whatever fantasies he created, his thoughts always returned to Burton.

Or his wife.

Had it all been a big mistake?

No, he had two beautiful daughters.

Did she still love him?

Had she ever?

What had he done wrong?

Since marrying her?

Was marrying her what was wrong?

Had he got it so wrong?

Were they both at fault?

He snorted. She would never accept any blame!

He could feel his stomach churning.

Is this how emptiness feels?

Should it hurt like this?

Ignore it and it will go away.

Is that was his wife was trying to do to him?

Twenty Two

"And what's the fucking point of them saying 'sorry sir we used to have it in stock', the daft buggers!" Elliott had been shopping, possibly for the first time in many years and he had not enjoyed the experience.

It was the last Wednesday in February and The Urra was relatively busy, other than around the regulars table. Only three had arrived, thus far. Elliott was recovering from a 'day out with the wife', Buster had spent all of an hour 'farming', and Eric had done 'nine tenths of fuck all'.

"Very very fucking helpful, 'no, we haven't got one but we used to' so what do you do?" Elliott wiped his mouth, "I'll tell you, you take up time travel, that's what you do! You ask the salesman exactly when they last had one, and then you travel back through time to get it...after first thanking the salesman for his help and politely declining the offer of twenty one years interest free credit if you buy one of a specially selected range of kitchen appliances right now, yes, 'fuck off and die' is the preferred response...followed by 'and could you please order me the jewel encrusted bird table when you have a free half hour you dim witted excuse for a member of some Gaelic tribe'."

"I've never seen any time travel equipment in any of the local superstores," commented Eric.

"That's because you are both blind and stupid," replied Elliott.

Eric stared at Elliott, considered a reply and then decided that silence was the appropriate response[59].

"Bit unfair, that," was Buster's contribution.

Grant was at his desk. On the wall behind him was a notice he'd stolen and had framed some years previously… "TOILET OUT OF ORDER…PLEASE USE FLOOR BELOW". It still made him smile; when he was in the mood to smile.

He sat slumped into his chair, staring at the fluorescent lights in the ceiling.

He scratched himself; well, that was the closest he'd come to any form of sexual activity for quite some time.

He looked around his office; his comfort zone. The walls were covered with framed photographs:

- 'famous' local footballers
- Grant with such 'famous' local footballers
- Grant with a number of properly famous rugby players – he particularly liked the one of him with Gareth Chilcott, the former Bath and England prop forward – it was always a topic of conversation…people often asked 'are you two brothers?'
- Grant with a number of clients at various race meetings and other corporate hospitality functions; he always seemed to be smiling. Was he always drunk?

He stretched his arms above his head. His shoes had long since been kicked off.

So how was he feeling?

Exhausted, frustrated, disappointed, lonely.

Scared?

---

[59] But why was Elliott becoming somewhat more cantankerous than usual? Well, rude, to be frank. "And what's he got to do with it?" you may ask. But, returning to Elliott, he seemed to have a comfortable and satisfying home life; a reasonably rewarding career; a healthy and seemingly happy family. Mid-life crisis?
Post mid-life crisis?

He looked at the small framed photo of his father. It was an old black and white photo of his father on duty in post-war Berlin; the only 'family' photograph in his office, other than one of his daughters at the nappy and crawling stage. No picture of his wife. No pictures of his family at any time during the last fifteen years.

What would his father have told him to do?

He always thought of his father as a spiritual conscience, looking over him; frowning in shame, occasionally criticising, rarely encouraging or praising.

They had never been close; and he'd been pretty much absent during Grant's formative years; the pressures of work?

Had he been a workaholic?

Was Grant?

Did he not get on with Grant's mother?

How similar were they?

Grant smiled. He'd been a poor son. Hadn't someone said something along the lines that when he'd been a boy his father had been that ignorant that he couldn't stand having him around? But a decade later he had been astonished by how much his father had learned in ten years. Mark Twain? Grant's gaze returned to the photo.

He could do with him now.

Ruffling his hair.

Telling him it would be OK.

Telling him not to worry.

And his Dad would make it OK.

He always had done.

Grant felt a shiver down his spine and tried to regain control of his thoughts. Control. That was what he had lost. Control. At work. At home. It had all gone. Lost. Totally.

He shook his head.

What have I done to deserve this?

The walls seemed to be closing in on his life. He hated going home. He was increasingly unhappy at work; the place which until recently had been his comfort zone. He really could not avoid the conclusion that he had health problems.

Had he done something really bad in a previous life?

Had he been a mass murderer of some sort?

Had he raped and pillaged?

Had he been a cannibal?

Or a particularly vicious pirate?

In all probability, if he had endured a previous life, he would have been some form of odious and completely insignificant clerk.

Running away seemed like a good idea. But he didn't have the courage necessary for such an action. Or any idea of where to go? Hopeless. He was absolutely hopeless. She was right.

Another reason for him to dislike himself.

That was part of the problem; he had lost respect for himself; he had been told so many times that he was every type of shit that he now actually believed that he was a total shit.

Only this morning she had reminded him of his numerous failings and misdemeanours; he could no longer differentiate between those he accepted because they were true, and those which he accepted simply because she had told him about them so often.

And as he lost his self respect he could see that his confidence – which had always been fragile – was going. This lead to the loss of his talent to 'bullshit' – perhaps his greatest personal strength – so he was losing the ability to bring in new clients and knew that he was inevitably going to lose the support of his staff.

'Never bullshit a bullshitter' had been one of his favourite sayings. Well, he couldn't bullshit himself out of a paper bag at present.

What would his father say?

Looking back he could see that his father had never been a particularly confident person; shy to the point of rudeness, he had been successful simply due to hard work and his outstanding intellect.

They had never been close. Grant had been the typical horrible son; typical but not acceptable. And for far too long.

Maybe she was right?

Perhaps he was nothing more that an overweight, bald loser?

His father had liked her. She had tolerated him.

What would his father tell him to do?

He would probably recite some piece of poetry and then leave it to Grant to work out what he meant; if anything. It would be some obscure but horrific piece from the Great War or a classic from the likes of Kipling. That was it; "If you can keep your head when all about you are losing theirs and blame it on you"[60].

He stood up. Looked at his briefcase; sod it; he left it where it lay. It was time to live for himself; everything couldn't be his fault; he wasn't a bad person; time for him to be a man, again.

But his stomach still ached; badly.

Grant walked into The Urra and received a round of applause.

"Where've you been?" asked Elliott.

---

[60] If you can keep your head when all about you are losing theirs and blaming it on you, If you can trust yourself when all men doubt you But make allowance for their doubting too, If you can wait and not be tired by waiting, Or being lied about, don't deal in lies, Or being hated, don't give way to hating, And yet don't look too good, nor talk too wise: If you can dream--and not make dreams your master, If you can think--and not make thoughts your aim; If you can meet with Triumph and Disaster And treat those two impostors just the same; If you can bear to hear the truth you've spoken Twisted by knaves to make a trap for fools, Or watch the things you gave your life to, broken, And stoop and build 'em up with worn-out tools: If you can make one heap of all your winnings And risk it all on one turn of pitch-and-toss, And lose, and start again at your beginnings And never breathe a word about your loss; If you can force your heart and nerve and sinew To serve your turn long after they are gone, And so hold on when there is nothing in you Except the Will which says to them: "Hold on!" If you can talk with crowds and keep your virtue, Or walk with kings--nor lose the common touch, If neither foes nor loving friends can hurt you; If all men count with you, but none too much, If you can fill the unforgiving minute With sixty seconds' worth of distance run, Yours is the Earth and everything that's in it, And--which is more--you'll be a Man, my son! Rudyard Kipling (1865-1936).

"Who are you?" asked Frank

Grant smiled. He shouldn't feel guilty about meeting nice people in a public house and drinking a little more than others would say he should; he wasn't doing anyone any harm.

"Alf my man" he shouted "Can I have a round for these young reprobates?"

Grant sat down next to Elliott, having placed everyone's drinks in front on the correct person. He looked around the table. No one had changed. Familiar faces. A few missing.

Familiar smells. The same old yarns, moans, insults…it was like an alcohol soaked comfort blanket. And what was wrong with that?

"Where you been then?" asked Frank.

"Around."

"Missed us?" enquired Elliott.

"So much it hurt."

"I should think so," replied Elliott, "mind, it has been a fucking improvement in here, no stories about numbers, no crap about football and none of your effing awful jokes!"

"So, you've not missed me?" Grant knew that there would be no positive answer, but felt that they had missed him. A bit.

Elliott leant forwards and pointed one of his stubby fingers at Grant "As it happens…you now owe us thirty two rounds."

Grant laughed.

Elliott persevered, "I'm not joking."

Grant grinned.

Elliott drained his glass, "So get a fucking move on!"

Grant took a sip and then wiped his lips with his cuff, "Elliott you have two chances and one of them is fuck all!"

Elliott smirked. He was pleased to see Grant, but he would never admit it. To anyone. Particularly to Grant.

"Have you been anywhere interesting?" asked a genuinely interested Frank.

"Not really...unless you think that the likes of Leeds and Manchester are interesting."

"You'd be sad if you did," interrupted Elliott.

Frank ignored Elliott ,"So, are you busy?"

"Yes, but bad busy rather than good busy."

Frank thought he understood.

Elliott didn't care. It was his turn to get the beers. He rose. "The usual." A statement, not a question.

Everyone nodded or grunted. It was sufficient. Elliott strode purposely to the bar.

"So" started Grant, "anyone been doing anything interesting?"

"Well, you've heard about Elliott getting into trouble at school?" asked Buster.

Grant shook his head, unsure as to whether this was the start of a wind up.

"Some parents reported him for demanding that one of his classes conclude a lesson with the singing of the national anthem."

"Brilliant, brilliant, only Elliott could get away with it," interjected Neil.

"But that's the point," continued Buster, "he didn't!"

Neil nodded, "Well, it was funny when he started answering questions with 'do you want fries with that', I mean he reckons the best that the most his pupils can aspire to is getting a few golden stars, working behind the counter of some burger joint."

Grant was silenced.

Pete pushed Grant on the shoulder, affectionately, before offering, "I loved the story about him paging himself over the school intercom."

Grant was stunned and could only muster a desperate, "Never?"

Buster leant forwards and whispered, "Aye, there's some that say that he's had a breakdown of some form."

Grant cracked, "Oh fuck off, not Elliott…he would do all of those things as some form of wizard prank, not as a result of some illness."

"Well, it's true," finished Buster before he swiftly changed the subject, "So Grant, who is that rather attractive brunette who keeps visiting your house?

"Eh?"

Pete stared at Buster.

"Very attractive, nice car as well, there most days."

"I've no idea," replied Grant.

"Did you hear about Elliott on the school trip to Edinburgh zoo?" Pete continued without waiting for an answer, "Seems he was seen running towards the coach park shouting 'they're loose, run, run' with the result that mass panic set in."

"Bollocks," laughed Grant.

Pete smirked. The direction of the conversation had been changed.

Twenty Three

The first Wednesday in March; the weather was miserable and had been for some days.

The log fire crackled in the massive stone hearth in the lounge of The Urra.

To the visitor, the group of middle aged and elderly men sitting around the table next to the fire could have seemed 'off putting'; clearly well oiled for the time of day, louder than necessary, using colourful language and being over familiar with the barmaids.

And immature.

They had been drinking since the rain had brought their golf day to a premature close. And like all young boys, drunken men like to play games.

"Right, breasts," shouted Elliott.

Grant giggled.

Frank smirked.

"Eh?" asked Pete.

"We go round the table, taking it in turns to come out with a word for breasts."

"Good one Elliott," replied Pete.

Grant rushed to reply, "I prefer them in pairs."

An immediate put-down from Elliott, "Grow up Granteebaby."

"I'll start," announced Frank, "Jubblies!"

Grant giggled.

Elliott, "Jugs!"

"Poor effort that," commented Pete, "How about funbags?"

Grant giggled.

Bill, "Knockers!"

Frank shook his head, "Showing your age there Billy Boy!"

"Melons," was Neil's offering.

Grant leant forwards, "Baby's dinners."

Pete, Elliott and Frank all recoiled in mock anguish.

Buster waved his hands about, his raised palms signifying his refusal to 'play'.

After much 'umming' and 'arring' Biggles provided, "Daddy dummies."

Eric laughed nervously, "Oh well, how about Bristols?"

"Pathetic…my favourite is Mammaries," offered Alf.

Frank scratched his chin, "Mmmmm, what about Sweater Fruit?"

"Fucking class, the best yet," interrupted Grant.

Pete went out of turn, "Baps!"

Bill followed him, "Tits!"

Neil erred, looked in pain and then offered, "Bumpers!"

"And he wonders why he gets called 'Forty' for fuck's sake," offered Grant.

Everyone looked at Elliott. "Have we had Boobs?"

The table erupted into moans of derision. Neil waved his hands about, "Poor effort."

"Forty before the dimmer switch!" sniggered Grant.

Pete shook his head from side to side, "Expected better Elliott, expected better."

Grant blew a raspberry.

"Fucking shocking," shouted Frank.

Alf became aware that the volume was increasing and that other 'guests' were looking in their direction; with looks of disapproval and annoyance. "OK guys, I'll get a round, Landlord's treat, you name it you can have it."

The table went silent until Grant spoilt the moment, "Bazoomas!"

Grant was more relaxed than he had been for sometime; the ale obviously had a contributory effect but he had been noticeably happier than normal all day. Such was his jovial mood that Frank had gone so far as to ask him if he'd been sexually entertained. The root of his happiness was that his wife and daughters were away – visiting her family. He had not been invited. This had been disappointing but, when the wife is away…

His house had become a home.

He had eaten well.

He had spent hours listening to old records; drinking wine.

Examining old record sleeves like they were long lost friends; remembering when he first listened to them. Carefree times. Happy days. Laughter. Parties. Smoke.

Some were warped. Many were scratched. The crackles were frustrating. Disappointing. Sad. Like the loss of a close personal friend. A sign of long lost days.

And he had the volume up.

All the speakers switched on.

Even Eric and Ernie had 'retired' to the laundry room. And he hadn't seen the cats for days.

Bliss. He could put up with this. The washing up, cooking and ironing were no problem. He was sleeping well.

He felt a bounce in his walk.

How long did he have before she returned? All good things…

Frank laughed and pointed at Grant, "That was a shite shot you played at the tenth."

Pete slapped Grant on the back, "Your tee shot on the eleventh was worse than shite."

Grant's diplomatic and perfectly timed riposte, "Fuck off, suckers."

Frank laughed, "No, Grant, you really are useless."

Elliott put his arm round Grant's shoulders, "Dear boy, have you considered euthanasia?"

"I'll help," offered Pete.

"We could have a competition," suggested Neil, momentarily bringing silence to the table.

"For what? asked Frank.

"In what?" countered Elliott

"As in how we help Grant to commit suicide," explained Neil.

"It's gotta be painful," slurred Bill.

Frank agreed, "With blood."

Biggles was clearly struggling from the exertions of the day but tried to rejoin the debate.

"He hasn't got any."

"What?" asked Bill.

"Blood," answered Neil and Biggles simultaneously.

"Time for another game," announced Elliott.

"How about, who wants to shag Lucinda behind the bar and why?" suggested Neil. Unwisely. And loudly.

Grant was a relative newcomer to the game of golf. Elliott, another relative novice, had persuaded him to 'give it a go'. Neither was in the same league as the likes of Frank, Biggles and Buster; and neither wanted to be. Golf for both of them was an excuse for a long 'chat' and some exercise.

Grant enjoyed a round if:

- There was no one 'up his arse'
- There were no slow inconsiderate bastards in front of him
- It wasn't too hot
- There were decent showers
- All day breakfasts were available (and could be washed down with a pint or three of Guinness)
- Frank and his electric trolley/ mobile drinks cabinet was at least two miles away

- Buster, who had a set of woods which were all larger than a British Leyland Mini, was at least three miles away
- Biggles, who was a boring golf expert, was at least five miles away.

Grant hooked the ball. He topped the ball. He swore. But when the Golf God was with him, he could hit a six iron further than most could hit a driver. He found it physically and morally impossible to ever play a safe or sensible shot.

And whenever he felt that he was improving, the Golf God would punish him.

But, with the right people, on an empty course, he enjoyed it and regretted not 'giving it a go' many years previously.

There was much about golf that Grant laughed at; the fact that Frank's golf clubs probably cost more than Grant's car was one such point. Then there were the clothes; and the rules (and knowing the rules was, to Grant and Elliott, a form of cheating); and the ethics; and the committees; and the plonkers who took it a tadge more seriously than was necessary.

And what the fuck was a Sandy Ferret?

Grant felt like an outsider, still. He had not broken into the 'golf set'; but did he really want to? He felt tolerated. Did he care? Of course he didn't. Or did he?

He had not disgraced himself today and was relatively pleased with himself. He had scored better than Frank and, as he had mentioned, on numerous occasions, "Frank's balls cost more than all of my clubs put together."

"Me!" shouted Pete, without thinking.
"I saw her first," pronounced Alf.

Grant stood and raised his glass to Alf, "You employ her, so get one of your staff to strip her, wash her and bring her round to my house."

Pete put his head in his hands.

"Sit down you daft bastard," suggested Elliott.

Pete corrected him, "Daft Bald Fat Bastard."

"Have I told you about my new 3 wood?" asked Frank.

Elliott looked at Frank, "Is that the one made out of the protective shield used by the Space Shuttle? The one that is made of the hardest, yet lightest material known to Man? The one which, if used by someone with a modicum of talent, would send the ball into orbit? The one which cost the same amount as a new BMW?" Elliott paused for effect; or was he waiting for Frank to take the bait?

"No."

Grant guffawed.

"Twats," was Frank's final contribution as he rose to leave.

"Are you leaving the money?" asked Elliott

Frank looked momentarily confused.

Grant rushed to his aid, "It's your round."

Twenty Four

The mid-March damp rotted the bones. Everywhere and everything seemed cold, wet and grubby. Other than the welcoming warmth and atmosphere of The Urra. Add to this the delights of daytime drinking and one gets a match made in heaven. For Grant and Elliott; given that Grant's wife was away and Elliott's appeared to be unerringly forgiving, this was life at its best.

They had played a morning round of golf and had agreed to meet in The Urra for a quick pint or two on the way home. That had been at lunchtime.

Grant was now sitting on a bar stool admiring Lucinda; obviously.

Elliott was standing in front of the fire in his best Churchillian pose, "And I said to the little wankers[61] 'why don't you all go home and fornicate with a loved one' and that shut the buggers up, I'll tell you!"

Other customers looked shocked.

Grant shook his head; he had long since given up trying to follow Elliott's line in conversation. His eyes followed a somewhat rotund woman on her way to powder her nose, "Last time I saw an arse like that it was pulling a cart." Grant slapped his thigh in self celebration. "In fact, in fact, she's got more chins than the Hong Kong telephone book." Grant guffawed, "And, and, she's so ugly that the tide wouldn't take her out!"

---

[61] Elliott's deferential term for his students.

Elliott slumped against the bar and looked at Grant, "You know my dim-witted little friend, you know it is impossible to kill oneself by holding one's breath."

Grant grinned "Bollocks!"

"Nah, is true," replied Elliott.

Alf looked on, uneasily. Was it time to ask his best customers to leave?[62]

Grant's gaze returned to Lucinda. Jeez, what a bottom. His mind wandered. He saw himself biting it. Licking it. Rubbing his face into her charms. He was lost in thought until Elliott slapped him on the back.

"And butterflies taste with their feet."

"Oh piss off," was Grant's considered response.

"No, 'onest, tis true."

"Yeah, and I'm a Rock Star."

Elliott looked puzzled, then his face lit up, "Yeah, in your dreams."

Alf attempted to calm the situation, "So guys, are you off now?"

"Nah!"

Elliott agreed "Feck orf," before continuing, "you know, you know, typewriter is the longest word that can be made from the letters on one row of a keyboard."

"Give me a break," replied a disbelieving Grant.

"Straight up, an', an' stewardess is the longest word you can type with your left hand."

"How fucking stupid do you think I am?" replied Grant, before he redirected his attentions to Lucinda.

---

[62] How does a Publican measure his best customers? How is value assigned? The amount of money that is transferred from wallet to till? The number of other guests he attracts? His contribution to the atmosphere? How often he complains. How often he upsets other regulars – not such a big issue as upsetting non-regulars – or is it? Incidents of "misbehaviour"? Potential future consumption – the Publican's equivalent of an order book. The profit margin on his preferred beverage? Bugger knows, but Elliott's value was clearly declining.

Lucinda was aware and increasingly nervous. Grant was a lovely bloke; old enough to be her father; harmless, but…

Grant's thoughts mirrored Lucinda's; to a degree. He was old enough to be her father; he was a lecherous, dirty minded old man, and he would love to have a go. He grinned inwardly, if it wasn't for security frisks at airports he'd have no sex life at all.

"You know Elliott," started Grant.

"I know him, I am him."

"No no no, I meant…you know…Elliott."

"Should have said that then."

"Well pardon me you academic piece of shite."

"Less of the academic."

Grant grinned.

Elliott prompted him, "You were going to say?"

"Oh yes, this morning I looked myself up and down in the mirror…then I got out of bed."

Grant giggled. Elliott didn't.

"Lucinda, sweetheart," shouted Elliott, "can we please have two more of your delicious Mount Grace Specials, please, thank you."

Grant shook his head, vigorously, "No no no, I hate that cloudy shite, I want a pint of Cod Beck Pale."

"Guys," suggested Alf, "do you want to go home and get something to eat so you can be back when the rest get in?" Alf hoped that the two would go home, and then go to sleep.

"Nah."

"Feck orf…"

"Well, can you lower the volume and moderate the language,"

Grant and Elliott both stared at Alf; he had never been so authoritarian before.

"Sure."

"Aye, sorry."

Grant broke the silence, "You know, the penalty for masturbation in Indonesia is decapitation."

Elliott took a short pull from his pint, "Yeah, but would you have to go that far to entertain yourself?"

"Guess not."

Elliott leaned over towards Grant, "Not that I'm suggesting that you're a wanker."

Grant nodded; he was beginning to struggle for any form of response.

"And if you were it would not bother me in the slightest," Elliott continued, "in fact it would imply, but by no means guarantee, that at least some parts of your cadaverous body still works."

Grant was realising that he was in the early stages of sleep deprivation.

"And, interestingly enough, in certain religions one is not allowed to inspect a corpse's genitals."

Grant was realising that he had now totally 'lost the plot'.

He was working hard at concentrating.

He felt bloated.

For reasons which he had never understood, he could see clearer out of one eye – either eye, if the other was closed – than through both of them.

He'd been working too hard. That and the golf. He was tired. He failed to convince himself.

Elliott continued his rambling, slurred monologue, "whilst elsewhere, Beirut and South Shields for example, men are permitted to have sex with animals, but the animals must be female." .

Grant asked, "So what if you have sex with a male animal?"

"Goolies off I'm afraid, then death."

"Not that I'd want to," interjected Grant.

"Of course not," replied Elliott.

Grant felt the need to clarify his position, "With any type of animal, male or female, dead or alive."

Elliott looked at Lucinda, "We're all animals you know."

Grant sat in his favourite chair, staring into 'deep space'.

The remnants of his evening meal – a failed attempt at Burmese Shrimp Curry[63] – lay on a tray on the floor.

Was it really legal to have sex with an animal as long as it was female?

He had changed from his golfing attire into a colourful ensemble comprising of a pair of bright blue Hartlepool United shorts, dating from the mid 1990s, a worn and once-upon – a- time white T-shirt, with the logo 'Let Me Play With Your Poodle' across the chest, and an odd pair of socks. He had acquired a substantial wardrobe of T shirts with logos over the years – bands, rugby tournaments, rude messages, all sorts – she hated them. He only wore them when she was away.

This shirt bore the marks of a lost battle with the Burmese Shrimp Curry.

What would it be like with an animal? He shuddered at the thought.

Attila The Stockbroker's Barnstormer[64] was attempting to entertain from his CD player.

---

[63] Use ½ kilo of peeled shrimp. Add pinch of turmeric powder to shrimp and set aside. Heat 5 tablespoons of vegetable oil; add one large chopped onion and stir fry until transparent. Make a paste of garlic and ginger (4 cloves of garlic and one inch of fresh ginger), add to onion and stir for one minute. Add ½ tablespoon of paprika, 1 teaspoon of chilli powder and ½ teaspoon of turmeric powder; stir fry for one minute and then add 3 chopped tomatoes. Stir fry for two minutes then add 2 tablespoons of soy sauce. Stir fry, then add 2 tablespoons of chopped coriander leaves and the shrimp. Cook on simmer for ten minutes and then serve immediately with rice. This should serve four growing, healthy adults. Mmm, tasty. Unfortunately Grant had no turmeric powder, so used extra chilli powder. Due to domestic difficulties there was also no paprika; being imaginative, he replaced this with chilli powder. To save effort and time he replaced the rice with sliced bread. He got what he deserved.

[64] The album 'Zero Tolerance' published by Roundhead Records in 2004, no. HELMET CD6.

They weren't doing too well.

He felt in need of a large belch or fart or both. Could he trust a fart? Given his consumption?

He thought about changing the CD; or of playing some vinyl. Too much effort.

The Daily Telegraph lay scattered across the floor; he loved having the time and space to read the Telegraph or Times. Unfortunately, outside of work the only things he seemed to read these days were menus and prescriptions – and her bills.

Eric and Ernie were trying to get his attention; both were in need of exercise, desperate to relieve themselves and somewhat peckish; in the Animal Kingdom the phrase 'pissed off' would have been appropriate.

"So, what's it called when you're damned if you do, and you're damned if you don't?" Frank paused for effect – badly – "Marriage!"

Pete sighed.

Neil shook his head.

"So, Tweedle Dum and Tweedle Dee have been and gone?" asked Buster.

"Been, wrecked, embarrassed and retreated, more like," offered Pete.

"Grant will be in trouble," observed Bill

"Nah, she's away," replied Pete

"She does appear to be somewhat difficult," commented Buster, "although she does have some very attractive friends."

"Well, I doubt that Grant gets to watch."

"Careful Frank," Pete asked rather than instructed.

"Aye, point taken, my round?" and Frank stood up.

Twenty Five

The last Friday in March; it was raining; it had been for some days; it seemed like it had been raining for weeks. The Urra was relatively quiet.

Alf sat at the end of the bar – on the punter's side – reading the evening newspaper and waiting for someone to offer him a drink.

Pete sat stroking his grey beard, deep in thought; his untouched pint in front of him.

Frank was reading a golf magazine; slowly.

Ben sat fidgeting; occasionally sighing; clearly wanting someone to talk to him or buy him a drink; ideally both.

Pete looked up and glanced around the table, "Another hard day at the chalk face, Elliott?"

Elliott grinned, but made no reply.

Neil was staring at a group of young women sitting on a table at the opposite side of the bar.

Elliott was watching Neil watching the girls.

Bill had tried, and failed to stimulate conversation on a number of occasions: "All this rain will be good for the lawns." He failed again.

Buster was concentrating on removing dirt from his finger nails; one could always tell when Buster was trying to concentrate as that was the only time he ever used his glasses – a half moon pair that he would take ages to delicately place on the end of his nose.

Pete looked up, smiled at Buster and then took a pull from his pint.

Frank moved to light a cigarette; Bill 'tutted', loudly. Frank put his packet away whilst commenting "You miserable old twat."

Ben coughed to clear his throat and then started, "You know there are some that say that the Romans should have built their wall along the banks of the Tees."

The silence returned.

Buster took a pen knife to his nails.

Pete continued to be lost in thought.

Elliott watched Neil, wondering what thoughts were passing through his mind.

Frank read on.

"Anyone seen Biggles?" asked Bill.

"They must have been hardier souls than current day Italians," suggested Ben.

"Not been seen for weeks," Bill answered his own question.

Elliott leaned forwards, "You dirty minded bastard"

"Am not," replied Neil, immediately, knowing what Elliott meant and accepting that he was correct.

"Eh?" asked Ben, "what have I missed?"

Grant was at his desk. Tie and shoes off; belt loosened.

He was working on a funding proposal for an abattoir; it was an interesting assignment; he was enjoying the work and felt in control. He was well within his comfort zone.

Should he take it home and do it over the weekend?

No, he would work as late as necessary so he would then have the whole weekend to spend time with…sod it, he'd finish it tonight anyway.

Neil had slipped into his nervous school boy persona, with complete ease and without thought, "The one on the left in the black leather trousers looks rather foxy, yes, I bet she'd be some fun, and I do like the look of the blonde in the middle, bet she's got no pants on."

"You're just like the shits I have to teach," commented Elliott.

"I'd like to teach them a thing or two," continued Neil, without pause for thought, "I'd give them all detention and then a good spanking."

"Does your wife know about this fetish?" asked Pete.

Neil blushed.

"Thought not, shall I talk to her for you?"

Neil sighed,. "No thanks, my wife is a sex object."

Before Neil could finish his sentence Pete and Elliott finished it for him, "every time you ask for sex, she objects!"

Neil grinned, "You twats."

Frank moved to sit closer to Pete before quietly asking, "Seen Grant? What the fuck is going on with his Missus?"

Pete shot Frank a 'shutthefuckup' glance before leaning over towards Frank, "What you mean?"

Frank, quietly this time, replied, "He's never at home, she is, and she's always got that good looking tart round there."

Pete took a deep drink.

Frank continued, "And her indoors reckons that she's seen them kissing."

Ben jumped, "Eh! What was that?"

"Grant's wife and that attractive tart," replied Frank.

"Haway man," warned Pete.

"What was that?" asked Bill.

"Nothing you daft old bugger," replied Pete.

"I may be old, I may be daft, but I'm not deaf and I'm not blind and I've seen some strange goings on as well."

Pete struggled to redirect the conversation, "So what about this fetish Neil?"

Bill continued, "Fetish is the right word, you youngsters might accept and understand such things, but I don't."

Pete continued, "You only appreciate school when you get older and you have to pay for a middle aged woman to spank you."

"No thank you," was Neil's hasty reply.

Bill rambled on, "And I just don't understand it"

Pete persevered, "Bet you beg for it."

Bill ignored Pete, "And she's got a lovely house, two lovely daughters and he's not such a bad lad."

"I guess begging for it and then being punished is one of your biggest kicks."

"Piss off Pete!"

Bill was now talking into his chest, "But, no, she wants to try it on the other side, whatever they do, I don't know."

"You love it, you little pervert," Pete was really trying. Trying to draw attention away from Bill; and trying Neil's patience.

"Give it a break Pete man!"

"Only if you tell me what she does for you."

"Just piss off."

Grant was scratching himself. And enjoying it.

It had always amazed him how much pleasure could be achieved from the simplest of bodily functions. How many times had he felt satisfaction, relief and pure joy within the confines of the lavatory?

His work was progressing well.

The phones were silent.

The only interruptions were when his mind wandered[65] or his stomach reminded him that it enjoyed pretending to be a contortionist.

He looked at the clock; he'd be finished by midnight.

Perhaps he would have a lie-in in the morning. Tea and toast in bed, with the Telegraph.

Fatfuckingchance.

---

[65] No, "wandered" is the wrong word given that his mind always returned to the same subject – HER. Or variations on a theme. Why did she hate him? What had he done wrong? Did he deserve this? Would it get better? What could he do about it?

She'd ensure that there was no chance of any relaxation, enjoyment or similar.

Twenty Six

The first Wednesday in April. The Urra was busy: the Easter holidays had brought with them a minor invasion; loud children, adults in track suits and teenagers in need of surgery to remove various items of electronic gadgetry from their ears, hands and personal bits.

"Good job Grant isn't around," commented Buster, "he hates it when it's like this."

"Don't we all?" replied Elliott.

Biggles laughed and nodded his head, "But Grant hates everything, everything from caravans – on the road and on driveways – remember his argument that you should have planning permission to park your caravan on your drive?"

"I haven't got one."

"I know that Elliott, but you know what I mean, he hates fog lights, he'd shoot able bodied people for parking in disabled spaces, he believes that the French are to blame for everything, and he cannot accept that the English are anything other than a superior race."

"So where's he wrong?" asked Elliott.

"I saw the Fat Bastard yesterday," announced Pete, to no one in particular, "Didn't seem too bright, looked like shit."

"Drink?" enquired Biggles.

"What? You offering or asking if the drink had wrecked Grant?"

Biggles considered Pete's reply.

"Both," he offered, as if he meant it.

"Well, that being the case I think the answer is 'yes' and 'no' and make sure you get them the right way round."

"What? You want a drink?"

"Yes, Biggles, my cuddly little winged wonder, you marsupial featured fighter pilot, yes I will have a pint of the most expensive bitter on offer," replied Pete.

Elliott leant forward, "I better keep him company."

Buster grinned, "Well, it would be churlish not to."

Biggles shook his head and rose from his seat, "Twats."

Grant was sitting in his car. He was parked in a lay-by on one of the major roads not far from his home. The engine was idling and he had reclined his seat. He was looking at the sun roof. The car was warm.

He felt safe.

Alone, but safe.

Alone, but in control.

On the passenger seat laid the remnants of his lunch – two crumpled plastic sandwich cartons and an empty juice bottle.

He smirked…he knew how to live it up, didn't he?

He didn't want to go to The Urra; he wanted to go home…well, to a home, and not necessarily his own.

He switched on his CD.

It went so well for you.

He grinned, the tune was familiar – a favourite – Just A Shadow – from the Big Country album 'Steeltown'[66]; he started singing along…

With a place right where you wanted and the ones to fill it too
But some blows break the spell
That it hits you every day until you need to hit as well

---

[66] Released in 1984, published by Phonogram, produced by the legendary Steve Lillywhite. Brilliant.

Like many Big Country songs, Grant pondered that it could be about him…

It's just a shadow of the man you should be
Like a garden in the forest that the world will never see
You have no thought of answers only questions to be filled
And it feels like hell

Shit, this was uncomfortable. He switched off the CD with a level of violence which both surprised and frightened him. "Got to sort this mess out," he shouted and pushed the stick down to drive and hit the pedal. It was time to sort it out; if he could work out what 'it' was.

"Just been up tae bonny Scotland," Biggles looked around to see if anyone was interested; he tried again, "You know, the most popular hotel in Glasgow is the Barlinnie." Still no reaction.

"I'm worried about old Grant," said Pete, scratching his beard with his right hand and holding his empty glass in his left.

"Why? Is it his round?" asked Elliott.

"I'm told," persisted Biggles, "that those taking the High Road were actually hung in Carlisle."

Pete shook his head, his eyes screwed up in mock pain. Elliott looked at Biggles and grinned, "Get it off your chest man!"

Biggles immediately put on one of those superior facial expressions which were guaranteed to invite, at the very least, a punch, "As I was saying, we've just been flying sorties over Scotland, bombing runs over Thurso and some seriously low stuff over Scapa."

Elliott interrupted, "Didn't Grant go up there a couple of years back?"

"Aye," agreed Pete, "He took an early morning boat trip around the wrecked fleet, said it was really eerie, one of those memorable experiences and-"

"As I was saying," continued Biggles, "we did some high skill, low altitude work, testing out half of the NATO force assigned to the exercise and-"

"What the fuck are you on?" asked Elliott, finally appearing to lose patience – something that no one, other than, perhaps, his wife, had ever witnessed.

Pete diffused the situation, "He's been on some unusual holidays hasn't he? I mean, didn't he go and visit a friend in Kuwait? And that place is dry. And then last year didn't he go driving around the Joshua Tree National Park in Nevada or California or wherever it is?"

Bill agreed, "Doesn't he always try to add an interesting visit onto every work trip?"

"So is that why he always goes by himself?" asked Biggles.

Grant arrived home. The house was in darkness. No one home and no messages.

Where had they gone?

Would they be back?

One of the cats walked in. He bent and stroked his head – of the two cats this was his favourite – a character Tom called Ginby – because it was a ginger tabby – the cat rolled over and he tickled its stomach until the scratching from its back claws became uncomfortable. He took a can from the pantry, opened it and emptied the foul fish-smelling contents into the cats' bowl. Having dealt with feeding the cats – not that he'd seen the other one - he looked in the fridge to find something for himself; he hadn't eaten anything warm since a bacon bun from a caravan by the A66 near Penrith early the previous morning; nothing attracted him.

He took his jacket off and threw it over the bar stool by the drinks cabinet.

Temptation.

No, he would make a hot drink and have an early night. He returned to the fridge. No milk. No option then. He took a bottle opener from the drawer and wandered over to the wine racks. There's got to be more to life than this.

Shit, he should walk Eric and Ernie.

And he could feel his stomach growl at him.

He shouted for the dogs as he went to collect a warm coat from the laundry.

Neither appeared.

Strange.

And he couldn't hear them.

Where were they?

Unconsciously he asked Ginby, "Where are the two daft lads?"

He ignored the absence of any reply.

"Have they been kidnapped by aliens?"

Still no reply.

He wandered around aimlessly, eventually arriving in his study. A pile of post – probably comprised of her bills – for clothes she would never wear – lay neatly in the centre of his desk. He slumped into his chair and grabbed at the pile. The top envelope bore her unmistakable hand writing 'Grant'.

Had she left him?

Was this her farewell letter of guilt and apology?

Was she intending suicide?

Was this her farewell note?

But what about the girls?

And Eric and Ernie?

His mind raced; with a perverse excitement.

Had she run off with someone?

Who?

Susan?

Why had she taken the dogs?

He felt the urge to open the envelope but also didn't want to; didn't want to for fear of being disappointed. But disappointed in what way?

That it was actually a shopping list or that it really was a suicide note and he'd never see her again? Never hear her laugh again. Never feel her arms around him again. Never nibble her ears again. Bollocks. That was all history.

He tore the envelope open.

Grant No 'dear'.

As you know Bit formal. Anyway, I know nothing. ***I've been under immense pressure recently and need a break*** Pressure from what? ***Accordingly I have gone on holiday*** Holiday! Fucking holiday! Another fucking holiday! ***with Susan*** That bitch! Fucking typical ***and have taken the girls and the dogs. We will be back sometime next week.*** Well thank you.

Where?

When?

What did she mean 'on holiday with Susan' with the kids as an add-on? Surely it should be the other way round? Fuck, I would have liked a holiday! And when was this planned? How come I only find out now?

He seethed.

He crumpled up the note before angrily reading it again.

Accordingly I have gone on holiday! Supercilious bitch.

And no 'love and kisses!' She hasn't even signed it! Cow.

Grant rose, wearily, from his chair and walked over to the window. If it hadn't been dark he would have been able to see the impressive, rolling peaks of the Hambleton Hills; instead he could see the rivulets of rain racing each other down the pane and the hazy lights of the village, shimmering through the rain on his window; like a watercolour painting where the colours have run. He loved the sound of heavy rain against a window; it brought back childhood memories.

Memories of long, boring days in his Grandfather's lounge. His Grandfather had a been a 'top bloke', it was just that his parents had always made him sit in his lounge – no toys to play with, no television, nothing – just his own thoughts[67]. It had been like some sort of torture. And it had always rained. Patter patter, against the glass windows.

Then, when he'd been a teenager, he'd spent many happy weekends camping.

Days spent orienteering.

Or canoeing.

Or climbing.

Or messing about – killing time on totally aimless fun like only a teenage boy could.

Then the camp fire meals. Tasteless canned food which seemed like a banquet fit for a king. Sometimes washed down by a few cans of illegally acquired beer. Luxury!

And at the end of the day, sleeping under canvas.

Laughs.

Dirty jokes for the immature.

Sneaked cigarettes.

Stories about certain sisters.

Stories which they laughed at, but didn't really understand.

And, if it wasn't icy cold, it rained. And however hard the rain was it would sound like a storm on the canvas. And the smaller the tent, the heavier the rain.

Happy memories. Happy days.

His mind wandered to the memory of a day at the cricket. There had been no play due to the rain and they had been 'forced' to spend the afternoon drinking in a corporate hospitality tent; one of his guests had referred to the sound of the rain and had likened it to a caravanning holiday; Grant smiled: it wasn't just him.

---

[67] And the thoughts of the average six to ten year old are not going to entertain anyone for long are they?

He turned away from the window, the proverbial storm clouds returning to his head.

It wasn't fair.

What had he done to deserve this?

Why couldn't it be made alright? Whatever 'it' was.

Why couldn't he simply turn into someone else?

Someone good looking. He could then enjoy shaving.

Someone successful but not over worked. He could then enjoy life to the full.

Someone in control of his life and his aspirations.

Someone in love with his wife and family.

Someone with well adjusted children who loved and respected their father; so they could all enjoy each others' company.

Someone with a happy, loving wife; a wife who was understanding, loyal, caring and pretty shit hot in bed.

"FATFUCKINGCHANCE." Grant was surprised by the fact that he spoke aloud and by the harshness of his voice.

He shook himself.

Was he going mad?

Had he gone mad?

Was he about to go mad?

Was this the early stages of his future suicide?

He was in the lay-by of life and it was far from comfortable.

Grant shrugged and then felt a shiver down his spine.

Bet that was her! The fucking cow!

Twenty Seven

The second Friday in April. It had been damp for days. It hadn't rained much. It had just been wet and cool. Misty. A damp mist, knowing at everyone's weak points; the future arthritis sites. Miserably wet and cool.

The bar in The Urra was relatively full. Drinkers stood two to three deep around the bar, causing access issues for the regulars who, as usual, were sitting around 'their' table.

Elliott was hugging his pint to his chest whilst issuing forth on the subject of the day, "Manchester United were nothing more than a flash in the pan."

Frank shook his head, "You're not serious?"

"Aye, and they've always been supported by footballing ignoramuses, fashion followers and your basic model prats."

"Oh come on Elliott," countered Eric, "the records speak for themselves."

Elliott shook his head, "I speak as I find."

"Oh now come on," blustered Eric, "you're an academic type of person, you should know better."

"And I do, and they were nothing more than professional cheats when they were successful."

Eric had taken the bait, "Oh Elliott that really is absolute nonsense."

"How many penalties were awarded against them at home?"

"Oh well, you can't expect me to know facts like that."

"So what about the way they were trained to intimidate the officials?"

Eric stuttered, "Well, er er er, I think that that is nothing more than a malicious rumour."

"So prove it."

Grant interrupted, "Elliott, why are you being such an awkward twat?"

Elliott grinned.

Eric squirmed.

Buster giggled and then started, "what do people mean when they say the computer went down on them?"

Eric was quick to answer, "It means it crashed."

General laughter erupted with a great deal of 'You stupid bastard' type comments aimed at Eric. He eventually got Buster's joke and blushed (internally).

Bill frowned, "I expected better from you."

Buster giggled.

Pete stroked his beard and asked, "Who[68] was it who said that the problem is that God gives men a brain and a penis and only enough blood to run one of them at a time?"

Frank looked up from his pint, "And your point is what?"

"Sid James[69]?" offered Grant.

"Your wife?" suggested Elliott.

"I loved the Sid James' laugh," continued Grant, to himself.

"Did you make it up?" asked Neil.

"No, you dim wit," replied Elliott, somewhat too harshly.

Bill nodded sagely, "It's true though, isn't it, a man carries his intelligence around in his pants and, as soon as he makes one little mistake, all Hell breaks lose and he's looking at a lifetime of poverty, shame, helplessness and solitude."

Grant grunted. That's what he had; and his Little Tommy had never been naughty.

---

[68] Robin Williams, a US comedian and actor, popular during the later part of the twentieth century.
[69] A typically British comedian and actor of the mid-twentieth century

"Your wife been away?" asked Pete.

Grant grunted and tried to change the subject, "Mind, I never liked Manchester United."

"Where she been?" asked Pete.

Grant didn't exactly know. The girls had mumbled something about 'the Lakes' but had been too preoccupied with homework, boys, shopping and boys to give him a full answer. She had barely spoken to him since they got back; other than to scold him for blocking the toilet in 'her bathroom'. He could not remember any discussion which concluded with a decision that the en suite shower room was 'hers' and the other bathroom was everyone else's' – which given the age of his daughters meant that he had big problems – unless he was up really early. And it spooked him how he always seemed to block, or be blamed for blocking, her toilet. As far as he was aware he didn't change his 'habits' between toilets – so why did this one keep 'blocking?' And why was it always him?

"Where did she go?" asked Pete.

And it always took some effort to unblock it. And every time he'd unblocked it he had then poured all sorts of cleaning fluids down it and had then checked the drains outside to see if he could see anything. But no, he never found anything to identify the culprit or cause so, in the meantime, which meant until the end of time, it was his fault.

"Which bit of the question don't you understand?"

"Sorry Pete, my mind was miles away."

"No probs Grant, everything OK?" Pete was genuinely concerned. And Grant realised and appreciated it. Grant winked at Pete before standing up "My round you bums, who wants what?"

"About fucking time too," announced Elliott.

Bill looked at Buster. Elliott's manner was changing, and not for the best.

Eric guffawed, unnecessarily, and replied, "Oh I'll have one of those Cod Beck thingies."

Elliott mimicked him, "I'll have one of those Cod Beck thingies."

Eric looked at Elliott, shook his head and turned to Buster, "Going racing tomorrow?"

Frank, sheepishly, asked for a lager, his requests being met with howls of derision.

Bill, Buster and Pete all requested the 'same again' and Grant turned and approached the bar, hoping that Lucinda would serve him.

"Now then trouble, what's it this time," asked Kate; blonde and young, for some reason Grant had never warmed to her.

"Thanks, four Cod Beck, three Whitby and a pint of the yellow fizzy with a cocktail cherry for old Frankie."

Grant watched Kate as she pulled the beers; each one was short and he quietly asked her to fill them up properly. She looked angry, hurt. Grant hated it when he was made to feel guilty when he'd done nothing wrong. He didn't ask if she wanted a drink. He could feel that, as a person, he was becoming 'harder' – perhaps more unlike-able. Bollocks to it. He took a long pull from his pint before transferring those he had just acquired to the table.

Pete was holding court. "So just read the label and do what it says."

"Eh?" asked Buster.

"Take two aspirin and keep away from children."

"Eh?" repeated Buster.

"Brilliant advice in my opinion," replied Pete.

"I think that those are two separate instructions," suggested Frank, missing the point as usual.

"Were you born stupid?" asked Elliott.

Frank ignored him.

Pete continued, "You know how the government tells us that we are eating too many pies and dying of heart disease, then in the next breath they're telling us we are living too long and there'll be no more pension money left for us. Well, I wish they'd make their minds up."

"Bollocks," commented Elliott.

"Did I hear that your family has been away," asked Bill, trying to change the subject.

Grant moved uncomfortably in his chair and was saved by Pete. "Do you know that it is illegal in some countries for a man to have sex with a woman and her daughter at the same time?"

"Is that true Grant?" asked Elliott.

Grant looked confused.

Elliott persisted, "Do you have sex with your wife and one of your daughters at the same time?"

Grant lifted the index finger of his right hand.

"Thank you Elliott," replied Pete.

Grant looked at the remains of his pint. He wanted another now; not when whoever's turn it was finished his. He couldn't go and get another round. Should he go home? What for?

He sat back, removing himself from the ongoing conversation, but listening for any more barbed comments.

"They're all a pack of wankers," concluded Elliott.

"If you say so," agreed Buster, to avoid any further discussion.

Bill was explaining the history of the local rail network; no one had asked him to; no one was particularly interested; not even Elliott could stop him. "So the junction was down at the end of the lane and tracks went up the valley to the mines, they closed years ago but the through line was there until just before the last war, in fact that lovely house where the Smithers-Jones clan live was the railway station and their garage was an engine shed or something similar. We walked along the line of the old route the other day and, do you know, it is fascinating what you see in hedgerows and so on."

Bill had Grant's full attention; others were fidgeting.

"Over the bank you can see the foundations of an old signal box and what may have been animal loading docks. Isn't it amazing to think that, once upon a time, you could have walked down the road and got a train to London?"

"It would have taken days though," interrupted Elliott.

"Yes, but that's not the point is it," countered Bill, "the point is that you could have taken a train to the coast, Whitby or Redcar, or down to Northallerton and then the world was your oyster."

Elliott interrupted, "Your oyster! What a daft phrase."

"Where's this signal box?" asked Grant.

Elliott folded his arms across his chest and leant forwards, "Bet you were a fucking trainspotter."

Grant looked at Elliott. What was his problem?

"Where the old lines meet over by Whorltone, you can see layout of all of the old foundations if you walk up the hill past the Smithers-Jones place and then look back down, over the wall, up near the phone box."

"Riveting!"

"Shut up Elliott!"

"Oh yes, Grant sir, yes siree, are you going to close me down?"

Grant shifted in his seat, "Haway Elliott, give it a rest."

Elliott grunted.

Grant turned his gaze back to Bill, "You were saying?"

"You were saying," mimicked Elliott.

Grant started, "You fucking," and then stopped himself.

Elliott stared at Grant and Grant returned it; both decided to let the moment pass.

Twenty Eight

Rain. Rain. Rain. Well, it was April. The third Wednesday in April to be precise. And the showers were keeping the numbers down in The Urra.

"Somewhat inclement isn't it," announced Buster, to no one in particular.

"Yes it is," mocked Elliott in a horsey accent.

Buster gritted his teeth.

Biggles put his glass down with a flourish, "I hear that Bannister is working away again." He had never liked Grant; he wasn't sure why. Perhaps it was Grant's annoying ability to see the funny side of everything; or his habit of hitting the spot every time he tried to goad him.

"It's not permanent or anything, he's just working on some deal down in North Wales." Pete paused, "I expect he'll be back in here on Saturday, talking in an awful Welsh accent, telling us tales of sex with sheep and recounting stories of how he found something earth shattering – or as earth shattering as anything could be in the life of an accountant."

Buster grunted, "But it must be interesting, seeing lots of different businesses and travelling."

"One number looks pretty much like any other fucking number."

"Interesting point Elliott, but it beats ploughing the same field everyday."

"But you don't plough anything Buster, you under pay some daft bastard to do it for you."

Buster recoiled in exaggerated hurt at the barbed comment, "No no no, I do plough, occasionally."

"Yeah, like fuck you do."

"Do you swear so much at school?" enquired Bill, who was becoming tired of Elliott's manner and language. Both were deteriorating; quickly.

"Only in retaliation, which I usually like to get in first."

"Do you think he enjoys it?" asked Buster, hastily changing the subject.

"He used to love it, talked about it all the time, but now," Pete paused, "not sure, but I don't think so."

"What changed?" Buster was genuinely interested.

Pete took a deep breath, "Well, where do I start? Firstly, the fun has gone out of it, if you know what I mean. Second, the wazzock factor has increased and third, it's just too damn hard to earn a decent wedge these days."

"Wazzock factor?" asked Buster.

"What fun has gone out of it? added Bill.

"Fuckwits" commented Elliott.

"Do we care," a statement not a question from Biggles.

"Well, bugger me, where do I start, if you're wanting a serious answer?"

And it was a long story, a story which started some fifteen years previously:

Pete had first met Grant at a lunch given by his Bank: Grant had been a guest, having recently joined a local firm of accountants as junior partner. Pete's first impression had been of a fun loving but shy, sharp minded but caring individual. Grant had always claimed that he had drawn the short straw in being seated between Pete and a characterless lawyer, some thirty years his senior; the truth was that the two of them were completely different in outlook and interests to all of the other guests and, as a result, spent three hours talking, eating and drinking, at the Bank's expense, before spending the afternoon in a number of hostelries. The purpose of the lunch was for the Bank to develop its network of income generating intermediaries; as such it prima facie seemed a success that Pete and Grant so quickly developed a close relationship.

And every month for the next decade Grant and Pete would lunch – liquid lunches, solids being banned. They would invite each other to numerous corporate hospitality events; they would entertain each other on their expense accounts; and they would religiously avoid spoiling such occasions by discussing anything to do with their respective jobs.

Pete's career in the Bank peaked as he struggled to adapt to the changing management style of his seniors and he was sidelined during a number of restructuring exercises: but this did not upset him and he was fundamentally happy.

Grant's career moved forwards at a phenomenal rate; he moved up his firm's hierarchy, steadfastly refusing to play 'politics' and focussing on client service issues; he overcame the negative attitudes of many of his senior colleagues by hard work and results. But many would not accept him: he recognised this but ignored it. And this upset many. Some saw it as arrogance. Some just didn't like the young 'upstart'.

Grant led by example; work hard, play hard. He expected the same from his staff; and looked after those who worked hard. He didn't suffer fools and struggled to hide his negative views of staff who failed to meet his high standards.

As his practice grew he was forced to delegate much of the work which had previously interested him, and expanded his management team; he was forced to focus more time on practice management, losing contact with many of his clients and being unable to undertake as much client facing work as he would want. And, over time, the rate of growth and profit performance deteriorated. Grant believed that the problems were caused by a number of underperforming individuals; those very same, politically astute individuals had started pointing the proverbial finger at Grant long before he started to realise.

Grant had developed a network of bankers and lawyers, who he socialised with, gave work to, received work from and who respected him. Socialising meant late nights, rich food and excess alcohol.

As time moved on this form of 'networking' became increasingly marginalised and the time he could commit to it became restricted – due to his internal management responsibilities.

Eventually, and not unsurprisingly, Grant's supply of new work dried up. And then the pressure and criticism had built up.

Grant was sitting in an office overlooking the production line of a food manufacturing plant in Oswestry.

"I'll never eat this shit again," Grant sniffed.

"Can't be healthy," agreed Kate, "and it doesn't taste too good."

"Fucking convenient, but probably carcinogenic!"

"Is it time to call a day?" asked Kate.

Grant looked at his watch, "Aye, you take the team back to the hotel and feed them, I'll do a bit more here and join you in the bar later."

"And so," continued Pete, "his success worked against him and there are as many people who love him as hate him; obviously it's the ones who hate him, for whatever reasons, are the most vocal."

"Bugger me," concluded Bill.

Pete nodded at Bill, "So now he is trying to run a practice with both hands tied behind his back and is getting grief from all sides."

"And he gets fuck all support at home," added Frank.

"So how long has this been going on?" asked Buster.

"Everything peaked for him about three years ago; he was doing excellent work, delivering top of the table results and then he seemed to lose it; and the poor bastard doesn't know why. And then, with changes in policy, policies with which he fiercely disagrees, he has been unable to turn it round."

Bill shook his head, "Poor bastard."

"You know he helped me out big style," started Frank, "so I've met a number of his partners and staff and I'll tell you that Pete has put his finger on it. There's a couple of halfwits who slag him off all the time, not realising that it is down to his efforts that they've earned good sums for the past few years."

Pete grunted.

"And the biggest mistake I made was in not doing exactly what he told me to do, but never has he said 'I told you so' or anything similar," Frank finished loudly, "The poor bastard!"

"Bollocks."

Elliott's contribution was immediately rejected by Pete, "You know, there are times that it worries me that the future of this country is in the hand of mindless losers like you. You haven't a clue about the big, bad, real world, have you? You inconsiderate, sarcastic twat."

Buster was visibly upset by Pete's tirade, "Steady on."

Grant was buying a round for his staff; he was tired and would have preferred to be in bed or in his own company with a decent bottle of red.

"Do you think we'll finish this week?" asked Kate.

"That purchase ledger clerk is a real beauty," commented Graham, an arrogant third year student who Grant would merrily thump if circumstances permitted.

David, one of the tax team, changed the subject, "I can't believe the fact that the vendor is paying our client to take the business away."

"Would you buy the business?" asked Will, an extremely naive but potentially able first year student.

I could do without this thought Grant. He fixed Kate with a stare and smiled, "Yes, I think so, as long as they produce the goods on time, your team has worked well so I think we will." He turned to David, "It does seem strange but it's all about opportunity costs; it would cost them more to close it or try and turn it around themselves so, to them, giving our lot six million to take the problem away seems good, and, of course, they don't know that we think that it can be turned round for less than four million and," he turned to Will, "that is why, yes, unless you guys find anything during the next couple of days, yes I would buy the business."

Both Will and David rushed to ask further questions but Kate, knowing Grant well, stopped them, "How about a game of snooker? Me and Will against you two? I guess you'll be off to read the draft report?" Grant nodded. He really liked Kate.

"So, anyway," Pete was in full flow, "Grant says to this girl 'Your face must turn a few heads' and she replies, without hesitation 'And I guess yours turns a few stomachs' and Grant, the daft bastard that he is, then says 'So, what do you do for a living' and she replies 'I'm a female impersonator' and Grant, for the only time in all the years that I've known him was completely and utterly silenced, lost for fucking words, dumb struck!"

"Bollocks!" uttered Elliott.

Biggles leant forwards, "I asked a girl once what her sign was, you know, like Cancer or Leo, and she says to me 'Do not enter', which I thought was pretty clever."

"Did you shag her?" asked Elliott.

Bill shook his head and sighed, "Elliott, you need to give it a rest."

Twenty Nine

It was one of those delightful May evenings; one when it is a positive pleasure to be outside, enjoying the smells and sounds of the countryside. The singing of numerous birds and the cacophony of sounds from the grazing animals; the lush sweet smell of the gentle breeze and the wonderful glowing ball of the sun slowly beginning to fall in the western sky. The brook through the centre of Watson Humphrey babbled away happily; if water bearing media could display any form of emotion.

The garden at the front of The Urra was populated by a mixture of courting couples, resplendent in shorts and tasteful T-shirts, bikers, suffering in leather leggings, and families with high volume offspring; offspring who made frequent visits to the cool and relative darkness of the bar in the unconscious hope of consuming sufficient fizzy to cover the rear seat of the parental motor car with projectile vomit.

"Should be fucking banned," commented Elliott on his delayed return to the table, "Grant was right in his views on learner drinkers and kids in bars."

"Someone rattled your cage?" More of a statement than a question from Biggles.

"And you?"

The Biggles jaw dropped, "Excuse me."

"You should be fucking banned as well."

Biggles knew Elliott well enough to appreciate that he was joking; or was he? Elliott had certainly seemed grumpy recently; strange, as Elliott had never been known to be anything other than

238

'Elliott'; piss-taker, happy drinker, laugher at bad jokes, and all-round good guy. Whatever, it seemed best to change the subject.

"Have you seen Grant lately?"

"No."

"Is he away?"

"How do I fucking know?"

"Thought you might have heard."

"Well I haven't."

Biggles looked towards the door, hoping that he would be saved by the arrival of Frank or Pete or Bill. Even Ben!

Elliott took a long pull of his pint and continued, "I think that he's been abducted by aliens."

"Excuse me?"

"I said that I think that he's been fucking kidnapped by fucking aliens."

"What's up with you?"

Elliott smirked, "Only the corners of my mouth."

Biggles shook his head and sat back in his seat, having decided that silence was the best form of conversation. Elliott drained his pint with some gusto and placed the empty glass, with a hollow sounding thump, on the table, in front of a surprised looking Biggles. Elliott folded his arms and sat back, waiting for Biggles.

The front door of The Urra opened and a beam of yellowy light stretched from the entrance to the bar; it was as if the sun's light was being purposely aimed directly through the doorway, the yellowy light seeming to move in the cigarette smoke atmosphere. This was an entrance which Neil could not have planned, but his silhouette in the doorway, resembling an alien being in 'Close Encounters of The Third Kind'[70], was both awesome and welcome.

---

[70] An epic and successful movie about aliens visiting the Earth; written off by Grant as complete "shite" as a result of the piece where the aliens and human beings communicate by musical fog horns. "Complete fucking shite"; another example of Grant being out of step with the views of the majority.

Biggles sighed and then clapped his hands in applause, "Neat entrance Neil, very neat."

"Seen Grant on your travels?" asked Elliott, the relevance of the question being completely lost on both Neil and Biggles.

"Not seen him for weeks," replied Neil as he walked over to where Elliott and Biggles were sitting, "Should be outside in gorgeous weather like this."

Two sharp intakes of breath.

Elliott leant forwards, "Sunshine gives you cancer, kids in beer gardens give you piles…and fresh air makes beer go off."

"Anyone like to join me in a pint?" enquired Neil, somewhat breathlessly.

Elliott scratched his chin, then shook his head, "Not enough room."

Biggles grinned, "And a tadge too wet for me."

"The usual then?" replied Neil.

Grant was driving north on the M6; approaching Lancaster: he and his assistant Kate had spent a long and difficult day in Wigan. Both wanted to get home; but for different reasons.

"Look at these fucking tossers sitting in the middle lane; lazy fucking bastards."

Kate said nothing.

"No one in the inside lane."

Kate understood Grant's point of view; agreed with him, but saw no point in letting it upset anyone.

"This lack of lane discipline is fucking illegal."

So's your speed, thought Kate.

"And these arseholes in Chelsea tractors think they own the bastard road."

"May be they do," replied Kate, wondering if they were being driven by the wives of rich men or drug crazed hoodlums.

"A mate of mine undertakes these tossers, I prefer flashing the bastards."

"What's the point?" enquired Kate, "neither of you are going to change their behaviour, whether it's wrong or not, and surely you're both guilty of illegalities."

Grant was silenced. He was shocked at Kate's outburst. And she was right. Why did he let the tossers annoy him?

Kate was looking out of the side window. They were now climbing towards Shap; a beautiful drive at anytime of the year. Grant looked at the tops of her legs. The lycra covered gap between her knees and the hem of her skirt. She always wore relatively short skirts, even though her legs were less than fantastic. She wasn't that attractive, physically, but she was a good person; she made him laugh, she worked hard and she told him when he was out of order. He felt an urge to touch her thigh; shook his head and gave himself an "internal talking to".

"All the same, it's a shame I can't have machine guns and rocket launchers fitted to the front of my car."

"You'd miss."

"True."

Poor, lonely bastard, thought Kate. "Thought the meeting went well until Rex started banging on about that tax fee."

"Aye, but he was right about that bill, it was unnecessary and unauthorised work, and, oh look at this convoy of fucking caravans! Shouldn't be allowed!"

"Yes, and you accepted that, but he wouldn't move on, he had to keep moaning about it."

"Attrition, it's his style, that and being a natural boring bastard, and I don't think his wife listens to him, or even lets him speak at home, so he has to go on and on at us and, after all, he is paying us for the pleasure."

Kate grinned "Bollocks, I bet he bores her to death as well!"

"Oh look at these farts in the middle lane."

241

"I bet Rex hogs the middle lane."

"Too right; and I bet he drives with his front and rear fog lights on as the response to some form of penile deformity."

"I expect he was good looking and a bit of a charmer in his younger days."

Grant laughed, "Now I know you've lost it Kate!"

Kate smiled. She liked Grant. Yes, he was a pain in the arse. Yes he swore too much. Yes, he worked people hard. But he was always fair; would never ask anyone to do anything he couldn't do himself, and he worked no one harder than he worked himself. And he was great company; at times.

And he had lovely blue eyes.

"Have I told you the story about the bloke who hired a hit man to kill his wife?"

"Twice."

"Sorry, oh would you just look at this daft bugger in the outside lane."

"Do you reckon that Rex will change auditors?"

"Given the poor service from our colleagues in tax, yes, I wouldn't blame him, but I think not" Grant paused "I think you did a cracking job on him this afternoon, regained his confidence, he clearly warmed to you, no, I think he'll stay with us."

"Thanks."

"No cause for thanks, it's your fault that we'll have to keep coming over here! Your fault that I'll have to listen to his stories of selling his equipment in various exotic corners of the world! Your fault that I'll have to suffer that fucking awful coffee which leaves a coating on your teeth for weeks."

Kate grinned; she knew that he was joking; and she was delighted that he was pleased with her performance.

"Think I'll cut the corner and join the A66 at Brough."

Elliott sat, scowling. His furrowed brow forcing his eyes to squint.

"You OK?" asked Neil.

"And what's it to you?"

"Give it a break Elliott" suggested Frank.

Elliott grunted. He knew he was out of order. He wasn't sure why. He just felt angry; all the time.

"Sorry guys, my shout."

"Pint of the Hedgehog for me please," asked Neil.

"Same," agreed Biggles.

"Have to be a lager for me."

"You puff, Frank," replied Elliott; smiling, this time.

Elliott walked over to the bar.

"What's got into him?" whispered Neil.

Frank leant forwards, "Look, I'm not sure, and keep this to yourselves, but I think his wife has done a bunk."

Neil sat back, shocked.

Biggles exploded, "You're joking!"

"Shhhhh!"

"Sorry Frank."

"When?" asked Biggles.

"Does it matter?" replied Frank.

"Isn't the question why?" suggested Neil.

Frank brought the discussion to an abrupt end, "Well, that's as maybe, but it's none of our business."

Elliott returned from the bar with the first beers, "Here you go."

"Thanks."

"Cheers."

Frank looked at the straw and cherry in his lager, "Tosser!"

Elliott grinned and returned to the bar.

Frank took a pull from his drink, "Poor bugger, got to feel sorry for him."

Neil couldn't help himself, "But why?"

"Shut it," growled Frank.

"And look at this tosser." Grant was in full flow.

"Who was it said that arrogance is the full sister of ignorance?"

"Ruben Zuniga," replied Grant, failing to pick up on the relevance of Kate's question, before continuing, "driving with a sodding caravan in the same style he would drive if he didn't have a mobile pre-fab hooked to his rear end."

Kate looked at the passing moor land. She looked heavenward. He couldn't help himself; he simply couldn't help himself.

"Mary had a little lamb, her father shot it dead, now it goes to school with her, between two hunks of bread," Elliott sat grinning, clearly proud of his poetry.

"Shite," replied Biggles.

"Or, or...how about Hey diddle diddle, the cat took a piddle, all over the bedside clock, the little dog laughed to see such fun, then died of electric shock."

Frank shook his head, "Absolutely awful."

"Mary had a little pig, she kept it fat and plastered, and when the price of pork went up, she shot the little bastard." Elliott guffawed.

Biggles looked at Frank and shook his head.

Neil broke ranks and giggled.

Encouraged, Elliott continued, "Jack and Jill went up the hill, to have a little fun, stupid Jill forgot the pill, and now they have a son."

Biggles looked at Elliott, "Worse, definitely worse," and rose to get another round of drinks.

Elliott folded his arms, with a look of smug pride on his face "Brilliant eh?"

"No," was Frank's succinct response.

244

"Do you use these rhymes in your lessons?" asked Neil.

Elliott laughed.

Buster waved his hands about in mock horror, "As Thomas Cardinal Wolsey is supposed to have said 'be very careful what you put into that head, because you will never, ever get it out' and may that be the end of the matter."

Thirty

The first Sunday in May. A lovely day by any measure; unless one was sitting in a characterless, functional, air-conditioned office, several storeys above street level in a pretty grim Northern city.

Grant sat at his desk; he had been working through files of an old tax case, which had been the subject of threatened litigation since October.

It wasn't his client.

It wasn't his area of expertise.

He wasn't sure that he knew what he was doing.

He could see what had happened.

It wasn't his fault.

It was always the same people who let you down and then avoided the resultant problems.

He looked at the pile of questions from the lawyers acting for his firm; whose side where they on? He knew it wasn't personal, but it seemed like it was at times.

Bastards.

It wasn't his idea of how to spend a Sunday afternoon.

It was his responsibility and everyone responsible for the problem had absented themselves.

Twats. Lazy idle bastards.

Grant was not in the most positive frame of mind.

He was pretty comfortable that the advice had been pretty sound; the problem was that it had not been communicated clearly; and none of the arse-covering clauses had been used in any of the advice letters. So the client, a complete shit, had ignored bits of the advice, had not told Grant's former colleague the 'full story', and was now attempting to recover his deserved losses.

Twat.

Why hadn't he opted for a career as a leotard fitter? Sure, there would be occasions when he would want to delegate duties, but overall it would be a rewarding career.

Grant shook himself. Weren't men supposed to think about sex every seven minutes? Or was it seconds? It was years in his case.

Fuck fuck fuckety fuck fuck.

Elliott leant over the table and stage whispered, "I understand that Grant has opened a florists shop, in business with a close personal friend."

"Get away!"

"Would I have you on Neil?" asked Elliott.

"Yes, you would, you bastard" replied Neil.

Elliott grinned "But not this time, young man."

Neil shook his head "Read my lips, F U C K O F F."

Elliott nodded.

"I can imagine him cutting the ends off" offered Buster.

"Eh?" Neil was bemused.

"I bet he loves his daffodils," suggested Frank.

"Nah," interrupted Pete, "he hates the Welsh."

"But he's an accountant," pleaded Neil.

Pete beckoned for Neil to lean towards him, "You should drop that unnecessary O."

Neil smirked.

Frank looked bemused.

Buster waved his hands about, "Yes, I get it." He was clearly pleased with himself.

"The ends off what?" asked Ben.

Frank took a long draw on his drink, "I can just see him selling flowers."

"He's that sort of man, isn't he?" agreed Elliott "A complete and utter flower arranger.."

Neil stood up, "Oh, you guys, this is bollocks, my round?"

Ben looked up, "Half a Hedgehog if you're asking."

Elliott looked at Pete, "I understand that the vicar's wife has fallen in love with her golf instructor."

Pete shook his head, "I thought she'd fallen pregnant to her aerobics coach."

Elliott slammed his empty glass on the table, "Bloody hell, does the golf instructor know?"

Neil's jaw dropped.

"Not sure about that," replied Pete, "but I understand that the Bishop is less than pleased."

Ben was concentrating as hard as he could.

Elliott nodded at Pete, "What about the story about the vicar and his wife's brother?"

Pete grimaced, "True I believe, but the less said the better."

Elliott looked around the table, his gaze finally landing on Bill, "So, what about the stories about you and the vicar's wife?"

"Who was the Bishop shagging?" asked Neil.

Ben leant forwards "Eh?"

Grant was sitting in a police car; totally confused.

He had been driving home; the roads had been relatively quiet.

He had started feeling weary; well, it had been a long day and he had enjoyed a good drink the night before.

He had started considering stopping for a cup of coffee.

He wasn't sure what had happened next.

It had been unreal.

And it still seemed unreal.

Sliding along, at ninety degrees to the direction of travel, with his front end pushing that small blue Fiat.

It had seemed to be in slow motion; as if he was dreaming.

He had felt no fear.

And then they had come to a stop; and then he became aware of the scraping noises.

It had still seemed unreal; he just wanted to go home.

His air bags had not gone off.

Could he drive off?

Would that be legal?

He wanted to go home.

Oh fuck.

His car was crushed against the nearside crash barrier. Three other cars were involved. His radio was still playing; the commentary on some Sunday afternoon football match.

What had happened?

Was it his fault?

What had he done?

The police, ambulance and fire engines had arrived quickly.

It had still seemed unreal.

He just wanted to go home.

He had been breathalysed; clear; just.

Details had been taken.

Everyone had seemed professional.

What had happened? No one would tell him.

"You really are an awkward bastard," concluded Frank.

Elliott nodded, a grin stretching across his well-worn face, "I only do it to keep your weary and retired mind active."

"Times like this are when I miss Grant!"

"Bloody hell Frank, you need treatment!"

Frank stared at Elliott, "True, but you know what I mean."

Elliott sighed and lifted himself up, "OK, I'll get Grant's round, you just make sure he pays me for it."

Buster interrupted, "Not for me thank you, time to go as dinner will soon be ready and I'm off to York tomorrow, so I must show willing."

"Show willing?" mocked Elliott, "I've heard about your twenty second foreplay."

Buster waved his hands and scurried out, ignoring Elliott's final insult.

Pete rose, "Buster thinks foreplay is confined to the golf course, and it's time for me to go too."

Ben interrupted, "So, what's all this about the vicar's wife?"

Grant had telephoned home in the hope of arranging a lift.

"You've done what?"

"What do you mean? A write off?"

"Have you been drinking?"

"Did you hurt anyone?"

"Bloody typical!"

"And don't even think about borrowing mine."

"You bloody fool!"

"I have to go now, some of us are busy"

He was sitting in Darlington bus station; cold: tired: sore: in a form of shock.

He still didn't know what had happened.

What would happen now?

How would he get to work?

Had he fallen asleep?

He had meetings to re-arrange.

Was he safe to drive?

Would he get points?

It could have been worse.

Much worse.

He could have hurt someone.

Or worse.

And he was alright.

Bruised.

Shocked: but by his apparent stupidity more than the crash itself.

His pride hurt more than his body.

He shivered.

"Fucking hell!" he groaned.

Thirty One

The second Tuesday in May. Disappointingly dull. The Urra is relatively busy but is pretty much a 'home from home' for the regulars.

"Oi, Alf," shouted Elliott, "any chance of you putting the television on? These fuckers aren't talking tonight."

"No," returned Alf.

"Did you see the England match?" asked Elliott.

No one replied.

"Shite, wasn't it?"

Again no one replied.

"Not paid your licences?"

Buster looked up from his pint, "Waste of bloody money."

"Like fucking Easter eggs," offered Ben.

Again, no one replied, but this time due to surprise rather than laziness.

Elliott broke the silence, "You're all rude bastards, we think that the kids of today are ignorant and rude, but it's always been the case and they have just learnt from ignorant fuckers like you lot."

"That's a bit rich," responded Buster.

"I bet you're the sort of old tosser who doesn't even acknowledge the soft tart who holds a door open for you."

"Well, I've never been so insulted," started Buster before Elliott started again, "Manners, you, I, we have lost the art."

"Come on Elliott," interjected Bill, "manners are about how we encounter strangers and the reason we turn to manners is because we want to have some sort of framework where there is a sense of mutual respect and ease, and that makes life easier to get on with."

"Bollocks!"

"No Elliott, listen to me," continued Bill, "we want predictable ways of behaviour."

"Bollocks, what has that got to do with some arsehole driving his Chelsea tractor down the road like he owns it, which is a form of rudeness or bad manners, if you want to be so polite?"

"Christ, Elliott has morphed into Grant."

"Fuck off Bill," Elliott grinned before continuing, "Anyway, it's as much ignorance in the way of being inappropriately educated, probably by the parents, and that's why you get shit-heads shouting into mobile phones, people eating with their mouths open, twats parking in disabled bays and all that."

"Bring back hat tipping."

"Oh piss off Buster."

Biggles chuckled – unwisely - "He has turned into Grant."

"Aye, well, he was right unlike you, you cardboard fighter pilot you, what the fuck do you know, gallivanting all over the skies then boring the pants off us."

"Haway Elliott, that's out of order," started Frank.

Elliott raised his hands in mock surrender, "I know, sorry guys, I was out of order."

She was spread-eagled against his bathroom door, hands tied to the top of the door by velcro fastened wrist straps. A rubber ball gag fixed firmly in her mouth. He lifted himself up from his knees, rubbing his hands up her lycra clad thighs and over her black corset, stopping as his mouth reached her neck; he began biting at her shoulders and neck, nuzzling the underside of her jaw. He loved it when she dressed up for him and she had made a special effort tonight – the high heel black knee boots they had bought in York, black silky stockings, a black semi-transparent basque and long black pvc gloves – he had hit the jackpot this time. She moved against his every move and then returned the force of his mouth with her neck. She loved these games. She had introduced these little sessions into their love making; he had found them quite intimidating at first but now would often take the lead - he preferred it when she took charge of him but it was 'her turn' and this little game would finish with her tied to a tree in the garden. She was moaning; it sounded vaguely like a constrained 'cuckoo', but he knew she was either telling him 'love you' or was playing 'fuck you'. His hand held her firmly by the waist and he pulled his face away from her neck and looked her straight in the eyes. Her bright blue eyes sparkled as she stared back. "Time the naughty girl was blindfolded." She writhed in disagreement but this didn't stop him.

The telephone rang. It rang again and again and then he heard his wife answer it; shouting at an unnecessarily high volume. The kitchen was naturally noisy but when she started talking, it became positively deafening. It was her sister. This conversation would be long and loud.

Fuck, thought Grant, as he rolled over and put a pillow over his head.

"Has anyone heard how Grant is?" asked Frank.

"Eh?" replied Elliott.

"Apparently he was in a pile up on Sunday night, wrote off his and several other cars," explained Frank.

"Get away!"

"Straight up Elliott, hadn't you heard?"

Elliott was silenced.

Pete took control of the discussion, "He's basically alright but is very shaken up; he has no idea what happened and is concerned that there may be something wrong, you know, making it unsafe for him to drive."

"Like what?" asked Bill.

"Some form of sleeping disorder or something to do with that head injury he got down in London."

"What head injury?" asked Ben.

Pete ignored Ben, "It's more like he's been over working, his mind wandered, as it does with all of us, and bang bang bang."

Elliott shook his head, "Fuck, but that could happen to any of us, I mean, who hasn't been driving along and then realised that they've lost it for a few moments?"

"What head injury?" repeated Ben.

Pete took a pull from his pint, "Poor sod, he could be in big trouble."

"Always knew he was mentally ill," concluded Ben.

Pete snapped, "It was a rugby injury, many years ago and he is fucking alright now!"

Ben looked shocked and decided that silence was the preferred response.

Elliott looked round the table, "Can you cry under water?"

"What?" asked Bill.

Elliott persisted, "Or how important does a person have to be before they are considered assassinated instead of just murdered?"

Biggles made an embarrassed laughing sound.

Pete grunted, acknowledging the validity of the question. Elliott nodded at Pete, "So, why do you have to 'put your two cents in'…but it's only a 'penny for your thoughts'? Where is that extra penny going? And we all know about spending a penny don't we?"

"What the fuck are you on about?" asked Frank.

"Haway Frank," replied Pete, "They are all questions deserving of an answer."

"My name is Martin!"

Pete nodded, "Well done, Frank."

Elliott smirked, "Why does a round pizza come in a square box?

"Do I care?" replied Frank.

Pete scratched his chin, "Cost? Production efficiency?

Elliott ignored the attempted answers, "What disease did cured ham actually have?"

Pete persevered, "I guess you'd struggle to manufacture a suitably robust round box lid?"

Elliott nodded at Pete, "That's a maybe, but how is it that we put a man on the moon before we figured out it would be a good idea to put wheels on luggage?"

"Now that is a good question," replied Bill.

"Did you get these out of a book?" asked Buster.

Elliott giggled, "Yes, Grant's book of unanswered and totally useless questions."

Ben looked up, "So he's mad is he?"

"Ben!" shouted Pete.

Elliott rescued the situation, "Why is it that people say they 'slept like a baby' when babies wake up like every two hours?"

"So, is it a sleeping problem?" asked Buster.

Pete sighed, "I don't know, all I know is that Grant is concerned. Personally I think that he is simply shagged out and generally worn down, by the parasites he works with and lives with."

She was still talking: loudly.

His stomach was hurting; he had not eaten properly for several days. It would be nothing serious.

Was there really so much to talk about?

She never had anything to say to him.

Would he listen?

Was he interested?

Maybe she had a point.

Christ, his stomach hurt.

Why had he crashed?

Just a moment's loss of concentration. Or had he fallen asleep? Or blacked out?

Fuck.

She seemed to be getting louder. Or was it just him being hyper-sensitive?

Was it a feeling of loss, which made him hate her?

He had loved her.

He was pretty sure that he had loved her.

There had been a time when the simple sound of her voice had made him smile.

Now her voice grated.

There had been a time when he read her text messages or letters, over and over again.

In hindsight, she had rarely communicated with him in those ways.

There had been a time when other people would disappear into the background whenever she arrived.

Now he would look for others if she approached him.

He used to smile at the simplest passing thought about her.

Now he would grimace.

While thinking about her his heart would beat faster.

No change there!

And he still thought about her all the time.

But different thoughts.

Was there anyway back?

Had it been good or had he been deluding himself?

"I can't go home," announced Elliott, "I'm still sober!"

"Do you have to be drunk to go home?" queried Bill.

"No, but it certainly helps," replied Elliott.

"What utter bollocks," commented Pete.

"Is 'utter' a bank word for large?"

Pete shook his head; he would not give Elliott's quip the respect of a reply.

Thirty Two

The third Tuesday in May. The damp clung to the lawn outside The Urra as if it had been sprayed with a silver silk. The dampness in the air made bones feel old; encouraged arthritic joints to misbehave and created a dull atmosphere – even in the bar of The Urra, even as afternoon effortlessly spiralled downwards into dusk.

Frank was smoking in a sort of peaceful, almost contented silence.

Ben, eyes screwed up, glasses gripped in his right hand, was attempting to read the evening newspaper, passing comment on the stories of the day. "Fourteen year old kids killed in a stolen car and the parents blame the fuzz[71], something is wrong somewhere."

Elliott was concentrating on his early evening rehydration.

Neil was staring at his pint, possibly in the hope that some great philosophical thought would come to him.

Eric was looking at the inhabitants of the other tables.

"Says here that the parents are going to sue the authorities."

"Why is phonetic misspelt?" asked Elliott, to no one in particular.

Eric coughed, "Sorry Ben, what was that?"

"These bloody folk from Redcar[72] are going to sue the authorities."

---

[71] Old fashioned slang for "the police".
[72] A town on the North East coast, east of Middlesbrough and across the Tees Bay from Hartlepool. Possibly once attractive, it has been blighted by the growth and subsequent decline of a number of basic industries. Long, wide, sandy beaches. Tatty. Even the donkeys ran away.

"Sorry Ben," Eric persisted.

"Their kids stole a car, raced it around and then totalled it into a lamp post."

Eric knew he would regret not changing the subject, "So why sue?"

"Money!"

"Yes, obviously, but on what grounds?"

"'Cos they're greedy, thieving twats?" suggested Eric.

"No, it is because the authorities should have stopped their perfectly formed children from misbehaving and finding themselves in danger," Ben folded his arms having finished this particular dialogue, in his opinion.

"But that's bizarre!" continued Eric.

"High dungeon," shouted Elliott.

"What?"

"That's what you are in, I think, not that I know what it means," replied Elliott.

Eric shook his head, took a long drink and continued, "No, how can these people sue the authorities when it is their offspring who broke the law?"

"Says here that a bloke has been caught drinking petrol from fuel pumps in petrol stations," mumbled Ben, folding the newspaper so that he could hold it closer to his eyes.

"Is he related?" asked Eric.

"Who to?" responded Elliott.

"The dead boys!" Eric was clearly becoming frustrated.

Elliott paused, thought and adopted a sincere, but somewhat pained expression, "Obviously."

Ben folded the paper in such a way that it was now less than inviting to any future reader, "Nothing on TV tonight, waste of money."

Eric was still troubled, "But it's so shocking."

Elliott nodded. Where's Grant or Pete he thought. I might have to go home in search of decent conversation and humour. He shook himself. "Righto, my round, who's on what?"

Grant was almost fifty miles away; tidying his desk and putting papers in his briefcase; rushing. He was supposed to be at home in forty minutes, to look after the girls while the wife went out for a 'much deserved evening out' – well that was how she described it. Her humour had totally lapsed when he had asked if they couldn't go out together. Well, it had been a daft question; had it? Why? Buggered if he could work it out! He hurriedly put his jacket on and raced out of his office and straight into one of the cleaning staff. He apologised, sincerely. She looked at him as if she had just stood in something. Another good night ahead, concluded Grant. And he couldn't even have a blast on the way home – he had forgotten to load the hire car with CDs and would be forced to listen to the radio – other peoples' choices of music or opinionated commentators talking to bullshitting officials or elected representatives of some form. Fuck.

Elliott had farted. He had the enviable ability to quieten down any group of people by silently dropping a mixture of gases produced by a lifetime's drinking. He would usually follow the 'drop' by staring at Grant; he was the easiest target; for anything. "I'm going to start a magazine," he announced, "in honour of, and dedicated to drunks."

"Now, now Elliott," Bill shook his head, smiling at Elliott like an embarrassed father frowning at his eldest child.

"Yes, this unrepresented and oppressed under class needs a mouthpiece."

"Elliott you are talking tosh."

"Billy baby, you are wrong, I am going to dedicate the remaining sober hours of my temporary existence on this old planet of ours to the publication of a monthly magazine for the professional drunk."

"No, you're teasing."

"Am not Billy, me old mucker, and you could be one of my first investors…oh yes indeedee, you could earn a subscription for life for a reasonable up front capital sum…shame Grant's not here to use some big words and talk general financial bollocks, but hey, I'll get by."

"No Elliott!" Bill sat erect, "And stop calling me Billy Boy!"

"Go for it Billy Baby, this is an act of the highest social responsibility you could imagine, or at least see in double through your average pair of beer goggles."

Bill drained his glass and looked at Elliott; he felt distinctly uncomfortable. Was Elliott serious?

"We'll have special sections for alcohol counsellors, reviews of drinks and bars, stories of record breaking vomiting sessions, and our very own specialist doctor…you know, dear doctor, I've just had fourteen gin and tonics and have a minor brain trauma, can I go hang-gliding?"

"Sheila, can I get you a drink?"

"You bugger," replied Elliott, "no bugger has called me that for yonks, but, cheers Bill, for that you get a free, autographed copy of the first edition."

Bill stood up. "Thank you."

Grant entered the kitchen to a decidedly chilly reception. No words were exchanged. The three women sitting at the breakfast bar finished their drinks and, in the style of formation dancers, got up, collected their belongings and walked past him. Not even his wife gave him eye contact. The kitchen door was slammed.

He took his jacket off and surveyed the kitchen.

The breakfast bar supported an assortment of spirits and mixers. Several empty glasses, with thawing ice cubes, cherries and the remains of drinks, were scattered about. The kitchen table was clear, other than for what looked like a pile of bills requiring his attention.

He looked in the fridge; to no surprise he saw that nothing had been left for him.

Grant sighed. Another day of toil in the name of his beloved family was coming to an end. Thank fuck.

Medoc or Chianti?

His stomach ached.

Straight to bed?

At my age!

He pulled a corkscrew from a drawer.

Thirty Three

The final Friday in May. One of those days when it is almost a delight to be in England[73].

The sun had shone all day. The clouds were high, white and wispy. The breeze was gentle and clean.

"Absolutely lovely walk round Wireltune, lovely summer evening, Audrey and I thoroughly enjoyed it, the sheep calling in the fields, an all pervading sense of peace about the place."

"Here we go again," groaned Biggles.

Elliott interrupted Bill, "Were the sheep worried about what you'd do to them or what you were doing to Audrey?"

"Grow up Elliott."

"Okay."

"Anyway, where was I?"

"See, his memory has gone."

"Shut up Elliott, yes, we were walking over Wireltune Ridge. Not too many flies, unlike the west coast of Scotland. Bloody unbearable, the flies and the locals."

Elliott nodded in agreement.

"That old church is really something special...you should get some culture in your life and go and have a look...12th Century but on the site of a Saxon church...site of a mass grave from the days of the plague...those bow and arrow trees everywhere and the grave of that Knight who fell at the Battle of the Standard over near Northallerton."

---

[73] Well, those bits of England covered in grass or trees; not those inner city deprived areas that are always, frankly, horrible – irrespective of the weather.

"Did we win that one?" asked Neil.

"Ignoramus."

"Thanks Elliott, I was only asking."

Bill sighed before continuing, "Depends on your definition of 'we' given that King Stephen was involved. Anyway, all these local battlefields are really interesting."

"Do they bring back memories?"

"Oh Elliott, please shut up."

"So what happened at the Battle of the Standard?" asked Neil.

"Which are unbearable, the flies or the locals?" asked Biggles.

"Pillock": an observation from Pete.

"Well," started Bill, "it all started in December 1135 when King Stephen was crowned."

"Was he already a King? asked Elliott.

Bill ignored Elliott "It was following the death of his uncle, Henry the First. Now, Henry had hoped that his daughter Matilda would succeed him and so King David of Scotland invades England in support of Matilda."

"What's this got to do with Northallerton?" asked Neil.

"I'm getting there. Well, Stephen and David sign a treaty at Durham settling land disputes. David's son Henry is granted Huntingdon, but Stephen keeps Northumberland, which has been claimed by the Scots for many years." Bill was clearly settling into what was going to be a detailed lecture.

"Haway man!"

"Yes, Elliott, so in 1138 King David invades Northumberland four times in support of Matilda. His aim may be the acquisition of Northern England, which has close religious, linguistic and cultural ties to lowland Scotland. He claims Northern England through his wife, who was the grand- daughter of Earl Siward, the pre-conquest ruler of the North."

"Alf will be calling time soon."

"Grow up Elliott, and so in August 1138 the Scots invade again and fight the English, whose army is almost entirely composed of Yorkshire barons, at the Battle of the Standard near Northallerton. Before the battle the English leader Thurstan, the Archbishop of York, who was once a close friend of David, set up a mast on a chariot with standards of Yorkshire saints tied to it for good luck. St Cuthbert's banner was not represented, suggesting a lack of support from Durham and Northumberland. Thurstan's supporters included the Mowbrays, Lacys and Percys along with the Balliols and Bruces of the Tees valley. David's supporters are Norman barons from Scotland, but he has some Yorkshire support. David's army is heavily defeated in the battle and he is forced to retreat to his castle at Carlisle."

"The sun's coming up."

"Thank you Elliott, and then a peace treaty was negotiated between Stephen and David at Carlisle. Of course, this doesn't stop the Scots and a year later another peace treaty is signed at Durham. David's son Henry is given Northumberland, but the castles of Bamburgh and Newcastle remain property of the English King. The Tees forms the border between England and Scotland, as Northumberland's territory extends to the district of Sadberge on the north side of the river. The district of Sadberge stretches from Hartlepool to Teesdale, but does not include Stockton and Darlington, which belong to the Prince Bishop of Durham. The Prince Bishop's territory remains outside Scottish control."

"Whoa, whoa," Elliott interrupts, "so that supports what Ben keeps saying about the Romans building the wall along the Tees."

Neil giggled, "My head hurts."

"And so it should," agreed Frank.

Bill was about to continue but Elliott moved in, "And so children, we then beat the French, Germans and Spaniards several times, we had a few minor difficulties with our supposed friends across the pond, we then had the Poll Tax riots, the mines were closed down and, and I blame the Scots for this, we got effing telephones."

Frank slapped his thighs and rose, "Excellent, and it is now time for yours truly to invest in Alf's pension fund."

"So, who was the Bishop shagging?" asked Neil.

Grant sighed "I just don't understand."

Kate remained silent.

"How could we fuck it up so bad?"

"Well," Kate started, but was given no chance to explain.

"I mean, it's every time, we work our proverbials off, get just about everything done, and then WALLOP, our tax department let us down."

Kate started, "They say they will be finished by-"

Grant stopped her, "Look Kate, we are supposed to report to the Bank on Monday, Monday, Monday next week, not whenever our little tax darlings can get their arses into action."

Kate concentrated on her shoes.

"So what do we do?" Grant leant back and placed his hands behind his head. "Oh bollocks! Look, I know it's not your fault, but I wish you'd told me before now that the little darlings were fucking you about."

"Grant has always been a salad dodger," argued Elliott.

"That's both unfair and incorrect," countered Pete.

"Is his tab still open?" asked Neil.

"That is a very good question matio," replied Elliott, "and for that you get a Blue Peter badge and the opportunity to visit the bar in Grant's name."

"You are a twat," commented Pete.

Grant scratched his head, "It's been a salmon day today."

"Sorry?" Kate was confused.

"We've spent the entire day swimming against the current, we've been screwed and now we are going to die."

"That's a bit extreme Grant."

Grant nodded and scratched his side. His stomach hurt. His eyes were sore and his knees ached. "Right, I'm not into blamestorming[74] and I'm too tired for anymore testiculating[75] so let's work out what we are going to do."

Keen to get back to work or go home, Kate pushed Grant for a decision, "So, are we going to work on this tomorrow, or Sunday, we don't need both days and I would prefer Sunday."

Grant smiled. "I'll fit in with you and the rest of the team; anyway I'll be in both days, so it makes no odds to me."

Kate gazed as Grant slowly got to his feet. *The sad, wrecked bastard, he needs some care and attention.*

Grant put his jacket on to go home and put on his best John Wayne accent, "Saddle up and lock and load."

Kate watched as he staggered out of his office door and then switched his lights off. *The daft bastard gets worse.*

---

[74] Blamestorming – sitting around in a group, discussing why a deadline was missed or a project failed, and who was responsible.
[75] Testiculating – waving ones arms around and talking bollocks.

Thirty Four

The first Tuesday in June. A delightful, early Summer's evening. Noisy: birds, lawn mowers and children screaming in The Urra's garden.

Grant took the chicken-ding out of the microwave. He dispensed with the wrapping and, ignoring the instructions, immediately put a fork full into his mouth; a monkey mouthful, he immediately started making falsetto monkey ooh-ooh noises. He'd over cooked it. He threw it in the bin and decided that was the end to his evening cooking efforts. Shit, but there must be more to life than this.

She was 'out' with Samantha.

He'd been told to be home early to look after the girls. He had been; they were both out.

He'd taken the dogs for a walk and was now fighting the urge to go to The Urra.

"Shouldn't we sit outside on a lovely evening such as this?" asked Bill.

Elliott took a deep breath, "Drinking in the outdoors, other than when associated with the burning of sausages and incineration of other meat products, is, without question, unhealthy and a complete no no in the good beer drinker's guide."

"Sorry I suggested it."

"Well, Billy Baby, don't let it happen again."

Bill nodded. Not in agreement; more of an attempt to move the discussion forwards in a positive vein.

"I hate barbecues," offered Neil.

Pete laughed, "Me too, mind it's a good excuse for a few tinnies but, bugger me, why does the bloke have to wear the apron and burn himself on the primitive, heat conducting utensils?"

"True, true," exploded Elliott, "why do barbecue tools all direct the heat straight to your hand? Eh? Eh? Answer me that one Billy Boy!"

Bill declined to accept the challenge.

"Everytime we go to a barbecue I end up getting bollocked when we get home."

"That's because you tried to enjoy yourself Neil, and you should know better than that," replied Pete.

Neil nodded.

Elliott stood up, "Right then, shall we try and open another tab in Grant's name? The Fat Twat hasn't bought us a round for some time and I, for one, believe this to be out of order."

"Sound idea, can't fault your logic," agreed Pete.

"Alf won't go for it," suggested Bill.

"And why not?" asked Elliot, "it's all profit to that miserable barsteward."

"Wonder how Fat Lad is," mused Pete before continuing, "Just tell Alf that Grant asked you to set up a tab in his absence and that he's promised to pop in on Sunday to settle it, and as we all know Grant, tell Alf that Grant's put a limit on the tab, that'll convince him."

Grant lifted himself off the couch and walked over to his music system – his pride and joy – and unloaded the CD he'd been listening to – 'Streetcore' by Joe Strummer & The Mescaleros[76] - and put the disc away in his perfectly ordered CD library. He tidied away his headphones – he hadn't been allowed to listen to music at any volume at home since…well, since his wedding.

---

[76] A superb album released after the terribly premature death of Joe Strummer; copyright and published by Hellcat Records in 2003.

Bloody tragic, he thought. He'd not learnt to appreciate the pure quality of Joe Strummer until too late…and Mick Jones and…should he listen to another CD and have another drink? No. Busy day tomorrow. He cleared away the detritus from his evening meal – an empty bottle of Medoc, an empty bourbon biscuit wrapper and a half empty packet of 'Ready salted' crisps. What did that mean? Could you get 'Unready salted?' What was wrong with 'plain' or 'fundamentally tasteless?'

He switched off all the downstairs lights, put on the porch lights and climbed the stairs. He looked in on his daughters; both asleep; had either of them conversed with him tonight? He shook his head and readied himself for bed.

"Two fish in a tank and one says to the other 'you drive and I'll fire the gun'."

"Fish can't talk Elliott."

"Can too."

Eric was beginning to suffer, "Don't be stupid."

"Oh, I get that," announced Buster.

"Have you thought about a career in nuclear physics," asked Pete.

"You should limit that to 'career'," suggested Biggles.

"Well, my little chums, I think it's time I took the wife home for some oral sex," announced Elliott.

Elliott's wife thumped him on the shoulder; his life being (temporarily) protected by her inebriated state, "It's OK, he thinks it's a lozenge for a sore throat."

"I'll have the packet then."

She hit him again. Harder.

Elliott's wife, Tina, was several years older than him and had clearly been attractive in her younger days. She was now by no means unattractive and, to quote Grant, 'she scrubbed up well'.

271

Grant had, on several occasions, caught himself staring at her legs, hips and bottom. A highly intelligent woman, Tina seemed to care for Elliott like a mother would comfort a wayward son; coaxing, encouraging, pampering and, on appropriate occasions, giving him a vicious public rollicking; perversely, Elliott seemed to enjoy these. Tina enjoyed the company of Elliott's friends and was viewed by some of the local women as a bit of a 'trainee piss head'; she would argue that she needed no training.

"Can Grant afford another round?" asked Pete.

Buster looked at Tina, "What do you reckon Doc?"

Tina grinned, "I reckon he can afford one, but not one for Elliott this time, he has some entertaining to do."

"Yippee," said Elliott, with a look of mock pain on his face.

"Yes Darling, and don't use the headache excuse tonight, it's becoming a bit tedious."

Buster tittered.

"Fuck off Farmer Boy."

Buster tittered again, "Sorry Elliott, do you need any medication to help?"

"Do your bulls get a Viagra substitute or anything similar?"

"Well," stuttered Buster, "I'm not sure how to answer that Tina, and I'm certainly uncomfortable with the idea of providing any such treatment to Elliott here."

"Well," sighed Tina, "he surely needs something. I've tried all sorts of treats, dressy ups, spankings, little games, all sorts, but he just can't stand up like he used to."

"Excuse me, but I am here you know," interrupted Elliott.

"And he used to be so good at it, if you know what I mean," continued Tina.

"I guess he gets enough of spankings at school," suggested Biggles.

"What sort of dressy ups?" enquired Pete. Enthusiastically.

"Excuse me," blustered Elliott.

Pete scratched his beard, "Nurses?"

"There's only so much a woman can do."

Pete kept scratching, "French maids?"

"Perhaps, and I've only just thought about this," Tina paused for effect, "But maybe he's changed, if you know what I mean."

Biggles burst into a fit of giggles.

Buster waved his hands about, "No no no, surely not, but possibly."

"Dominatrix?" Pete wasn't going to let it drop as his imagination was beginning to get the better of him.

"Oh fucking hell," exploded Elliott, "Now I'm beginning to really miss Bannister!"

"Slave girl?"

Tina shook her head, "Peter, you need to broaden your mind."

Pete grinned, "Go on then, give me a clue."

Tina giggled, "In your dreams."

"You don't want to go there!" suggested Biggles.

"Fuck off."

"OK Pete."

Tina crossed her legs, her tight black skirt hitching itself up her thighs, revealing a flash of leg.

"So," started Pete, "just how many people, people here in this village, do you think play sex games?"

Tina leant forwards, "Well, I think the question is how many want to, but can't or won't."

Pete nodded; hoping she would continue.

Bill joined the discussion, "Name, names."

"I think we can assume that Elliott isn't involved," offered Buster.

Tina grinned.

"I reckon Frank's wife would be up for it."

"Get real Biggles!"

"Sorry Bill."

"Got it!" Everyone stopped and stared at Pete, "Neil and his missus, if there's a dominatrix in the village it's got to be the remarkably attractive Helen!"

"But Neil?" asked Biggles.

"Got to be," Pete sat back, a smug grin on his face.

Elliott stood up, "Time for bed said Zebedee."

"Boing," agreed Tina.

Grant lay in bed: his mind racing.

Big day tomorrow.

Meeting with a potential new client and did he not need a few successes!

Was he prepared?

Would the team perform?

What had they missed?

Who were they up against?

He heard a car on the drive. A door banged after a surprisingly long gap. He heard a key in the front door then a loud, pleasingly solid bang. For a fleeting moment he wondered if she would join him for a brief moment of pleasure; it had happened before; there was that time she'd been out and appeared in his bed and announced that, on the way home in the taxi, she had been talking with her mates about sex and now she fancied some. It had been pretty unsatisfying as he remembered it. She'd have to beg, he decided.

She didn't.

Grant lay on his back, concentrating on the darkness.

His knees ached.

What had gone wrong? Fuck, the same unanswerable question.

His stomach hurt.

He rolled over and tried to sleep – and trying is not the right thing to do when your mind immediately starts racing to important meetings, declining performance statistics, and how cold and empty the bed seems.

Thirty Five

The second Wednesday in June. A delightfully sunny and warm afternoon.

Grant and Elliott had started 'early'. Their moods were dark and cold.

"So, what's your funeral going to be like?"

"I'll miss it," replied Elliott.

"Nah, twat, I mean have you planned it all?"

"What! You mean like scattering my ashes by a corner flag or at sea?"

"Aye."

"No, not really, although I like Frank's idea of having his ashes fired off Wireltune Ridge in a big firework."

Grant nodded, "Cool."

" 'Bout you?"

"On the basis that my dearly beloved wouldn't collect my body from the morgue I have given it some thought."

Elliott's interest was aroused, "Like what?"

"I've got it in my Will, well, a letter of wishes which is attached to it."

"You're joking!"

"No, straight up, I've got details of the post funeral booze up, you're invited, and details down to the order of service."

"Fuck me!"

"Chosen the music so that she, or some other fucker, won't play hymns or some other wrist-slash inducing crap."

Elliott was now intrigued, "Like?"

"Well, on my arrival, dans box, I want The Final Taxi by Wreckless Eric[77], then as all the buggers are sitting down I'll have the amazing, anthemetic, if that's a word, Stranger Than Fiction by Split Enz[78], bloody awesome track with the spoken line 'It's the story of my life' in the starting passage."

"Never heard of it or them."

"Twat, anyway, then, during the service we have two singalongs with Chance and In a Big Country from Big Country[79], both thought provokers with great chorus lines."

"Bizarre."

"Shame, no one would come!"

Elliott grinned, "Would you care?"

"Yes, I have this vision of looking down and seeing old friends enjoying themselves and saying nice things about me."

"Fat chance," laughed Elliott.

"True, bet the daughters would be 'shopping' and work would send a 'representative' and that would be about it."

"I'll be there mate."

"Thanks Elliott, but you'll die before me."

"Thanks."

"No sweat."

"What about the eulogy?"

"Very good question Elliott" Grant smiled "Given the complete absence of friends, I guess I had better pre-record my own."

Buster arrived. Despite the barmy weather, as on the other 364 days of the year, Buster was resplendent in dark corduroy trousers, a dark grey polo neck jumper and his hacking jacket. "Evening guys, I suppose it's my round."

---

[77] By Eric Goulden a.k.a. Wreckless Eric, published by Street Music Ltd., available on numerous Stiff records.
[78] Written by Tim Finn and Phil Judd, this Split Enz classic was first released in 1975 with Mushroom Records Pty. Ltd as publishers.
[79] Both taken from the 1983 album The Crossing, copyright Phonogram Ltd.

"Quickly please, I'm about to die," replied Elliott.

"Excuse me?"

"Just get two pints of the Summer Haze please, and don't upset Elliott; he could go at anytime now."

Elliott coughed.

"Are you in serious pain?" asked Grant.

Elliott coughed.

Buster shook his head and retreated to the bar.

"Have you chosen the menu?" asked Elliott.

"No solids, liquids only."

"Might have to out live you."

But it was true. Grant had planned his funeral. And he had given a lot of thought to his death; and the later years of his life.

He wanted a quick and painless death.

Ideally in heroic circumstances.

He accepted the reality, however, that he would spend several lonely and painful years in an old folks home; surrounded by the sort of people that he had spent years avoiding, and bathed in the smell of stale urine.

"How long have you chaps been in here? asked Buster.

"Given how little time I may have left, not long enough."

Grant grunted in agreement with Elliott.

"It pains me to think of all those days, weeks, no months, of my life, my only life, that I have wasted working," Elliott paused "Being nice to people that I fundamentally dislike and, and, being sober!" He shook his head.

"Does your drinking ever bother you?" asked Grant.

"Only if I don't have enough," quipped Elliott.

"No, seriously," persisted Grant, "There are some that would argue that many of us are alcoholic."

Buster waved his hands about in mock horror, "Surely not!"

278

Grant took a long pull of his pint, "Straight up, you must have seen these questionnaires? You know the ones, do you drink to build up your self confidence? Do you drink alone? Has drinking affected your reputation?"

Elliott smirked, "They are bollocks, just like those that can tell you if you're a great lover or not!"

"I'm not so sure," continued Grant, "I mean I never want a drink in the morning, or anything daft like that, but, haway, we do consistently drink more than is healthy for us, we all admit to memory loss, and I admit to having felt ashamed after some of the things I've done when I've been pissed."

"Like what?" demanded Elliott.

Grant refused to bite. "No, seriously, I read one of these tests in the dentists the other day and if you answered yes to three questions it meant you were a definite alcoholic."

"So what did you score?"

"Haway Buster man, it's not high score wins!"

Buster chuckled.

Elliott placed his glass down with a thud, "I bet you got five or six."

"Yes," agreed Grant.

Elliott laughed, "Beat that easy and, no, I am a piss head, not an alcoholic."

"Here here! concluded Buster, "and that calls for another round."

Grant shook his head, "Not for me thanks."

Elliott looked shocked, "Don't be so fucking stupid and anyway, what are you going to do when you get home, other than hide in your study with a glass of malt?"

Grant sat in his study; a cup of coffee slowly going cold.

Was he an alcoholic?

He never felt like he needed a drink.

And he never hid his drinking or his drinks.

Why did he keep finding half full or empty white wine bottles in cupboards? She must be getting forgetful in her middle to old age.

Is it a disease?

His father-in-law had died an alcoholic.

That had been horrible. The drinking habits and irrational behaviour had been symptoms, so he had been told, of the disease.

He had been an amazing liar.

Resentful.

Jealous.

Self pitying.

"He hates himself more than anyone else." That is what the doctor said. Grant had taken some convincing.

Was he now an alcoholic?

Did he drink to escape his troubles?

No, he was just a lush.

Did he crave a drink at a certain time of day?

No.

Did his drinking affect his efficiency?

Well, he was getting older.

Did his drinking cause sleeping problems?

No, just the need to relieve himself several times.

Did he drink to build up his self confidence?

No, but…

Did his drinking affect his reputation?

Don't know…

Thirty Six

The third Tuesday in June. It was damp and surprisingly chilly. The bar of The Urra had filled up relatively early; all of the usual 'suspects' were present.

Elliott was recounting tales of his day at school "Little bastards, mind, I blame the parents".

Frank had been golfing, "An absolutely superb shot at the fifth'.

"Bollocks, you fluked it,". Buster had played with him.

Pete had spent the day doing nothing, "Day time television gets no better."

"Wish I could watch it rather than waste my time attempting to force feed unnecessary education to a group of loathsome jerks."

"What do you mean; it was a tremendous shot with my lob wedge."

"Well, I thought you fluked it!"

Neil sat in silence.

Grant was quiet. Grant had spent the morning at Hartlepool Magistrates Court. And he was less than happy about the experience.

"The way it ran to within two feet of the pin was intended."

Buster laughed.

"How was your day Grant?" asked Pete.

Grant shifted uncomfortably, took a long pull and then exploded "Treated like a common fucking criminal, that's me. Did I go out intending to hurt anyone? Or to do anything wrong? Did I bollocks! But, wahay, let's get the accountant in his suit, treat him like a common criminal, and then fine him more than the twats who steal, mug and assault! Why? Why! I'll tell you why! Because they can hit me with a fine and I will pay it! They wouldn't have to chase after me or settle for fifty pence a week for the next millennium! A bloody fine, costs and five more points!"

"Sorry," started Pete, "I'd forgotten that today was the day."

Grant waved a hand in apology.

"What happened then?" asked Frank.

"You remember my Sunday afternoon crash? Well the Police, who clearly have nothing better to do with their limited time and resources, did me for driving without due care and attention. Fair I guess. I had lost concentration; momentarily. And with no intent or malice. But whatever, they prosecuted and I was up in front of three worthies today."

Frank shook his head, "You're joking?"

"Nah, I was in after the bloke being done for stealing numerous bottles of under-arm deodorant and before the three thugs who pushed over a pram; with the baby still in it!"

"Haway, you're exaggerating?"

"No Frank, wish I was, but it's totally true. And if I hadn't taken advice and instructed a local brief, who described me in such glowing terms that I thought he was talking about someone else, anyway, if it hadn't been for him, I dread to think what would have happened. I would probably have lost my temper and could have got myself sent down."

"And you really got a heavy fine, costs and points?"

"Yes Frank! And I felt dirty, sort of abused and totally insulted."

"Have you had a bath or have you come straight here?"

"Fuck off Elliott."

"Sorry, I'll get them in." But Elliott didn't move.

"So what happened then?" persisted Frank.

"I've told you," replied a clearly irritated Grant, "Do you want the fucking gory details or something?"

Frank nodded.

"Come on," encouraged Buster, "Get it off your chest!"

"Did the judge wear a black handkerchief?" asked Elliott.

Frank followed Elliott's lead, "Did one of them say, 'Take him down' and did someone bang a hammer?"

Grant shook his head. What had he done to deserve this? He wasn't a bad person. A waster of sorts. Probably difficult to work with. A bit of a piss-head. But not a bad person.

Neil joined the conversationm, "Was it a proper court room sort of thing?"

Grant smirked, "Sadly not. It was a surprisingly large room with walls that looked like partitions. The ceiling seemed low and the lights not quite bright enough. Very Nineteen Sixties. I sat on a chair; a wooden chair, against one wall. On the other side of the room; what seemed like miles away, sat two blue perm old dears and an angry looking middle aged bloke. My brief was over on my right and the chief prosecutor, who clearly based herself on something out of some witchcraft movie, was over on the left. And half way through a couple of yobs walked in, asked if they were in the right room, swore and walked out! All I said was that I was sorry; the brief made me out to be the Mother Teresa of the accountancy profession and the prosecutor seemed to compare me with some criminal master mind, intent on wreaking carnage across the face of the civilised world. Kept referring to 'his Mercedes' and photographs of 'the Mercedes', like driving a nice German car is an offence in its own right. The prosecutor, a very maudlin looking women, probably in need of a good shag, seemed to think that I had just crawled from beneath some stone."

"She had a point," suggested Frank.

Neil looked astonished, "Bugger me."

"No thanks," an unnecessary quip from Elliott which drew the expected response from Frank, "Or you'll be in Court with Grant."

Grant sighed. He craved a cigarette. A kiss and a cuddle would be nice. He could feel an urge developing in his loins. No chance of that. He shrugged, "Anyway, they should bring back hanging for those able bodied twats who park in disabled spaces. You never see those buggers getting dealt with. And they, unlike me, do it intentionally! Right, my round I guess."

"You better settle your tab as well," suggested Elliott.

Grant laughed, "I haven't got one!"

Frank laughed, loudly and Elliott explained, "Wrong again Granty Baby!"

Grant stared at Elliott.

"Silence in Court," shouted Frank.

Grant shook his head and turned to face the bar. Alf was waiting for him, "Suspended sentence or time off for good behaviour?"

Thirty Seven

The final Saturday in June. June had not been 'flaming'; it had been pouring; for days; without a break. At least it provided an excuse to avoid the gardening.

Alf started closing the curtains in the front bay windows of The Urra; there was a large crowd of locals in and it had been some time since he'd let them have a 'locky back'. He'd called time thirty minutes previously and all the "incomers" had now left; he knew everyone else and rarely saw any police out and about at this time of night. He let the staff leave (or change sides of the bar) and took over serving duties; Elliott was first at the bar.

"Not well Guv?"

Alf stared at him.

"Cash flow problems then?" Elliott persisted; Alf stared.

"If you've got financial type problems, well, Grant is your man!"

"Do you want a drink or what?"

"I'm only saying, you working suggests a profit problem and me old chum Grant could help you out."

"Do you want a drink or shall I go and serve the Springsteen Twins[80]?"

---

[80] The twins weren't really twins – they were brothers who looked alike, behaved the same, and lived together, alone. They weren't called Springsteen either; they'd got this name after ruining many an after wedding party with their own renditions of various Bruce Springsteen classics; they meant no harm, but now received few invitations....to anything.

"Right my man, I'll have a bottle of your cheapest white for the ladies and five pints of the Newman Whalley Ale please, and a fine pint it is too."

Alf started pouring the Newman's and Elliott turned away from the bar and wandered over to a table where Buster and Eric were in the middle of a serious discussion about the state of various local golf courses.

"It might be nice, it might be relatively challenging, but it is always waterlogged and the members are tossers."

"You're wrong Buster," replied Eric.

Buster looked annoyed.

"No no no," interrupted Elliott, "he's right and wrong…it's not nice or relatively challenging."

Buster continued to look annoyed.

Eric stroked his chin, and a very proud chin it appeared to be, before concluding in unexpected style with an unusual relish, "Fuck off Elliott!"

"You want a drink then Eric?"

Elliott turned back to the bar as Alf finished putting his drinks on the bar. "Been practising short measures again?"

"Piss off Elliott."

Grant was in his study; reviewing the wreckage of the last week. A week during which he had seen a deal he had been working on for four months 'crash and burn' – leaving him frustrated and in the path of an exceedingly annoyed client. The bank had said 'yes' and then, at the eleventh hour, had retracted the offer for 'reputational reasons'. Reputational reasons! Well, his was in tatters!

A week during which his wife had not spoken to him. He had no recollection of a row – or any other event that could lead to this form of punishment. Perhaps it was not a reaction to some recent event, but was now the way it was.

A week during which he had become intensely frustrated with a number of colleagues, both senior and junior. And the senior ones annoyed him more. Why wouldn't they listen? The facts were obvious. The problems were clear. Clear and fundamental. Fundamental and in need of early resolution. And capable of early resolution, if the will was there. Fuckwits.

Then there was the court appearance. He knew that he was over-reacting; that it was, fundamentally, a case of 'fair cop', but he still felt abused by the whole process.

He sipped his coffee. Stale; too strong; stewed. Horrible. He was having an alcohol free day. Was it just to make him feel more miserable? He grinned. No, it was so he could start a career in male modelling. Assuming that his Hollywood career failed to prove successful.

He wandered over to the window; rivulets were racing each other down to the patio; the rain hadn't eased up all day. The dogs would need some exercise. Bugger. Time to get wet then.

Elliott stood up and swayed, "Let's raise a pint to our little fat friend."

Pete stood to join Elliott in the toast, "Who, the bald one or wee Buster here?"

Buster looked annoyed but remained silent.

"Alf!" shouted Elliott, "we need a round here, on the Bannister account, as soon as you can, dear chap."

"I'll drink to that," agreed Pete.

Grant stopped outside the front door to The Urra. There was a 'locky back' going on. All the tell-tale signs. Curtains closed. Outside lights off. Lights still shining from the window in the gentlemen's toilets.

He could feel water running down his back. His socks were wet. Should he 'pop in', just for one? For medicinal purposes?

It seemed like a long time since he had last enjoyed a Hedgehog.

Or a Newman Whalley Ale.

Or a Whitby.

He wiped the rain from his face; well, there would be no harm in a couple of pints.

He felt a wet dog rub against his already wet trousers.

He could tie them to one of the garden benches.

Not in this weather!

That would be cruel.

What had they done to him?

He looked down; two pairs of eyes looked up at him: sad eyes, pleading with him:

CAN WE GO HOME?

NOW?

ANY CHANCE OF A NICE RUB WITH A DRY TOWEL, A TIN OF MEAT, A BOWL OF WATER AND THEN A SNOOZE?

OR WE MIGHT NOT BE YOUR BEST FRIENDS FOR MUCH LONGER.

LOOK, IT IS PISSING DOWN, SO WHY ARE WE STANDING AROUND?

He felt the leads around his wrist as they started pulling towards home.

Not tonight then.

"Shame Grant's not in tonight," commented Pete.

"He'll be enjoying himself somewhere."

Pete nodded, Neil was probably right…and that was a rarity, a rarity worthy of another round of drinks. Pete jerked to his feet and, somewhat unsteadily, made his way to the bar.

"Shame again," slurred Pete.

"Pardon," Alf not at his most helpful.

"The shame ash befour please,"

"Beerlarious," Alf grinned and started pulling the required beers.

The sound of unnecessarily loud laughing started from near the fireplace. A stool fell over as Frank stood up; Neil moved his chair backwards with a loud scraping noise. Elliott's head appeared to rise from the middle of the commotion.

Bill started clapping, "Come on Elliott, show us what you can do."

Elliott stood on the table. Amazingly, and much to Alf's pleasure, every glass had been removed.

"Fans, my dear dear fans, you asked nicely so I cannot disappoint'.

"Elliott calm down," shouted Alf.

Elliott interpreted the instruction as an invitation and started dancing on a bar table. His own version of the Springsteen Twins doing "Dancing in the Dark[81]".

Biggles was encouraging him.

His wife was ignoring him.

Eric was laughing.

Pete was smirking.

Buster was giving serious consideration to undertaking a tactical retreat – it was his round next.

"Get down Elliott!"

"Only if I can jump into your arms!"

Alf shook his head. Elliott jumped.

Grant couldn't even raise the enthusiasm to torment himself. He looked at the clock; was it too early to get up? He got out of bed and went to the window, drew the curtains and stared at the silhouette of the hills against the dark blue night sky. It had finally stopped raining. Thoughts of a late night walk passed through his

---

[81] A track on the critically acclaimed and commercially successful album "Born in the USA" by Bruce Springsteen.

mind. He looked at the distant lights of the village and wondered what was going on in those lit bedrooms. Fuck. What a life. What do I have to do?

He climbed back into bed and again tried to sleep.

Saturday was going to be a long day.

Thirty Eight

The first Friday in July. The beer garden was full; and loud. The regulars hid in the relative cool and quiet of the bar. A full squad was in residence.

"So, if you had a band, what would you call it?" demanded Elliott.

Pete was speechless.

"Haven't you done this before?" asked Frank.

"Bad breath dogs?" suggested Elliott.

"Haven't we been here before?" asked Frank.

Neil sat forwards, "Penile dysfunction."

Elliott sighed, "No, Neil, names for bands not your problems."

Neil slapped his forehead, "Oh, how remiss of me!"

"Dinner with Mandelson," proposed Grant.

"Nice one," replied Elliott, "but what about Phlegm?"

Buster was confused, "Well, er, I'm not sure what point you are trying to make."

"The Strangulated Hernias?"

Frank shook his head.

Elliott persisted, "The Amazing Skinned Aardvaarks?"

"What's the point?" asked Frank.

"Not bad," replied Elliott, "but not a winner."

Frank shook his head and reached for his cigarettes, "Elliott, you are one mother."

Grant pushed Frank's shoulder, "Good one, you're getting the spirit, what about 'Frank's a miserable bastard' or The Amazing Twat Flaps?"

Frank took a long drag on his cigarette, causing his head to be surrounded by a blue haze, caught in the sunlight cascading through The Urra's windows.

"Neat," commented Grant.

"Alf's a shite landlord," proposed Elliott.

"Suggestion or comment?" asked Grant.

"Hey," started Elliott, suddenly changing the subject, "Have you finished your eulogy yet?"

Grant smirked and took a few moments considering his reply, "Well, I'm not finished yet but I am focussing on a number of sound bite type lines."

"Like?" pushed Elliott.

"He was a better man than Biggles, a fairer man than Buster, a better drinker than Pete, smarter than Frank, nicer than Neil, a good friend to all and totally lousy at marriage."

"Deep and somewhat provocative," commented Elliott.

"What are you two twats on about now?" asked Frank.

Elliott folded his arms, "It's a secret." Frank stubbed his cigarette into the ashtray with some force, "Yeah, right!"

Grant had enjoyed his day: it had been hard work but ultimately satisfying. He had enjoyed the early evening drive home. Until it had ended.

He had been greeted by Samantha's car in his place on his drive.

She had been drinking his wine in his kitchen.

With his wife.

Talking about his children; although he wasn't sure as they had adopted a strained silence when they had realised that he had walked into the kitchen.

No welcome.

No dinner.

No warmth.

He had exercised the dogs, changed his clothes and repaired to The Urra.

Bollocks to them.

"You seem happier tonight," commented Pete.

Pete and Grant were talking at the bar.

Grant shrugged his shoulders, "Time to stop letting the bastards get me down," he paused and smiled, "And I've finally learnt 'don't get angry, get even' which is making me look at things a bit differently."

Pete looked bemused, "Eh? You're speaking in tongues."

"Any connection between your reality and mine is purely coincidental."

Pete shook his head, "Forgotten your medication again?"

Grant grinned, "No, it's just that now, eventually, I think I'm beginning to work out the plot, realising that you can't fight every battle, that you must choose your battles wisely and that, at the end of the day, I've been suffering from the mental equivalent of blue ball."

"Blue ball!" splurted Pete.

"You know, when your balls swell because you've been excited and, for whatever reason, you've been unable to fire it."

"I think I know what you mean, but I've never heard it called blue ball[82] before."

"I guess it's a distant memory to you," replied Grant.

"Fuck off."

"So, what's this life changing event, then?"

"Well," started Grant, "I've been getting messed around at work and have been trying to sort things out in completely the wrong way, resulting in further grief for yours truly and the one step forwards, three steps back type of result, you understand?"

"Not really."

"Anyway, I'm going to focus on what I'm good at and leave everything else to others, and if I see anything going wrong, I'm leaving well alone, it's not my problem, I'm not going to try to sort it out, thereby getting shit for sticking my nose in or being blamed for any resultant shit, and let them get the shit."

"How old are you?"

---

[82] Blue balls is a slang term for a temporary fluid congestion in the scrotum and prostate region. It is most commonly associated with adolescents but can occur in any sexually mature male. It is often accompanied by a deep, agonizing, cramping ache.

The main cause of blue balls is prolonged sexual stimulation of the erect penis, either by direct or indirect contact, that does not result in orgasm and ejaculation. During arousal in a sexually mature male, the sympathetic nervous system is disrupted, resulting in increased blood and lymphatic fluid flow to the scrotum, testicles and prostate areas. As this happens, other fluid outflow muscles constrict, causing more bodily fluid to enter the area than leave, ensuring a high enough regional blood pressure to allow a sustained erection for penetration during sexual intercourse. Because orgasm is not achieved, the blood tends to pool and become oxygen deprived. In some men, this pooling of oxygen-starved blood may result in a bluish tint to the scrotum.

The easiest way to relieve the symptoms of blue balls is through an orgasm either by masturbation or sexual intercourse. The resultant ejaculation jump-starts the sympathetic nervous system, which increases blood flow through the groin area, dissipating the fluid buildup. Even without orgasm, the symptoms of blue balls usually subside within an hour of onset. The symptoms can also last much longer.

One folk remedy for blue balls is the cold shower, which stimulates increased blood flow throughout the body, including the groin area. Putting cold substances (such as ice) on the crotch region significantly helps. Also, physical exercise like walking, climbing stairs etc, can ease the engorgement.

So, women described as 'cock teasers' or similar are dangerous to men's health.

"Fuck off."

"You can't do it Grant, you can't help yourself, you're a perfectionist, through and through, a class A pain in the arse, for all the right reasons, but a class A pain in the arse."

Grant smiled. He knew Pete was right. But so was he. And he was doing his head in and so had to change something.

"You need to start by getting some enjoyment back into your sad little life."

Again Grant knew that Pete was right. "Bollocks you old git!"

"Perhaps, but they're not blue, like yours!"

It had been a strange week for Grant. Amazing highs and lows. No individual event seemed to be life changing; but en masse?

He had suffered another meeting with Burton on Monday. Facts and figures. All unchallengeable. But the two of them drew completely different conclusions. Burton wanted to reduce the scale of operations; Grant wanted to invest. Burton wanted Grant to extend his service area; Grant believed that he was already losing credibility by trying to specialise in too many areas. Burton was making implied threats; Grant wasn't reacting to these in the manner expected by Burton. Grant's gut reaction was to walk away.

He had enjoyed Tuesday; a full day away from the office and Burton. A long, hard day with a group of his staff, finishing off a project in Cumbria. The work completed on time and well, Grant had entertained the team to a boisterous dinner.

Wednesday had been pretty awful. Burton had called him and had told him that he had received a complaint that Grant was refusing to hand over some personal study records to a junior member of staff. This simply was not the case; but Burton refused to listen and terminated the call abruptly. Grant was stunned. The girl involved had requested the records the previous week. Grant had asked his secretary to pass them to her. If there had been a delay why had the girl not asked his secretary, or called him?

Why had she complained direct to a rather loathsome member of the personnel department?

Why had that loathsome toad then not bothered to check the facts? A simple telephone call would have sufficed.

Why had the loathsome toad called Burton direct? And why had he chosen to accept the complaint without checking?

Why? He had done nothing wrong, but several people had chosen to not give him a chance.

Twats.

Thursday had started with the news of a significant new client gain. Excellent news for all concerned and a great morale booster for the office. On hearing the news Burton had decided that the new client should be serviced by a team based in Leeds. A proverbial kick in the balls for all concerned and the office in general. As usual Grant didn't understand or agree with Burton's logics. Grant had spent several hours wandering around various city centre public houses, in search of humour, solace and friendship. He had been unsuccessful and had returned to the office in a less than sensible state of mind; he had fought, however, the urge to hunt out the silly bitch who had complained about her "withheld" records.

He had been desk bound on Friday morning and had spent the afternoon visiting clients; visits organised in a manner to ensure his early return home: well, that had been pointless.

"I don't suffer from insanity," explained Elliott, "I positively enjoy every minute of it!"

"He stopped to think," replied Pete, "but forgot to start again."

"Enough, enough," pleaded Bill.

"I smile because I don't know what is going on," continued Elliott.

'Good line, very true,' thought Grant, "Right chaps, I need to absorb some more alcohol."

"Your round," suggested Pete.

"By Jingo, I believe you may be right, my turn, your tab?"

Pete guffawed, "Try it Fat Boy!"

Thirty Nine

The second Tuesday in July. Not a cloud in the sky. It had been a beautiful summer's day. The birds had sung, the flowers had blossomed and everything in, and around, The Urra appeared perfect.

Grant was on the A1, north of Leeds, driving towards 'home'.
His mind was full of dark clouds.
Another awful day.
Dark thoughts and unwelcome voices cluttered his thinking.
Bad day at work; then she called as he was leaving the car park.
Can you pick up some things for me?
Why not? Scott would for Rachel.
Everything is a problem to you.
Why can't you be like Scott? Or Richard?
It's me, me, me, isn't it?
What did I see in you?
My greatest mistake, which I'll regret forever.
And Richard has just bought Annie a new motor.
Mine's needing replacing; it's nearly two years old if you hadn't remembered!
Well, you'll have to get some tea for yourself.
He looked at the clock: too late to call in for a beer or four. Would have had time; if it hadn't been for all these anti-social, inconsiderate, selfish, middle lane-hogging arse wipes. What was their problem? He raced up behind some sort of people carrier, skipping along in the middle lane at 65 mph. He moved into the inside lane; no vehicles; the lane was clear as far as the eye could see. Did he undertake? No, why should he lower his standards. He moved back into the middle lane and flashed his head lights. Why?

He wasn't going to change their behaviour. Where were the Zippies[83] when you needed them? He moved into the outside lane and stamped on the accelerator, passed the people carrier and then indicated and swerved into the inside lane.

Who was the tosser now? Grant laughed.

Him!

Me!

Both of us!

He pushed the on switch on his CD player. Bollocks. The first notes of an old T Rex hit started playing. He wasn't in the mood. Another car in the centre lane came into view. He switched the volume up. What did these ridiculous lyrics mean? He flashed his headlights, it moved over, he sped past, feeling marginally happier.

Then a myriad of conflicting thoughts started bombarding his mind.

Who did he think he was?

What was his problem?

Why were there so many tossers on the road?

He was by no means a good driver.

Why were there so many tossers in his line of business?

Why was he such a self-centred, selfish, ignorant tosser himself?

Was she right?

"So, by jingo, as Grant would say, I guess it's my shout."

No one disagreed and so Pete got up and walked to the bar.

"Eight glasses of water a day can prevent colon cancer," announced Bill.

"Is that a semi?" asked Elliott.

Bill frowned.

---

[83] Traffic police; so called as they unzip their foreheads to assist in pre-patrol brain removal.

Neil joined the conversation, "Drinking water is supposed to make you lose weight."

"So, is Alf doing his bit for our health when he waters this stuff?" asked Frank.

Elliott tutted.

Neil continued, "Helen says I should drink water when I come here."

"When did you last have a semi?" Elliott asked Neil.

Bill fought the urge to question the relevance of Neil's comment, "Water makes you feel full and stops hunger pangs."

Elliott tutted, loudly.

"And only a small shortfall can make you dizzy."

Elliott shook his head and sighed, "Change the subject, I'm beginning to feel healthy!"

Bill folded his arms across his chest, "You should know all this, being a teacher."

Elliott tutted.

Grant spotted the police car in his rear view mirror.

He took his foot off the accelerator and fought the urge to press the brake pedal.

How long had he been there?

How fast had he been going?

Was it going to light up like a Christmas tree and pull him over?

Fuck.

What a great way to end a bad day.

"Do you drink enough water, Pete?" asked Bill.

"Give it a rest," pleaded Elliott.

"What?" replied a clearly puzzled Pete.

"Do you drink enough water?"

Elliott tutted.

"Are you taking the piss?" replied Pete.

Elliott sniggered, "No, clean water."

He was doing just over seventy.

The police car was maintaining its distance.

Good job he hadn't had a drink, as he had wanted to, after leaving the office.

Come on, get it over with.

Bill was still holding court, "And people don't drink milk like they used to, and that can't be good for the bones."

Elliott slammed the table with relish, "John Wayne."

Bill looked confused, "John Wayne. John bloody Wayne! What has he got to do with it?"

Elliott drawled, "Get off of your horse and drink your milk."

Pete sipped his beer and chose to join the conversation in the hope of stopping Bill's lecture, "He never said that but I like the bit when he says 'he surely is the son of Gawd' in that movie about Jesus."

"He was a centurion," agreed Neil.

"Saddle up," continued Pete, in an awful American accent.

"Westerns or war movies? asked Elliott.

"Got to be Westerns," started Neil.

The blue lights started flashing.

Grant's heart started pounding.

Shit.

He indicated and slowed down.

Pete and Elliott had succeeded in redirecting the conversation

"He won the Second World War single handedly,"

Elliott sniggered, "And he exterminated the Red Indian."

"Now, he would have made a great president," concluded Pete.

301

"Of what?" asked Neil.

"Fuckwit," replied Pete.

Pete scratched his bearded chin, "Would he had to go back to his proper name?"

"Good question," acknowledged Elliott, "Marion wasn't it?"

"Shirley," said Neil.

Pete and Elliott glared at him.

The police car stopped close behind his.

Did he get out?

Did he stay in the warmth?

He took off his seat belt.

The officer got out and placed his hat on his head.

Officious bastard.

Grant got out.

"Evening Officer, what's the problem?"

"Who would be his vice president? He always had the same blokes around him in the movies, do you reckon it would have been one of those guys?"

"Another good question, Petey Baby."

"Thanks Elliott, but less of the baby."

"What about Clint Eastwood?" offered Neil.

Pete spluttered, "Christ, the yanks would have invaded everywhere with Clint and Big John in charge."

Elliott laughed, "Can you imagine him ending every speech with a line like 'saddle up' or 'Yo!' you know when he put his hand up to lead his cavalry charge."

"Mental, you're all mental."

"Thank you Bill, from you that is a compliment."

"Peter, from you that is sarcasm."

"In a hurry, sir?"

Forty

The third Tuesday in July. The sky was bright blue; the swallows were high and all seemed tranquil. The Urra was quiet inside and a hive of activity in the Beer Garden.

Elliott, Grant, Pete and Ben were the only occupants of the bar.

"And the bastard says 'in a hurry, Sir?' You know, the sarcastic tone for Sir, and then he asks me to get into his car and blow into his friggin balloon! And they wonder why no one co-operates with them. You know the score, 'sorry we can't attend to your burglary, let's hope the intruder doesn't hurt you, got to go and give a parking ticket out, bye', the bastards." Grant paused for air "So, 'What speed were you doing' says he, I felt like saying, 'why ask you twat, you know the answer' and anyway I was only doing eightyish."

"Three points then?" asked Elliott.

The energy and angst seemed to leave Grant, his shoulders fell and his chin touched his chest, "Aye."

"Sorry, what was that?" asked Ben.

Grant wanted to punch Ben but common sense prevailed; it was his own fault, "I said, yes, I got three points."

"I bet her indoors was not amused," offered Pete, almost sympathetically.

Grant grunted. He had not told her. Mind, he had not seen her.

"The breath test was alright then?" asked Ben.

"Of course," snapped Grant.

It had been a strange day for Grant. Pretty average at work; no real problems.

He had enjoyed a social lunch with an old school 'friend': 'friend' as in she hadn't really been a friend when they had been at school.

She had been, and still was, beautiful. He remembered the short blue skirts she used to wear; that seemed to cling to her perfectly formed bottom. The loose cotton shirts and blue striped tie. The shiny tights – stockings in his fantasies.

She still had a lovely head of dark hair; cut in an almost tomboy style; highlighting her sparkling white teeth, bright blue eyes and a strong, but delicate nose. And she had a laugh which was little short of infectious; like her personality.

He had lusted after her; but had never managed to overcome his overbearing 'fear' of the fairer sex; he had opted to study Biology at A level, simply to be close to her. And he had, on two cider fuelled summer afternoons, attempted to 'ask her out'; his timing had always been impeccable and she had always been "out" when he had called.

They had met by accident at a dinner; and had enjoyed an intense rapport almost immediately; it had been as if they really were 'old friends'; and so well had they got on that Grant, given the courage of an evening's alcohol, had told her all about his youthful lust. She did not say that his lust had been reciprocated, but she had asked if they could meet up again; and so lunch had been arranged.

"Not seen you for a good week or so," a question disguised as a comment by Pete.

"Not really fancied beer or socialising," replied Grant.

Pete thumped Grant's back, "You miserable twat."

Grant smiled: he had really enjoyed lunch with Gillian: female company, a woman who seemed interested in him, gentle but humorous conversation.

"Oi, fat twat. Are you day dreaming or what?"

Grant smiled, "Sorry Pete, I was miles away."

"I told you that you couldn't change," started Pete, "you've got your head right up your arse again, work, work, fucking work! Everytime you announce that you are going to sort yourself out, we get nothing more than a dead cat bounce[84]!"

Grant grinned. Pete was half right. "You've got a point, but I'm not sure that it's all to do with work, or even the dearly beloved."

Pete sighed. His friend was a mess. "You need to sort yourself out, you seem to live life in some sort of rage."

"A rage against who?" asked Grant.

"Yourself, you daft fat twat!"

Grant pondered this sudden outburst. Pete was right. He did seem to go through life in a sort of rage.

A rage against all sorts of other drivers; centre lane huggers; idiots with their fog lights on; inconsiderate drivers; Chelsea tractors; big white motor homes with trailers or small cars attached.

A rage against queues; not because he felt he shouldn't have to queue; it was simply a question of his time. How many times had he walked out of shops, going without whatever he had gone in for, simply to avoid standing round gormlessly for ages?

How long did it take him to bank cheques? Simply because he didn't trust the holes in the wall and hated queuing to pay them in.

---

[84] The "dead cat bounce" is a term used by the poor buggers working in the "world of finance" to describe a small, and probably temporary improvement in the market's fortune, after a long downward movement—even a dead cat dropped from a dizzy height may bounce a little.
"If you threw a dead cat off a 40-storey building, it might bounce when it hit the pavement. But don't confuse that bounce with renewed life. It is still a dead cat."

How often had he left fully laden trolleys in supermarkets because the queues are too long or slow?

How annoyed did he get if people were late for appointments? However, how often was he late?

How impatient did he get with shop assistants if service was not immediately forthcoming?

How could he never understand delivery delays?

Was he simply intolerant?

Had he always been like this?

If not, when had he become such a pain in the proverbial, and why?

"Oi, fat twat!" Pete was becoming increasingly frustrated.

"Sorry, I'm a bit tired. And I am not a dead cat!"

"Well fuck off then, or get the beers in!"

There was no option: no need for consideration, "Same again?"

She had never married.

She had lived with a bloke for ten years.

She had a daughter by him.

"And so," started Elliott, "out comes the Yorkshire war cry of 'how much' and Alf tells the bloke to sling his hook! First time in the many years that I have been warming this seat that I have seen anyone thrown out!"

"Bugger me," a comment not a request from Pete.

Grant returned with the drinks.

Pete showed his appreciation, "About time too."

"Has Biggles been kidnapped?" asked Ben.

"What's your view on impatience?" Grant asked Elliott.

Elliott looked vacant.

Pete replied to Ben, "We live in hope."

Grant continued, "As a teacher?"

Elliott shrugged his shoulders.

Grant tried again, "I know that I am now an impatient old bugger, probably due to the feeling that life is accelerating away from me. But I was patient and tolerant in my younger days."

"Bollocks," observed Pete, "You've been a fat twat all the time I've known you."

Elliott sighed, "You have a point, the young of today are more impatient than we were. I don't know why. I mean, you become impatient because you have too much to do, you don't have enough time or some shit further up the hierarchy is giving you shit. And what pressures do the young darlings of today have? I mean, everything is spoon fed!"

Ben grunted.

Grant had clearly hit on a sore subject for Elliott, who was now unstoppable, "Just look at the way that the buggers communicate with each other and this all leads to a complete break down in basic manners. And then the little shits get cars off mummy and daddy and we have a whole new breed of road ragers."

"Fog lights," interrupted Grant.

"You seem them pushing past old folks, showing no sensitivities to pensioners, pregnant women or people with any form of disability."

"This upsets you then?" asked Pete.

"Nah! The key problem is that these friggin' youngsters think that they have a divine right to everything, by which I mean every fucking thing."

Ben stood up, "Ta ra like well as they say in Hartlepool."

Ben was ignored, Elliott continued, "And the charmless fuckers have no manners, expect total respect and believe that they warrant fat salaries and glorious careers."

"Why?" asked Grant.

"Fucked if I know," replied Elliott.

"Got to be the parents," proposed Pete.

"Like us!" concluded Grant.

All three of them laughed.

He hadn't been allowed to be a proper parent.

She had always made all of the decisions and hidden things from him whenever she thought that he might disagree.

Gillian would be a good parent.

A wonderful mother.

She could read him a bedtime story anytime.

Rock him to sleep in her arms.

"Where will it all end?" asked Pete.

"I'm telling you Petey Baby, it can only get worse, it will eventually lead to the end of society as we know it."

Elliott punched Grant's shoulder, "Oi, are you still with us, or have you left us to join an alien civilisation?"

"I wish," replied Grant.

Pete leant forwards, "You know, there was a time when the conversation in here was mildly amusing, frequently abusive, but rarely depressing! And you Grant, you used to be decent company!"

Forty One

The final Wednesday in July. The Urra was busy; most of the Regulars were present.

"Been cheating at golf, again?" Elliott questioned Frank.

"Excuse me?"

"I said have you been cheating at golf again?"

Frank took a deep breath. Elliott was trying to goad him but he didn't know why. "Why do you ask?"

"Why does it bother you?"

"What's your problem?" asked Bill.

Elliott turned to Bill, "Who asked you to join this conversation?"

Bill sighed and turned to Pete, "How are things with you?"

"How are things with you?" mimicked Elliott.

Pete scratched his chin, "Alright, thanks, got a holiday planned?"

"Couple of weeks in Dubai."

"Lucky bastard," commented Elliott.

Grant was still at work.

He had been presented with a draft report some hours earlier; it had to be finished, printed and bound and in London by Friday morning.

It could be done.

But he was supposed to be having lunch with Gillian tomorrow; lunch, that was all. He could rearrange; she would understand. But he didn't want to. He wanted to see her again. She made him laugh. And smile.

So, it would be a late night.

He tugged his tie down and turned the page; he still preferred reviewing hard copy documents than on screen; he had no problem with amending the soft copy as he worked through it, but he simply preferred paper.

He smiled at himself.

Old fashioned bastard.

"What are you doing with your holidays?" Pete asked Elliott.

"Fuck all and it's none of your fucking business anyway!"

"That's a bit out of order," commented Bill.

Elliott glowered at him.

Grant sat back in his chair and sipped at the cup of coffee that Kate had made him.

"It's looking alright, you've done well."

Kate smiled at the compliment.

"I think your conclusions and recommendations are pretty much spot on, but we need to work on the recommendations as I can just imagine the client saying "we knew all this and were going to do it", which is complete bollocks but you know what I mean."

Kate nodded. He was right. And she needed his help to add some obvious value to the report.

"Let's think outside the box for a minute," Grant got up and walked over to the wipe board.

"Here we go," thought Kate, "This could take hours, it could involve lots of Grant's ramblings and bad jokes, but we'll get there."

"Shall I go and put another pot of coffee on?" she asked.

"So," asked Pete, "if a deaf person has to go to court, is it still called a hearing?"

Bill grinned, "Good one."

"Bollocks," added Elliott.

Pete ignored him, "So, answer me this, why are you in a movie, but you're on TV?"

"Do we care?" asked Ellliott.

Pete persevered, "Why do people point to their wrist when asking for the time, but don't point to their crotch when they ask where the toilet is?"

Bill laughed, "Very true, very true."

Elliott tutted. Loudly.

Frank stood up, "My shout, same again everyone?"

Grant had written a series of lists on the board and had numerous lines crossing the board, joining comments, questions and suggestions in a logic, which only he understood.

Kate sat making comments and observations as he stood at the board. His trousers were hanging off his waist, she thought. He must be losing weight.

"Let's get back to the three Ps basics," started Grant. Kate sighed inwardly: she had done: she knew that Grant was not being critical: it was his way of thinking.

Kate stood and walked over to the window: she felt an immediate urge to go out and join the vibrant city below. She turned sharply, "We have some issues with each P: the People need improving, there are doubts over the Product and I think that the Price is too high."

Grant scratched his chin, "What the asking price or the borrowing cost or both?"

She braced herself, "Well, I think that the basic asking price is excessive and I would argue that the vendor should provide a significant cash contribution for the management team to take it away."

Grant stopped writing on the board: Kate prepared herself for some potentially high volume criticism. She had read the situation wrongly. "Good point, in fact a very good idea, but not really ours to make and it's a bit late in the process. But, what the fuck, let's get it into the report somewhere. I guess that you'd be suggesting a net asset adjustment at completion?"

Kate stuttered and then composed herself, "Yes, that was my approach."

Grant smiled to himself. "So, if the problem is that we question the long term sustainability of both the product and the management team, the financing cannot be anything more than medium term."

Kate nodded.

"What if we improve the management team, address the gene pool theory, remove the related inbreds and replace them from a mix of internal and external sources?"

"Like in a bimbo[85]?" asked Kate.

Grant grunted.

"The product line, current and potential, isn't good enough," suggested Kate.

Grant scratched his head. There must be a way through this, but he couldn't see it. Yet.

"Could you please chill?" Bill pleaded with Elliott.

"Could you please chill?" mocked Elliott.

"It's getting late," commented Frank.

"Aye, time for me to hit the sack," agreed Pete.

They all murmured their agreement, all wanting to leave what was rapidly becoming an unpleasant atmosphere.

Kate had left for home.

Grant sat with his feet on his desk.

---

[85] No, nothing rude or sexist! A Buy In, Management Buy Out – a mixture of a Management Buy In and a Management Buy Out. Confused? Uninterested? If the answer to both of these is anything other than 'yes' you should worry for your ongoing sanity.

It was late.

He scratched the back of his neck.

He was tired.

His mind wandered.

What would tomorrow bring?

The report should be finished by mid-morning.

He was beginning to feel good about it; happy to sign it.

The team had done well.

He sipped at his coffee; it was cold and tasted rancid. Bollocks.

What would Gillian be doing now?

Sleeping?

In a large bed, covered with crisp, fresh-smelling sheets.

Would she have thought about him?

She was a teacher.

In Durham.

Not too far away.

The sixth former's dream teacher.

The perfect fantasy.

She could teach him a lesson or two.

And he probably deserved a caning.

And detention.

He groaned.

Time to drive home.

Forty Two

The first Wednesday in August. A pleasant day followed by an equally pleasant evening. Warm enough to attract a number of the regulars to a table on the lawn. "Drinking outside is for feminine sorts," noted Pete, as Frank, Buster, Neil and Biggles opted for fresh air.

She had called him today.

Just for a chat.

He had been overjoyed to hear her voice.

They had talked for twenty minutes or so about nothing in particular.

The weather.

Her daughter.

Her plans for the school holidays.

He had been sad and frustrated when she had ended the call.

Frustrated that something had not been said. Something that needed to be said. And he felt that she seemed similarly frustrated.

His mind had filled with numerous, conflicting thoughts and emotions.

If only things were different.

"What's up with you?" asked Pete.

Grant lifted his head, "Nothing much, just a heavy day at work and I guess I'm a bit tired."

"Retire."

"Too young."

"You're never too young!"

"Fair point, but I can't afford it."

"Can you afford a round, cos if you can't, fuck off, I'm not drinking with you anymore!"

Grant laughed, "You have to, you've got no mates."

Pete grinned, "Yes, because twats like you scare them away."

Grant bowed his head, conceding the point.

"So, what have you been up to today?"

Grant sighed, "Nothing more than a time wasting, internal, navel gazing, deckchair rearranging meeting in Leeds; a waste of time, energy and money; yet more evidence that my firm is fully committed to our own early destruction." Grant paused, took a pull of his beer and continued, "We are now run by a group of sycophantic arse wipes, who spend their time justifying their own existence by criticising those who do the actual work and thereby earn the money to pay their vastly inflated salaries."

"You don't like them then?"

Of course, as usual, Grant had not recounted the full details of his day. His meeting had gone less than well. It had been with a number of his senior partners; John Naylor, a man who Grant frequently described as a gentleman, a man possibly past his prime but an individual of loyalty and integrity; John 'Myopic' Burton; and Howard Marsh, a man who raised one question in Grant's mind, 'why?'.

Grant disagreed with everything Burton said. Marsh agreed with everything Burton said. Naylor appeared to be repeatedly over-ruled.

Burton had called the meeting; irrespective of previous discussions he wanted Grant to specialise into what he saw as his best areas and wanted to combine the management of a number of operational units; this would free Grant to cover a wider geographic area. It was non-negotiable. It was now 'policy'. Grant was less than comfortable with the proposals and was incensed with the way in which the policy was being communicated, and would then be implemented. It gave Grant two options.

He felt uncomfortable with the 'shut up and get on with it' option, but this seemed marginally more attractive than the 'fuck off out of it' scenario.

What was he to do?

He was convinced that the proposals would not succeed. And he would ultimately be blamed for the failure.

He simply did not enjoy work as it was.

Would he be happier with another firm?

Would he get another position?

The money was good.

Pride, dignity and integrity never paid the bills.

Was he getting too old?

Was she right?

Was he a spent force? An ignorant, intolerant and generally unlikeable person?

Perhaps he needed a change?

A change of job.

A change of location.

A change of wife.

A change of personality. Grant smirked. Fuck fuck, fuckety fuck fuck.

Some chance.

Some hope.

Grant shook his head: an attempt to clear his mind and focus his thoughts on his beer and Pete.

"So, by jingo, here comes old Frank."

"Are you boring bastards going to stay in here?"

Grant and Pete looked at each other and replied in unison, "Fuck off Frank."

"You won't be wanting a pint then?"

"Well, it would be churlish not to," countered Grant.

Frank looked skywards and shook his head, "You are a pair of twats!"

Pete raised his empty glass, "A compliment! Thank you Frank."

"Will you please stop calling me Frank?"

"Sorry Frank," replied Pete.

"Frank," asked Grant, "Have you seen Elliott recently."

"No, thank God!"

Grant looked at Pete, "I can understand that response but can't help myself from thinking that something is not right. In all the years that I have known him, however drunk he has got, he has always been amiable, a bloke with no edge, a bloke with hardly anything bad to say about anyone, even Frank here and, let's be frank, it is very difficult to say anything positive about him."

Pete nodded in agreement, "But he has hardly been pleasant recently."

"Yes, but you know that that is not the Elliott we all know and love."

"Love! Steady on, darling!"

Forty Three

The first Thursday in August. It was lunchtime and it was raining, heavily. Grant had thought about giving lunch a miss and of working through and leaving for home before the evening rush hour. He had convinced himself that this would be pointless and had opted for a quick liquid lunch in one of the city centre hostelries.

"I was late in this morning as I had to drop the girls off at school and I underestimated the stupidity of the mothers dropping their broods off," moaned Grant, "and why do they all drive excessively large cars, which they clearly can't handle, or, even worse, effing people carriers or four by fours that never see anything muddier than the blessed bairn's dirty football boots?"

Grant would argue that frequenting pubs over the lunchtime to mid afternoon period was part of his job and came under Marketing on his weekly timesheet.

At best, he was living in the past: at worst, he was delusional.

"I mean, they can't reverse…biological fact…put two of them in a car at the same time and you've got a shopping trip…both looking at ninety degrees to the direction of travel…indisputable fact…rear view mirrors are totally fucking redundant…they have no conception of the needs of other road users…fact…and," Grant was stopped in full flow by Mike, a corporate banker and regular lunchtime drinking companion, "Next you'll be saying that the Arabs have got it right."

"Why not," replied Grant, "although the reference to Arabs as a generic grouping may be crap?"

Mike stretched, towering over Grant (they had been described as the Laurel and Hardy of the business community by many observers), "So, they shouldn't have the vote then?"

In his late thirties, Mike hailed from somewhere in the Black Country and still carried a dull Midlands tone in his accent. Standing at well over six feet, with head of thick blond hair and piercing blue eyes, Mike possessed a successful and dangerous interest in the fairer sex. Now on his third marriage, with a regular girlfriend on the side, Grant looked up to Mike because of his clear sexual prowess rather than his ability as an effective corporate banker. Regular drinking partners, they occasionally 'did business' together, Grant and Mike shared the same cynical sense of humour and a passion for liquid lunches[86].

"Good point my son," laughed Grant.

"Perfect circle," offered Grant's assistant and regular drinking companion, Simon.

"Eh?" was the best that Mike could manage.

"A queue of Arabs is a perfect circle," continued Simon, seemingly in control of the conversation for the first time in living memory (or this lunchtime at least).

Grant saw Simon's logic and attempted to encourage his usually silent chum. "Too right, female drivers queuing are reflections of the Arab queuing mentality but create less than perfect circles."

"You can do courses in queuing theory," continued Simon.

"Are they open to the fairer but more dangerous sex?" enquired Grant before he quickly drained his fourth "lunchtime quickie".

---

[86] As addressed in the second book of the Grant Bannister trilogy, the aptly titled "Liquid Lunch".

Mike turned and signalled 'same again' to Ethel, the lady who appeared to have been in charge of The Lion since the beginning of recorded time. Thick set, but not fat; short, but not stooped; Ethel had seen it all before and managed the establishment as if the days of The British Empire had never ended, and that anyone not wearing a tie before seven at night should be treated like an uneducated native.

"Like fog lights," suggested Simon, who was struggling with his pint.

"Nah," replied Grant, "Women don't read the instructions so drive around with their fogs on due to stupidity…usually the bright red bastard at the back of their cute little Nova or whatever…no, it's the boy racer tossers who piss me off with the front fogs."

"It's the tossers who park in the disabled spots who do my head in," commented Simon.

Grant grunted in agreement and, after a suitable pause for thought added, "And in the mother and child bits…it's always the boy racers or the arrogant, over-dressed thick bint in hubby's over the top four wheel drive jobby."

Simon nodded sagely, "Great word"

"Tosser or jobby?" enquired Grant.

Mike took his latest cigarette from his mouth, "I saw a copper do a woman for using her front fogs unnecessarily."

"Top man," was the limited reply from Grant who found his attention being drawn to something floating near the bottom of his new pint, "Ah shit, look at that, looks like a wedge of skin off someone's big toe."

Within seconds Ethel was next to Grant, peering into his glass. Grant daren't move or say anything; stories of Ethel throwing drunken builders into the back alley were the stuff of legend. "Hop" was Ethel's contribution before seizing the pint and disappearing behind the bar.

Simon looked at Mike; Mike looked at Grant; Grant looked at Simon. Checking that Ethel was out of earshot, Simon spoke for them all, "Bollocks was that a hop."

Grant nodded, "So has the whatever it was that was in your pint melted?"

"Ah shit," concluded Mike, "time to go back to the bank."

"Before you go, have you had a chance to look at the business plan I sent over?

Mike looked blank.

"The one for the market testing business," clarified Grant.

"Yes, thanks, not interested."

"Twat," replied Grant.

"Why?" asked Simon.

"Why what?" replied Mike.

Simon grinned, "Why do you not want to finance the market testing business?"

Grant sat behind his desk, staring out through the wet windows over the shiny rooftops of the city centre.

He couldn't drive home.

Should he stay over? Have a few beers?

Should he get the train home?

How would he explain his arrival home by taxi?

Would she notice?

Would she care?

It would certainly provide more "ammunition".

Should he work late, by which time the effects of the lunchtime drinks would have worn off?

Yeah, right.

He shovelled his papers about.

He was bored.

He had no enthusiasm.

Did he go for a wander round the office? Walk the shop floor?

No.

Should he make some calls?

Perhaps not advisable.

He was on top of all of his client work.

He was ahead with his administration.

Should he go home?

Or back to the pub?

He scratched the back of his neck. He was bored and frustrated.

Should he call her?

Why had she not called him recently?

To be fair, she usually called him.

Perhaps it is his turn?

Perhaps she was bored with him?

Fuck.

There must be more to life than this?

He was in a rut and seemed unable to get out of it.

Unable or unwilling?

He could design and implement complicated financial transactions.

He could secure and manage a wide and impressive range of assignments.

He managed a office employing over seventy professionals, delivering a cocktail of professional services.

Yet he was seemingly unable to manage his personal life and seemed unable to say 'no' to the offer of another unnecessary drink.

Forty Four

The first Friday in August. It was lunchtime and it was raining, heavily. Still. Grant had again thought about giving lunch a miss and of working through and leaving for home before the evening rush hour. He had convinced himself that this would be pointless and had again opted for a quick liquid lunch in one of the city centre hostelries: adamant that he would control his intake.

Grant stood at the end of the bar, entertaining a number of bankers. He was in his element.

"If Wiley E. Coyote had enough money to buy all that ACME crap, why didn't he just buy dinner?"

"Spoken like a true accountant," laughed one of the bankers, "And thanks for that market research company opportunity, I think we'll be able to do something with it."

Grant smiled, "Smashing, let's have a drink to celebrate that!"

"Beep Beep!" agreed Simon.

"That was Roadrunner, you twat!" laughed Grant.

Grant turned into his drive and was forced to swerve to avoid his wife's car, which was leaving at some speed.

What the fuck has got into her?

The house was empty: other than for the dumber members of the menagerie.

Grant walked then fed the dogs.

He fed the cats.

Then fed himself: leaving fat all over the hob surface. And leaving the undeniable smell of a greasy fry-up throughout the downstairs.

That will piss her off.

Then he changed clothes and repaired to The Urra.

"We'll get along just fine, once you learn to worship me appropriately."

Bill shook his head, "Please don't start Elliott."

"I'll try being nicer if you try being smarter."

Bill rose, "Gentlemen, I bid you farewell."

"You off, Bill?" asked Grant as he arrived.

Bill nodded, wearily, "I am afraid so."

Grant patted him on the back, "Have a good weekend," and turned to the group around the table, "Well! By jingo, I would delight in the opportunity to procure a beverage for one and all."

"Tosser," replied Elliott.

Grant grinned at Elliott, "I can already visualise the duct tape over your mouth."

Elliott stared at Grant, "Yeah, you kinky bastard."

Grant returned with the round of drinks.

Frank was in deep conversation with Buster. Golf, assumed Grant.

Neil was listening to what sounded like Biggles' life story.

Ben sat staring at his drink.

Elliott sat staring at the ceiling. What was up with him?

Pete stared at Grant; like one of the dogs *Please give me some attention.*

"How you doing Big Man?" asked Grant as he sat down next to Pete.

"Ticking along, ticking along, what about you?"

Grant took a long pull from his pint, "I honestly don't know is the true answer to that question, so ask me another."

"Well, I'm not going to ask you about business or your family, as the replies will be bollocks."

Grant laughed. Pete was right again.

"So, do you fancy a lunch time session next week? Like the good old days."

Grant smiled widely, "Tremendous idea, let's go for it."

Pete grinned, "Yeah, I'll look forwards to that."

Grant had returned home early. He was in a positive frame of mind and was intent on developing some quality time with his family.

No one else had returned.

The kitchen stank of his fry-up so he opened a few windows and cleaned the work surfaces.

He wandered aimlessly about, debating in his mind whether he should worry about the whereabouts of his family:

Or open a bottle of one of his favourite wines and listen to some music or read a book:

Or go to bed; he felt relaxed and would sleep well.

He lay in bed.

He felt relaxed. On top of his work.

He had no need to attend to any work during the course of the weekend.

Two days to do with what he liked.

Two days to spend with his family.

Two days which could be so nice or so...

What will Gillian be doing this weekend?

He was going to strive to avoid any form of escape to The Urra.

What could they all do together?

A family day out?

Go for a meal?

Go to the cinema?

Or theatre?

Grant smiled at the darkness.

We'll see, we'll see.

Forty Five

Saturday lunchtime in The Urra was rarely busy. This one was no different. The weather had encouraged the vast majority of locals to attend to out door chores or to simply enjoy the summer warmth and sunshine.

Grant sat on a stool at the end of the bar, focussing on the business pages of The Daily Telegraph.

His 'family' weekend had not lasted; it hadn't really started.

Eric and Ernie had been pleased to spend some time with him.

The girls had gone 'shopping' with friends.

He had shared a brief and succinct conversation with his wife[87].

He had been spoken to as if was a simpleton, and as a result he understood that, in her eyes, he was generally inadequate – as a husband, provider, companion, and so on.

He was socially inept; he under-performed in every respect.

He was an embarrassment.

"Alf, another pint of the Middleton Mild please."

Alf pulled the pint, "Early start Grant." A statement, not a question.

Grant handed the necessary money to Alf without reply.

Fifteen minutes later.

"Alf, another pint of the rather tasty Middleton Mild please."

---

[87] The words 'share' and 'conversation' are inappropriate. It had been one-sided in every respect – once he had mentioned that he had no work commitments to attend to.

Alf pulled the pint, "Nothing to do today." Another statement, rather than a question.

Grant folded his newspaper and placed in on the bar, "Tell me Alf, why do people pay to go up tall buildings and then put money in binoculars to look at things on the ground?"

Alf stared blankly.

"Rightio, so why do doctors leave the room while you change? They're going to see you naked anyway."

Alf grunted and rang the price up on the till. Grant took the correct change from a pile of coins he had built from the change from his earlier drinks. "If corn oil is made from corn, and vegetable oil is made from vegetables, what is baby oil made from?"

Alf shook his head "Sorry Grant, I'm too busy to play today."

Fifteen minutes later.

"Alf, another pint of your delicious Middleton Mild please."

Alf pulled the pint, "Will you be coming in later?" A question with a hidden purpose.

Grant folded his newspaper, roughly and placed in on the bar, "Not sure I'm going in the first place, and when I go I doubt if I'll be able to return."

Alf nodded.

"Tell me Alf, why do people pay to go up tall buildings and then put money in binoculars to look at things on the ground?"

Alf ignored Grant. "Rightio, so why do doctors leave the room while you change? They're going to see you naked anyway."

Alf grunted and rang the price up on the till. Grant again took the correct change from a pile of coins he had built from the change from his earlier drinks. "If corn oil is made from corn, and vegetable oil is made from vegetables, what is baby oil made from?"

Alf shook his head, "Give me a break Grant.

"Is pop corn a vegetarian food?"

Alf started to walk away.

"Oi, Alfie I'm talking to you. What's your problem? I'm good enough to take money off, but not good enough to talk to."

Alf turned and smiled at Grant, "It's not like that, I'm busy that's all."

Of course, Alf was being disingenuous and Grant realised this. "Bollocks."

Alf attempted to calm the situation: a path that further incensed Grant.

"It's nice beer that isn't it?"

"I'm not fucking playing Alf."

"Come on Grant, play nice."

"Play nice! Play nice! At these prices!"

"Seriously Grant, I've got work to do down in the cellar so why don't you finish reading your paper?"

"You never go down to the cellar and I've finished my fucking paper, you condescending fuckwit."

"I've got pipes to clean."

"Not during bleeding opening hours, how daft do you think I am? Anyway, your beer is crap, your prices are shocking and you are a humourless shit."

"Sorry Grant, can you lower the volume and stop swearing, I've got other customers to consider."

Grant stopped. He realised that he had stepped well over every line of decency, courtesy and behaviour, "Sorry Alf, I am really sorry, I don't know what came over me. Sorry."

It was a glorious evening and The Urra was busy.

"Alf tells me that Grant was in earlier on and was in a right state," Biggles was clearly enjoying his tale, "Seems he was loud and abusive, pretty typical really."

"That's unfair," started Pete, "Grant can be a piss head but something must have happened to get him going, if he did start misbehaving."

"Aye, give him the benefit of the doubt," agreed Frank.

Biggles felt uncomfortable: like a child who has been caught telling tales.

"Well, that's what Alf told me and he should know!"

Pete shook his head, "Yeah, yeah."

Biggles stood up, "My round then?"

As Biggles walked to the bar, Frank leant over to Pete and quietly asked "So is Grant's wife having an affair?"

Pete shifted in his seat, clearly uncomfortable with the question.

"You're his mate, you'll know, it's just that I've heard from several people that she is having an affair with that woman who is always round at their house."

Pete stared at Frank, "He has said nothing to me. So, if it's true perhaps he doesn't know. Or if he knows he is keeping his own counsel. And whichever, I'll respect his right to privacy."

Frank nodded, "Fair point, Pete. Mum's the word."

Pete smiled, "So, how are your dahlias?"

Frank laughed, "Better than my chrysanthemums!"

Grant lay on a sofa.

Staring at the television without watching whatever was on.

Struggling with a sense of frustration: a frustration with himself, he felt angry and lonely.

He felt hungry.

He had not been welcome at the family dinner table.

He had grazed on various bags of crisps and biscuits.

Unfulfilling and far from enjoyable.

Even the dogs were avoiding his company.

Grant walked into The Urra and approached the bar.

"Evening Grant."

"Evening Alf."

"Mild?"

"Please, and I'm sorry about earlier."

"No problem and this one is on me."

"Thanks Alf."

Pete greeted Grant, "Now then Fat Lad."

"Now then Old Man."

Pete laughed.

Frank chided the pair of them, "Children, children."

Forty Six

An extremely mild late-August saw trade booming at The Urra; the bar was becoming virtually a no-go area for the locals and on at least one occasion a 'tired' Grant had threatened to call the licensing authorities, his complaint being the number of 'ignorant townie[88] buggers' shouting into mobile phones. He threatened to complain so often that he had now become something of a joke himself.

Grant, like many of his colleagues, had a 'thing' about mobile phone users; this ranged from the suited 'tossers' on trains (who would be heard 'buying' and 'selling' exotic, and probably fictitious, stocks and shares, telling various members of their family that they loved them and hoping that they had eaten all of their breakfast or tea {depending on the time of day}...and be good for mummy {or the child-minder}, through to those who would be heard explaining how marvellous they had been today, or how awful someone else had been: 'and, to top it all, he was wearing white socks') to those who had no apparent need for such modes of communication (and would clearly be unable to string two or three words together if a pen was involved), who would be often found wearing worryingly skimpy vests (exposing their off white bra from various angles) and would force all those within fifty yards to marvel at the excitement of their lives ('our mam and our Kylie are having chicken nuggets and chips for our tea'; 'you should have seen all the yellow pus when the nurse took the bandage off our

---

[88] Grant himself was something of a "townie", given that he had spent much of his life resident in urban masses and continued to work in such areas, merely spending part of his leisure, and much of his sleeping time in a semi-rural area. Grant enjoyed a phenomenally short memory.

nan's leg'; 'our Kirk is a good lad, it's the coppers with nowt better to do').

Grant had a mobile phone[89].

And then there were the women in supermarkets "Eee Pet, they are on offer so shall I get three cans for our Michelle?"

Grant hated shopping.

Then there were women drivers and white van men manoeuvring with one hand holding the phone "Aye Pet, I'll be back in time for the bingo."

Grant often wondered if he was actually the problem. Was everyone else all right and he was just a narrow-minded bigot?

Perhaps he was the worst narrow-minded bigot and his dearly beloved was in fact correct.

"Sharon is that you? You gotta watch Celebrity Snot Firing tonight, did you see it last night, eeee, did we laugh and then our Craig came round and you'll never guess what we did."

And then there were the no hopers with bits of phones sticking out of their ears. Who the fuck would call them? "Yes, Commissioner Gordon, Robin and I will there within ten bat minutes."

Grant hated his phone.

He hated its ringtone. Whichever one he was currently using.

It was like a harbinger of doom.

Every call seemed to carry a problem from work.

Or her voice.

He smiled.

And sometimes it was Gillian.

Just past seven in the bar of The Urra and the early evening drinkers are already in full flow...

---

[89] Which he only used in the car. Which he drove too quickly. So that's all right then.

"It's the bloody metal music that does my head in…why can't they just say hello…it's like all those years ago when everybody with an answerphone had to be Jim Rockford," was Elliott's standard contribution to discussions on all matters telephonic.

Frank, "It's people who use their mobiles while walking the dog that gets me."

Grant laughed, "I had a slash in the bogs of The Monkey at lunchtime and this twat next to me was having a piss and talking to his kids on the phone at the same time."

Elliott sighed, "And women say we can't multi-task."

Buster, "No, women in supermarkets…the grapes look very good today, shall I buy a bunch?"

"I hate piles," commented Elliott, but no one saw the joke.

"You know," offered Grant, in an attempt to change the subject before Elliott introduced the internet and email to the discussion, "I can't stand people who pull individual grapes off the bunch, leaving behind soggy lumps of grape detritus and bare twigs."

"Your life must be pretty frustrating," commented Frank.

"Or just plain sad," added Elliott.

Grant had strong views on many things; usually little things; things that most mature, intelligent individuals would ignore. As his frustrated wife had once observed, his views were nearly always negative; she had turned on him one day, commenting that he 'never said anything nice' and had cited the example of the 'lovely daffodils along the hedgerows' when he had asked what he could pass 'nice' comments on. She had pretty soon regretted this as, in his sincere attempts to be 'nice', every car journey had become a horticultural tour burdened with 'look at those lovely tulips', 'ah, look at those dahlia' and 'the yellow ones are my favourites' type comments; she thought that he was taking the piss; the sad thing is that he wasn't!

In the work environment, Grant's cynicism was encouraged by many of the bankers with whom he enjoyed liquid refreshment; in The Urra, Elliott was his partner in moaning.

The relationship between Grant and Elliott was strange.

A very masculine relationship.

They made each other laugh.

They both enjoyed drinking with the other.

They both understood and observed the drunkards' code of conduct[90].

They never complained to or confided in each other.

They had known each other for many years: but didn't really know each other.

They never provided advice to one another.

They rarely talked about themselves to each other.

They never spoke about their respective families, careers or feelings.

But they clearly missed each other when one was absent from The Urra for more than a couple of drinking sessions.

And they seemed to share similar senses of humour and appeared to be able to communicate without spoken words when wind up opportunities presented themselves.

"I'm not sad," replied Grant, "it's just that I am not blind to the rest of the world, I observe and occasionally comment."

"Define occasionally."

"Piss off Elliott."

"So you can't?"

"Ladies," interrupted Frank, "my round I believe."

Grant looked at his watch. He should go home. She'd ignored him this morning. He wasn't sure why but was pretty certain that

---

[90] As in you never, ever refer to someone's mistakes or bad behaviour, if caused by an excessive intake of the amber nectar.

the atmosphere would still be icy. He had pretty much given up trying to understand what he had done or was doing that was wrong. He knew that this in itself was wrong. But what chance did he have? She wouldn't talk to him but accused him of not communicating. She would never say what she wanted, or explain why she was unhappy. And he wasn't a mind reader. Although she seemed to expect him to be. And was one herself. Who seemed to misread his mind on purpose.

"Just a pint for me," replied Grant

"What do you mean with the just?" asked Frank

Grant smirked, "As in I don't want two pints at this time, but thanks anyway."

"Tosser,"

"It's the closest I get," muttered Grant, to the amusement of Frank.

"Aye, my hand never says no," agreed Elliott. Grant kissed his palm.

Bill cleared his throat with a polite cough, "You know Grant, for someone in such an exalted position as your good self, you are phenomenally coarse."

Elliott sniggered, "Aye, you can take the boy out of Hartlepool…but you can't take Hartlepool out of the boy."

"They hung a monkey in Hartlepool you know," was Ben's immediate, unnecessary and unwanted contribution.

"Where's Pete?" asked Frank.

"Down in Nottingham, visiting one of his kids," replied Grant.

Pointing at a group of youths who had just entered the bar, Bill asked, too loudly for comfort, "Why do people wear those bloody hats back to front?"

"Baseball hats," noted Ben, unnecessarily.

Elliott leant forward, "'Cos they're selling drugs…it's like a sign over a shop."

Bill clasped his hands, "Now Elliott, you are joshing aren't you?"

Elliott shook his head, a serious expression locked on his face.

"And the Germans bombed Hartlepool United," added Ben.

"Is that true?" asked Neil.

Ben stuttered, "Yes, and they still send letters asking for compensation."

Elliott laughed, "Not that, he's on about the drug pushers because his daughters are both going out with baseball-hatted youths."

"Is 'hatted' a word?" asked Bill.

Neil waved his right hand, palm facing his drinking companions, "No, I meant did Grant really stand next to a guy on the phone to his children in the toilets?"

"Which toilets?" asked Elliott.

"Which kids?" asked Frank.

"Grant!" pleaded Neil.

Grant shifted uneasily, his mind had wandered.

He was tired.

He was frustrated in so many ways.

He wanted to talk to Gillian: but felt guilty with the mere thought of it.

He wanted to shoot half of his staff and half of the clientele in his pub.

He knew he needed to rest; and proper rest: but how could he?

His new suit, yet another one, was already looking well lived-in and his shirt had not been introduced to an iron since its most recent immersion in hot water.

He looked at Neil, "If the peak is forwards it means that they are just a common or garden prat...but backwards, it means I've got drugs for sale."

Bill looked shocked, "Well, blow me"

"No thanks," commented Elliott.

"But whatever," blustered Bill, "they should still take their hats off when they enter a building."

"Ahah," interrupted Grant, "and who was it was moaning about me whingeing about things that annoy me?"

Elliott nodded his head, folded his arms and leant forward, "No, but he's got a point...I've seen people eating, wearing baseball hats and, worse than that, get into lifts without removing them."

"Serious shit," agreed Grant, with excessive sarcasm.

Frank returned from the bar with pints for all but Ben. "Young Sarah behind the bar is looking very tasty this evening."

"Hands off," replied Grant, "She is starring in my dreams tonight."

Buster looked startled, "Excuse me?"

Elliott grinned, "You've no chance, even in your dreams."

"But she's one of Eric's girls," finished Buster.

"So?" questioned Elliott.

"At least we know she's clean," added Grant.

"Quite," finished Elliott.

Again with a total disregard for his personal volume control, Ben made a further contribution to the increasingly ridiculous conversation, "I expect that they've just popped in here for a quick drink before they go and steal a car or two...let's hope that they nick one with a personalised plate."

Frank looked somewhat confused. He, like several others around the table owned not one, but several personalised number plates. Grant retaliated first. "Well, unless they've got wild senses of humour, there's no fucking way that they'll nick your Volvo!"

"Unless they're undercover collectors for some eccentric museum," added Bill.

Elliott attempted to change the subject, "I think that men who wear jackets with the sleeves rolled up are more dubious than baseball hat wearers…and," now looking directly at Grant, "overweight old men who spend weekends in jeans and bright white training shoes are especially spooky." He failed.

Ben persevered, "The young Lee girl had a car stolen the other week."

"That was some special edition Toyota sports thing and it was last year," replied Frank.

"Was that the lovely low slung job?" asked Grant.

Frank nodded, "Aye, with the skirting"

"Low slung," commented Elliott.

"The car and the daughter," replied Buster.

"And Mr Williams had his BMW stolen," continued Ben

"From Darlington railway station," added Frank.

Ben, "And Mike Barron lost his Rover."

Elliott, "Anyone seen Mike Barron recently?"

Grant, "Losing a car is pretty daft isn't it."

Bill, "Can you get insurance cover for losing things?"

"Of course you can," replied Elliott.

"Any chance of you losing your voice tonight?" asked Grant.

"Mrs Westwood had her Landcruiser stolen from outside the supermarket."

Frank shook his head, "That was two years ago, Ben."

"She's a scary woman," commented Buster.

"And didn't Mrs Robinson lose hers?"

Elliott, "Great film."

Grant, "Decent music."

"What?" asked a clearly confused Neil.

"That music about the bloody rabbits did my head in," added Grant.

Frank, "Lose her what?"

Elliott rejoined the conversation, "Her virginity!"

Buster, "Now now."

Frank, "You really do have a mind like a sewer."

Grant, "Comes from working with all those pigs."

"And then there was that time that someone broke into the Tinklers and then used their Range Rover to take away all their electrical stuff."

"I wish," started Buster before he was interrupted by Elliott.

"Be careful…remember your blood pressure."

"No, no, no…I was going to say that I wish that someone would steal my old Land Rover."

Elliott laughed, "Buster me little old chum, you lost your Land Rover to my friend Mr Bannister last year. You remember. You lost the bet over the England Wales game at Twickenham."

Buster grinned, "No, no, I don't quite recall that."

"Liar." A simple statement from Frank.

"What rabbits?" asked Neil.

"Shall I have a word with Ben's mates over there?" enquired Grant.

"They are no friends of mine," corrected Ben, unnecessarily.

"Would you be so kind?" replied Buster.

Grant, "For you, my cuddly little farming friend."

Elliott, "Less of the cuddly."

Frank, "And the farming."

Buster, "Or the friend."

Grant, "OK Tiny"

Buster grimaced, shook his head and stood to leave.

Elliott, "Stand up for yourself."

Frank, "He is standing up."

Elliott, shocked, "No!"

"Can I have my Land Rover back?" asked Grant.

"You'll get it when it needs taxing," suggested Elliott.

"Quite," grinned Buster.

"What rabbits?" repeated Neil.

Forty Seven

Thursday lunchtime, late August. The bar of The Lion is comfortably busy. The usual flotsam of the professional and banking[91] communities are present.

"You're just jealous 'cos the little voices are talking to me," Grant took an unnecessarily long pull from his pint. He had been working exceptionally long hours, under mental pressure at home and at work, and he was clearly suffering the effects of the beers quicker than would normally be expected.

Pete was clearly becoming frustrated, and somewhat concerned, by Grant's obvious exhaustion and increasingly erratic behaviour, "Howay man, you need to slow down, there's no point working yourself into an early grave."

Grant ignored the well intentioned comment. "Me, I'm boldly going nowhere."

Pete looked heavenwards; long lunches were usually entertaining, had been a perk of the job, and Grant was usually top company, but not on current form. He shook his head. Grant had suggested a 'lunch time session like the old days' and it had seemed like a good idea. But, on reflection...

To Grant this was the closest to a day off in many months. And he had been looking forward to a boozy trail around the city centre hostelries with his old mate. He had got into work early and had crammed a day's work into four hours; and he felt that he now

---

[91] Bankers no longer deserve the classification of "professionals" given that, and through no fault of their own, they have now all become suited insurance salesmen or the frontline defence system for call centre operatives.

deserved a good slurp. He had no intention of returning to work: despite the fact that he had given everyone the impression that he would return.

Pete too had been looking forward to a long lunchtime with Grant. It had been part of the rich tapestry of banking life: before he had been persuaded to retire. But Pete was becoming increasingly concerned for his friend's state of mind and general well-being: at times he seemed hell-bent on self destruction and was clearly unable to take his foot off the peddle: he was driving himself into an early grave or a bed on a secure ward.

"Howay Sunbeam, let's be moving on."

Grant turned back towards the bar and attempted to attract Ethel's attention "My body is evil and must be punished." Ethel had seen it all before and, from his language alone, could tell that Grant had reached 'sensible' capacity and should be on his way. "Sorry, son…time to go."

Grant nodded, knowing he was beaten.

The chill wind whistling down the alley to the rear of The Lion had an immediate effect on both Grant and Pete. "Jeez, my bowel is about to explode," grimaced Pete.

"Uh, need a quickie in The Monkey," agreed Grant.

They both jogged down the alley, accepting that a quickie would amount to a rapid visit to the facilities, followed by a pint or three; well, it would be churlish to use the facilities without providing some revenue for the proprietor.

They stood next to each other: staring at the ceiling in the gents toilets of the Monkey.

"How many bowels you got then?" asked Grant.

"What the fuck?" replied Pete.

Grant sniggered: like a little schoolboy.

Pete decided to ignore whatever it was that he had said, "Say, do you fancy a week away somewhere? Somewhere nice and hot? Just the two of us?"

Grant looked blankly at Pete.

"I fancy a week or so away, maybe golf, maybe just a few days in the sun, lazy days, cold beer and good foreign food."

Grant was stunned. It was a superb suggestion. He wanted to say 'yes' but struggled. Surely there were reasons why he couldn't or shouldn't. She would go off on one. It was a bit selfish. But he deserved a break. Shit, even he knew that he needed one. What about the office? He grinned. They would be delighted if he buggered off for a while. He shook himself from his thoughts as he realised that Pete was talking to him.

"Come on fat lad, indecision is a virus. You're supposed to be the boss. It's your call, just say yes!"

Grant sighed and pulled up his zipper, "You know it's not as easy as that."

Pete shook his head as he adjusted himself, "You really are a tosser."

Grant and Pete stood, backs against the bar, attempting to hold their stomachs in, whilst observing the female clientele of The Monkey. A tall blonde entered the room, clearly cognisant of her beauty and dress sense, and its effect on the opposite sex. The lemon suit was closely tailored to enhance every curve, her long silky hair lying round her shoulders emphasising her assets and her legs; 'up to her armpits' commented Pete.

"Come to Papa," was all Grant could muster.

"Did I tell you about the secretary I entertained when I was last in Darlington?" enquired Pete.

"Frequently."

"But did I tell you about the time in the strong room?"

Grant shook his head.

"In her early twenties she was, could not get enough of me, it was tremendous."

"Fucking hell Pete, you talk about your sexual experiences like a former member of the Education Corps talking about his war exploits."

"You taking the piss?"

"Nah, but I'm going for another one…once I start I cannot stop. Once I break the seal, I'm done for!" Grant meandered off in the general direction of the conveniences.

Pete remained leaning against the bar, a smug smile breaking out from his beard as his memory wandered back to that time in the strong room…she'd complained about one of the metal drawer handles digging into her back, but she'd enjoyed it enough to invite him home…when hubby the fire bobby was on duty."

Grant returned, "We going for lunch then?"

Pete looked at his watch, albeit he already knew that, yet again, just like in the good old days, the noontime pint followed by lunch had deteriorated into a three hour session and everywhere would now be closed. "Bag of crisps or back to The Lion for a ham-n-pease pudding sarnie?"

Grant shrugged, "Bugger, I could have done some serious damage to a curry. It is ages since I last had a real hot curry, a curry with all the works. Popadums. Naan bread. Cucumber riata. Chicken Tikka Jalfrezi. And a gallon of good Indian beer."

"You have no chance," laughed Pete.

"Fuck!"

"Not with the tart in the lemon… you've got no chance," laughed Pete.

"One last pint then?" suggested Grant.

Pete scratched his beard and stared at Grant, "How the effing hell are we going to get home?"

"We could have an early evening curry and then get the last train home."

Pete smiled, "Sorry matio, I'm too old for this sort of pace. I'm all done in and need my bed in the very near future!"

Forty Eight

The last Tuesday in August.

Lunchtime in The Urra was generally a quiet affair. That is why Grant had wandered in; that and the fact that he couldn't think of anything better to do.

Grant was staring at a man – late-forties he would guess – wearing fawn polyester slacks, a powder blue, Crimplene safari jacket and grey slip-on shoes.

Grant smirked. Why was he wearing so much gold jewellery?

Was that comb-over necessary?

Expect he does most of his shopping in catalogues, concluded Grant before taking another drink.

Bet he supports Manchester United! What was it his father had said to him? Yes, that was it, "You can change your wife as many times as you like…but your football team is for life."

Elliott had seen him walking through the village and had assumed that he was on his way for a swift drink or three. Elliott was not to know that his friend didn't want company and was concentrating on his own thoughts and space; such concentration being made the easier (or more palatable) by an injection of the amber nectar, particularly when his mind was filled with an assortment of dark thoughts and frustrations.

Grant was sitting on a bar stool, staring at the previous day's evening paper, tucking into his third pint when Elliott sauntered in. "Hello stranger."

Grant looked up and saw Elliott's beaming smile; his first instinct was to tell Elliott to leave him alone; he overcame the urge, "Now then, what are you drinking?"

"A pint of the Worthy would do the trick."

Grant folded the newspaper and banged on the bar to attract Alf's attention, "Yoh!"

Alf looked at Grant with a less than welcoming expression. Grant immediately resolved never to buy Alf a drink…well, why break the habit of a lifetime?

"A pint of Worthy for my educated friend and I better have another pint of your exceedingly overpriced guest ale."

"Educating friend," corrected Elliott.

"Day off?" asked Grant.

"Sort of," was the stilted response. Elliott looked at his shoes and then blurted, "actually, I've been to the hospital, have been having some problems, anyway seems it's not as bad as I thought."

"By jingo! So is that why you've been down a bit recently?"

Elliott looked embarrassed, "If I have been, I guess so. Thought it was the Big C. And I can't say that I was ready to face such a challenge in any sort of heroic way. Anyway, sorry if I've let it get to me."

"You have been a class one pain in the arse, as it happens. But I can understand why," blurted Grant.

"Shit, er, what can I say other than sorry?"

"Well, I hope you're alright and at least it means the stories about you having marital problems are wrong."

Elliott laughed, "Of course I'm having marital problems! I'm a married man!"

Grant grunted and reached for his pint.

They sat in silence: both comfortable with their own thoughts. Eventually Elliott drained his glass, "Another?"

"It would be churlish to refuse," replied Grant.

They finished these pints more quickly than the previous drinks, "I love lunchtime drinking," explained Grant, to no one in particular, "Time for another one?"

Elliott did not need to answer: Alf swiftly served the new drinks.

"Drinking in the afternoon is a fine sport too," commented Elliott.

Grant raised his glass, "Yes, a toast to afternoon drinking."

Elliott joined him, "To drinking at anytime."

Grant laughed.

They both emptied their glasses with unnecessary haste.

"So," started Elliott, "What brings you in here on this fine afternoon?"

"Because I'm totally pissed off with work and I believe that the feeling is pretty much mutual."

Elliott raised his eyebrows, "Oh."

"And I am so incredibly pissed off that you should wish that you hadn't asked."

"Sorry."

Grant shook his head, "No, I'm sorry. It's good to hear that you are alright and I apologise to you, and every other living creature, with the possible exception of my wife, for my feeling sorry for myself."

"Frank tells me that your wife is having an affair," Elliott recoiled as soon as the words had left his lips.

"Poor bugger," was the stilted response from Grant, "I hope he enjoys himself while he can!."

"No, no," Elliott was clearly suffering from the effects of the lunchtime session, "with another woman!"

Grant took a long pull from his glass, "Well, I've never claimed to have the cure for lesbianism."

Elliott sat hunched, at a loss as to what to say or do. He was surprised by his crassness, and the unemotional simplicity of Grant's answers.

"Although I'd argue that I never had a chance to see if I could cure it."

Elliott was lost for words – a first.

Grant broke the silence, "That's why I've got the penis of a nineteen year old."

Elliott asked why with his expression.

"Rarely got used at University, infrequently when I was a trainee accountant," he paused, "shite, being a trainee accountant is a bigger sexual turn-off than being an inbred transvestite," he giggled, took a pull from his drink and continued, "do you know, when I was a trainee accountant if I ever got to talk to a woman in a pub or night club, I'd tell them I was a sparky on the rigs. Straight up. This explained why I could only go out a couple of times a month, you know, because I was on the rigs, although the truth was I was skint and had to study. Anyway, eventually I pass my exams, life is now ready to commence and, kabooom, along she comes, I fall in love, or think I do, few shags later I beg her to marry me, didn't get a sniff on my wedding night and the meat and two veg have seen fuck all action since."

"Fucking hell," was Elliott's considered response.

"And I can remember the time and place of all of them. Does that make me sad? That I had so few? Or that I can remember irrespective?"

Elliott started worrying.

"Rachel was the first and she fell asleep under me. Then there was Carole, oh dear, I think that she now teaches history somewhere in mid-Wales, I should have married her, but she frightened me off."

Elliott wanted to ask how, but missed the opportunity.

"Then there was Rosemary, lovely girl but she had a smelly afghan coat, and then there was Sue from Carshalton, gorgeous but a real teaser and then there was Paula, she had a broken nose you know."

Grant paused, took a drink and continued, "I think she's a copper now, down in South Yorkshire. She was wild, reckoned that everyone should be killed at the age of thirty something, you know, so no one suffers in old age and the young don't have to support the decrepit."

Elliott forced himself not to make any 'women in uniform comments'. Or to ask how Grant now felt about this novel idea about euthanasia or mass slaughter.

"And she lived with a girl called Pat, Pat was a tadge too skinny but had gorgeous blue eyes, come to bed eyes, and shiny blonde hair, the hair was short, aggressively so for those days, but my oh my could she get me going."

Grant stopped moving, his eyes fixed on his pint. Elliott struggled to think of something sensible to say. He failed. "See Hartlepool United got beaten last night."

Grant grunted.

Elliott tried again.

"Have I told you the story about the little boy in the bath who points at his testicles and asks his mother if they are his brains?"

Grant ignored him, "Pat was really something, not great to look at but smashing to be with."

Alf pushed Elliott's arm, "No!"

Elliott continued, "So his mother says no son, not yet," and he burst into forced laughter.

"Eh?" asked Alf.

Grant smirked, "Heard that before, anyway, what did Frank say?"

Elliott felt and looked distinctly uncomfortable, "Not sure I can quite remember."

"Guess I should have known, it never seemed right."

Elliott sat up straight on his bar stool, "You mean you had no idea?"

"What? That she was batting for the other side, that she has been having an affair or both?"

Elliott wondered whether he should change the subject or let Grant carry on; Grant helped.

"Oh well, it runs in her family you know. Do you think that she will she let me go free without too much hassle?" He answered his own question, "No fucking chance, well me fine young friend, time for me to buy a round?"

Alf, who'd been 'hovering', attempting to listen to the conversation, served them promptly. "How's it going, lads?" he asked.

"Fucking brilliantly," replied Grant.

"Have you got the cure for lesbianism?" asked Elliott.

"Need to water the horses," announced Grant as he dismounted from his stool and made his way to the gents.

"Poor bastard," commented Elliott, quietly.

"You what?" replied Alf.

Grant stood staring at the white porcelain target area.

He fired.

The relief was immediate.

Who was it said that 'indecision was a virus?'

He realised that he was suffering from splash back. Bollocks!

He shook his head.

It wasn't his fault.

Was it?

He hadn't changed.

Or lived a lie.

Why had he been doing his brains in at work?

Was that the reason?

His absence from the marital home?

Too many late nights?

Had she become lonely?

He shook himself. Of course not, he had started working so much to avoid her!

There had been no other men.

So how could he be to blame?

How had he not seen it?

Had his head been up his arse? Had he proved her right in her frequent assertion that that is exactly where his head had been for so many years?

Was he blind?

Insensitive?

Naive?

Fuck, fuckety, fuck fuck. Maybe she had been right all along.

Shit, what a complete tosser he had been.

He finished up.

Washed and dried his hands.

Indecision is a virus.

He looked at himself in the mirror above the sink. He didn't like what he saw. The aged face. Tired eyes. The spineless twat staring back at him. He smiled at himself. Expect this has provided some top quality entertainment to the local women! He grinned.

He felt like thumping himself.

He had failed in so many ways.

Was he deaf, blind and stupid?

Probably, and he could do little about it now.

Indecision is a virus.

Hedgehog Remembrance Ale is a fine antibiotic.

He grinned as he pulled his mobile telephone from his jacket pocket.

It was the answering machine.

Thank God.

"Hello Gillian, how are you? It's Grant. I am really sorry. Really sorry. Can we start again? Think about it and call me. If you want to. I won't call again in case, well, in case. Bye."

If you keep saying that things are going to be bad, you have a good chance of becoming a prophet **Isaac Bashevis Singer**

The Back Bit

This book is the result of many hours of research in those quaintly British establishments, pubs, and specific mention is warranted by the following. It is emphasised that mention of these should not be construed as up to date recommendations; they were good when I was there, but they may now be child friendly, lager selling, purveyors of microwave cuisine; or, as they should be known, shit-holes.

The Crown Possada, Newcastle upon Tyne
The Sutton Arms, Faceby
The Commercial, Herne Hill
The Red Cow, Hammersmith
The Rugby Tavern, Twickenham
The Mill House, Hartlepool
The Red Cow, Market Harborough
The Bacchus, Newcastle Upon Tyne
Rosie's Bar, Newcastle Upon Tyne
The Woodcutter, Hartlepool
The Hole in the Wall, Waterloo
The Princess Helena, Hartlepool

The Dudley Arms, Ingelby Greenhow
Dr Brown's, Middlesbrough
The White Swan, Stokesley
The Sun, South of Chop Gate
The Greenside, Hartlepool
The Blackwell Ox, Carlton in Cleveland
The Royal Scot, Kings Cross
The New Bridge, Hartlepool
The Fox on the Hill, Camberwell

I always wanted a job as the pub, restaurant and car reviewer for a quality national newspaper!

Dinner with Mandelson is the third book in the 'Grant Bannister Trilogy'. 'Business Breakfast' and 'Liquid Lunch' are in progress and the fourth and final book, 'The Last Supper' has not yet left the author's scribble pad.

The author believes it to be fashionable to have four books in a trilogy and cannot spell 'quadrilogy'.